Caroline Anderson is a[n] armchair gardener, unof[ficial...] and eater of lovely cake[s... in] that order! What Carolin[e loves: her family. Her] friends. Reading. Writing contemporary love stories. Hearing from readers. Walks by the sea with coffee/ice cream/cake thrown in! Torrential rain. Sunshine in spring/autumn. What Caroline hates: losing her pets. Fighting with her family. Cold weather. Hot weather. Computers. Clothes shopping. Caroline's plans: keep smiling and writing!

Three-times Golden Heart® finalist **Tina Beckett** learned to pack her suitcases almost before she learned to read. Born to a military family, she has lived in the United States, Puerto Rico, Portugal and Brazil. In addition to travelling, Tina loves to cuddle with her pug, Alex, spend time with her family, and hit the trails on her horse. Learn more about Tina from her website, or 'friend' her on Facebook.

A VET
TO HEAL HIS HEART

CAROLINE ANDERSON

LAS VEGAS NIGHT
WITH HER
BEST FRIEND

TINA BECKETT

MILLS & BOON

First published in Great Britain 2024
by Mills & Boon, an imprint of HarperCollins*Publishers* Ltd,
1 London Bridge Street, London, SE1 9GF

www.harpercollins.co.uk

HarperCollins*Publishers* Macken House, 39/40 Mayor Street Upper, Dublin 1, D01 C9W8, Ireland

ISBN: 978-0-263-32179-1

12/24

A VET
TO HEAL HIS HEART

CAROLINE ANDERSON

MILLS & BOON

Huge thanks to SarahRossi@TamingTwins
for the Marry Me Chicken recipe,
the missing ingredient in the story
without which this book would not be the same!

And, as ever, to my long-suffering and apparently
endlessly patient editor Sheila Hodgson, whose
guiding hand has hauled me back from the brink on
countless occasions over the past almost twenty-five
years. Thank you from the bottom of my heart.

CHAPTER ONE

FINALLY!

Ellie turned onto the drive with a sigh of relief and stared at her little house for a long moment.

She'd saved hard for a deposit and since she'd bought it three years ago as an investment she'd let it to tenants to cover the mortgage. She'd never lived in it herself because she hadn't needed to, but she did now, so thank goodness it was available.

It shouldn't have been. Wouldn't have been, if it hadn't been for her tenant doing a midnight flit a few weeks ago. She'd been furious at the time, but now she was grateful that it was empty, even if, in the words of the agent, it needed 'a little attention'. But that was fine. Thanks to Craig she had time on her hands now, if nothing else. Certainly no job security, that was gone and the rent-free flat that went with it…

No. She wasn't going down that rabbit hole again. Time to find out what 'a little attention' actually meant.

She sucked in a deep breath, then turned to look at Lola in the back seat. After six horrendous hours in heavy traffic, it wasn't just Ellie who was more than ready to get out of the car. Her little black Lab was sitting up now, her face expectant, tail wagging, and Ellie dredged up a smile.

'This is our new home, Lola. It's going to be great!'

Maybe her voice had been more convincing than she

thought, or maybe the dog was just as relieved as she was, but she jumped up, and Ellie got stiffly out of the car, let her out and led her to the front door.

The paint was a little chipped and faded now, but that was hardly a major issue. She slipped her key in the lock, turned it and stepped inside.

And stopped.

A little attention? It smelt stale and unpleasant, and she wouldn't feel happy until she'd scrubbed it from top to bottom and cleaned all the carpets. Lola was busy sniffing, and she led her through the sitting room to the kitchen at the back and peered out of the window.

The light was fading, but she could see the once-tidy garden was a mess and heaven knows when the grass was last cut. Well, her agent had warned her, and it wouldn't take long to get it in order. Like the house, it was only tiny and easily manageable. She let Lola out for a wee and a sniff and left the door open while she went to check out the rest of the house.

She'd furnished it sparsely when she'd bought it three years ago, but everything was tired and dirty now, the mattress grubby, the bathroom filthy, and her optimism hit a brick wall. She came back down and sat with a plonk on the bottom step, her usually relentless optimism crushed.

What had she been thinking? Yes, she owned the house, but she knew nobody in Yoxburgh, and her rose-tinted family holidays here seemed worlds away. And the house was awful now. Beyond awful, really. 'A little attention' didn't even scratch the surface.

She sat up straight. No. She just needed to clean it, get the paintbrush out and—

The loud yelp made her turn her head sharply, and she ran out through the kitchen and found Lola limping towards the door. Even in the fading light she could see the thin spurt of blood from her right hind leg, and her heart went into overdrive.

'Lola! Oh, sweetheart…'

She needed a vet fast, but how to get her there before she bled out? She laid Lola down on her side, pressed her thumb firmly over the femoral artery high up in her groin above the wound to stop the bleeding, and studied it carefully. Whatever Lola had slashed herself on, she was pretty sure it wasn't glass. The cut wasn't clean enough for that, more a jagged tear, and it was just above her knee on the inside of her thigh, so she could get a pressure pad on it. If she had one…

She held her fingers on the artery while Lola whined and struggled to get free, stripping off her sweater and thin vest-top, swapping thumbs, then she balled the top up into as firm a wad as she could manage one-handed and wrapped her scarf tightly around it to hold it in place over the wound.

Lola did her best to resist, and at one point she put her teeth on Ellie's hand, not hard, just a gentle protest, but Ellie knew it must be very painful for her.

'Good girl, it's OK, I've got you, sweetheart, it's going to be all right,' she murmured, but she wasn't sure if it was. Tying it tight enough to stop the bleeding was next to impossible, and Lola wasn't helping, but it was as tight as she could get it and at least it had slowed the blood flow down.

So now what?

Back to the car and head to the nearest vet. She'd been scoping out the practices online this morning with the intention of visiting them to ask about locum work, and the closest by miles was just three streets away in a big old Victorian house. She'd driven past it on the way here, and they had excellent reviews. She tugged her sweater back on hurriedly, carried Lola to the car and set off, praying that the makeshift tourniquet would stay put until she'd got there.

Please be open, please be open, please be open...

There! Yoxburgh Veterinary Practice. She swung through the open gates into the empty car park in front of the building, jumped out and ran to the door. She could see lights on at the back, but the entrance was in darkness, and her heart sank. She rang the bell and pounded on the heavy old door.

Please be open...

Nothing. She fumbled for her phone and rang the practice, and was automatically transferred to the night service. It was miles away, but she'd been watching the wound as she'd phoned, and she could see the blood slowly seeping through the wadded-up top and her scarf every time she took her hand off the pad.

If she didn't get help soon, Lola was going to die.

She felt a sob rise in her throat as she hung up and pressed hard on the pad, and Lola whined and licked her hand.

'Oh, baby. I can't lose you, not like this, not now after everything else...'

She fought down the sobs, kneeling on the edge of the back seat and stroking her sweet, gentle dog with her other hand while she tried to work out what she could do. Move her to the front seat so she could reach to press on the pad as she drove? No, the front seat and footwell were packed to window height and it would take too long.

So—leave her in the back and drive fast? She couldn't, not that fast. If she took the pressure off she'd bleed out in minutes, and the tourniquet, such as it was, had already been on nearly ten minutes.

Five more minutes and the leg would be compromised...

Stay there all night pressing on it until the surgery opened again, and resign herself to Lola losing her leg?

Or just pray for a miracle?

So much for their new start. If only she'd stayed put—but she couldn't have, not after what had happened, and now everything was falling apart and Lola was going to die. She'd never felt so helpless in her life.

She went back to the door and pounded on it again.

'Where *are* you?' she wailed. 'Why won't you open the door?'

But they didn't. Whoever was in there was ignoring her, and she went back to Lola, leant on the pressure pad again and stroked her head gently with a hand that shook with grief and guilt and horror.

'I'm sorry, sweetheart. I'm so, so sorry...'

The pounding on the door seemed frantic, and Hugo hesitated another few seconds and gave in.

He went out through the staff entrance, Rufus at his heels, and saw a car in the car park, the back door hanging open. A woman was half in, half out of it, giving him a distractingly tempting view of a gently rounded bottom in snug jeans.

He ignored the inappropriate urge and was gearing up to explain that the practice was closed when he heard a wrenching sob that made his heart sink. So much for his quiet Friday evening walk with Rufus...

He peered in at her. 'Can I help you?'

She turned her head, her face streaked with blood and tears, a strand of dark hair clinging damply to her cheek. He didn't wait for a reply, just told Rufus to stay and ran round to the other side of the car and opened the door.

A dog, a black Labrador by the look of it, still alive but

bloodied and whimpering, and the woman was leaning on some kind of makeshift bandage on her hind leg.

'What happened?'

'No idea. I let Lola out into the garden and heard a yelp and she was hosing blood—'

'OK, let's get her inside. I'm Hugo, by the way. And you are?'

'Ellie.' Her eyes held his and he could see hope in them. 'You're the vet?'

'Yes.'

Another wrenching sob made her whole body convulse, and he took over, lifting the injured dog into his arms and carrying her swiftly round to the side door. He opened it with his elbow and went inside, Rufus beside him, and he sent him to his bed and headed straight through to the prep room, putting the dog down on the table.

'It's OK, Lola, I've got you, sweetheart,' he said gently, and the dog licked his hand and gave a quiet whimper. A trembling, bloodied hand reached out and stroked the dog's head, and he leant on the makeshift pressure pad and looked up and met Ellie's distraught eyes.

'Right, tell me everything you know.'

Her voice had a tremor, but her words were calm and concise. 'It's her femoral artery. No idea what she tore it on, I'd just let her out for a wee, but it's a jagged cut, so most likely not glass. I did what I could to contain it, but she's probably lost two hundred mils, maybe more?'

He gave an inward eyeroll. She'd probably spent her life watching vet programmes. 'That's a wild guess,' he said, but she cut that off with her next words.

'It's an educated wild guess. I'm a vet.'

He met her eyes again. 'Seriously?'

She rolled her eyes, echoing his thoughts, which under normal circumstances he would have found funny, but this wasn't exactly normal. But if she really was a vet...

'Do I look as if I'm joking? My dog is bleeding out, and that pressure has been on for about twelve minutes now! Can you please just give her a GA and clamp the artery before she bleeds to death or you have to amputate her leg?' Her voice cracked on that, and he frowned.

'I'll call my nurse—'

'You don't need a nurse, Hugo, I'm a vet! I've got all my paperwork in the car, or you could call my old boss James Harkness, but we don't have time for that now. Please— before it's too late?'

His mouth opened, but then he clamped it shut and held her eyes.

Come on, come on...

'You know Jim?'

'Yes. He owned my old practice. I worked with him for eight years.'

Another pause, then, 'OK,' he said at last, and her shoulders sagged with relief. 'Right,' he went on, stepping up a gear. 'You hold this while I get everything ready, and once I've got her under I can clamp that artery and get a proper look at it. Meanwhile tell me a bit more about her, please.'

She watched him, heart pounding, itching to do it herself, hoping he'd do things the way she would, and while he prepped at lightning speed, she filled him in.

'She's got no pre-existing conditions that I know of, no contra-indications, she weighs twenty kg. I gave her a general anaesthetic to drain an abscess at the back of her mouth three and a half weeks ago, she was fine for that and it's healed well. She hasn't eaten since this morning, she had a drink about three hours ago.'

'Good.' He was moving briskly and efficiently, doing what she would have done. Warming a bag of Hartmann's in hot water because Lola would need the compound sodium lactate solution to replace her lost blood volume, pulling up the induction agent, checking the anaesthetic gas in the vaporiser, selecting an ET tube, and she began to think they might after all be able to save Lola and her leg.

He clipped the hair on the front leg that hadn't been recently cannulated, asked her to hold it while he slid the needle in, and moments later Lola was asleep, intubated and out of pain. 'OK, let's move her into Theatre,' he said, and they carried her through and he connected her up to the gas. He was setting up fluids, injecting pain relief and antibiotics, checking Lola's stats, moving reassuringly swiftly. Then he looked up and met her eyes again.

'Right, we're good to go,' he said, then added, 'Which end do you want?' which surprised her.

The leg, because she wanted to know exactly what was going on in there, but she didn't know where anything was in his theatre, and anyway, her hands were shaking too much and vascular surgery needed steady hands. And she realised she trusted him.

Not that she had a choice…

'You do the leg, I'll monitor her.'

To her relief, he did exactly what she would have done.

Keeping his thumb on the artery, he removed the makeshift pressure pad, then released the pressure carefully.

Blood welled in the wound, but at least it didn't spurt.

'It might have closed up a bit,' she said hopefully, but as

soon as she said that it started again, a thin stream streaking out across the room, and he shook his head and clamped the artery.

'OK, let's clean this up and get a better look. Up the fluids, please. We need to boost her circulation now.'

She'd already done it as soon as the artery forceps were on, and she watched as he filled the wound with sterile gel to protect it from the clipped hair, ran the clippers over the inside of Lola's thigh, scrubbed the skin with chlorhexidine, sucked out the gel and irrigated the wound thoroughly.

Just what she would have done. She heaved an inward sigh of relief.

'How's she doing?' he asked without looking up.

'She's fine. All good.'

He nodded, laid out all the instruments he'd need, then while he scrubbed she opened the outer packets ready for him.

'OK, let's get a good look at this.'

He laid a sterile drape over the leg, blotted the wound with a swab, and she leaned over and studied it with him. The artery was punctured, but it was also grazed, not extensively but enough that it would need a skilled vascular surgeon to fix it.

'That's a nasty graze. Can you repair it?' she asked without any real hope, but he shook his head.

'No. If it was just the tiny hole, I'd give it a go, but the graze has damaged the vessel wall and I don't have the equipment or skills for fine vascular surgery. It needs a graft.'

'So what do we do?'

'Tie it off and hope? The artery's been clamped for a few minutes but her foot's still warm, she has good perfusion of the tissues, so I reckon she's got a good enough supply from the other vessels. She should be fine, but realistically, we have no other options.' He looked up and met her eyes. 'Unless you want her to go to a specialist? We can probably get her stable enough. Up to you.'

She shook her head. 'No. I've tied it off in a similar case, and frankly, if she's got enough of a blood supply to that leg for it to survive the journey, it's probably fine anyway.'

He nodded, and his gloved fingers explored the wound carefully.

'Nothing in there that I can feel. You've got no idea at all what she cut it on?'

'No, none. I'd literally just got the keys off the rental agent and walked in, and I'd got no idea what's in the garden, so I should have been more careful.'

He raised an eyebrow. 'X-ray?'

She nodded. 'Might be an idea, as I haven't got a clue what it was. She was probably racing round like a mad thing. She'd been in the car for six hours.'

He winced, and she pulled a face.

'Yeah. Long story. I'll tell you later.'

He wondered what the story was, but it would keep.

He X-rayed the leg, studied the images closely and tried not to think about the scent of something delicate and delicious drifting from her hair as she leant close to look at the screen.

'I can't see anything,' she said.

'No, nor can I.' He straightened up and told himself to focus. 'OK, let's close it.'

He tidied up the wound, debriding the edges so they'd come together in a clean line, tied off the artery and then hesitated.

'Does it need a drain in the dead space so she doesn't get a seroma?' she asked, echoing his thoughts, and he nodded.

'I'd rather put it in and take it out if it's not needed than have to do it later. Negative pressure drain?'

'I would.'

He made a tiny hole through the skin to the centre of the wound, slid in the fine flexible tube and taped the drain in place, then repaired the muscle damage before he drew the edges of the wound together and closed it with a continuous soluble suture. Then he squeezed the empty drain bottle and attached it to create suction in the wound and watched as a thin trickle of pink-tinted serum filled the fine tube. He gave a satisfied nod and looked up. 'How's she doing?'

'Fine. Stable.'

'Good. I'll get some local into that so it's not too sore when she wakes up, and then let's bring her round and see how she is.'

He stepped away from the table, pulled off his gloves and gown and binned them while she monitored Lola.

She was slowly coming to, but still sleeping, her breathing slow but steady, and together they put her into a mesh vest, tucked the suction bottle into it up against her tummy and then Hugo carefully moved her into a kennel and covered her with a warm blanket.

Ellie sat down onto the floor beside the kennel, her legs suddenly too weak to hold her. Lola was alive, her foot was warm, and she wasn't going to die. She realised she was shaking uncontrollably, and she felt a gentle hand on her shoulder.

'Hey, it's OK. She's going to be all right.'

Hugo hunkered down beside her, his hand still on her

shoulder, warm and reassuring, and she turned her head and met his eyes. They were the kindest eyes she'd ever seen, and she couldn't hold that gentle, understanding gaze. She turned her head away again and blinked back tears.

'Have you had anything to eat or drink recently?'

Recently? Hardly. She shook her head. 'Not since this morning. I had a bit of water when I stopped to let Lola out, but—no, not really.'

'I'll knock something up. You OK with pasta and pesto?'

'Um—yes, fine. Sounds lovely. Thank you.'

'Good. I might even have some parmesan.'

She dredged up a smile, suddenly realising how hungry she was. 'Even better.'

He went through a door into what she assumed was a staff room. She could hear him talking to his dog, the sound of a food bowl being chased around the floor, and he came back a couple of minutes later with a large mug full of steaming tea.

'It's got sugar in it—and don't argue, just drink it,' he said over his shoulder as he walked away again.

She didn't argue. She was beyond arguing, and his kindness suddenly overwhelmed her. She put the tea down, buried her face in her hands and gave in to the tears.

She was crying. He could hear her as he ran back downstairs from his flat with the ingredients from his fridge, the quiet sobs tugging at his overused heartstrings.

He wondered again what the 'long story' was. Something that had taken her alone on a six-hour journey, ending up in a rental place with a garden that was clearly unsuitable for a young, energetic dog like Lola. Or any dog, really, by the sound of it.

He dumped the fresh pasta into boiling water, drained

it, stirred a hefty dollop of pesto into it, grated the parmesan generously over their brimming bowls and carried them through.

'Here you go,' he said, and sat down cross-legged beside her.

She'd stopped crying now, and he could see why. Rufus was curled up in her lap, and she was stroking him with one hand and nursing her mug with the other. He called the dog over to his side, and he lay down between them, sharing the love. She got the head end, he noted wryly.

He handed her a bowl, and she put the tea down and took it with a smile and a hand that was still shaking. Low blood sugar? Shock? Exhaustion?

All of the above, probably.

They ate in silence.

She was glad of that. She was too tired, stressed and hungry to engage in polite conversation, and it seemed he was, too.

But then it was done, her bowl scraped clean, and she put it down and met his eyes. They were slate blue, and she thought they could see to the bottom of her soul, but that kindness was still there in them and she felt oddly safe. 'Thank you. That was amazing. I really needed it.'

'Yeah, me, too.' He smiled, his mouth tipping up a little on one side. 'You'll feel better soon.'

'I do already,' she told him honestly. 'I can't believe how kind you've been. It's restored my faith in human nature.'

'I haven't billed you yet,' he reminded her with a wry smile, and she gave a fractured little laugh.

'No, you haven't, but I'm sure you will.'

He chuckled, then held out his hand. 'It's probably time

we introduced ourselves properly,' he said. 'I'm Hugo Alexander, and this is my practice.'

She knew that already from her research last night, but she took his hand—the warm, strong and yet gentle hand that had squeezed her shoulder and reduced her to tears, that had saved Lola's life and leg with quiet competence—and she smiled at him.

'Eleanor Radcliffe. Ellie to my friends,' she added, and he cocked his head on one side, a smile playing around his lips.

'So, *Ellie*,' he said with quiet emphasis, 'this long story…'

She looked away from those kind yet piercing eyes that would see too much and gave a little shrug. 'Oh. That. I'm sure you've heard it before. I was working in Jim's practice in the Cotswolds. He was a brilliant boss, but he was getting on and he wanted to retire, so he stepped back and made me senior vet, which was great for a while, but things had moved on, some of the equipment needed upgrading, and he didn't want to invest any more in it, so he decided to sell it to a corporate.'

'Was that a problem?'

'Not initially. The building needed investment, and it was going to get it, which had to be a good thing. And then within a year the corporate sent in a new senior vet over me.'

'Ah…'

She threw him a wry smile. 'It's not what you think. He was an ex from uni days. We'd had a brief relationship, I'd dumped him when I realised he was a lying, cheating snake, then he'd said stuff about me that wasn't true that caused a rift with my best friend—and then he reappeared in my life and got his revenge.'

'How?'

'Oh, picking fault here and there, snide remarks, trying to

undermine me with my colleagues—it went on for months, then we had a row over Lola, and I lost it.'

He frowned. 'What kind of a row?'

She sighed and looked over her shoulder at Lola. 'Her owner brought her in. She'd been off her food for a day or so, could barely open her mouth and her eye was being pushed out of the socket by something—a tumour, an abscess—I didn't know and I couldn't see without an anaesthetic, but her owner said she couldn't afford it, didn't have insurance because it was too expensive—she was heartbroken.

'She loved Lola to bits but she wasn't well herself, she was struggling to look after her properly, and she was utterly distraught. She'd tried every rescue place she could find without success, and now, with this issue, she thought it would be better for Lola if she was dead than facing an uncertain future, so she asked me to put her to sleep. And she's three. There was nothing wrong with her apart from whatever was going on in her mouth, she's a beautiful dog and she didn't deserve to die. I couldn't let that happen.'

'So you treated her for nothing?'

She shook her head. 'No, because that wouldn't have solved the problem going forward, but I said I'd take her on, keep her myself, give her a home for life and she signed her over to me on the spot. It turned out to be a massive abscess at the back of her jaw. She'd yelped when she'd been chewing a stick in the woods a few days before, her owner had said, so it was probably blackthorn or hawthorn, but I drained the abscess and flushed it, it healed up really quickly, and I paid the bill.'

'So what was his problem?'

She sucked in a breath. 'I'd used my staff discount for her treatment, and then Craig refused to give it to me, billed me in full for the initial consult, the op, the drugs, the dispensing fee, the kennel time, the overnight care, even though I'd done all that myself while I was off duty… He said it was company policy, which was a crock of nonsense. A staff discount was in my contract and he knew it, but he said the dog hadn't been mine at the time of the first consultation, so technically it was down to the previous owner, and if I didn't pay up he'd bill her.'

He frowned. 'That's horrendous. So what did you do?'

'I paid it, because I didn't want her being hassled and I don't want a bad credit rating, so I told him exactly what I thought of him, finished my shift, wrote a stinking letter to the company, went up to my flat over the practice, packed up all my stuff, put it in the car and drove away with Lola. I spent last night in a dog-friendly motel, got up this morning, spoke to the rental agent and drove here.'

His eyes widened. 'So this was only yesterday? You were lucky to find a house to rent so quickly.'

'Oh, no, I didn't, it's mine. I've been letting it, but a few weeks ago the tenant did a flit and left it in a bit of a state, so I thought—well, I don't know what I thought, really, but maybe I'd been naïve imagining I could just drive up here and move in, but I can't live in it, not like it is. Maybe I should have been less impulsive and stayed, but I just—I couldn't even look at Craig any more I was so angry.'

'I can see that. So when was her op?'

'Three and a half weeks ago. The Monday.'

'And he's only just now decided to bill you?'

'Yes. He didn't know anything about it. He started a three-week holiday the day Lola came in, so he didn't know. Then someone said something about Lola, and he looked at the accounts yesterday afternoon, and it all hit the fan.'

* * *

Hugo leant back against the wall, taking it all in.

'Wow. That's quite a twenty-four hours you've had.'

She laughed, but it ended on a tiny sob. 'Tell me about it. And now my poor little house turns out to be lethal, filthy and—I can't take her back there, not with a wound, and I have nowhere else to go.'

'No family?'

'No, my mother's in Spain.'

No mention of a father. He wondered why. 'No boyfriend, partner, significant other?' he asked, realising as he'd said it that he was blatantly fishing.

'No other at all. Just me and Lola.'

She shot him a smile, but it didn't look convincing. 'So there you are. I'm jobless and unemployable, I have a broken dog, and my house is bordering on uninhabitable.'

He frowned again. 'Why?'

She stared at him. 'I just told you why. The tenant—'

'No, I mean why are you unemployable?'

'Are you serious?' She gave a tiny huff of laughter without a trace of humour. 'You didn't see my letter! And I'm in breach of contract because I didn't give three months' notice, so who's going to employ me with a record like that? And I didn't hold back when I talked to him, so I wouldn't fancy his reference,' she added with a wry smile.

He grunted. 'Yeah, I can imagine.' He studied her face. It was still streaked with blood, her sweater was on inside out, her tired green eyes were red-rimmed and exhausted, but she still had fight in her. Impressive.

He took a deep breath, let it out again, and said, 'I have an idea. Feel free to say no, if you want to, but I'm short-staffed tomorrow.' He rolled his eyes. 'That's nothing new,

I'm permanently short-staffed, but the locum who was doing tomorrow morning is sick. If you can show me all the appropriate certification, how do you fancy covering the shift?'

'But what about Lola?' she asked without missing a beat, and he smiled. He wasn't in the slightest bit surprised that the dog was her first thought.

'Lola needs to stay in overnight, probably for at least two nights, and we have a bed in the office that the night vets used before the staffing situation got ridiculous. You're welcome to stay and look after her tonight, do the shift tomorrow, and when that finishes we can go over to your house and blitz it together.'

She stared at him. 'You'd do all that for me? For a perfect stranger you know nothing about?'

Her eyes were welling with tears, and he had to stifle the urge to wrap his arms around her and kiss the tears away. He gave himself a mental kick and stuck to the facts.

'I know quite a lot about you. I know you're a competent vet, I know your dog comes first, I know you did exactly what I would have done under the circumstances, and I'm not being entirely altruistic. I do need a vet for tomorrow. I need another vet, full stop, so you could look on it as an interview, if you like?'

'An *interview*?'

'That's what I said.'

She looked away, then looked back at him, her face awash with a whole raft of conflicting emotions, and he held his breath.

Ellie, please say yes...

CHAPTER TWO

ELLIE STARED AT HIM, trying and failing to read his expression.

Could it really be so simple?

She blinked away the tears and felt one slide down her cheek. She swiped it away crossly with her hand, and it came away tinged with blood.

She tried to laugh, but it cracked in the middle. 'Gosh, I'm such a mess. How can you even consider employing me?'

'How?' he asked, sounding incredulous. 'Because I need a vet? Because you clearly know what you're doing, and you're passionate about your job?'

'How on earth do you know that?'

'Because you took Lola on and treated her because it was the right thing to do, and today you stood your ground and made me help you. So that's twice she would have died if you hadn't stepped in to help her. You saved her life today under really tricky conditions—'

'No. *You* saved her life.'

'No. You did, by getting that tourniquet on, getting her here and making damn sure I helped you fix her.'

She felt her cheeks colour. 'Sorry, I'm not normally that pushy.'

'It's fine, you were fighting for Lola, and if it helps, I would have done exactly the same thing.'

She stared down at herself and laughed in despair. 'Look at me! My sweater's on inside out! How on earth did I do that?'

His mouth twitched, and he gave a soft chuckle that resonated inside her in a weirdly unsettling way.

'Er—one-handed, while you wrestled with a dog that I'm guessing wasn't being too cooperative? It's not rocket science and I imagine you had bigger things to think about.'

A vivid image of Lola struggling as she tied the scarf around her leg flashed into her mind, and she shuddered.

'I guess I did.'

Behind her, Lola gave a little whine, and she reached out and laid a hand on her head, stroking it gently. 'It's all right, Lola. I'm still here. It's OK, there's a good girl.'

Her tail thumped gently, and a wet tongue came out and licked Ellie's hand. She struggled up onto her elbows and looked around, clocking Hugo, and her tail thumped again.

'What a sweetheart,' he murmured, shifting in beside Ellie, so close that she felt the breath jam in her throat as he held out his hand for Lola to sniff.

She licked it, then looked round at her leg.

'Leave it, Lola,' he said, easing her head back down gently and stroking her to distract her, and she sighed and settled again.

Then he sat back on his heels, and Ellie breathed again.

'She's going to need the cone of shame,' she said, trying to focus on Lola and not the lingering masculine scent of his body, and he nodded ruefully.

'Yes, she is, otherwise she'll have that drain out in a minute.' He cocked his head on one side. 'So—what's your answer?'

She turned her head and looked at him, just inches away,

and the breath jammed in her throat again. Those slate-dark eyes, so kind, so mesmerising, so intense...

'Did you mean it?'

'What, that I need a vet? Absolutely.'

She laughed softly. 'No, I believe that. I meant about helping me clean the house.'

He frowned. 'Of course I meant it. Lola needs to rest, anyway, and the first thing we need to do is find out what she cut herself on and deal with it. So—locum tomorrow?'

'On one condition. I do the shift for free in exchange for your help.'

'That's ridiculous.'

'You haven't seen the house yet,' she pointed out, and then added, 'I don't want your charity, Hugo. Take it or leave it.'

She held her breath, and then he gave a soft huff of laughter that echoed through her again as he gave in.

'OK, I'll take it—but only if you do the shift in exchange for Lola's treatment.'

'What? No! Absolutely not.' Ellie shook her head firmly. 'Anyway there's no need. She's insured.'

That expressive eyebrow quirked at her. 'Is she? Even though you've had her less than a month?'

She had. Damn. 'I can pay you,' she said, wondering exactly how she was going to do that, but his mouth twitched, drawing her attention again to those firm, sculpted and oh-so expressive lips.

'Lord, you are stubborn.'

'I am,' she retorted, dragging her eyes and her mind off his mouth. 'So what's it to be?'

He let the smile out then, and her heart quickened. 'I'll take it.'

She smiled back, relief flooding her, her pride restored.

'Good. My paperwork's all buried in the car somewhere but I could call Jim?'

His smile was warm and it made her heart hitch. 'Yeah, do that. I did a practice rotation with him when I was training. He's a great guy. Be good to talk to him again.'

She pulled her phone out of her back pocket, glanced at the time to see if it was too late and decided that nine fifteen would be OK. She rang him, and he answered immediately.

'Jim, it's Ellie. I have an odd request. I'm with Hugo Alexander, and—'

'Hugo? Really? How is he?'

She laughed. 'Stressed and overworked, I think. He's looking for a locum. Could you vouch for me, please?'

'Of course I can. Put him on.'

She handed the phone over, and watched Hugo's face as Jim spoke. At length. Hugo looked across at her, his eyes alight, that expressive mouth twitching. 'So you rate her, then, Jim?' he asked, and Jim started again.

'I'll take that as a yes. Thank you.' He was silent for a moment, then added, 'Ah. You'd better ask her that,' and he handed the phone back. 'He wants to know how come you're here.'

Jim's voice was concerned. 'Ellie? What's happened?'

'Yeah, I had a bit of an issue with the new senior vet. We have previously, and I—er—I walked out. Long story, I'll tell you another time, but it's not your fault. This was strictly personal and a bit of a vendetta on his part.'

'Oh, Ellie, I'm so sorry,' Jim said heavily.

'Don't be. It's not your fault, Jim, you did what was right for you and right for the practice. You had no control over who they hired, and neither did I.'

'No, apparently not, but it sounds like you're well out of

it. You'll be all right with Hugo, though. He's a good lad. You can trust him.'

She hoped so, because right then she was all out of options. She said goodbye, hung up, met his eyes and raised a brow. 'Well?'

'According to Jim, you're the best vet he's ever had. I reckon that'll do me.'

He unfolded his legs and stood up, picked up their empty bowls and held out a hand, pulling her to her feet and sending tingles all the way down her arm.

'Why don't you get some fresh clothes from your car and see if you can find that paperwork, and I'll get the buster collar for Lola and keep an eye on her. There's a shower out the back, I'll find you a towel. And leave your clothes outside the shower, I'll throw them in the washing machine to get the blood off.'

She emerged from the shower feeling infinitely more civilised, to find he'd taken her clothes away. He'd also changed, so she guessed his scrubs were in the wash, too. And he'd put a pile of bedding in the office for her.

'I thought you might want to sleep next to Lola. You know, so you can hear the second she moves?'

She felt her shoulders drop as yet another worry fell away from her. 'That would be amazing. I was contemplating setting an alarm to check on her every half hour.'

He frowned. 'You can't do that. You need your sleep. You've got another long day tomorrow. I've topped up her pain relief, but she'll need to go out before you go to bed.'

She nodded. 'Where can I take her?'

'I'll show you, I've got to take Rufus out anyway now. I normally set the burglar alarm when I knock off, but I'll show you how it works so you can set it and unset it in the night if you need to take her out again.'

He led her out through the kitchen at the back, and into a garden. She wasn't expecting that, somehow, but as the light came on automatically she could see a large square of lawn with shrubs and trees around the sides against the old red brick walls, and an area of paving with some seating.

Rufus trotted off and started sniffing around, and Lola followed, limping a little unsteadily down the gentle ramp, then making her way onto the grass. She didn't bother to sniff, just bopped down awkwardly.

'Good girl,' Ellie said softly when she was done, and the dog turned and made her way back inside to her kennel without a fuss, lying down and letting out a big sigh.

'She's doing well.'

'She is. I'm so grateful to you—'

He rolled his eyes. 'You're like a stuck record. Wait till tomorrow, I'll get my own back.'

She somehow didn't think so. Nothing she did could ever make up for his care and kindness, but doing that shift for him might go some small way to redress the balance.

'I found my paperwork,' she told him. 'It's on the desk in the office.'

'Great. I'll take a look in the morning. Right, let's get this cone on Lola so she can't rip the drain out while you're asleep, and then I'll move your bed.'

They had to shoo Rufus off the folding bed before they moved it out beside Lola's kennel, and he showed her where the light switches were, put on a dim nightlight so she could see Lola, and showed her how to set and unset the alarm, a necessary evil because the drugs on the premises were a prime target.

Then he handed her a slip of paper. 'My mobile number. Call me if you're worried about her and I'll come down. I live over the practice.'

That didn't surprise her, she'd done it herself until last night, and lots of vets with small practices did the same. It was the 'I', not 'we', that struck her, but it might not be significant. And anyway, it was none of her business.

'Thank you. I'm sure she'll be fine. Will my car be OK outside? It's just it's got my whole life in it right now.'

'It should be if you've locked it. I'm about to close the gates and there's CCTV on the drive.'

She felt another layer of stress peel away and smiled at him. 'That's great. Thank you.'

He went out through the side door and she watched him go, her mind whirling as she made up the bed.

He needed a vet. He wanted her to 'interview' for the post by doing the shift tomorrow. Was he serious? And would she contemplate it, so soon after the fall-out of the last one? But Jim had called him a 'good lad' and said she could trust him, and he'd been nothing but kindness…

He came back in then, cutting off her tumbling thoughts.

'Right, that's me done. Help yourself to anything you want in the kitchen, and shout if you need me. I'll be down here by seven. Sleep tight.'

Not a chance. She had far too much to think about. She dredged up a tired smile. 'You, too. And thank you, Hugo. For everything.'

His eyes creased into an answering smile that did something strange to her midsection. 'You're welcome. Rufus, come on, you're not sleeping there,' he said, and Rufus hopped down off her bed and trotted after him.

They went through a doorway, and she heard his footsteps

recede as they made their way up, leaving her alone with Lola and her thoughts.

Did she want to work here? Maybe—and maybe not, or not long term. But—locum? At least that way she'd have an income while she decided.

She lay down fully dressed, with her head close to Lola's kennel so she could see her just by turning her head. She'd settled down, and after a moment Ellie heard a gentle snore.

Poor Lola. What a start to their new life together, but at least they wouldn't starve, so maybe it wasn't going to be so bad after all…

She slept surprisingly well, and so, to her relief, did Lola.

She picked up her phone and looked at the time.

Six forty-three. He'd said he'd be down by seven, so she threw off the covers and got up, turned off the burglar alarm and checked on Lola.

She wagged her tail but didn't move. Not surprising, really. Her leg would be sore this morning, now the pain relief had worn off, but she hadn't complained once in the night and she'd accepted the cone without argument.

She put the fold-up bed away in the office, coaxed Lola out of her kennel, took her out for a sniff and a wee, then put her back in her kennel, had a quick wash and was heading for the kitchen when she heard the light patter of little feet running down the stairs, followed by a heavier tread, and Hugo and Rufus came through the door.

'Morning,' he said cheerfully, all freshly showered and smelling delicious. He handed her a neatly folded pile of yesterday's clothes.

'Gosh, that was quick! Thank you.'

'Pleasure. How are you both today? Did you sleep?'

'Better than expected,' she said with a wry laugh, trying not to think about how good he smelt. 'That bed is seriously comfy and Lola slept all night.'

'Good. I'll have a look in a minute. Ready for the fray?'

'I will be when I've eaten something. Can I make some toast?'

'Sure. Stick a couple of bits in for me while I have a look at Lola. Has she been out?'

'Yes. She seems fine, but a bit sore, I think.'

'I'm sure. I'll give her another shot. I just want to check her leg for the circulation, make sure it's not cold or swelling—'

'It isn't. It feels fine, which is a relief. I just wish I knew what she'd cut it on.'

'Well, we'll find out later, won't we? How about the drain?'

'The bottle had a little in. I left it for you to see.'

'Have you fed her?'

'No, not yet. Her food's somewhere in the car, but it's buried. I'll get it.'

'Is she a fussy eater?'

She laughed. 'She's a Labrador. What do you think?'

His mouth twitched. 'I'll give her something bland, then, see how she gets on with it. She may not want much.'

'Tea or coffee?'

'Coffee. White, no sugar. There's a machine in the corner and pods on the side.'

To his relief, Lola's foot was warm and not swollen and the drain was doing its job. She greeted him with a wag of her tail and a lick, and didn't even flinch when he gave her the painkilling injection, just inhaled her breakfast and lay down again. She was very lame, but that was to be expected, and she'd accepted the plastic cone around her head without too much fuss.

She seemed an utter sweetheart, and he could absolutely see why Ellie had refused to put her to sleep. He would have done the same under the circumstances. *Had* done the same, hence Rufus, and he hadn't regretted it for a moment.

He sorted out the suction drain, then went back to the kitchen, drawn by the smell of toast and coffee. They took it through to the office and after he'd looked through her paperwork they went through the morning's appointments together.

'OK, I've switched things around a bit, given you all the routine stuff, but we've got Kerry in, she's our head nurse, and she'll be able to give you a hand if you can't find anything. Oh, and I've found you some scrubs to wear.'

He showed her how the computer system worked, then swivelled round and met her eyes. 'Any questions?'

Too many.

She was still reeling with the shock of the last forty-eight hours, and she was glad he'd given her the simple consults, but there would still be much she didn't know about the practice.

'Can you give me a quick guided tour?'

'Sure.'

He got up and led her through a door to the reception desk in a corner of the waiting room. It was a lovely room, with a bay window to the front, high ceilings and ornate plaster cornicing. There was a screened waiting area for cats, and across the hall, past the lobby with the beautiful old front door she'd pounded on last night, was the main waiting room and doors to the two consulting rooms. They had doors at the back leading via a corridor to the stock room and pharmacy, the X-ray room and the areas she'd already seen. These areas, unlike the waiting rooms and entrance at the front, were modern, crisp and clinical. Pretty standard fare, really, and nothing she hadn't seen before, but spotlessly clean and very well equipped.

'Happy?'

She nodded, feeling a flicker of nerves, the word 'interview' hovering in the back of her mind. Actually, make that front...

'I'm fine.'

Her list of consults had been, as he'd promised, simple and straightforward, and Kerry had been a huge help. She'd also kept an eye on Lola, and said she was doing fine.

One less thing to worry about.

She saw her last client of the morning and was just filling in the details on the computer when there was a tap on the door and Hugo stuck his head round.

'Are you done?'

'Pretty much. I'm just writing the last one up.'

He closed the door and propped himself against it, somehow sucking all the air out of the room. 'How did you get on? Was everything OK?'

Was it? She'd thought so, but maybe Kerry had raised some concerns?

'I think so.'

'Kerry thinks so, too. She basically told me if I don't offer you the job she's going to walk.' He shrugged away from the door and shot her a grin that turned her heart inside out. 'Fancy a quick sandwich before we go and tackle the house?'

'Um—yes, please, that would be great. I'll just finish up here.'

He nodded and walked out, and she stared after him.

Had he just offered her a job?

Maybe… And maybe she was reading too much into it. She closed the file, shut down the computer and followed him out.

While Ellie took Lola out to the garden for a moment, he loaded his car with milk, teabags and a packet of biscuits, the carpet shampooer and cleaning stuff and some gardening tools, then once Lola was settled he put Rufus in his crate in the office and followed Ellie to her house.

It was small, modern, unprepossessing but innocuous— until you got inside.

'Hmm,' he grunted, and Ellie looked over her shoulder and gave him a wonky little smile.

'See what I mean?'

His answering smile felt every bit as crooked. 'Well, you didn't lie, let's put it like that.'

He followed her through the tired and grubby living room into the kitchen. 'This looks OK. I think you can rescue it with a bit of elbow grease.'

'I can, it just needs a good scrub. The rest is harder— especially the garden.'

He nodded, a glance through the window enough to make his heart sink. Then she opened the back door, and the full story of last night's horror with Lola was revealed.

'Wow,' he murmured, staring at the stains all over the paving. 'She really was hosing blood.'

'She was. It's a miracle I managed to slow it enough to

get her to you. Goodness knows what's lurking in the grass
to tear her to shreds.'

Whatever it was, he couldn't see it. It was well and truly
hidden by the overgrown grass and the tangle of weeds. No
wonder she'd felt so defeated last night. Time to sort it out.

'Right,' he said briskly, 'I'll find out what tried to kill her
in the garden while you tackle the kitchen, then we can have
a cup of tea and work out a plan for the rest of the house.'

Ten minutes later she was on her knees scrubbing the kitchen
floor when he propped himself up in the open doorway.

'I think I've found the culprit. There's a coil of barbed
wire with a loose end hanging out into the grass, and there's
blood and hair on one of the barbs. I'm guessing that's what
she caught her leg on. Come and see.'

She followed him out and studied the wire thoughtfully.
'I think you're right. It's the right height, and it looks vicious
enough. Poor Lola.'

He shot her a sympathetic smile. 'Absolutely. And poor
you, too. Did you say you had a letting agent?'

She suppressed a sigh. 'Yes.'

'Well, I have to say I don't think they earned their commission, not by the look of it. I would have thought at the
least they'd have had it cleaned up.'

'I told them not to bother. He said it needed a little attention, so I'd already booked a week's leave to come up here
to clean it. I just ended up coming a day early, but I think he
might have been a tad frugal with the truth.'

The snort said it all, and she smiled wryly. 'Yeah. My
thoughts entirely. Shall we drag the wire out of the grass so
you can mow it and find out what else lurks beneath?'

'I've got a better idea. You go back in and finish cleaning up the kitchen, and I'll sort this out.'

It wasn't just the barbed wire—not that that wasn't bad enough, but he ended up going over the mercifully small lawn with a fine-tooth comb and pulling out all sorts of stuff that had just been dumped. Plastic bottles, nappies, broken crockery, a bamboo cane from some long-dead house plant, the occasional brick…

And until it was all out, he couldn't cut the grass.

He tipped the last lot of rubbish into the bin and headed for the kitchen door, just as she opened it.

'I've made some tea. Are you finished?'

He laughed at that. 'Not exactly. I've got the worst of it, so I might run the strimmer over it next and then rake it all off.'

'After you drink tea and have a biscuit,' she said, handing him a mug. 'Sorry about the chip, the crockery seems to have suffered along the way.'

'Yeah, I found some in the grass, along with everything else.'

'I'm not surprised. Come in and sit down. You should be safe, I washed the chairs.'

Two hours later they were back at the practice, tired but satisfied with their progress. The kitchen was clean, the sitting room was almost respectable, and she felt much more positive.

And grateful, because Hugo had been a Trojan in the garden, and it looked worlds better—which was just as well, as Lola was going to have to start using it very soon.

Immediately, if it hadn't been for Hugo's insistence that Lola couldn't be moved yet, and she couldn't argue with that.

'I should be able to stay there tomorrow night,' she said, for the umpteenth time, but he just leant back in his chair, Rufus curled up on his lap, and raised an eyebrow, his eyes sceptical.

'What, on that mattress? You need to wash it first at the very least—or replace it. And anyway, there's Lola to think of. At least here it's reasonably sterile and she can stay as long as she needs to.'

She sighed. 'I suppose you're right, and she's fine in the kennel while she recovers, but I'll go back there tomorrow and carry on until I've finished, then we should be able to stay there.'

He gave her another of those looks. 'On a wet mattress.'

'Or a new one.' Although she couldn't really afford it…

'Or you could just stay here?'

'What, sleeping by her kennel?'

He hesitated for a moment, as if he was about to say something else, then shrugged. 'Or in the office. It makes sense, at least as long as she's got the suction drain. She looks wiped, and after you took her out when we got back she went straight back into her kennel and went to sleep again. She needs more time, Ellie, you know that. There's no rush, and if you're with her you can keep a better eye on her, and reassure her.'

He was right. Of course he was right, but she felt like she was imposing on him, taking advantage of his good nature, and he'd already done enough. More than enough. Starting with saving Lola's life…

'OK. Just until Monday, though. That should give me time to get a replacement mattress from somewhere, and get everything clean.'

'We should be able to make some decent progress on it

tomorrow,' he said then, taking her completely by surprise, and she stared at him.

'We?'

He frowned. 'Well—yes. I said I'd help.'

'You said you'd help *today*. I can't ask you to do that—'

'You didn't ask. I offered. And anyway,' he added with a grin, 'I'm trying to convince you I'm a decent human being so you'll take the job.'

She stared at him blankly. 'What job?'

Hugo did a mild double-take. 'The one I offered you this morning?'

Her heart thudded against her ribs. 'That was a serious job offer?'

'What did you think it was?'

She blinked and looked away. 'Uh—I don't know. I didn't realise you meant it.' And then she looked back and met his eyes, sincere and oddly intent. 'You seriously want me?'

Her words hit him like an express train, and he realised they were true—in every sense.

His heart thudded against his ribs, and he swallowed the sudden lump in his throat. 'Yes, I want you,' he said honestly. 'I need you.' And as he added that, he realised it, too, was true in every sense.

He ignored the thrashing of his pulse as he forced himself to hold her searching eyes. 'I desperately need another vet,' he said, to himself as much as to her. 'I think last night and this morning were a pretty good interview, Jim Harkness couldn't pile enough praise on your head—what else is there to think about?'

Apart from the fact that every time he caught the waft of scent from her body his gut tightened, every time she smiled or frowned or scraped that unruly tendril of dark hair back out of her incredible green eyes he wanted to kiss her—

He looked away, unable to hold that steady gaze for another second, not knowing what she might read in his eyes. He'd been told more than once that he'd be a lousy poker player.

'Can I think about it? I'm not sure I'm ready to commit to anything permanent yet. It's all been a bit sudden.'

He made himself meet her eyes again. 'Sure. I don't suppose you want to locum while you think?'

He held his breath while she hesitated, and then she nodded slowly. 'OK. Just for a while, until I decide what I'm doing with my life, and Lola's a bit better.'

That sounded a hugely sensible idea, and it meant neither of them would be committed to what already felt like a complicated relationship, at least on his side. And that was the last thing he needed. Thank goodness he hadn't offered her the flat. He'd been so close to it just now. He allowed himself to breathe again and hauled out a smile.

'Excellent. I think that calls for a celebration. How about a takeaway? I'll let you choose.'

By the end of the next day the upstairs was cleaned, the mattress included, and the bathroom had been scrubbed within an inch of its life, and with the windows open and a lovely fresh breeze blowing through the house everything was drying nicely.

'Better?'

She smiled at him and laughed. 'Much better. So, so much better. I don't know how to thank you, Hugo. You've been amazing.'

He chuckled softly and turned away before he did something stupid like haul her into his arms and kiss that smiling mouth.

'I had to do something to keep you on board,' he said lightly, and then picked up the carpet shampooer. 'I'll put this lot in the car while you shut the windows, and then we need to get back to the dogs. I think Lola's drain's probably ready to come out now, but I want to have a proper look at her first.'

'If she's OK and you've got a crate I can borrow, she and I can stay here tonight now.'

He frowned. 'Really? You've got no food, the mattress is still damp—what's the rush? And anyway, Lola isn't out of the woods yet, she'll need cage rest for another two weeks and you're working tomorrow, so you might as well be there or you'll have to move her backwards and forwards, which won't be comfortable for her. Besides, I've got a lasagne thawing and I can't eat it all.'

His logic was unassailable, but she still felt as if she was taking advantage. Plus, she was worried about the bill for Lola's in-patient treatment. All of it, really, because she'd taken out insurance for her after her abscess, and that wasn't yet a month. And anything in the first month was excluded, as he'd pointed out.

She thought about that all the way back, and as soon as they were in and the dogs were fed, she tackled him about it.

'You need to bill me for Lola's treatment and her care,' she said, and he raised an eyebrow and smiled.

'I think we've gone a little past that now, don't you?'

She frowned. 'But—'

'No buts. We'll be horrendously busy tomorrow morning with all the people who've hung on over the weekend so they didn't have to pay the out-of-hours rate, on top of an already full clinic, so I'll well and truly be getting my own back. And anyway, you're doing most of the caring, and we're hardly short of kennel space.'

He wasn't going to budge, she could tell that just from the look he gave her, but there was still room to negotiate.

'On one condition,' she said firmly. 'I don't want the standard locum rate, I want you to work out what you'd pay for a full-time vet, divide it by the number of hours they'd work, and pay me that pro-rata. And I'll pay her bill. You can give me a staff discount if it makes you feel better.'

One eyebrow quirked up. 'You're cheating yourself.'

'No, I'm just not cheating *you*. I don't need to rip you off, I just need to earn enough to live on. Take it or leave it.'

'And if I say no?'

'Then you're a vet down tomorrow.'

He held her eyes, then a slow smile tipped his mouth at one side, and he nodded, and she felt the tension seep out of her. 'You're a very stubborn person, do you know that?' he said mildly, and then with a little shake of his head and a tiny huff of laughter, he looked down at Lola, resting in her kennel and watching them.

'We need to check that drain,' he said, and closed the subject.

CHAPTER THREE

THERE WAS NO 'easing in gently' or giving her the simple stuff on Monday morning. After an early start to sort Lola out, she was straight in with a dog spay, a cat castrate and then a cruciate repair on a terrier who'd snapped a ligament in his knee joint.

Kerry must have given him a heads up on that, she realised, as he stuck his head out of his consulting room.

'I think he probably needs a lateral suture. Are you happy to do that?'

'Sure. I've done it before—I've got an ortho certificate.'

He nodded. 'Good. Kerry'll give you a hand, help you find what you need and assist. Shout if you run into any issues.'

'Will do.'

She didn't, to her relief, and after she'd finished the operation and they'd X-rayed him and Ellie was confident the joint was going to be stable, she and Kerry put him into a small kennel cage in the area where Lola was lying, looking bored.

At least her drain was out and her leg was healing nicely. It would still take a good while, but she'd be left with a fine, neat scar and a functional leg, thanks to Hugo.

She was relieved by that. Poor Lola had had enough to deal with. 'Hello, sweetie,' she said, giving her dog a little tickle through the bars, but there wasn't time for more, even though Lola was pleading and pawing at the door.

'I'll take her out for a wee,' Kerry said, and Ellie left them to it and went to see if there were any more consults she could help with.

She was on the last one, a little spaniel puppy called Mr Wiggles in for his second vaccinations, when the door at the back opened and Hugo stuck his head round.

'I hear there's a puppy,' he said with a grin, and he came in and gave the wiggly little pup a cuddle while she drew up his vaccinations.

He obviously knew the owner, and they chatted while she gave him the injection.

'Oh, you're such a good boy,' Ellie said, ruffling his long floppy ears, and he wiggled and licked her.

'They're so forgiving,' his owner said with a laugh, and carried the puppy out, leaving her alone with Hugo.

'So how's it been?'

'Busy? Good? Let me fill this in and we can talk about it.'

'Tell me over lunch, I'll make you a coffee,' he said, and she glanced up at the clock. Half past one, and consults started again at two.

'Thanks,' she said, and he left her to it. By the time she emerged three minutes later there was a coffee and a sandwich waiting for her in the kitchen, and she took it into the office and sat down with him.

'So, tell me all about your morning. How did you get on?'

'All right, I think. The spay and castrate were routine, and the cruciate repair seems stable.'

'Yeah, I had a look. Nice tidy job.'

It had been and she didn't really need his praise, but nevertheless it was good to hear, and she felt a silly little glow of pride. What a contrast to Craig, still bitter because she'd dumped him ten years ago.

Hugo, on the other hand, seemed like a genuinely decent human being. To date he'd been nothing but generous towards her, and she owed it to him to do her best in return.

'What are you doing tonight?' he asked, and she swallowed her bite of sandwich and shrugged.

'Moving my stuff into the house, I guess. Taking Lola home with me, settling her in, buying some food—is it OK if I borrow a crate for a while?'

Hugo frowned. 'Ellie, you're welcome to a crate, but I don't think she's ready yet. She can't jump into the car, she can't do steps, she has to be on cage rest—I've been thinking, why don't you keep her in the kennel here and move into the flat upstairs till she's better?'

She stared at him. 'Hugo, you—I can't just move into your flat, it's ridiculous!'

'Not *my* flat,' he said hastily. 'There's another one, at the top. I'll show you later. I'm assuming you'd bring Lola to work every day anyway, wouldn't you?'

'Well, yes, if that's OK, but—'

'That's fine, then. She can lie here in the crate in the day for a change of scenery, and she can go back in the kennel at night. She'll have plenty of company, lots going on, you'll be able to keep an eye on her, and it won't stress the wound.'

She stared at him, slightly stunned. 'But—I thought you'd want us out of the way?'

'You're not in the way. And she's a sweetheart, she's no trouble. The flat's fully equipped, so you'll only need clothes and anything else you might want, so after we shut up shop I'll give you a hand to empty your car, and you can sort out what you want up there and put the rest in the store room, if you like?'

Did she like? She wasn't sure. He'd done so much for her,

and being independent was hard-wired into her DNA, but nevertheless it seemed churlish to refuse his help after he'd already been so generous. And then there was the question of the rent, but she had no choice really while Lola was so immobile, she knew that. She just hoped she could afford it.

'Thanks for the offer, but I've got plenty of room for my things at the house, if you don't mind me leaving Lola here while I go and dump them?' she said, and he got to his feet.

'Sure. We can sort out the details later,' he said, drained the last of his coffee and headed out, and then Kerry came in, followed by Jean, the practice manager.

'Ah, Ellie, I need your bank details and all the other HR stuff for the records,' Jean said to her as she stood up to follow Hugo out. 'Not urgently, but when you can?'

'Sure. I've got to empty my car later, it's all in there. I'll give it to you tomorrow if that's OK?'

'That's fine. It's good to have you here, by the way,' she added. 'Hugo's been struggling for too long, and with our only other full-time vet off on maternity leave it's been ridiculous, so we're all really relieved that you turned up when you did.'

'I'm only locuming,' she said, feeling the net of commitment tightening around her, and Jean smiled knowingly.

'So he tells me, but you're still very welcome.'

And now she felt guilty for refusing to consider a permanent job.

Although the door to that was also still ajar...

As soon as she'd finished for the day she fed Lola and let her out, then put her away again and headed for the house.

It was the first time she'd been in it alone since Lola's accident, and she stood for a moment, listening to the silence.

Would it ever feel like home?

Weird thought. She'd never lived in a home that she owned, but it still felt like someone else's. Moving in might help, but Hugo of course had had a view about that and the moment Lola's leg was healed enough she'd be here like a shot.

She ferried all her belongings into the house, dumped them on the floor and stared at the pathetically small pile. It was everything she owned, but now she had a permanent base—

Did she want it to be that? Not necessarily. It didn't need to be, although apparently it could be, if Hugo had his way.

Did she want to take the job he'd offered, live here in Yoxburgh, start to put down new roots in a place she'd always loved but never really known?

A bit of her—the bit she didn't trust, because it had shown pretty lousy judgement in the past—said yes. The rest, the bit that had told Craig exactly where to stick his job, said no.

She didn't know enough about Hugo.

Yes, he'd been kind, yes, he'd been highly spoken of by her old boss, but what would he be like to work with? Fair, definitely, she was sure of that, but it all seemed too easy, and she didn't trust 'easy'. Not now, after all that had happened. And another job going wrong, if it did, would firmly put the kibosh on her CV. No. She'd locum for him, but that was it. She really, really wasn't ready to commit herself again so soon, and especially not to someone as charming as Hugo. She couldn't trust it. Couldn't trust *him,* whatever Jim had said.

She went through the pile of bags, pulled out the things she might need, stacked the rest under the stairs and then headed back to the practice with—not dread, exactly, but reluctance.

She knew it made sense, she knew Lola couldn't easily be moved backwards and forwards yet, but right now she felt so dislocated that she was desperate for a home of her own.

And she was going to be living in Hugo's flat. Well, not *his* exactly, but as good as. Was that a good idea? It didn't sound like it, but he was frankly too kind for his own good and she owed him so much already that she didn't really want to put on him any more. But she felt stressed and a bit cornered, and if it hadn't been for Lola...

If it hadn't been for Lola she'd still be working with the odious Craig, but she wasn't, and Lola had to come first.

She drove into the car park just as Hugo was parking his car, and he got out and waved a shopping bag at her.

'Supper,' he said, and she felt another wave of guilt to add to the stress.

'Hugo, you should have sent me a shopping list! I didn't even think about food, but I can't keep sponging off you.'

'Don't be ridiculous.'

He closed the gates and locked them, and she followed him in through the staff entrance, bags in hand.

'Right, I'll just get Rufus and we'll take all this up and go and eat.'

'What about Lola?'

'She's fine, I checked on her before I went out. She's sleeping and there's a camera so we can keep an eye on her on my phone. Let's get this food cooked. I'm starving.'

He let Rufus out of his crate and she followed them up what must once have been the wide main stairs of the house, past a glorious stained glass window and onto a large, open landing with a high ceiling and ornate cornicing. The flat was much bigger than she'd imagined, certainly bigger than the one she'd recently vacated, thanks to Craig, and significantly nicer. Much bigger than her house, too, but that wasn't difficult.

His bedroom door was open just enough to see a large sleigh bed, the duvet neatly turned back to air. She dragged her eyes and imagination off it and followed him into the kitchen, light and bright and spotlessly clean, with a range of integrated appliances and a table by the window.

'Right, food,' he said, and unloaded the shopping. 'Are you OK with fish pie?'

Her stomach rumbled, and he chuckled. 'I'll take that as a yes.' He put the oven on to heat, and she leant against the worktop and tried not to watch him as he removed the film from the top of the ready meal and put it in the oven.

'This is a lovely flat,' she said, and he smiled.

'It is, isn't it? I've redecorated it and refitted the kitchen and bathroom, but I don't spend nearly enough time in it. I'll show you the other one now while the food heats, if you like?'

'Sure.'

They went through a door off his hallway, onto the landing of what must have been the old back stairs. She followed him up into a much smaller but equally well-presented space, with a double bedroom, a shower room, a small but well-equipped kitchen and a welcoming living room, all with sloping ceilings at the sides making it seem cosy and intimate. And homely.

She stood in the dormer window of the sitting room looking down into the garden and felt him move to stand behind her.

'You can see the sea from here,' he murmured, pointing towards the gap between the houses. 'Look along my finger.'

She did, leaning altogether too close to him to look and

feeling the brush of the soft hairs on his forearm teasing her cheek and making it tingle.

'Found it? It's only a glimpse.'

She had, the line of the horizon peeping through the roof-tops, but it wasn't nearly as fascinating as the scent drifting off his body, an intoxicating combination of citrus and the rich, warm note of musk from his skin, and her cheek was still tingling.

'Yes, I can see it,' she murmured, and he dropped his arm so she could breathe again.

'So what do you think?'

She thought he smelt more delicious than a man had any right to smell, but she put the thought firmly out of her mind. She inched away from him and sucked in a quiet breath.

'It's lovely. Perfect,' she added, and felt some of the stress drain away.

'Tell me if you think it would be any kind of incentive to a new vet. I was thinking of putting it in the advert.'

Her eyes widened. 'Goodness, yes, I would have thought anyone would be tempted by it, especially as you live here, too, so it means they don't have all the responsibility for the practice at night. I found that quite challenging, some-times, and I was always the first person to any emergency, of course.'

He laughed and moved away. 'Yes, I know how that works,' he said, and headed towards the door. 'Come on, let's go and have our meal, then you can settle in.'

'We need to talk about rent,' she said, and he turned back to her with a frown.

'Rent? What rent?'

'For the flat.'

He gave a soft huff of laughter and shook his head slowly.

'There is no rent, Ellie. If it goes with the job, it goes with the job. And right now, you're doing the job. End of.'

Feeling slightly stunned and a lot relieved, Ellie followed him back down.

The fish pie was delicious, and after they'd eaten it he made them coffee and picked the mugs up.

'Let's go and sit down somewhere comfortable,' he said, and led her to the sitting room, with a beautiful marble fireplace and the same original plaster cornicing. It must have been a very grand house in its day.

Not that it wasn't grand now, but in a more relaxed way—especially since Rufus had made himself at home on the sofa.

'This is a beautiful room,' she said, and he smiled.

'It is, isn't it? I really should spend more time in here.'

She settled herself into what had to be the comfiest sofa in the world and cradled the mug in her hands.

'So how come you're a vet?' she asked, partly out of curiosity and partly to fill the silence, and he gave a soft grunt.

'Oh—long story.'

'I've got time. And you've had to put up with mine.'

She looked at him and he smiled, but it didn't reach his eyes and he looked away before she did.

'Well, you asked, so here goes.' He hesitated for a moment, then started to speak, his voice flat and matter-of-fact.

'My father was a consultant surgeon at Addenbrooke's in Cambridge, my mother was a GP until I came along, then she stayed at home and looked after me and did all the admin for his private work. They got a dog, because I nagged, and every time she needed the vet I went along, and I was interested. I told my father I wanted to be a vet like my godfather Peter, and he said no. Be a doctor. If you're a vet, you'll spend all your time killing things. If you're a doctor, you'll be saving lives.'

Ellie stared at him, stunned. 'We save lives. We save lives every single day!'

'I know. That's what I told him, and I told him lots of people die, doctors or no doctors, but looking back I think he didn't want me to be a vet because he regarded it as inferior. And then our dog got sick, and our vet couldn't save her, and she was put to sleep—which just proved his point.'

'So why *aren't* you a doctor?'

'Because I've never wanted to be. Peter's influence, probably, and because I've always loved animals. This was his practice, and I used to love it when we stayed here and I could spend time with his menagerie. And then when I was ten, Mum was diagnosed with cancer, and Dad had a heart attack. They inserted a stent, put him on all the drugs, and he was fine and she was responding well to the chemo, but then two years later she was told it had spread and it was terminal, and a week later he had another massive heart attack and died.'

She sucked in a breath, her heart aching for the boy he'd been. 'Oh, Hugo. I'm so sorry. How old were you?'

'Twelve. But in a way it proved me right, because the doctors couldn't save him, any more than they could save my mother. She died two years after him, when I was fourteen, and I spent a lot of time here with Peter and Sally during her last few months. Mum had made Peter my legal guardian when she knew she was dying, and they took me in and welcomed me with open arms. They'd never had children, and Peter would have been a brilliant father. He *was* a brilliant father, and Sally was a wonderful mother figure, so kind, so understanding. And after Mum died, I was horrible to them.'

'Horrible?'

He gave a tiny huff of laughter. 'Yeah. I was fourteen, and I was an orphan. That's all I could hear, that word, and nothing could take it away. I was utterly broken with grief and anger, but they understood why, and they gave me the little flat. I still ate with them, lived with them, really, but it became my bolt-hole, my sanctuary, and it saved my sanity because I had a private space to grieve in and to come to terms with what was now my life.'

Her eyes welled over and she blinked to clear them. 'That must have been so hard.'

'It was, but I left my old school and went to one in Woodbridge, and I never told anyone there that my parents were dead, so I didn't have to deal with their sympathy, which made it easier. Peter took me under his wing, gave me his time unstintingly, and when I'd got over the initial trauma, he showed me everything he could. He had me doing stuff in the practice every holiday, and when that got boring he fixed me up with some farmers so I could learn about sheep and cattle, then he sent me off to a stable yard where I spent a glorious summer mucking out the horses and learning how to handle them, and all the time he was keeping me on target in school, making sure I got the grades I needed.'

He threw her a wry smile. 'Not that he had to push me, I was all the way there myself, but then they supported me through uni until I got my first job in a mixed practice, then he took me on himself when I decided I wanted to specialise in companion animals. He mentored me, taught me everything he knew, and when he retired eight years ago at sixty I bought him out. I'd moved back into the little flat when I started work here, and I lived in it until Peter and Sally moved out, and then I renovated this one, moved into it and did up the little one.'

'So it really is home to you,' she said, and he nodded.

'Oh, yes, absolutely. This place has been a lifesaver, one way or another, and it's been my home and sanctuary for the last twenty-five years.'

So he was thirty-nine, and he'd been a year younger than she was when he'd bought the practice. There was no way she could even dream of doing that.

'It feels like it wraps itself round you,' she said softly.

'It always did. I think it was their love that did that. I owe them everything, him and Sally, and my parents. They left their estate in trust for me until I was twenty-five, which meant I was able to buy the practice, but—yeah, everything I am today, I owe to Peter. He literally saved my life and gave me a reason to go on, and I owe him more than I can ever say.'

'He sounds pretty special,' she said softly after a long pause. 'You were lucky to have him as a father figure.'

'I was. I've been so, so lucky to have them both in my life, and without them there's no way I'd be here doing the job I love.'

'And Jim? How did you end up there?'

'Rotation via college. Peter knew him, though, so maybe that was another string he pulled, but he never said so. It wouldn't surprise me. They've stuck by me through thick and thin, and some of it's been pretty tough.'

He drew in a long, slow breath and turned to look at her, and she knew from the shield that had come down over his eyes that there was something else that he wasn't telling her.

'So that's me,' he said, done with the confessions. 'How about you? Why are you a vet?'

* * *

She held his eyes for a long moment, then gave him a strange little smile and looked away.

'Good question. I don't really know the answer. It just sort of…evolved. I wasn't sure it was what I wanted, but there was nothing else that was ever on my radar, and I had to do something.'

'Had to?' he asked, probing a little.

'Well—yes. I had to earn a living, but I needed a career that would give me job satisfaction, I was bright, I loved animals—it just seemed a bit obvious really.'

'But?'

She shrugged. 'But I was never really sure. I found it all a bit intimidating, but my mother was very keen that I should make the best of myself and take whatever opportunities were presented to me.'

My mother?

'What did your father think?' he asked, probing a little.

She gave a hollow little laugh that spoke volumes. 'I have no idea. He left my mother when I was little and I haven't seen him since, so I've never had a father figure.'

That shocked him. 'You've never seen him?'

'No, and there's never been any father figure in my life. You don't know how lucky you are.'

'Oh, I do. Believe me, I do. So how did your mum cope?'

'I don't know. It must have been tough. She had to work hard to support and house us on her own. There were times when it was really hard, and after all she put into it, I couldn't let her down.'

'And if she hadn't been like that?'

'Then maybe I would have found something else to do, something less challenging, less complicated, less—difficult.'

That was odd. 'Difficult?'

She looked at him, then away again, a slightly twisted smile on her lips. 'Difficult. Yes, we save lives, but as your father said, we also take them, and we have to break a lot of bad news. I always find that hard. It breaks their hearts, and—I don't know, sometimes there just seem to be days when you have to do it over and over, and it drains you.'

'But not as much as watching animals suffer because the owners, often for good reason, can't bear to let them go. I watched my mother die of cancer, and I wouldn't wish that on anyone, human or animal.'

She nodded slowly. 'Yes, I get that, and I absolutely agree. It's a privilege to be able to spare them that, but—then you get a dog like Lola, otherwise fit and healthy, who can easily be saved with a simple operation and some antibiotics, and you have to put it to sleep, because you can't just take them all in or you'd end up running an animal shelter.'

'But you took Lola.'

She looked down at Rufus between them, and he watched a tear slide down her cheek as she stroked him gently.

'Yes, I did, and I'd do it again, but look where it got us both. And what if it happens again? What if there's another Lola? When do you stop?'

He reached out and put his hand over hers and gave her fingers a little squeeze, then left it there, his thumb absently stroking the back of her hand.

'There'll always be another Lola. That's how I got Rufus. Elderly owner, unaffordable bill, energetic pup she couldn't cope with. Her kids had bought him for her to cheer her up after her husband died, but she wasn't ready for it and she couldn't cope with a puppy. And her family weren't able to take him on, because they all worked full-time, and they couldn't pay the bill either, so I did what you did, I took him on.'

She looked up and met his eyes, her lips tilting in a sad little smile that made something inside him ache to comfort her.

'We're a right pair, aren't we?' she said, and he chuckled.

'You could say that,' he said, and gave her fingers another quick squeeze and retrieved his hand before it got too used to holding hers. 'And talking of dogs, we need to take them both out, and then you need to settle in.'

She followed him down the stairs, and while he took Rufus in the garden she went into the kennel area and found Lola fast asleep.

'Lola? Wake up, sweetie,' she murmured.

She opened the kennel door, and Lola lifted her head and stared at her, and she took the cone off and stroked her gently. 'Come on, poppet, let's take you out in the garden and then put you back to bed. We've got another busy day tomorrow and I need some sleep.'

They went out, and after Rufus had sniffed Lola and she'd returned the favour, she bopped down for her wee and then led Ellie back inside and went straight into her kennel and lay down.

He's right, Ellie thought. *She's not ready for anything other than rest right now.* She sat with her for a while until Hugo came in, and he crouched down beside her, the tantalising waft of warm male body drifting over her again as he gave Lola a gentle stroke.

'She's a good girl,' he murmured, and she swallowed hard.

'She is—and you were absolutely right, she's not ready for

anything other than lying here and recovering. Thank you for letting me use the flat while that happens.'

'You're welcome. Shout if you need anything, you know where I am.' His mouth tilted in a slight smile, and after a second he straightened up. 'I'll take your bags up for you. See you tomorrow. Sleep well.'

'You, too—and thank you.'

His mouth tipped again into that smile she was getting all too fond of, and he went upstairs with Rufus, taking his warmth away but leaving the faint lingering trace of his scent that teased her senses and made her think things she really, really shouldn't. Not if she wanted to keep her sanity.

She put the cone back on Lola, changed her water and settled her for the night before heading up the back stairs, past the door that led to his flat, on up the second flight to her temporary home.

At least the bed was made, presumably in readiness for a guest, and she was more than ready to crawl into it and find some oblivion. He'd put her bags on the chest of drawers, and she found her wash things and cleaned her teeth, then lay down in the welcoming, comfy bed, desperate for sleep and yet wide awake, her thoughts tumbling.

Yet again, Hugo had come riding to the rescue. Yes, sure, he needed a vet and if she'd taken Lola home, she could only have worked restricted hours for a while, so he might have had a vested interest, and of course there was the permanent job he kept dangling in front of her like a nice juicy carrot.

But she knew enough about Hugo now to realise that his offer might simply have been an act of kindness. Did he really need another vet? Jean had said someone was on maternity leave. Did he know that she wasn't coming back? Or coming back part-time? Or was it just Hugo being Hugo…?

She rolled onto her side with a little growl of frustration, tugged the pillow into the crook of her neck and shut her eyes firmly.

One day at a time. Starting with tomorrow.

CHAPTER FOUR

ANY DOUBTS SHE might have had about Hugo's motivation vanished the next morning. By the time she'd dealt with Lola and was ready to start it was a quarter to eight, but there were already three cars in the car park, and she could hear Hugo's voice rattling off instructions in the background.

She followed the sound and found him surrounded by nurses, all working furiously on a puppy. Her little spaniel puppy of yesterday, Mr Wiggles.

'Anything I can do?' she asked, and he shook his head.

'No, short of teaching puppies not to eat stuff they shouldn't. Right, let's open him up and find out what's going on. Ellie, could you pick up the consults, please? I'm going to be tied up for a bit.'

'Sure.'

She left them to it, and for the next half hour she did mostly routine things—until it all hit the fan with Chester, a two-year-old Dalmatian that had eaten chewing gum.

His owner was distraught. 'I wasn't sure if it mattered, but I looked it up on the Internet and I thought I ought to bring him in. He hadn't wanted to go for his walk, and then he seemed floppy and started to vomit, and a bit of gum came up, and then I saw the pot lying on the floor. He must have got it off the worktop—'

'How much was in the pot?'

'About a third? I don't know. I brought it to show you.'

She pulled out a small pot, her hands shaking, and Ellie's heart sank. Sugar-free gum with xylitol—and a third of the pot?

'OK, I'm going to have to admit him and get him on a glucose drip fast because his body thinks he's had a lot of sugar and will be pumping out insulin. Get Reception to give you a consent form to sign, and I'll get the drip in now, but don't worry, I think we've got him in time.'

She scooped the floppy dog up and carried him quickly out to the prep room. 'Can anyone help me, please? I've got a dog who's ingested xylitol.'

Kerry detached herself from the puppy group and came over. 'I'll warm the dextrose. Can you get a line in?'

'Sure.' She shaved his front leg, slid in the cannula, withdrew bloods for analysis and flushed the line, and by the time she'd done that and given him a bolus of dextrose to kickstart his blood sugar recovery, the bag of dextrose was warmed and she hung the drip up and checked the blood results as soon as they came up, with Kerry monitoring him constantly.

His glucose levels had been at rock bottom, but he was slowly starting to wake up, to her relief.

Then Hugo arrived at her side, a brush of warmth against her arm, sending distracting tingles through her body.

'How's he doing?'

Focus!

'OK, I think. We might just have caught it in time. Do you have any hepatoprotectant, in case his liver's affected?'

'Yes, I'll get you some. Kerry, what does he weigh?'

'He was twenty-six point four kg last time he was

weighed,' Kerry said promptly, and Hugo nodded and disappeared, coming back a minute later with the drug.

'So how's Mr Wiggles?' she asked as they worked, and he rolled his eyes.

'Better without a rubber toy in his gut.'

'What? How on earth did he swallow that?'

'No idea. It's a special skill dogs have. Do you want me to update Chester's owner on how he's doing?'

'Sure, if you've got time. I'm just going to check his bloods again, but I think he needs hospitalising. He's not out of the woods yet. He's going to need his glucose and liver enzymes monitored hourly for seventy-two hours.'

He gave her a wry smile. 'I'll go and break the news. I'm sure Mrs Grey will be delighted.'

Mrs Grey *was* delighted. Not by the fact that she'd have to drive him to the specialist centre, but because he was still alive and they'd hopefully managed to start his treatment in time.

She sat and waited for an hour until they were sure he was stable, then Hugo carried him out to the car for her.

'Thank you, Hugo. And please thank Ellie for me,' she said. 'She was so lovely to me, so quick and efficient and yet she still found time to be kind. I'm so, so grateful to you all.'

'I'll pass it on,' he said, and he went back inside. She was in consults again, and he checked on Mr Wiggles before he started his next op, a routine spay that had already been delayed two hours.

Thank God for Ellie. If he hadn't been sure of her before, he was now. He needed her in his practice. He just wasn't sure how to persuade her. Maybe Mrs Grey's message would do the trick…

* * *

The rest of the day didn't get any better.

Apart from a snatched biscuit, Ellie hadn't eaten since breakfast and by six she was running on adrenaline alone.

She said goodbye to her last client with a sigh of relief, and went out to Reception.

'Right, that's me done for the day, unless you've got anything else that's come in?' she said to Jean.

'No, we're done. Hugo's last client didn't turn up, so he's in the office and I'm going to lock the door.'

'Thank goodness for that,' she said. 'I can't believe it's still Tuesday.'

But before Jean could get to the door, a woman burst in.

'Where's Hugo? Nell's had a dreadful accident—'

'Find him, I'll go,' Ellie said to Jean without hesitation, and she ran out with the woman and found an elderly Labrador lying in the back of a car, shaking and whimpering, one leg bent at an ominous angle.

'I was bringing her to Hugo to put to sleep because of her cancer, but she slipped off the ramp getting into the car and...'

She broke off, sobbing, and Ellie gave her a quick hug. 'I'll go and get the drugs and find Hugo. Don't worry, I'll be really quick. You stay with her.'

She ran back in and found Hugo on his way out to them.

'What's up with Nell?' he asked.

'Fractured femur. She slipped getting in the car.'

He swore. 'I'll get the stuff. Can you help, please?'

It wasn't really a question that needed answering. They went out together, and found Nell's owner sitting under the tailgate by her head, stroking her side, her face grief-stricken, and she looked up at Hugo through eyes filled with tears.

'Hugo, this is all my fault, please don't let her hurt any more,' she said, and he hugged her briefly.

'Don't worry, Jenny, it'll be quick and I'll be very gentle.'

She moved out of the way, and he leant into the car.

'Hello, sweetheart,' he murmured tenderly, stroking Nell's head, and the dog looked up at him with pleading eyes. 'It's OK, Nell, it's all going to be OK, good girl,' he said, his voice low and soothing, and as soon as Ellie had clipped the little area of hair on her front leg and pressed her thumb on the vein to raise it, he took the syringe and slid in the needle, and as Ellie stepped out of the way, Nell's head sank down and she gave a quiet sigh.

'There we go, Nell,' he crooned softly, stroking her head with gentle fingers. 'It's all over now.' He put the stethoscope on her chest to listen to her heart, then turned to Jenny. 'She's gone now,' he said quietly, and stroked the old dog's head again tenderly as he straightened up.

'It's my fault,' she said, sobbing and cradling Nell's lolling head against her. 'I should have listened to you before...'

'You weren't to know she'd slip like that,' Hugo said, his voice gentle, one hand rubbing her shoulder to comfort her. 'Will you be OK to drive home?'

She nodded. 'I will be now. Thank you so much.' She sniffed and straightened up, visibly pulling herself together. 'Um—I need to pay you.'

'Don't worry about that now. Do you still want her cremated?'

'Please. That would be so kind, Hugo. We've buried the others but since I lost George...'

He squeezed her shoulder. 'It's no problem. You take care. I'll be in touch.'

Hugo lifted Nell out of the car as gently as he would an

injured child, her owner kissed her goodbye and he carried her into the back of the practice while Ellie held Jenny as she sobbed, her own eyes filling with tears.

She felt Jenny drag in a huge breath and straighten up, swiping at her eyes and fumbling for a tissue.

'Are you going to be OK?' Ellie asked her.

Her smile was sad, but her face was calmer. 'I will be. It's just the shock. She was our fifth dog, and I don't know why we kept doing it, setting ourselves up for heartache. I don't know why anyone does it.'

'Because we love them, and they bring us so much joy in their short lives. Just try and remember the good times.'

'I will, but I'll never forgive myself. Since George died she's always been by my side, and the guilt will live with me for ever. She was my best friend in my darkest hours, and I let her down...'

'No, you didn't, it was an accident. You loved her till the end, and she knew that. Don't worry, we'll take good care of her and Hugo will give you a call about her ashes.'

'Thank you,' she said, and as she drove away Ellie watched her go, tears blurring her view.

She turned and went back inside, and walked straight into Hugo's arms. They wrapped around her like a protective cocoon, and she rested her head against his shoulder for a moment, soaking up his warmth and strength. She could have stayed there for ever, breathing in the scent of his body, listening to the steady, reassuring thud of his heart beneath her ear.

'You OK?' he murmured softly, and she nodded and straightened up, and he gave her shoulders a quick squeeze before letting her go.

She followed him into the prep room where Nell was lying on the table, and she walked over to her and stroked her head tenderly. 'Poor Nell. Such a sad end. You know I hate it, we were talking about it last night, but when it's like that...'

He nodded. 'I know. I'm just sorry Jenny didn't let me do it the last time she was here and then this wouldn't have happened.'

'She told me Nell was her best friend and she let her down. She said she'll never forgive herself.'

'It's always easy to be wise after the event. They've listened to advice in the past, but maybe Nell was the last link to George. I wonder if she'll get another.'

Ellie looked down at Nell and stroked her again. 'I expect she will, the house will seem awfully empty without a dog. She said they've had five.'

'They have. I've known them all.'

She studied his face, searching his eyes as he held her gaze. There was something in his eyes, something dark and—angry? No, not angry. More...

'There's something else.'

He gave a soft laugh that wasn't a laugh at all, and looked away. 'You don't miss much, do you?' he murmured, then went on, 'My mother had a pathological fracture of her femur—she stumbled in the garden and it went. Luckily I was there with her. They took her to hospital and pinned it, then she moved to a hospice and never went home again. That was when I came to live with Peter and Sally. So—yeah, pathological fractures are a bit of a sore point.'

She could see why. How traumatic for a fourteen-year-old to witness that. 'You hid it well from Jenny.'

He shrugged. 'That's what we do. We keep our own feelings under wraps, and manage theirs. And sometimes it's harder than others. Nell was a lovely dog. I was very fond of her, and so was Jenny, but I understand how hard it is to say goodbye. It's a difficult decision. Grief is always difficult, but this just made it a whole lot harder for them both. And yet we do it to ourselves over and over again,' he added quietly, looking down at Rufus who was leaning devotedly against his leg as if he knew he needed comfort.

He reached down and Rufus licked his hand, and she smiled round the lump in her throat.

He straightened up, his eyes glittering a little before he turned away. 'I need to take Nell to the cremation guy, and I've got a couple of others to drop off as well. If you're not busy you could come with me?'

She stared at his back, trying to work out if he wanted her there or not. Should she go?

Probably, but Lola had had a boring day in her kennel, and Rufus had been in the office all day. 'Is it far?'

'About twenty minutes away.'

She hesitated again. 'Wouldn't it be better if I stayed with the dogs? And I need to go and buy some food.'

'Do that tomorrow. I've got stuff in my fridge that needs eating—I could knock us up something when I get back?'

She was so tempted, partly because of Nell and how it had affected him, but—another meal eaten with him? That would make it the fifth night on the trot. Every night, in fact, since she'd arrived at the practice with Lola trying to bleed to death. And he hadn't turned *her* away, either. No wonder he looked exhausted. The man didn't know how to say no.

'It's not that hard to decide, is it?' he asked, a smile tugging at his lips, and she gave a little laugh.

'No, it's not that hard, but I'll cook. It's definitely my turn.'

'Well, use the food in my fridge or it'll turn up its toes. I shouldn't be more than an hour. I'll take Rufus, he likes a run in the car.'

* * *

While he loaded the car and set off, she removed Lola's cone and took her out into the garden briefly, and then fed her and sat beside her on the floor in the office, Lola's head on her lap and her good leg raised for a tummy rub.

The wound on her other one was healing nicely, thanks to Hugo. She chewed her lip and wondered how much her bill was going to be. She owed him so much for last Friday night, not to mention the inpatient fees, and every time she raised the subject Hugo brushed it aside.

She'd have to pin him down—or ask Jean. She'd do that tomorrow.

Lola rolled her head round and stared up at her. 'Yes, I will,' she said to her. 'I'll ask Jean tomorrow, but right now, sweetie, you need to go back in your kennel and I need to go and see what Hugo's got in his fridge.'

Lots, was the answer. Some chicken thighs with a short date, lots of fresh green veg, a small pot of crème fraiche, again with a short date, the remains of the parmesan he'd used on Friday night, and there was even a pot of basil growing on the windowsill.

She found dried herbs, stock cubes and olive oil in a cupboard near the hob and another rummage in the fridge came up with garlic and a small jar of sundried tomatoes.

She smiled. Excellent. She had everything she needed.

She'd just finished cooking when she heard his car pull up, and by the time she'd put the veg in the pan ready to steam and a pouch of rice in the microwave, she heard the door at the bottom of the stairs open.

Rufus arrived first, of course, rushing in to greet her and

sniff around for anything she might have dropped, followed by Hugo, also sniffing.

'Wow, what are you cooking? It smells amazing.'

'It is amazing, and it's also super easy and you just happened to have all the ingredients. I hope you weren't saving any of them for anything special?'

'No, nothing. So what is it?'

She felt him close, his breath teasing her cheek as he peered over her shoulder into the pan.

'It's vaguely Italian. For some ludicrous reason it's called Marry Me Chicken,' she said, turning her head as his eyes widened, and she gave a stifled laugh and turned away again, wishing she hadn't told him. 'Don't panic, that's not significant, it's just one of the few things I can cook.'

She heard a low chuckle. 'Well, if it tastes as good as it smells I can imagine why it got the name. How long will it be?'

'Three minutes? I just need to steam the veg.'

'I'll go and change. Dish up when it's ready, I won't be long.'

He walked into his bedroom, closed the door and leant on it, letting out a long, slow breath.

Yes, it smelt amazing, but so did she, and standing that close, the combination of the rich sauce and the drift of something tantalising from her hair had sent a shiver of something powerful and potent streaking through his body.

Three minutes? He'd need three hours in a cold shower to unravel that. But then again, Marry Me Chicken? Really?

In another world, at another time—but not here, not now. Not ever. Not since—

He felt his chest tighten and slammed the door on that

thought, peeled off his clothes, dragged on a pair of jeans and a long-sleeved T and went back out to find she'd laid the table under the window and was about to dish up.

Good. He wouldn't need to make small talk.

'Thanks for your help with Nell,' he said, propping himself up against the worktop and folding his arms.

She looked slightly surprised at that. 'You don't need to thank me. And for what it's worth, if I was ever in any doubt about you genuinely needing another vet, it's gone. Today was crazy.'

'It was, and I was very grateful for your help. My job offer still stands, just so you know. Oh, and I have a message for you from Mrs Grey, she wanted me to thank you. She said you were very kind to her and really great with Chester. She was impressed. And he's doing fine so far. I rang and checked on the way back and his blood glucose level's picked up and he's stable now.'

'Good. We weren't sure how much he'd had, really, but I didn't want to take any chances.'

'No, very wise. Right, let's eat this, I'm starving,' he said, and he sat down with his plate and took a mouthful.

Wow. His taste buds all but cried with joy, and he gave up any attempt at small talk and scraped the plate clean. If he'd been on his own, he might even have licked it. Instead he swallowed and met her eyes.

'That is *the best* chicken dish I've ever tasted. I don't care what it's called, I want the recipe.'

She gave a tiny laugh and looked away, and he wasn't sure if her cheeks were turning a soft shade of pink or if it was just the heat from cooking. Whatever, he had to fight the urge to kiss her—

'Sure. I'll zap the link to your phone. There's enough left for you tomorrow.'

He swallowed. 'Excellent. And thank you.'

'You're welcome—and thank *you*. It was your food.'

His laugh sounded a little hollow. 'If you can do that with my ingredients, you can cook for me any time you want.'

This time her laugh was real. 'Don't push your luck. It's about the only thing I can cook apart from pasta and jacket potatoes. Right, I'll clear this lot up, and then I'd better get Lola settled for the night.'

'And I'd better take Rufus for a walk, and then I really need to do some admin. See you tomorrow?'

'Sure, since you clearly need me.'

Something flickered in his eyes for a second, and then he bent down and ruffled Rufus's ears again, her words hanging in the air between them.

'Yes, we need you,' he said, his voice oddly gruff. He pushed back his chair and headed for the door without meeting her eyes. 'Thanks again, Ellie. I'll see you in the morning. Rufus, come.'

Ellie stared after him, trying to work out what if anything had just happened there.

No. She was imagining it, trying to make something out of nothing. He was simply grateful for another pair of hands, and it was nothing more than that, however much she might want it to be.

And anyway, now wasn't the time. She had a new life to build, to find her place in the world now it had been turned upside down.

He'd be such a wonderful father...

And where had that thought come from? She'd barely met him and she was dreaming about his babies!

She felt a curious stab of longing, and stifled it. Getting tangled up with Hugo would be silly right now.

However much she wanted it…

How could it *be* so difficult?

She wasn't interested in him—or at least not in the job. She'd made that clear enough—and yet there was something that drew him relentlessly to her.

Why? She was a vet, and he needed a vet more than he needed anything else in the world right now, or his health would start to suffer and his practice would collapse. And that wouldn't help anyone. And even if he *was* interested in her, there was no way, not with the little he had to offer. Apart from the fact that his dedication to his job screwed up every relationship before it really got off the ground, like it had with Emma, he couldn't offer her anything like the relationship she deserved.

She needed someone kind, someone who was able to love her whole-heartedly. Someone who'd give her the family life she'd never had. And that wasn't him. Didn't stop him wanting her…

He swallowed hard. Time to start advertising again. Maybe if he chucked in the flat he might get a couple of decent candidates. With rents sky-rocketing and an uncertain housing market, free accommodation could be a winner. If he could get anyone else competent enough to do the job.

Someone as competent and capable and caring as Ellie…

Never going to happen.

'Come on, Rufus,' he said with a sigh, and he put the little dog on a lead and headed out of the door. A good brisk walk along the sea front would clear his head and sort it out.

Except he'd only got halfway to the gates when he realised there was a cardboard box outside them. Rufus tugged him towards it, and as he unlocked the gate and bent to open it he heard a distressed miaow coming from inside the box.

His heart sinking, he picked up the box carefully, went back inside, shut the confused Rufus in the office and went into a consulting room, closing the door behind him before he opened the lid in case the cat escaped.

There was no way the tiny little cat was going anywhere. She stared up at him, hugely pregnant, utterly exhausted and clearly in need of help. He lifted her out carefully and examined her, and as her abdomen went rigid with a contraction, he noticed a tiny paw protruding.

The kitten was still alive, the paw flexing slightly when he touched it, but it was clearly obstructed. And he didn't have much time. Damn.

He called Ellie and she picked up on the second ring.

'I've got a very pregnant cat in obstructed labour. Fancy some overtime?'

'Give me ten seconds to change and I'll come down.'

He hung up and carried the poor little cat through to the prep room, laid her down, shaved her leg in readiness then put her back in the box and quickly got out all the things they'd need for a C section, then stripped and pulled on some scrubs. By the time he'd done that Ellie was there. She'd had the sense to put scrubs on, too, and they anaesthetised the little cat and opened her up and carefully eased out the kittens. Six were alive, and the seventh, the one that had been stuck and that he finally managed to free by easing it back, was borderline.

He took the borderline one and worked on it while Ellie rubbed the live ones and got them mewling and tucked them under a heat lamp, and then she took the limp, barely alive kitten from him and breathed into its mouth while he closed up the mother.

'How is he?' he asked.

'I think he's trying to breathe—yes, he's breathing!'

'Wow. I thought he wouldn't make it. I reckon he'd been stuck for ages, but I think we deserved some luck after Nell. But there you go, you win some, you lose some. Right, can you monitor mum while I finish closing, please? And then we need to get these babies snuggled up to her.'

She put the little kitten down with the others under the heat lamp, and turned back to the mother with a quiet groan.

'Problem?' he asked, and she shook her head.

'No, she seems OK at the moment, but it's going to be a long night and my bed's calling me already,' she said, and he gave a short laugh. Her bed was calling him, too, but hey...

'Tell me about it,' he said, his voice irritatingly gruff. 'We'll finish off and then you can go up to bed. I'll sit up with them and feed them.'

She cocked her head on one side. 'Does this happen often?'

That dragged a laugh out of him. 'Things rocking up at the door when we're shut? All the time—like you with Lola. If I had more cover, I'd still be running a night service, but I just haven't been able to recruit enough staff and when I do they leave because their partners have moved away with jobs or they're off on mat leave or they want a senior vet job—it just got relentless. So if this happens, it's all down to me to sort out.'

'Does everyone know you don't turn anything away?'

He grunted. 'Probably. I've no idea where she's come

from, she was in a box by the gate. I expect someone got her on a whim and didn't follow through with a spay, and then didn't know what to do.'

'Is she microchipped?'

He shrugged wearily. 'I don't know. I haven't had time to check her yet. I'll do it when I've finished this, but I doubt I'll find anything. Let's get this done and get her settled and we can worry about it then.'

The little cat survived her ordeal, and so did all the kittens, but after a night spent taking it in turns to feed them, Ellie was drained.

So, by the look of him when he came down just before seven, was Hugo.

'You look about as good as I feel,' she said, and he gave a grunt of laughter.

'Don't. Coffee?'

'Please. Lots. And toast.'

'You do it, I'll check on the kitties and scan her for a microchip. And then I really need to take Rufus out for a run before we start.'

She looked at him a bit more closely and realised he was dressed in running gear. 'Really a run?'

'Really a run. We do it every day.'

'Wow. Where do you get your energy?'

His hollow laugh echoed in the empty air behind him as he went through to check on their little patients, and she went into the kitchen and realised she was smiling.

He was really getting under her skin...

The little cat had been microchipped, to his surprise, and she'd been reported as lost by her owners three months previously on the day they'd moved from Yoxburgh to Norfolk. Hugo rang them and they were delighted to hear she was OK, and came later that day. They left smiling with their little cat and her family, armed with cat food, kitten milk to supplement if necessary, and an advice leaflet.

'Nice to have a happy ending,' Hugo said to Jean after he'd waved them off.

'Nice to have your bill paid, even if it was heavily discounted,' she pointed out, and he laughed.

'Yeah, well, it wasn't their fault and I had to do it. Oh, and Ellie needs some overtime pay for that, too.'

'Overtime pay for what?' Ellie asked, walking into the office at the critical moment, and he left Jean to explain that to her. She'd only argue with him.

'What overtime pay?'

'For the cat. Her owners just came and collected them all. Didn't Hugo tell you?'

'No, I haven't seen him all day. So, what overtime pay?'

'Last night.'

'I don't need overtime pay for last night. And he needs to bill me for Lola.'

'Take it up with Hugo. I'm just doing as I'm told,' Jean said, and Ellie gave a little huff of irritation and went to find him.

'Why overtime?'

'Because you worked all night.'

'So did you. We did it for the kittens.'

'The owners came and got her and they paid the bill. It's covered.'

She tilted her head on one side and studied him. 'What, all of it, the whole, proper, everything-accounted-for bill?

Or a figure you pulled out of the air because you felt sorry for them and the cat?'

'I'm not that magnanimous, but there may have been an element of that,' he admitted, but then trashed it by adding, 'and regardless of that, you still need paying for the overtime. And incidentally, while we're on the subject of magnanimous, you won't let me pay you locum rates, so you actually don't have a leg to stand on.'

'Fair cop,' she said with a chuckle, and walked away, but she hadn't forgotten that she owed him for Lola's treatment. She'd sort it out with Jean in a quiet moment, if there ever was such a thing...

CHAPTER FIVE

MERCIFULLY THE REST of the week was quieter—not that it was quiet, exactly, but certainly more manageable with the other two vets there on alternate days, and then it was Friday night.

To her relief she wasn't scheduled to work on Saturday morning, and she'd have time to spend with Lola at last.

She was still on cage rest, but she was well enough to move now. And Ellie really, really wanted to go to her house, even if it was only for the weekend. It would get them out of Hugo's hair and give her something else to think about apart from him.

She found him in the office at the computer, and she perched on the edge of the desk and waited for him to pause.

'Give me two seconds,' he said, and then pressed save and looked up with a smile. 'Sorry. You OK?'

'Yes, I'm fine. I'm going to my house tonight with Lola.'

He blinked. 'Really? I thought you were staying until she was off cage rest?'

'I know, but I'd like to be there, at least for the weekend, to give Lola a change of scenery if nothing else, and I need to get on with tackling it properly, as well. She can lie and watch me while I do stuff.'

'I'll give you a hand,' he said, without asking her if she needed help. Typical Hugo, and actually it was the last thing she needed when she was trying to get some distance between her and the man who was occupying all too much of her head space.

She shook her head. 'Don't worry, I can manage, but could I borrow your big crate for a while? Just until her stitches are out?'

'Sure, if you really feel you need to go, but you're welcome to stay here, you know that. The flat's just sitting there.'

'Yes, I know, but—'

'You want your own home,' he said softly, because of course, being Hugo, he understood.

She smiled. 'That sounds ungrateful, and I'm not, not after all you've done for me and Lola in the last week, but I thought if I spend the weekend there, I won't have to worry about her, I can get on with sorting my stuff out, and we can see how it goes. I'm assuming you won't mind if I bring Lola to work every day if I decide to stay there?'

'Of course I won't. She can lie in here in the day. She'll have plenty of company.'

'She will, and she was fine doing that at the other practice. If you don't mind, that would be brilliant.'

'Of course I don't mind. The crate probably won't fit in your car, but I can drop it over later, after I've taken Rufus out. Then I'll give you a hand, if you like?'

Did she like? She was torn, for all sorts of reasons. He'd done so much for her, and being independent was hard-wired into her DNA, but nevertheless it seemed churlish to refuse his help, like throwing his kindness back in his face.

'That's very kind of you, Hugo, but I can probably manage if you could drop the crate off,' she said, and hoped she could and it wasn't just a big fat optimistic lie…

* * *

Ellie pulled up on the drive with a feeling of déjà vu.

Was it really only a week since she'd arrived here so full of optimism and then everything had fallen apart? Just seven days, and without Hugo she had no idea what she would have done. Would Lola even have survived?

She felt her eyes prickling, and pulled herself together. No time for sentiment, she had things to do. She opened the front door and carried Lola in from the car and put her down, then looked around. She'd forgotten how tired it all was, how much in need of some love. She really needed to phone the agent and have a serious conversation.

She opened the back door and led her reluctant dog out into the garden. It was the first time Lola had been here since her accident, and she was a bit wary of it, but after a few moments of hesitation she was persuaded to step onto the grass—only for long enough to bop down and do a wee, and then she was back on the patio and staring pleadingly up at Ellie.

She clearly hadn't forgotten that the garden was full of terrors. Maybe tomorrow in full daylight would be better— under strict supervision, because even though Hugo had been meticulous, there might still be something lurking there and she'd never forgive herself if Lola was hurt again.

They went back inside, and Ellie took Lola's cone off. She wasn't allowed to jump up or go on the stairs until her sutures were out, so Ellie dug a throw out of the pile of bags still decorating the living room, spread it out in front of the sofa and sat down, patting the space beside her. Lola looked at the sofa, then at her, and lay down beside her with a sigh, head on Ellie's lap, and she fondled her ears.

'You're such a good girl,' she murmured, and Lola

thumped her tail and sighed again. She could understand that. She'd be sighing all the time if she didn't stop herself.

'What am I going to do, Lola?' she asked, her voice weary. 'I wish I knew, but there's no hurry now, thanks to Hugo. Shall we see how it goes?' she asked the dog, and got another little tail thump in reply.

Not much of an answer, but heart-warming. Maybe it *could* be a home. And maybe Hugo really was as decent as he seemed. Should she take the job he'd offered?

Her chest tightened a little at the thought, and she shook her head. Too soon. There was no hurry, and besides, he still had to find a replacement, so she'd be locuming anyway for a while. She'd do as she'd promised and stick it out until then...

A car pulled up outside, and she heard the dull thunk of a door closing, then footsteps. She glanced out and saw him walking up her path, as if she'd conjured him up out of her imagination, and her heart gave a little skip. He was carrying a bag, and she opened the door as he rang the bell.

'Hi.'

'Hi.' He held the bag out to her, his mouth tipped in a crooked smile. 'I brought you something to eat. I wasn't sure if you'd had time to do a shop, so I dived into the supermarket.'

'Oh, Hugo, you didn't have to—thank you! That's so kind of you—or are you still trying to buy me?' she added, only half joking, and he gave a soft huff of laughter.

'You don't take anything at face value, do you?' he said, giving Lola a little tickle, and turned away and went back to his car.

Now she'd offended him—except he opened the boot, pulled out the crate, then leant in again and emerged carry-

ing a plant in a pot. An orchid, the beautiful white flowers
almost luminous in the dusk.

'What's that for?' she asked, expecting him to say yet another thank you for bailing him out, but he didn't.

His mouth tipped into another of those crooked smiles.
'Housewarming present. A little something to cheer the place
up a bit—oh, and I've brought a body sleeve for Lola,' he
said, and for a second she had the ridiculous urge to cry.

'Thank you, Hugo,' she murmured, absurdly moved by
his simple but thoughtful gestures. She took the plant and
beckoned him in.

'Sorry, it's still a mess. I haven't done a thing since I got
here except sit down with Lola. Come on through.'

He followed her and Lola into the kitchen and put the
shopping bag on the worktop. 'Does the microwave work?'

'I think so. I've cleaned it so I hope so.'

She put the orchid on the kitchen windowsill while he
emptied the bag. Milk, eggs, bread, butter, tea, coffee, Greek
yogurt, some fruit—and two ready meals.

'They're not exactly the healthiest, but I didn't think you'd
want to start cooking on top of everything else. And I bought
two, in case you fancied company?'

She searched his eyes, and all she found was that bone-
deep kindness and consideration that seemed to be his trade-
mark, and possibly her undoing.

'I don't have to stay,' he added, when she said nothing, and
she swallowed another urge to cry—where was that coming
from?—and found a smile from somewhere.

'Sorry. Yes, of course stay. What do I owe you for the
shopping?'

'You don't give up, do you?' he said mildly.

'Not often.'

His lips twitched, and he pulled the receipt out of his pocket and glanced at it. 'Twelve pounds and seventy-four pence.'

She didn't believe him for an instant, but the receipt was back in his pocket and she tipped out her purse and found something close to it while he pricked the top of the ready meals and stuck them in the microwave.

While they heated she put the body sleeve on Lola and he erected the crate. He'd even brought a new sheet of thick vet fleece cut to fit it, something she hadn't even got round to thinking about.

She found a couple of plates that weren't too chipped, and they took their food into the sitting room and settled down on the sofa, Lola on the floor between them looking hopeful.

'Where's Rufus?' she asked, to break the yawning silence.

'In his bed. He's fine, he's had a busy day keeping an eye on things and he's had a bit of a run around in the garden, so I'll take him out later.'

The silence descended again, and she finished her meal—surprisingly delicious and very welcome—and then picked up their plates and took them back to the kitchen. He followed her and propped himself up against the worktop as she dumped them in the sink.

'Anything I can do? Carry stuff upstairs, shift furniture, help you make the bed?'

No way was he going anywhere near her bed, but the carrying...

'That would be great. I'll stick Lola in her crate while we do that, or she'll try and come up.'

'I'd put the cone back on, she'll need that unless she's under supervision,' Hugo said.

Lola wasn't impressed, but she went into the crate reluctantly and lay down with a great sigh, the plastic cone framing her mournful face.

'She does that martyr thing for England,' Ellie said with a chuckle, and led him back to the sitting room. 'Well, this is it. Grab a bag or two and follow me.'

She took the garment bag on top, followed by a couple of carrier bags, and went up into her bedroom—*her bedroom? How odd*—and turned to find him right behind her with three bags in each hand.

'Where do you want them?'

'On the bed. That way I'll have to deal with them before I can go to sleep. Otherwise I won't get round to it.'

And it avoided the issue of him helping her to make it.

Except, of course, he had a better idea.

'Why don't we make it first, then dump the stuff on it? That way when you've finished emptying them you can fall straight into it.'

It made sense. Of course it did, so she searched the bags, found the bedding and quickly whipped out the mattress protector, the sheet and the pillow cases and dropped them on the mattress.

By the time she'd wrestled the duvet out of its bag he'd nearly done the sheet. In seconds the bed was made, and if it hadn't been for common sense she would have been tempted to fall straight into it there and then.

With him?

As they straightened up their eyes met, and she looked quickly away before he could see what she was thinking.

Madness. Tempted or not, there was no way she was going there. Not with Hugo, or any vet who was a prospective employer. Not after Craig, who'd made it impossible for her to stay in the job she'd only stayed in out of loyalty to Jim.

And Hugo was a charmer. Her father had been a charmer, according to her mother, and she was never going to let herself fall for that.

But he was hoisting the bags back onto the bed, and she forced herself to meet his eyes again over the top of the heap.

'Coffee?' she asked lightly.

'Sure, if you've got time?'

'Of course I've got time.' And as he'd brought the coffee, it would have been churlish to kick him out without offering.

They ended up on the floor in the living room, Lola lying between them making the most of stereo cuddles, her head draped over Hugo's lap this time. The body sleeve had hind legs to cover the stitches, and she was groaning softly as he scratched her neck where the cone had been, and tugged her ears gently.

The movement of his hands was mesmerising, and Ellie looked away. She had to work with him, at least for the next few weeks or maybe months, and letting herself fantasise about his gentle, knowing hands on her body wasn't the way to do it. Especially with that freshly made bed right overhead…

Get a grip!

'So, what's your plan?' he asked, and she blinked at him.

'Plan?'

'For the house.'

She looked fleetingly relieved, for some reason, and he wondered if she'd thought he meant about the job. He already knew the answer to that, and it wasn't even as positive as a maybe.

'I don't really have one yet. Obviously it needs decorating

from top to bottom, so I'll presumably start there, a room at a time, and then it'll need new carpets and furniture, really.'

'Especially if you're going to live in it for any length of time.'

She shot him a sideways glance and gave a wry smile. 'Nice thought, but I can't afford to replace anything yet.' She sighed. 'I need to phone the agent tomorrow morning. It's time I told him what it was like. And I still need to wipe down all the woodwork.'

'I can give you a hand tomorrow after we close if you like?' he offered without engaging his brain, and she glanced at him with that wry smile and looked away again.

'Hugo, I'm fine. I just need to put on my big-girl pants and get on with it.'

Why did she have to say that? He really, really didn't need to think about her pants...

'Well, the offer's there if you want to take me up on it,' he said, and looked down at Lola. 'Sorry, sweetie, you need to let me get up, I have to go home and get on.'

'Admin again?'

He laughed, and it sounded hollow even to his ears. 'Always admin. Well, admin and Rufus. He needs a walk, or at the very least I need to play with him in the garden for a while. And I need to get that advert out there.'

He waited a heartbeat in case she picked it up, but she didn't, so he lifted Lola's head gently and slid out from underneath it.

'I'll see you out,' Ellie said, but he shook his head.

'You stay there with Lola. She looks comfortable. I'll let myself out. See you tomorrow?'

She tilted her head and smiled up at him, and he felt a

jolt of something warm surge through him and settle in the region of his heart.

'You really don't need to help me. You've done enough already—more than enough. I can cope.'

'Big-girl pants,' he murmured, trying not to think about her bed right over their heads, and she smiled.

'Absolutely—and, Hugo?'

She reached up and caught his hand as he passed her, and the warmth turned to fire and burned through his body.

'Thank you. I don't know what I would have done without you this last week. You've been a lifesaver. Literally, for Lola.'

He gave a little huff of laughter, and his smile felt crooked. 'I only did what you would have done, and as for Lola, that's what we do, isn't it? That's why we're here.'

He squeezed her hand, then disentangled his fingers and made his escape before he did something really, really foolish that would only hurt them both.

The front door closed with a firm click, and she rested her head back against the arm of the sofa and listened to the sound of his car driving away.

She could still feel the warmth of his hand in hers, still feel the unexpected quiver that had travelled through her like lightning, leaving longing in its wake.

No! No, no, no! She wasn't going to go there. Not that he'd suggested anything in any way, but...

'You're an idiot. He's just being nice.'

Lola lifted her head and stared at her, and she stroked her gently. 'Come on, baby, let's take you out in that beastly garden again and then put you to bed, hmm?'

She put their mugs in the dishwasher, then took Lola out,

put the cone back on her and settled her in her crate before heading up to bed.

A strange bed, in a strange room, with all her worldly goods piled on top of it, but she was too tired now to deal with that, so she dumped the bags on the floor, found her wash things and cleaned her teeth, then lay down on the unfamiliar mattress, staring at the ceiling.

Her own bedroom, in her own home.

It should have felt wonderful, but it didn't, it felt oddly wrong, temporary, uncertain. There was still so much that was undecided, so many ways to go, different paths to travel.

Should she take the job? Or just locum for now and take the time to do up the house a bit and then re-let it and move on? But where to? She'd have to find accommodation that would take Lola, and that was tricky. And she couldn't take her with her into practices if she was locuming, it wouldn't be fair on any of them.

Only one thing was certain. If she stayed here, she'd definitely need a better bed...

She spent Saturday morning washing the woodwork downstairs with Lola, but she needed to pull out the washing machine and dishwasher so she could clean under them.

Except that meant asking Hugo for *another* favour.

'Oh, Lola, what am I thinking? I need to leave him alone! He's got a life, and he doesn't need us clogging it up.'

Lola lifted her head and thumped her tail gently on the floor. Thank goodness she'd got her. She'd go mad otherwise.

And she'd still be in her old practice working with the odious Craig.

'It's a lovely day, let's go and have a look in the garden, shall we?'

She managed to drag and lift the crate out onto the patio, and Lola went hastily into it the moment she opened the door. She left it open, so Lola could come out if she wanted to, and then spent an hour or more peering down into the grass to see if she could find anything else that might present a hazard.

Not easy, as it needed another cut already and of course the lawnmower in the little shed was useless, the cable sliced through as if it had been mown by accident.

By the time she was satisfied that it was safe, Lola had come out of her crate and was lying on the patio in the sun watching her, so she sat down beside her, a hand on her side, and stared blankly at the garden.

If you could even call it that. Another thing on her endless to-do list.

She took Lola inside, hauled the crate back in—harder than bringing it out, of course—and put her back into it, then went into town. First stop the rental agent, only the office was closed, so she found a supermarket, bought a few food essentials, a pot of violas in full bloom to cheer up the garden, a packet of drawer liners and some dishwasher and washing machine cleaner, then headed back.

The first thing she did was run the empty dishwasher and the washing machine on a hot wash with the cleaner, then spent an hour adding to her to-do list and emailing the letting agent, then went for a short stroll while Lola was napping, trying to find some nice walks for her once she was able to start controlled exercise again.

She did the same thing the next day, heading towards the sea this time, and of course she bumped into Hugo and Rufus out on a run.

He slowed to a halt and stopped in front of her, his chest heaving, sweat dribbling down his neck and into the running vest that clung to his lean, toned frame, and her heart lurched in her chest.

How is it that, even hot and sweaty, he's so darned sexy?

'Hi,' he said, his eyes crinkling into a smile, and she smiled back and bent to say hello to Rufus. Not that Rufus really cared, but it was a good excuse and got her eyes off his body.

Except his legs were now right in front of her, and they were every bit as distracting as the rest.

'You look hot,' she said, and then could have kicked herself, but he just laughed.

'I am hot. I'm steaming. We've just done ten K, ready for the race next weekend.'

'Race?'

'Yes, there's one every year in aid of the local children's hospice. I've been tapping the clients for sponsorship.' His grin was cheeky and made her heart hiccup, and she had to look away again. 'So how's it going?'

'Oh, OK. I'm just taking a little stroll to keep my muscles working and to get to know the area ready for taking Lola out,' she told him, distracting her brain from the subject of his hot sweatiness and his support for charity, both of which made him even more attractive than he had been.

Why does he have to be so nice?

'How's she doing?'

'OK, but she's bored to death. I reckon in another week her leg should be healed enough so she can come out of prison. She'll love that.'

'She will. It's nine days now.'

'Yes, I suppose it is.' Ten since her world had been turned upside down, and nine since she'd met him—

He shifted from foot to foot. 'I'd better go or I'll stiffen up, I need a shower and some stretches, but what are you doing later?'

How to find an excuse to avoid him? 'Trying to tame the house?' she said truthfully, and then without permission her mouth tacked on, 'Why?'

He shrugged. 'I thought, as the weather seems so much warmer today, I could crack out the barbecue? Then Rufus and Lola can spend a bit of time together and it'll give her a change of scenery. She must have serious cabin fever.'

She wasn't alone, just the thought of tackling the house made Ellie want to run away, and the offer was so tempting. Still, she really shouldn't…

'That sounds lovely. Anything I can bring?' her mouth asked, and she contemplated sewing it shut.

'No, nothing. I've got some stuff in the freezer and I'm going shopping after I've showered. Two-thirty?'

She nodded, cross with herself for being weak and yet looking forward to it because she felt oddly lonely here. Lovely though everyone here was, she missed her friends in the old practice, and her house with all that needed doing was overwhelming. And a barbecue with Hugo…

'Two-thirty's fine. Are you sure I can't bring anything?'

'Just yourselves,' he said, and she told herself that the invitation was as much about Lola as it was about her. If not more so.

'OK. I'll see you then.'

He threw her a smile and set off again, Rufus running beside him, and she watched him go, those long, strong legs eating up the pavement, and kicked herself for being so weak-willed.

Maybe she should start applying for other jobs.

And leave him in the lurch, after all his kindness?

No. She couldn't. And she knew in her heart of hearts that

she ought to put him out of his misery and take the job, but she was scared of doing it, scared of making another mistake, another wrong decision, another error of judgement—

'He's nothing like Craig,' she told herself crossly as she walked back into the house, and Lola looked up at her and whined. She opened the crate and stroked her head.

'I'm sorry, sweetie, you have to stay in there. You need a rest before this afternoon, and I need to get *something* done on the house. Maybe it's time to fire up the washing machine. What do you think?'

It didn't really matter what Lola thought about that as an idea, because the washing machine needed another hot cleaner wash before she'd want to use it, and anyway, she didn't have time to dry the clothes before tomorrow. She phoned Hugo.

'Can I ask a favour? Can I use the practice washing machine? I'm running out of clothes.'

'Of course you can. Bring everything over when you come. In fact why don't you just come back today instead of tomorrow? It would save moving Lola backwards and forwards and you won't have to rush in the morning.'

She hesitated, torn between her need for distance from him and the lure of the blissfully comfortable bed in the flat.

The flat won hands down, and she didn't really want the distance, anyway, if she was honest. 'Thanks, you're a star. I'll do that.'

She hung up, had a shower, threw all her washing into a bag and then rummaged through her clothes.

'It's not a date!' she told herself crossly, and threw on a pair of jeans and a top, then changed the top for a nicer one, grabbed a jumper just in case it got chilly later, and then loaded Lola and the laundry into the car and headed back to the practice.

He'd opened the gate for her, and she shut it behind herself and parked in her usual place, then picked Lola up and carried her round to the staff entrance. She could see Hugo in the office, and she put Lola gently on the floor and took her in there so she could say hello.

'Are we interrupting?'

He gave a wry, tired laugh and reached out to give Lola a little love. 'Not really. I'm posting an ad for the vet job. I thought I'd throw in the flat, see if it tempts a few applicants.' He tilted his head to one side. 'Since I clearly can't tempt you?'

Oh, she was so tempted, but there was no way he was knowing that...

'What?' he asked, his brows crunching together, his eyes searching. 'Are you having second thoughts?'

She looked away. 'I'm not sure. Right now I'm not sure about anything.'

He gave a grunt of laughter. 'Well, if it helps give you a little certainty, how about I take you on as maternity cover for Lucy, then that gives you time to decide and me time to find a permanent replacement if you really don't want to stay?'

'When's she due back?'

'Six months, give or take.'

Six months...

She held his eyes for a moment, then looked away again. 'Can I think about it?'

'Sure. Of course you can. And I'll hold fire on the advert for now.' He pressed save, closed his laptop and got to his feet. 'Let's go and cook. I'm starving.'

'Can I put my washing on first?'

'Help yourself. I'll get started, come on out when you're done. I'll take Lola with me, I can tie her to the bench and she can lie in the sun and hang out with Rufus.'

CHAPTER SIX

BY THE TIME she'd put the first load into the washing machine there was a delicious waft of barbecue in the air.

She went out into the garden and found Hugo, armed with tongs, standing by the barbecue with the contented look of a man making fire, Rufus and Lola gazing up at him hopefully.

'It really smells of summer out here,' she said, and he turned his head and grinned.

'About time. It's been cold too long. I've got a very attentive audience.'

'Yes, I can see that,' she said with a smile. 'Lola's leg certainly hasn't affected her appetite.'

'Have you had a look at it today?'

'Yes. It's healing beautifully, thanks to you.' She peered at the laden griddle. 'That looks delicious. Anything I can do?'

'Yes, you can relax.'

Relax? It was so long since she'd truly relaxed she wasn't sure how to do it, but she parked herself on a sun lounger, lay back and closed her eyes and let the sounds of the garden wash over her.

She could hear the hiss and spit of the barbecue, the scrape of the tongs as he turned things on the griddle. A bird was singing somewhere in the garden, and she could hear another answering it. Blackbirds? Maybe.

The sun was warm on her skin, not the fierce heat of summer, but the gentle warmth of spring that relaxed her muscles, emptied her mind of her worries and lured her into sleep...

It was ready. Hugo turned the barbecue down, piled all the food on the warming rack and closed the lid.

He turned, his mouth open to speak, and then stopped.

'Ellie?' His voice was low, no more than a murmur, but she didn't respond, and his mouth softened into a rueful smile. He didn't have the heart to wake her.

Her chest was rising and falling slowly, her limbs relaxed, and he made himself look away. He really didn't need to know what she looked like when she was asleep, her face unguarded, her body motionless apart from the gentle lift of her breasts towards the sun with every slow breath...

God, he wanted her. He wanted her so much it hurt, but she deserved so much more than he could offer.

He closed his eyes, but he could still see her, see the soft curves, the peep of cleavage in the vee of her top—

Should he wake her? She clearly needed to sleep.

He opened his eyes and saw a wasp on her cheek. Her eyelids flickered as her hand came up to swat it away.

'Don't move, it's a wasp,' he said quietly. 'Just keep still and it'll go.'

It flew off, and she sat up and turned towards him, looking a little confused, her eyes blinking against the sun.

'Sorry, I must have dropped off. How long have I been asleep?'

He shrugged. 'I don't know, I've been busy. Five minutes, max? I was about to wake you when the wasp landed. The food's ready when you are. I'll bring out the salads.'

* * *

Had he been watching her sleep?

Idiot, of course he hadn't. She was reading far too much into it. Why would he want to watch her anyway?

He came back out with a tray and set it down on the table, and her smile felt awkward. 'I'm sorry, I didn't mean to drop off like that, but it was just so relaxing in the sun.'

'You obviously needed it.'

She nodded. 'Yes, I guess I did. I didn't sleep well last night.' Or the night before...

He paused in mid-unwrapping of the salads and turned to look at her searchingly. 'Why?'

She shrugged. 'I don't know. Maybe the bed? It's not because I'm not tired, but—I don't really know. I just feel so unsettled.' Partly because of him, but there was no way she was telling him that—

'I'm sure you do. There's been a lot of sudden change in your life and it must have been pretty overwhelming. I know how that feels, but you've got a job here for as long as you want it, and a very decent reference if you want to move on, so you don't need to worry about that.'

Except she did, because somehow it all seemed too cosy. And it wasn't that she couldn't trust Hugo professionally, that was a given, but she felt this weird pull towards him, an almost visceral yearning, and it was herself she didn't trust. She was in danger of falling in love with him, and that wasn't in any way a good idea. Not personally, not professionally, and certainly not now.

'I know,' she said, breaking away from that searching gaze, 'and I am very grateful for all of that, but it's everything else as well,' she said, making excuses now. 'There's so much to do on the house, and I don't know where or how to begin. I need to speak to the letting agent, really. I've emailed him asking for a meeting. I might need to take some time off for that, if it's OK?'

'Sure.'

'Not that it'll make any difference. He'll probably just say it was "wear and tear", knowing my luck.'

Hugo grunted and picked up the tongs. 'Very likely. Right, we're good to go. Grab a plate and come and load it up.'

They ate in silence, the dogs lined up watching every mouthful while he watched Ellie.

She looked troubled, and after what she'd said, he wasn't surprised. He could offer to help with the decorating, but he really didn't have time while they were so short-staffed. And if he offered to pay a decorator, she'd only say no.

'Do you want this last sausage?'

She shook her head, so he put the leftover salads in the fridge for lunch tomorrow and shared the sausage between Rufus and Lola.

It was starting to cool down now, the sun dropping lower in the sky, and despite her thin jumper he saw her shiver.

'Coffee?' he suggested, and she gave a tiny shrug.

'I feel so guilty. I really ought to be at home getting on with something,' she said. 'My to-do list is ridiculous.'

And she didn't sound as if she wanted to do any of it.

'It'll keep. Come on, let's go and get a coffee. It'll be warmer inside and we can talk through what needs doing before you speak to the agent.'

She hesitated, a host of emotions flickering in her eyes, and then she nodded. 'That sounds good. You're right, the house can wait.'

She had a message from the agent just before eight the next morning, suggesting he meet her at the house. Now.

She stared at her phone, sighed and went to find Hugo.

He was in the office with Kerry, running over the list of consults and electives while Jean answered the phone and slotted in another client.

'Hugo, I'm so sorry to do this, but is there any way I can meet the agent at my house now? He's just messaged me.'

He hesitated for a second, holding her eyes, then shrugged. 'Sure. We can cope.'

'Thanks. I've fed Lola and she's been out, so she should be fine. I'll be as quick as I can,' she promised, and headed off armed with a list of issues and very few expectations. It was going to be a difficult meeting and it needed to be done, but she was so not looking forward to it…

While Jean went out to Reception, he and Kerry rejigged the first couple of appointments. Difficult, as he didn't know how long she'd be. Would she get any joy from the agent? He doubted it, and he certainly wasn't holding his breath—

'Hugo? Hello?'

He shook his head to break his train of thought, and looked back at Kerry. 'Yeah. Sorry. What?'

'Is Ellie OK?'

'Yes, she's fine, she's just got issues with her house. The tenants pretty much trashed it.'

'Mmm, she said that the other day. It sounds a nightmare.'

'It is a nightmare, and it all needs decorating, which is difficult when she's living in it.'

Kerry pounced on that immediately.

'Let her stay on in the flat as long as she's here. You aren't going to find a new vet that quickly, not anyone worth having, anyway. They'll have to give notice. And it's just sitting there doing nothing. It's the obvious solution.'

It was, and he'd already thought about it.

'It would give you a chance to get to know her better, too,' Kerry went on, and he searched her eyes and turned away, letting out a frustrated huff of laughter.

'Don't start that. I don't need you matchmaking.'

'But she's lovely, Hugo, and you're lonely—'

'I'm not lonely, I don't have time to be lonely, and I'm hardly a monk.'

'I'm not talking about your sex life, Hugo, I'm talking about a meaningful relationship. You've been on hold for ten years—'

His heart crashed against his ribs. 'You don't have to tell me that, I'm well aware,' he said shortly.

'Don't you think it's time—'

He glared at her. 'Don't go there, Kerry. I'm warning you…'

'She'd be so perfect for you.'

She would be. She was. She wasn't the problem, he was. Not that he was telling Kerry that. 'Just because you're all loved-up—'

'That doesn't mean you can't be. James and I don't have the monopoly. You deserve to be happy.'

He shoved a hand through his hair. 'Dammit, do I have to fire you to get you to shut up?' he growled, his pent-up frustration threatening to boil over, but she'd known him a long time and she just smiled gently and shook her head.

'Have it your way, Hugo, but you know I'm right. I just want you to be happy,' she added over her shoulder as a parting shot, and he waited till she'd gone and punched the wall.

Hard.

He rubbed his knuckles, the pain bringing him to his senses. Kerry was right. Ellie was perfect for him, in every way. But he was very far from being perfect for her, and the past kept coming back to haunt him.

He clenched his fist again, but it was already sore enough so he left the wall alone before he broke a metacarpal and went and called in his first client.

The flat idea was still kicking around in his brain, though. He'd initially offered it to Ellie as the obvious solution while Lola was on cage rest, but she was almost better now, and Ellie still hadn't committed to cover Lucy's mat leave.

Even though he knew letting her stay on in the flat for longer was the ideal solution for her, it would put them in very close proximity for however long it took to fix her house, which would do nothing to help keep any distance between them.

Except she needed to get the house sorted, and that would give her a chance. And then there was his other idea that would help her even more—although it would throw them together for even longer, so that was still kicking around in the back of his mind.

He was such a sucker for punishment...

Ellie headed back to the practice, still not quite believing how the meeting had turned out, and Kerry grabbed her on the way in.

'How did you get on with the agent?'

'He's agreed to refund his commission, which means I can afford to get it decorated. I can't believe it.'

Kerry blinked. 'Wow. That's a result.'

'Isn't it?' She just hoped Hugo wouldn't mind her staying on in the flat a bit longer, but then Kerry pre-empted that.

'You won't be able to live in it while that's happening, of

course,' she said, ever practical, 'but Hugo won't mind if you stay on in the flat. It's sitting there doing nothing.'

'At the moment, but he's going to offer it to a new vet so he won't want me there for long.'

'You're covering Lucy's mat leave, aren't you?'

'Well—only for now. I haven't agreed to stay—'

'Well, that's fine, he can still advertise the job with the flat. The decorating won't take long, will it?'

It wouldn't, once she'd found someone to do it, but...

Then Kerry moved on. 'Anyway, enough of that, I've been meaning to ask you if you'd like to come to my wedding in three weeks? The day's for family, but the evening's a party and I'd love you to be there. Everyone here's coming, and you're one of us now.'

Was she? Was she really 'one of them'?

She waited for that familiar feeling of the net tightening, like it had in her last practice whenever Craig had organised social events for them and she'd felt obliged to go, but it didn't happen, because this wasn't Craig, it was Hugo. His practice, his head nurse. All she felt was the steady, gentle warmth of welcome, and she felt her eyes fill with unexpected tears.

'Oh, Kerry, that's so sweet of you. I'd love—'

Kerry beamed. 'Great. I'll add you to the list. You can be Hugo's plus one.'

She stared at Kerry. 'Hugo's...? But surely he's got someone to bring? A girlfriend?' she added, now blatantly fishing, but Kerry just shook her head.

'Hugo? No, or certainly not one he'd bring to the wedding. He doesn't have time.'

Didn't he? Or was he just lonely, and filling time with busy work? What a waste of his life—and actually, none of her business.

* * *

'Kerry's invited me to her wedding,' she told him later be-tween consults, and he gave a wry smile.

'I didn't think it would take her long.'

Really?

'So how did you get on with the letting agent?' he asked, changing the subject swiftly.

Ellie shook her head slowly and laughed. 'Weird. He was a bit defensive, but then acutely embarrassed when he looked through my photos, said he'd sent a new member of the team out to deal with it and should have done it himself. And, amazingly, he's refunding me all the commission from the last six months, which means I can afford to get it decorated.'

She let it hang, wondering how to bring up the flat, not wanting to put him in a difficult situation because knowing Hugo he'd just say yes regardless of his own feelings.

'That's great news. Look, I don't have time to talk now, I've got a Lab with an obstruction, but let's get this morn-ing out of the way, and we can talk over lunch. I've got an idea I want to put to you.'

'Is this the mat leave thing?'

'No. Later.'

Except that lunch didn't happen for either of them, not surprisingly, and it was after six before her last client left. She walked out of Reception and bumped into him in the corridor.

'Sorry about lunch,' he said, 'the Lab took longer than I thought.'

'What was it?'

He rolled his eyes. 'Foam balls from the park. He'd eaten at least two, judging by the colours, and his gut was choked with bits, some of them huge. I don't know why people give them to dogs. They get chopped up when they mow the grass and some dogs just can't resist. Have you got time now to talk?'

'Sure, I'm not busy. I just need to eat pretty soon, so as long as it doesn't take more than a few minutes I'm fine, otherwise we can do it after I've eaten. And I need to spend time with Lola.'

He laughed. 'It'll take seconds. Let's do it now, and then I'll cook us something while we talk about it.'

'It's not your turn,' she pointed out, but he just laughed and headed upstairs anyway.

She left Lola in the kennel and followed him up, curious. His door was open, so she walked in and propped herself against the worktop in his kitchen while he pulled stuff out of the fridge.

'What have you done to your hand?' she asked, eyeing a nasty bruise on his knuckles.

'Oh, nothing, I misjudged a doorway,' he said, sounding a bit short, and carried on sorting through the fridge.

'So what did you want to talk about?' she asked as he straightened up.

'The flat.' He had his back to her as he chopped veg, so she couldn't read his expression, but his shoulders seemed a bit tense. 'I know what it's like trying to work on a property and live in it, and it's not easy, but if you're going to get a decorator, it'd be much easier for you and for him if you'd moved out, and the flat's the obvious answer.'

'Kerry said I should ask you about doing that, but I thought you might not want me in it for that long,' she said carefully.

He glanced at her then looked away again, turning his attention back to the onion he was dicing into a million pieces. 'Why wouldn't I want you in it?'

Why wouldn't he look at her?

'I don't know. Because you want it for the permanent vet, when you get one? Because I'll be in your way?' she tacked on, wondering if that was it, but he shook his head.

'You won't be in my way.'

'But it's not necessary. I don't have to move out, Hugo, I can just stay there and they can work round me.'

'You don't need to do that, not when the flat's just sitting here, and anyway, I'd already assumed you'd be here. That's not really what I wanted to talk to you about,' he said, scraping the onion into the pan before turning to face her and coming up with something that took her completely by surprise.

'I've been thinking. If you cover the rest of Lucy's mat leave, which is six months, that takes us to mid-October. If you move into the flat and stay here all summer, rent free, which is the vet's deal, then you could get the house done up a bit and rent it as a holiday let. They're in very short supply at the moment, and Yoxburgh's really popular in the summer.'

She stared at him, vaguely stunned because it had never occurred to her, and it was a genius idea. Except...

'I know. We used to holiday here when I was a kid, and I loved it, which is why I bought the house, but that isn't the point. What if you find a really good vet who's available sooner and they need accommodation? I'd have nowhere to go.'

He shrugged. 'Then let your house as a late last-minute deal. If you want to, of course. I just thought it might help pay the mortgage.'

She stared at him, stunned.

It would. It absolutely would, and the money would be really useful, because having lost nearly three months' rent due to the tenant, she didn't have much of a buffer, even with the commission being refunded. But…

'Can I think about it?'

'Sure. I'm doing Thai paneer curry. Red or green?'

She stared at him blankly for a second, then gave a soft laugh. 'Green would be lovely. Thank you. Let me go and feed Lola and take her out for a minute, and I'll be with you.'

By the time she'd done that he was dishing up, to her relief, and they sat at the table and ate without speaking until their plates were cleared.

Then he pushed his plate away and looked up, his head cocked on one side as he met her eyes. 'So, has the agent suggested a decorator?'

Ellie swallowed the last delicious mouthful and shook her head. 'No, and I wouldn't know where to start looking.'

'I spoke to Ryan, the guy I use, while you were downstairs with Lola. He's got a gap next week if you're interested. I said I'd call him back if you were.'

Another thing to be beholden to him for? He'd picked up their plates and headed over to the dishwasher with them. Was it her, or was he really avoiding her eyes?

'Is he expensive?'

'Yes and no, because he's quick, so he doesn't waste time and he's very, very good, and he clears up after himself. He used to do work for Peter, and he's done quite a bit for me. Or you can find someone else? Up to you.'

'How is he available, if he's any good?' she asked sceptically.

He shrugged. 'People pull out for all sorts of reasons. Financial pressure, mostly.'

She stared at his back, knowing that it made sense, debating the 'beholden' thing again, since they were talking about financial pressure. But if he was a known quantity…

She gave up. 'OK. If you give me his number I'll call him.'

'I'll do it, I said I'd come back to him.'

Which probably meant he'd offered him some financial incentive, she thought, knowing Hugo, but he handed her his phone after a few brief words, and two minutes later she had a decorator lined up, an appointment to meet him at the house tomorrow evening at six thirty, and a promise that he could start on Monday.

She gave Hugo his phone back and chewed the inside of her cheek.

'What?' he asked, studying her with those eyes that saw altogether too much and right now gave away too little.

'Nothing. It just seems too easy—'

'That again? Life doesn't have to be difficult, Ellie, and you can trust Ryan. Yogurt and berries?'

'On one condition. I'm cooking tomorrow, as soon as I get back from the house.'

He held her eyes, and one corner of his mouth twitched. 'You're on. Do you want some colour charts to look at? I've got some somewhere.'

The decorator was bang on time, and she was back in the practice by seven. Hugo, predictably, was in the office, Lola and Rufus at his feet, and he turned to her as she went in, his eyes searching her face.

'How did you get on?'

'Quite well, I think,' she said, giving Lola a love. 'He said he could get it all done next week. He's sending me a quote this evening. It'll probably be hideous.'

'Great. I've done my run, so are you cooking, or am I ordering a takeaway?'

'I'm cooking. Give me ten minutes.'

The quote pinged into her phone while she was cooking. It made her wince a little, but the house would be transformed in a few days and she could move on with her life. If nothing else, she'd have options, and Hugo's suggestion of letting it over the summer was growing more tempting by the minute.

She showed the email to Hugo when he appeared. 'What do you think? Is that fair?'

He nodded thoughtfully and handed her phone back. 'I would say so. It's about what I expected, maybe a bit less. I'd bite his hand off. What colour are you going for on the walls?'

'White everywhere except the front door, because it's cheaper and easy to touch up. I'm just worried it'll look too clinical.'

'No. It'll look clean and fresh, especially if you're going to let it?'

She searched his eyes. 'Are you really OK with that? Because it seems a brilliant idea—short term, only, obviously, and no longer than Lucy's mat leave, but it would give me a buffer.'

'Of course I'm OK with it. I wouldn't have suggested it if I wasn't.' He leant over and peered into the pan she was stirring. 'That smells good. I'm starving. Anything I can do?'

She emailed Ryan and accepted his quote, and then the next two days were so busy she didn't have time to worry about her house. Hugo's charity ten K was coming up on Sunday and he went running every evening after work, sometimes for half an hour, sometimes for longer, and she took the time to take Lola out into the garden and let her wander around for a good while before going inside to cook for both of them.

He argued, of course, but she pointed out she owed him, and if nothing else it was good for her pride.

'Chosen a colour for the front door yet?' he asked on Thursday while she was cooking, and she shook her head.

'I have no idea.'

So after they'd eaten they went down to his flat and he dug out the colour charts and they sat together on his sofa poring over the coloured squares and drinking coffee.

'That's nice,' he said, pointing to a very dark blue. 'Sort of charcoal navy. It could look very smart.'

She peered at the colour he'd picked out, leaning closer and catching a delicious whiff of shampoo and warm skin. She straightened up, her own skin warming, her heart rate kicking up a notch.

Why? Really, why? I need to get out of here...

She shifted away. 'Yes, I think that one could look great. Can I hang on to the chart and show it to Ryan?'

'Of course. Or drop him a text. He'll pick it up then before he starts. More coffee?'

'Uh, no, thanks, I've got stuff to do, and I want to take Lola out for a little stroll. I think she's healed enough now and she must be so bored.'

'I'm sure she is. That's fine. I'll see you in the morning.'

He listened to the door close, and dropped his head back and blew his breath out slowly. Why on earth had he suggested she should do this? It was bad enough bumping into her during the day, but the evenings, eating together, sitting together over coffee, chatting about this and that, it was all too cosy, too—dammit, too tempting.

That worried him. There was no way this was going anywhere, however tempted he was. He wasn't in the market for anything other than a decent vet to cover Lucy's mat leave. Nothing more, and certainly nothing like what his body was screaming at him to do. He saved that for women who didn't expect anything from him but a good time. And now he and Ellie would be living cheek by jowl for months.

This was all Kerry's fault.

No, it isn't. You brought it on yourself.

He flexed his fist, but it was still sore, so he left the wall alone…

Ellie ran upstairs, closed the door of her flat and leant back against it. Why was she reacting like this to him? She'd known him two weeks now—two weeks tomorrow. She worked with him, ate with him, and mostly it was fine, but then every now and again he'd be that little bit closer, close enough to smell the scent of his skin, feel the warmth radiating from his body, and her heart would somersault in her chest and she'd feel breathless until he moved away.

It was ridiculous. And if she was going to be living here over the summer, letting her house, she was going to have to get a grip. And maybe a bit more space. Fewer cosy evenings…

That was fine. She could do that. Lola was almost better now, so every evening she could take her for a walk, a nice slow stroll onto the clifftop to look at the sea, then a stroll back via the other road. Starting now.

She put on her trainers, ran back downstairs and let Lola out of her kennel. 'Come on, sweetie, I've got a lovely treat for you. We're going for walkies.'

Lola's ears pricked, and she seemed more than ready to go

out. They wouldn't be long, Ellie wouldn't do that to her on her first proper outing, but she needed to build her strength and have a change of scenery, and so did Ellie.

Especially scenery that didn't have Hugo in it...

The sun was setting as they reached the clifftop, and she watched the light on the water, the slow, lazy swell of the waves washing away the stress. The tide had reached its height, she guessed, and she sat on the grass, Lola lying down by her side, and they watched the sky turn a glorious orange streaked with purple while all the tension faded away.

Lola nudged her with her nose, and she gave her a hug and got to her feet. 'Come on, little lady, let's take you home.'

And hopefully Hugo wouldn't be in the office...

Sunday dawned cool and sunny, with a light breeze, to Hugo's relief.

The run kicked off at ten, and he was mercilessly collecting last-minute sponsorship from anyone he could.

He'd already tapped the practice team, and Ellie had chipped in with twenty pounds that he knew she couldn't afford until she was on a better footing, but he'd taken it anyway.

He couldn't see her here today. Maybe she was at the house getting it ready for Ryan to start tomorrow, or maybe she just didn't want to come, but as he scanned the crowd he saw Peter and Sally waving as they made their way towards him.

Bless them, they never failed to support this event, and he knew they'd sponsor him generously. They always did.

'Hugo,' Peter said, wrapping him in a hug and slapping his back fondly. 'How are you? Ready for this?'

'I reckon. I've been putting in some pretty good times.'

'I'm sure you have,' Sally said, kissing his cheek and hugging him. 'Where's your form?'

He handed it to her, and over her shoulder he caught sight of Ellie. He beckoned her over. 'Ellie, I'd like you to meet Peter and Sally. Ellie's the vet covering Lucy's maternity leave.'

'Good to meet you, Ellie, I've heard great things about you,' Peter said, shaking her hand warmly.

'Good to meet you, too, and I've heard wonderful things about you both. It's nice to put faces to the names.' Her smile seemed warm and genuine to Hugo's eyes as she shook their hands, but he noticed she didn't really look at him. Well, not in the eye, at least—

No! He didn't need to think about her now, he needed to focus on the run and remember why he was doing it. Not that he could ever forget… 'Right, guys, I'm going to shoot off and warm up. I'll see you when it's over.'

'We'll be here,' Sally told him, and handed back the form.

He glanced at it. 'That's ridiculously generous.'

'It's not for you,' she pointed out, and he hugged her hard and headed for the group gathered behind the start line, his heart pumping.

As he jogged away, leaving Rufus with Peter, Ellie's shoulders dropped a notch, as did her heart rate, and yet again she wondered what on earth she'd committed herself to by agreeing to locum until October—never mind living in the flat!

Sally smiled at her, but her eyes were assessing and Ellie wondered what his godmother was thinking. Peter, thankfully, had better things to do making friends with Lola.

'This must be the invalid we heard about,' he said, rubbing her tummy and studying the faint line of the scar on the inside of her thigh.

'Yes—well, she was. She's not now, she's pretty much healed, but Hugo was—amazing. Not that I gave him much choice, I pretty much bullied him into treating her, but without him I don't know what would have happened to either of us.'

Peter gave Lola a last pat and straightened up. 'No, he told us a little about it and I don't think you had to bully him. He's a good lad. Always has been. Priorities in the right place, but he—he's had a lot to deal with.'

She met his eyes and read a warning there, a gentle reminder that Hugo, too, had been damaged and needed care.

'I know, he told me. He also told me how wonderful you both are, and how much love and support you've given him. And judging by you being here today, I guess you still do.'

'We do. Right, I think we need to head over there, Sally. We can catch up later, Ellie. I think we're all going to the pub.'

He and Rufus walked away, heading after Hugo, but Sally hung back.

'Peter's right, we do try to support him however we can, but there are some things we can't fix,' she said, her eyes following Peter as he walked towards Hugo at the race start point then looking back at her as she added softly, a gentle warning in her eyes, 'Please don't hurt him.'

Ellie shook her head. 'I—I'm just working there. We're not...'

'He said you've become a friend.'

'Did he?' That warmed her in a way she hadn't expected. 'Yes—yes, I suppose I have, in a way, but—that's all it is. We're not...'

'That's a shame,' Sally said softly under her breath, and followed Peter to the start line, leaving Ellie staring after her, not knowing what to make of that.

'Hey, Ellie, come on, we have to watch them set off,' Kerry said, linking her arm through Ellie's and towing her and Lola towards the start.

She went, a little reluctantly, Sally's words echoing in her head. 'Please don't hurt him.'

And what about me?

CHAPTER SEVEN

THEY WATCHED THEM set off, Hugo at the front of the pack, and as the runners streamed past them, Kerry turned to her.

'Right, let's go and find a coffee and a doughnut and have a look round the stalls. There are all sorts of things—puzzles, books, clothing, local produce, tombola, splat the rat, a bouncy castle for the kids, and it's all in aid of the hospice so I hope you've brought lots of money?'

'I brought some,' she said, wishing now that she'd brought more cash because she'd had no idea there'd be so many stalls. 'How long have we got?'

'Before the front runners get back? About forty-five minutes.'

'And Hugo?' she asked, wondering if that sounded too needy, but Kerry just chuckled.

'Hugo won it the year before last, but last year someone pipped him, so he'll be right up there trying to get that title back.'

'Is that why he's been training so hard?'

'Oh, no, he always pushes himself. He's a bit driven, really, but it's not surprising. He's had so much to deal with.'

'Yes, he told me. It was awful.'

'He told you?' Kerry glanced at her, her face surprised.

'Yes. We had a long heart-to-heart,' Ellie said softly, remembering their conversations about his parents, and his mother dying in a hospice would explain his support for this one.

Kerry sighed. 'I'm so glad he felt he could open up about it. They took such wonderful care of them all for the short time he was in there.'

He? Ellie stopped in her tracks. 'He?'

She stared at Kerry blankly, and Kerry stared just as blankly back, then let out a long groan.

'He didn't tell you, did he? Oh, no…'

'Tell me what?'

Kerry closed her eyes and bit her lips. 'Oh, Ellie. I should have realised he wouldn't have told you. He never talks about it.'

'About *what,* Kerry? What does he never talk about? I know he lost both his parents. I thought you must mean his mother dying in a hospice?'

Kerry shook her head, and Ellie could see she was fighting back tears. She felt a cold chill spread through her.

'Who is "he", Kerry?' she asked, dreading the answer.

She hesitated, then said softly, 'His baby.'

His baby? His…son?

'No…'

'Don't say anything to him, please? I shouldn't have told you, and it'll only upset him.'

She shook her head. 'No, no, of course I won't. I…'

'Come on, let's go and get a coffee and sit down for a bit,' Kerry said, and steered her towards a picnic bench by a refreshments stand.

'So—what happened? Where is he now?' she asked, half of her not wanting to hear the answer, but Kerry's face was enough. 'He died. Didn't he?'

Kerry nodded wordlessly, and Ellie felt the air sucked

out of her lungs. Her eyes filled with tears and she blinked them away, but they slid down her cheeks and she swiped them away. 'I had no idea,' she said, heartbroken for him. 'How—that's...'

'Sorry. Look, I'll get us a coffee. Stay here.'

Stay? She couldn't have moved if she'd tried. She sat down on the bench as if her strings were cut, staring numbly across the field while Lola sat pressed against her leg. To comfort her?

She could see runners in the distance through a gap in the hedge, streaming past. Was Hugo at the front, driven by the need to support the place that must mean so much to him? Or just running away from it, trying to forget...

No. He'd never forget. You couldn't. But how could he live with that? Live with such a horrendous, soul-destroying loss? It must have torn his heart out...

She closed her eyes, the tears leaking through her lids and streaming down her face, and she felt something pushed into her hand. A paper napkin, offered to her by Kerry who was sitting beside her with a coffee in her hand and a bag of doughnuts on her lap.

She scrubbed her face, blew her nose and sniffed hard. 'Sorry. It just—'

'I know. And I'm the one who's sorry, I didn't mean to dump that on you. I shouldn't have—'

'When?' she asked, her voice sounding weird and some-how remote. 'When did he die?'

'Nearly ten years ago? I'd just started there. It was before Peter retired, and Hugo dropped off the face of the earth for a lot of the time in those few months. How he would have coped without Peter and Sally I don't know, and of course it was the nearest they'd get to a grandchild, so they felt the loss almost as deeply. And he hasn't had a meaningful relationship since. It broke him, and I think he's scared of the what-ifs.'

'What what-ifs?'

'In case it happens again—maybe. I don't know. He just shuts down if you raise the subject. He'll talk about anything else, but not that.'

That made sense. 'He told me about himself, about his parents dying—and actually, when he was telling me that, I was sure there was something else. There was just some undercurrent, and he suddenly changed the subject and asked me about myself. It was right back at the beginning—I hardly knew him at all, and we told each other all sorts of stuff, but not that. Never, ever that—'

She pressed a hand to her mouth to hold in a sob, and Kerry put an arm round her shoulders and hugged her.

'I should have realised he wouldn't. I don't think anyone else at the practice knows apart from Jean who's been there for ever, and she never gossips. Here, have a doughnut. They're still warm, and you probably need that sugar hit.'

She took one, the sugary crunch followed by soft, sweet dough and the comforting squelch of jam. She took another bite, and another and another, almost absently, then handed the last bit to Lola, dusting off her fingers and dredging up a smile.

'Thanks. You were right, I needed that.'

'You're welcome. Come on, let's drink our coffee and have a wander round before we go back and wait for them. We've got twenty minutes or so.'

They stood at the finish with Peter and Sally and other members of the team. While she was still trying to make sense of what she'd been told, they were yelling and cheering as he ran through the timer beam, then slowed and ducked under the tape to join them. He bent over, hands on his knees, chest heaving, his body driven to the limit, slowly getting his breath back.

Then he straightened up and checked with the stewards, and came back to them with a broad smile.

'Ten seconds off my PB,' he said, but the smile didn't quite reach his eyes—not now she knew what to look for.

'Congratulations,' she said, and then turned and slipped quietly away, the tears threatening again as she left him, surrounded by the nearest thing he had to family.

Ten years of sorrow, ten years of loss, ten years of denying himself a family, the children he'd be such a good, kind, loving father to.

Don't hurt him.

We're just friends.

That's a shame.

She walked quickly away, taking a reluctant Lola with her, and a moment later she felt a firm, warm hand on her shoulder.

'Hey, where are you going? I thought we were all going to the pub?'

She couldn't look at him, not now, with those tears still threatening, not knowing what she knew.

'Sorry, I need to get on with the house. Ryan's coming in the morning and I need to get it ready. But well done. I'm really pleased for you.'

She glanced up fleetingly then and caught the flicker of a frown on his face as she forced a smile. 'I'll see you tomorrow.'

'OK,' he said, the words coming after the briefest hesitation. 'Shout if I can help.'

'I'll be fine,' she told him, her voice much firmer now, but her smile was probably no more convincing, so she turned and walked away, taking a still reluctant Lola with her.

Hugo watched her go, torn between the people behind him and the woman in front.

Something was wrong, he had no idea what, but she didn't want to talk to him. Sure, there must be things she had to do at the house, but he didn't think sorting the house was enough to make her cry. And she'd been crying, without a shadow of a doubt. Why?

He turned and walked slowly back to the others, endured a stream of hugs and back-slapping and handshakes as the results revealed that he'd won, and then he caught Kerry looking at him with an odd expression on her face.

He moved to her side. 'What's up with Ellie? Why's she crying?'

She shook her head slowly, biting her lip. 'We need to talk.'

'Well, go on, then, spit it out.'

She closed her eyes and shook her head again. 'It's my fault, Hugo, I'm so sorry. She was asking why winning was so important to you, and I said you always push yourself hard. I said you were a bit driven, you'd had a lot to deal with, and she said she knew, you'd told her, and I just assumed...'

'You told her.' He crushed it down, the rush of emotion he thought he'd outrun, but he hadn't. He never could.

'Not in so many words, but you seem to be so close—'

'Not that close.'

Never that close, not to anyone, never again...

'I just said the hospice had been very supportive while he was in there, and she just stared at me. She thought I was talking about your mum, and after that I had to tell her—had to explain. I'm so sorry, Hugo, you know I would never have told her if I hadn't thought she knew.'

Her eyes were welling up, and he sighed and gave her a quick hug. 'It's OK, it doesn't matter, it's done now. I'll talk to her later. Right now I need a shower, and then we're going to the pub to celebrate.'

'Really?'

'Yes, really. We don't have a choice. Chin up, Kerry, what's done is done and it's not the end of the world.'

She heard a knock at the door in mid-afternoon, and she froze.

Hugo? Who else? Anyone else, hopefully, because if it was Hugo she wouldn't know how to look him in the eye.

She peered out of the window, but there was no car outside. Not that that meant anything, he was quite likely to have walked. Or it could be one of the neighbours come for a nose round. Please God...

Except Lola was whining and scratching at the door. The knock came again, and she braced herself and opened it.

He was standing there with Rufus, hands rammed in his jeans pockets, unsmiling, and she could see the pulse beating at the base of his throat.

'Hugo, I said I didn't need your help.'

'I know.'

She closed her eyes, not sure what to say, not sure what to do, but he took the decision out of her hands.

'Can we go for a walk?'

She looked at him again, her heart pounding, but his eyes were blank, giving nothing away. Not so the tension in his body. Had Kerry told him?

'Yes, of course. I'll put Lola in her crate.'

They walked side by side in an awkward silence, Rufus sniffing along the way, and when they reached the cliff top they made their way down the steps and along the concrete walkway, the sea stretching away to their right, the water glinting in the sunlight.

She didn't say anything, she had no idea what to say or where to start, so she left it up to him. A couple passed them, going the other way, and still she waited. And then finally they reached a point where the concrete ran out and the rocky sea defences took over, and at last he stopped walking.

'I spoke to Kerry.'

What was she supposed to say to that? She had no idea, so she said nothing, and he carried on.

'I asked what was wrong with you. She said—' He sucked in a breath, then let it out in a shaky rush. 'She said she'd told you about Samuel. Thought you knew.'

Samuel. She hadn't known his name, and somehow knowing it made her hurt for him even more.

She closed her eyes, and the tears slid silently down her cheeks. She felt him brush them away with a gentle hand.

'Hey, come on. Let's sit down.'

They sat side by side on the shingle, shoulders not quite touching, Rufus wedged between them.

He laid a hand on the dog's head, stroking it gently, and then he started to speak, his voice low, sombre.

'We weren't married—we'd been on and off for a bit and we weren't together any more, and it was a while before Emma realised she was pregnant. She had a scan at twenty weeks which showed that the baby had all sorts of issues and he might not even survive the pregnancy. She contacted me then to tell me about it, so even though we weren't together,

I was there for her. I had to be. He was my child as much as hers, and I blamed myself for her getting pregnant. She didn't want a termination, she wanted to let nature take its course, and he was born at thirty-seven weeks.

'His DNA had three copies of chromosome eighteen in each cell, instead of the usual two. It's called Edwards' syndrome, or trisomy 18, and the fault could have come from either of us. They said it wasn't a heritable defect, just one of those things, a failure in the cell division of the ovum or sperm, but in his case it was incompatible with life.

'His head was small, and he had cysts in his brain, which meant sometimes he stopped breathing, and he had difficulty swallowing so he had to be tube-fed. His heart wasn't plumbed right so his circulation was impaired, so he was on oxygen, but he wasn't in pain and he wasn't in imminent danger of dying and he didn't need to be in the noisy hospital, so we got him moved to the hospice so we could be with him in a quieter, more normal environment for as long as he had.

'And they were wonderful in there. He needed round the clock care, so with their support we took it in shifts, and then when he was eight weeks old he got a chest infection, and he died in my arms—'

His voice cracked, and she rested her head against his shoulder, her hand on his arm.

'I'm so sorry, Hugo.'

His hand covered hers. 'Don't be. He couldn't have lived, his body was too compromised, but that time we had with him was so precious. It'll be with me for ever, but I couldn't go through all that again.'

'What about Emma? She must have been devastated.'

'Oh, she was, of course, but she's moved on. She's married now, she's had three children. I don't know how she could do that. It would seem all wrong to me, somehow, to have another child, as if I'd airbrushed him away because he didn't matter. But he did—'

His voice cracked again, and he stopped talking, the tension vibrating through him, and a single tear leaked out of the corner of his eye.

Oh, Hugo...

She closed her eyes, and he put an arm around her and leant his head against hers as they sat in silence, listening to the sound of the sea lapping on the shingle, each lost in their thoughts.

And then he straightened up, sucked in a breath and gave her a crooked little smile. 'We need to go and get your house sorted out.'

He stood up, held out his hand and pulled her to her feet, then wrapped his arms around her, folding her against his body as if to comfort her, and as he spoke she could feel the low rumble of his voice.

'Don't be sad for me, Ellie. I'm OK.'

Was he? Was he really? She didn't think so, not for a second.

She kissed his cheek, and he turned his head and his mouth brushed hers and lingered for a moment, then he lifted his head, leaving her lips bereft and her body aching to comfort his.

She laid her head against his chest, felt the slow, heavy thud of his heart against her ear, and after the longest moment she straightened up and moved out of his arms, but he didn't let her go, just slid his hand down her arm and took hold of her hand and held it all the way back to her house while she thought of his baby and tried not to cry.

She unlocked the door and went in, and he followed her

and the silence closed around them, still unbroken, the tension now replaced by sorrow.

'I don't have any dust sheets,' she said inconsequentially, dragging them both back into the here and now, and his mouth twitched into a smile that didn't quite reach his eyes.

'Ryan has hundreds of dust sheets. Let's get your stuff out, give him a clear field.'

An hour later her possessions were stacked in her bedroom at the practice.

All except the beautiful orchid he'd given her, and she'd put that on the worktop in the kitchen so she could see it every day.

'Have you eaten?' he asked, and she shook her head.

'You have, though, haven't you? You went to the pub.'

His smile was a little twisted. 'I didn't eat a lot. How about we try again, just the two of us and the dogs?'

So he took her to the Harbour Inn, and they had fish and chips and shared some with the dogs, and gradually she began to relax again.

He drove them home—funny how the practice and not her house seemed like home—they went upstairs together and he kissed her, another gentle touch of his lips on hers that left her heart and her body aching.

'Goodnight, Ellie,' he said after a breath-stealing pause, and turned away.

She nearly called him back, but that would have been foolish, and anyway she needed some time alone to think. She heard the door on the landing click shut, and she closed her eyes.

'Goodnight, my love,' she whispered, and closed the door, walked into her bedroom, lay down on the bed and cried for him.

* * *

Within days the house was transformed.

So was her relationship with Hugo.

She felt she had a much greater understanding of him, and she could absolutely understand Sally's 'don't hurt him'. Her 'that's a shame' was echoed in her heart, but there was no way he was going to take their relationship any further, so they focussed on the friendship that they'd formed.

With the run over for another year, their evenings were spent walking the dogs, often strolling along the beach or beside the river. Sometimes they'd eat out, sometimes she'd cook for them, sometimes he would.

And as soon as Ryan was finished, she got her house ready for holiday letting, found a site where she could advertise it and within moments she had her first tenants lined up.

'Wow, that was quick,' he said when she told him.

'It was. I'm stunned. I just hope they don't trash it. And of course it's taken my eye off the ball for this wedding and I don't even know if I've got anything to wear. What's the dress code? And do you have any idea what I could buy for them?'

'Black tie, and no. She's got a gift list on a website, I believe. Ask her.'

'I will. And I might have to go dress shopping. I've only got three days and I've got to get the house ready, they come on Sunday.'

'That's fine, you can do that whenever. There are some good shops in Yoxburgh, nice little independents and they aren't outrageous.'

They didn't need to be outrageous, because she didn't have money to fling around after the expense of the house.

She asked some of the others what they were wearing, and they were all going in long. And she didn't have a long dress.

Unless she wore the wrap dress she'd got for Jim's retirement party...

It was hanging in her bedroom in the flat, and at lunchtime she ran up and pulled it out. Would it do? She'd felt good in it, she'd only worn it once, it had been expensive, and it was long.

Well, it was at the back, but not at the front where it wrapped across. That was mid-calf.

Long enough? Probably. And it was a beautiful dress.

She stripped off her scrubs, put it on, tied the waist and looked in the mirror, but it wasn't a full-length mirror so it was hard to judge. A bit too much cleavage? And if it was windy...

But she owned it, it suited her, and it picked up the colour of her eyes.

'It'll be fine,' she told herself, and hung it back up.

Job done. Now she just had to buy a present.

Hugo gave his bow tie a last little tug to straighten it, looked at himself in the mirror and closed his eyes.

He really, really needed to find a smile or he'd upset everyone, but he wasn't looking forward to the wedding.

It would have been easier without Ellie being his 'plus one' as Kerry, so blatantly matchmaking, had described it. They'd grown closer since the race, and he was finding it difficult enough to keep his distance as it was, especially since he'd kissed her. OK, it had been pretty platonic, but that had only been because he'd firmly kept it that way.

If she'd been anyone else, they would have ended up in bed weeks ago, but she wasn't a woman he could sleep with and kiss goodbye, and that was as much of a commitment he'd been prepared to make for years. And he cared about her far too much to want to treat her like that.

But with all the romantic wedding vibes, the alcohol, the dancing—hell, especially the dancing.

His heart sank. He'd be expected to dance with Ellie. They'd all be watching and waiting for it, and he'd bet his life that as soon as they were up on the dance floor Kerry would get the DJ to play some slow numbers, and she'd end up in his arms.

No alcohol, then. The only thing left for him to influence. Unless she hated dancing. He could only hope—

There was a quiet tap on the door, and he opened it to find Ellie there, looking drop-dead gorgeous in a beautiful dress that did absolutely nothing for his increasingly fragile self-control. It was bad enough when she was wearing scrubs—

'Will I be all right in this?' she asked doubtfully.

If it was any more all right he'd die of a heart attack, but that was his business, not hers. He dragged his eyes off the soft swell of her breasts so perfectly framed by the vee.

'Yes, it's fine,' he said, his voice gruffer that usual because that dress had totally emptied his brain. 'It's lovely. Are you ready?'

'Yes, I'm good to go.'

She needn't have worried about her dress. It was just right for the tone of the occasion, and she felt good in it.

They'd left the dogs together in his flat and walked to the venue, arriving bang on time, and after she'd changed into heels and left her wrap and flats in the cloakroom, they'd gone in and found some of the others from the practice there clustered around the bar talking to Kerry and her new hus-band James.

'Oh, she looks gorgeous,' Ellie said softly, 'and so happy, both of them.'

'They are, and she deserves it. I'm really happy for her.'

Kerry turned then and spotted them, and after all the kisses and hugs and handshakes were done and they moved on, Hugo turned to her.

'What would you like to drink?' he asked her, and she hesitated, then threw caution to the winds.

'White wine? Just a small one, not massive, I'm a bit of a lightweight and I haven't eaten yet.'

'No, nor have I. We'll have to raid the buffet later.'

He ordered drinks for all the practice members there, got himself an alcohol-free beer, handed her the wine and they mingled with the others.

'Hello, you,' a voice said behind them, and Hugo turned and gave the woman a warm hug.

'Lucy! Great to see you, I'm so glad you're here. Lucy, this is Ellie, she's covering your mat leave.'

Ellie met her eyes—curious, assessing—and smiled at her. 'Hi.'

'Hi. I've heard a lot about you from everyone. I hope Hugo's not working you too hard.'

She laughed, wondering what she'd heard, hoping none of it was idle speculation. 'Not as hard as he works himself, that's for sure. And everyone's been lovely.'

'They are lovely. I miss them.'

'I hope that means you're coming back,' Hugo said, and Lucy laughed.

'Never say never,' she said, 'although I might pop in soon.'

'Do. You're always welcome. So, how's it going?'

'Great. I love being a mum. Sleep would be nice, but—yeah, it's all good. Anyway, I need to mingle, we're not here for long and I've got loads of catching up to do. See you soon?'

'Sure.'

Lucy turned away and went back to the others, and Ellie met Hugo's eyes and smiled. 'She's nice.'

'She is. Right, somewhere there's a buffet table, and I need to eat. I had half a sandwich for lunch.'

They grazed on the buffet, mingled a bit more, and then it was time for the first dance.

They all clustered round to watch, phones clicking as photos were taken, videos filmed, and then everyone clapped and cheered and headed onto the dance floor.

Hugo looked down at her with a smile she couldn't quite read. 'Shall we?' he said, and held out his hand.

She put hers in it, and a shiver of something strange ran up her arm and settled in her chest, robbing her of breath. She should have had a bigger glass of wine, she thought, and let him lead her onto the dance floor.

The music was typical wedding dance stuff, and despite his apparent reluctance, he was a natural. It didn't surprise her, because he always moved fluidly, but it was years since she'd danced with anyone who didn't have two left feet, and it was a joy to dance with someone who loved it as much as she did.

And then the music slowed, and he held out his arms and she moved into them. Not too close, but close enough that she could smell the subtle fragrance of his cologne, feel the light touch of his hand on her back, the occasional nudge of his legs against hers, and her body caught fire.

She glanced at his face and met his eyes, and with a quiet

sigh he eased her closer; she rested her head on his shoulder, his cheek against hers, his body close now, his legs brushing hers as they swayed together to the music. She felt his lips graze her cheek, and she turned her head a fraction and his mouth met hers, a light, fleeting kiss that seared all the way down through her body, leaving her feeling more alive than she had for years.

He swore softly, then turned his head a fraction, his mouth by her ear, his voice a low murmur.

'We need to get out of here.'

They did, but she had no idea where it would lead, and she had no more idea where she wanted it to lead, either.

She just knew that for now, she wanted Hugo, and he wanted her, as simple and as complicated as that.

Except there was nothing simple about leaving, because Kerry caught them on the way out and gave them both a knowing look.

'Damn,' he said after they'd made the feeble excuse of needing to get back to the dogs and headed for the foyer.

'Don't worry, she's had way too much to drink, she probably won't even remember,' Ellie said, hoping it was true.

She retrieved her ballet flats, slung her wrap around her shoulders and they walked back to the practice, not quite touching, not quite apart.

So what now?

What was he doing? What was he *thinking* about?

He had no idea, he just knew that the only sure way to find out where this was going was to go with it, and go with it they would, he knew that much.

Either that or he'd die wondering what it would be like to—

He put his key in the lock, let them in and led her up to his flat.

The dogs gave them a rapturous welcome, and he took them out into the garden for a moment and came back up, wondering if she'd still be there or if she would have come to her senses and gone up to her flat.

No such luck.

'Stay and have a drink?' he suggested, leaving her a way out, just in case, hoping to God she didn't—

'Sure.'

She didn't look sure, and he wasn't, either, but it made no difference. He headed to the kitchen. 'Coffee or wine? I have both.'

'What are you having?'

Second thoughts, but he didn't say that, because she turned and he caught a flash of leg where the two sides of the dress met, and his brain left the building.

He swallowed. 'I don't really want a drink,' he said, and held her eyes.

Then what...?

'Nor do I.'

He held out his hand, and she let him draw her into his arms.

'I want you.' His voice was gruff, and she could feel the tension vibrating through his body. It matched the tension in her own, and she lifted her head and met his eyes.

'I want you, too,' she whispered, and he closed his eyes.

His mouth found hers, tentatively at first, then bolder, his teeth nipping lightly at her lips, his tongue teasing, coaxing, and then hot, so hot as she opened her mouth to him.

He rocked against her, his erection hard against her abdomen, one leg nudging between hers as he lifted her against him, his mouth doing incredible things to hers.

And then he broke away and let her go.

'I think we need to take this somewhere—'

'Horizontal?' she offered, and he gave a strangled laugh.

'I was going to say without the dogs, but yeah, that too.'

He shut the dogs in the sitting room, then caught her hand in his and led her into his bedroom and closed the door.

'So, where were we?'

'Not horizontal yet,' she said with a shaky smile, and tugged at his bow tie. 'Oh. It's real.'

'Of course it's real.' He slid it out from under the collar and laid it on his chair, shrugged off his jacket, heeled off his shoes and turned back to her. Then he stopped, took her by the hands and stared down into her eyes.

'This isn't going anywhere, you know that, don't you?'

She nodded, not at all sure if that was how she felt but willing to go along with it. So long as he was…

'If you don't want this, I can go,' she said, but he shook his head and his mouth tilted into a wry smile.

'Oh, I want. Believe me, I want.'

He cupped her face in his hands and kissed her again, slowly and thoroughly, then let her go and took a step back. 'We have way too much on,' he said, his voice hoarse, gravelly with need, his eyes so dark they looked almost black.

He turned off the top light, put on a bedside light and stripped off his shirt—or tried to. 'Stupid cufflinks,' he muttered, and she took his hands and slipped the cufflinks out one by one, dropping them on his bedside table.

When she turned back his shirt was gone, and his hand was on his belt buckle. She stopped him, removed his hands, undid the buckle, slipped the leather free, then reached for the waistband. Two clips. Why so many?

And then his zip was sliding down, and she let go and his trousers slid down his legs and puddled round his ankles.

She closed her eyes then, unable to look at him without touching. She heard the soft rustle of fabric, a muted clunk as the belt buckle hit the floor again, then his hands were on her waist.

'How does this undo?'

She reached for the bow and he caught her hands and eased them aside, then she felt the waist fall away, the cool air of his bedroom brushing her skin as he opened the front of the dress.

She heard the sharp hiss of indrawn breath, felt the touch of his hands on her shoulders brushing the dress aside so it slid to the floor, then his hands reached around her and un-clipped her bra and freed her aching breasts.

She opened her eyes and they locked with his as he reached for her and drew her into his arms, his chest heav-ing as if he'd been running, the soft hairs chafing lightly at her nipples with every breath.

His kiss was long and slow, one leg nudging between hers, the thin layers of fabric between them annoying now.

'Hugo, please,' she said, her voice cracking, and he tugged back the covers, stripped off his shorts and then slowly, inch by inch, he drew that last tiny scrap of lace away, his mouth following it.

She sucked in her breath, and he straightened up, lifted her and laid her on the bed, following her down and strad-dling her. Then he reached into the bedside table and pulled out a small foil packet, tore it open and took out a condom.

'I'm on the pill,' she told him, but he just shook his head.

'I still want this.'

'Let me,' she said, and, in the gentle light that gilded his body, she saw the muscles in his abdomen clench as she touched him, carrying out the intimate task with deliberate and meticulous care. He tipped his head back and swore softly as she trailed her trembling fingers slowly back up.

He took her hand away. 'Are you done torturing me?' he said, his voice uneven, his breathing ragged.

She couldn't stop the smile. 'I think so. For now.'

He stared down at her, his mouth tipping into an answering smile, and then the smile faded as his hands reached down and cupped her breasts, taking his sweet time as he rolled her nipples gently between thumb and forefinger, then shifted down her body, bending his head to draw her nipples one at a time into his hot, hungry mouth.

His tongue toyed with them, his teeth nipping gently, his lips closing over them as he suckled. She bucked and writhed under him, and finally, when she thought she was going to cry with frustration, he nudged her legs apart and slid slowly, deeply inside her.

A long, shuddering groan echoed through his body and into hers, then his mouth found hers in a kiss that nearly sent her over the brink as he began to move. His hands were everywhere, nothing off limits, and so were hers. She loved the feel of his body, the taut muscles of his shoulders, the feel of his hair sifting through her fingers, the slight roughness of his beard against her cheek as his tongue flicked against the pulse in her neck. The tension she could feel building in him…

She was close, so close, and then he shifted again, his clever, knowing fingers touching her, coaxing her, taking her over the edge and then following her with a guttural cry as his body stiffened against hers.

He lowered his head and rested it against hers, and she could feel his breath hot against her shoulder.

And then, as the echoes faded and their breathing slowed, he rolled away from her, got up and went into his bathroom, closing the door behind him with a soft but definite click.

CHAPTER EIGHT

HUGO DEALT WITH the condom, then propped his hands on the washbasin and stared at himself in the mirror, shaken to the core.

What the hell just happened?

Apart from the fact that he'd just had the most profound sex of his life. He closed his eyes and groaned.

Why? Why the hell did you do that?

No idea. No idea at all, except it had seemed like a good idea at the time, get rid of the urge, take the edge off it. But it hadn't, had it? No. It was worse than ever, because now he *knew*. He knew just how good it was with her, and it scared him, because sure, the sex had been good, but it had been more than that.

Far more.

He felt like he'd given her his soul, and taken hers. So now what did he do with it? Hand it back? Tell her it was all a stupid, rash mistake and they should never have done it?

He had no idea. He just knew he wanted her like he'd never wanted anyone ever before and, whatever happened, it was going to hurt them both.

She tugged the covers over herself and lay there motionless, staring at his bathroom door, her body still thrumming with the last echoes of her climax.

So what happens now? Is that it? Is he done with me now?

No idea. Should she get up and leave before he told her to go? Get up and put her dress back on and go and sit with the dogs? She could hear them whining in the other room, wondering what was going on.

They weren't alone.

The bathroom door opened and he walked out, gloriously, beautifully naked, and she wanted to touch him, to hold him, to make love with him again. But she didn't have the right to do that, because it would make it more than just a one-off drunken quickie.

Not that it had felt like that, at least for her. Quick, yes, but something much more powerful, more meaningful than she'd expected. And neither of them were drunk, or at least not on alcohol, so that meant—what, exactly?

'The dogs are whining, and I'm still hungry. Fancy a snack and a cup of tea?'

He turned away before she could read his eyes, and she stared at his back. He was lifting a bathrobe off the back of the door, shrugging into it, covering that glorious, wonderful body that had just taken her to places she'd never been before and stolen her heart along the way.

'Sure,' she said, although she wasn't sure of anything right then. 'I'll run upstairs and put something on.' Something sensible that didn't give out such blatant signals…

'I'll be in the kitchen.'

He left the room, and she scrambled out of bed, flung her dress back on, scooped up her underwear and shoes and ran up to her flat, closing the door behind her and leaning back on it with a shaky sigh.

She had no idea what was going on in his head, and his

eyes had been unreadable. Mostly because he'd had his back to her for nearly all of that very brief conversation…

She hung up her dress, pulled on fresh underwear and her jersey PJs, and then after a glance in the mirror she took off her makeup and went back down to his flat, her heart beating a tattoo behind her ribs.

He'd pulled on sweat pants and a hoodie, and he was busy in the kitchen, the dogs at his feet looking hopeful.

'That smells good,' she offered, trying to sound normal.

'I made cheese on toast,' he said over his shoulder. 'Hope that's OK.'

And he turned then and smiled at her, and she still couldn't read his face, but at least he wasn't frowning. He picked up the laden plate.

'Here, you take the tea and I'll bring this. I don't want Rufus to steal it, he loves cheese.'

'He'd have to fight Lola for it,' she said drily, and smiled back, not sure if it would look like a smile or some kind of weird rictus, but it was the best she could do. She picked up the mugs and followed him.

Rufus and Lola, as predicted, were all about the cheese, dancing around under Hugo's feet, their eyes fixed on the plate.

'No. Lie down.'

They lay, obeying him but eyeing the plate longingly as Hugo sat down beside her with it on his lap.

'Here, let's eat it quick while it's still hot and before they drool everywhere.'

She took a slice, the melted cheese running off the edges of the toast, stretching into strings as she lifted it. She scooped it up, wiped it off on the crust and sucked the tip of her finger, then glanced at Hugo.

He was watching her, transfixed, and she could read his face easily now. Want, need, the white heat of that visceral urge that had brought them together just a short while ago.

'Did you have to do that?' he said, his smile wry, his voice not quite managing to be casual.

'I'm sorry—'

'Don't apologise,' he told her, and leant over and kissed her. Just a touch, a light brush of his mouth on hers, the flick of his tongue to catch the taste of that melted cheese.

Then he leant back, his shoulder against hers, and picked up a slice, biting into it with a groan that dragged her mind straight back to his bed. 'Oh, that's *so-o-o* good! I'm starving.'

She couldn't watch him. Too tempting, too—just too *Hugo*…

His arm settled round her shoulders, pulling her in against his side as he rested his head against hers.

'Are we OK, Ellie?'

His voice was low, a little gruff, and she turned her head a fraction so she could see him, the food forgotten.

'I don't know,' she told him frankly. 'Are we?'

His mouth twisted a little. 'I hope so. But I think we need to talk.'

She looked down at her cheese, cooling now, congealing on the toast as it cooled. 'Can we eat and talk at the same time?'

She felt as much as heard his chuckle.

'Yes, we can eat and talk.'

But he didn't talk, so she prompted him.

'So what did you want to say?'

He'd just taken another bite, so he shook his head and chewed and swallowed, a smile playing on his lips. She was happy to see the smile, because she had no idea what was coming and until he got on with whatever it was he wanted to say—

'Sorry. OK. Firstly, I have absolutely no regrets about what happened. But if we're going to do it again, we need some ground rules first,' he added, his smile fading.

Ground rules? 'OK,' she said slowly. 'Such as?'

He hesitated, his smile well and truly gone, his face serious now. 'I don't do permanent. I don't do long-term, I don't make promises I can't keep—and I don't want anyone else here knowing. And there's no way you're getting pregnant if I have anything to do with it.'

The last one was clearly a veiled reference to Samuel, and maybe all the rest of his rules, too. She chewed and swallowed, taking her time while she tried to work out exactly what he was saying. 'So, is that it?'

He turned his head and studied her face for a moment. 'I think so, for now. Your turn,' he added, but she shook her head.

'I haven't—I didn't ask for permanent, I didn't ask for long-term—'

'You didn't ask me to leave the wedding with you so abruptly and come back here and—'

He broke off, and she wondered, for a moment, what he'd been going to say.

'Make love to me?' she suggested, her words hanging in the silence, and he met her eyes again, his utterly unreadable this time.

'I don't do love,' he said.

Because love hurt, she realised, and he'd already lost too much. Oh, Hugo...

She felt something in her chest squeeze a little tighter. 'OK, so what do you do?' she asked, and then added bluntly, 'Apart from having mind-blowing, earth-shaking no-strings sex?'

She'd felt it, too?

The blown mind, the shaken earth.

The soul-sharing? She hadn't mentioned that. Maybe she hadn't felt it the way he had.

'That's pretty much it,' he said, his voice a little terse because he wanted to deny it and couldn't. He wasn't going to talk about the soul-sharing, not now, not ever. He had nothing to offer her. Nothing that would expose him to any more losses in his life. His heart was like a hollow shell already. Letting himself fall for her would just tear out the little that was left of it when she went. Which she would, in the end. And she deserved better than the little he had to offer.

'OK.'

He stared at her, his mind distracted. 'OK?'

'Yes. OK. Your terms.'

He pulled himself together. 'And what are yours?'

Something raw and hurt flickered in her eyes and was gone before he was sure.

'I don't do Ts & Cs, Hugo, and I'm on the pill and you're using condoms, so that takes care of that one. All I'd ask is that you don't slag me off to all the practice staff when you decide you're done with me.'

He swore, dumped the plate and turned her face towards him, appalled. 'I would never do that to you. *Ever.* And the last thing I want to do is hurt you.'

He leant in and kissed her, just a fleeting, gentle touch, an apology for sounding like a—

'No!'

He swore again, snatched up the empty plate and glared at the dogs. They were gulping down the last few pieces, and they didn't even have the grace to look guilty...

'Come back to bed,' he said, and then added, as a belated afterthought, 'Please?'

She couldn't have said no to him if her life had depended on it.

They took it slower this time, savouring every touch, every tremor, every kiss, and when it was over he kissed her gently, rolled away and went into the bathroom.

She watched him go, wondering what would happen now, what his protocol was for this kind of event. Would he expect her to go up to her room for the rest of the night? Stay here with him? And what about the dogs? Lola was used to being upstairs with her now. Where would *she* sleep?

Maybe she should just be proactive and get up—

The bathroom light clicked off, and he walked back to the bed, turning off the bedside light as he got back under the covers. 'Come here,' he said softly.

He rolled towards her, drawing her into his arms again, and his kiss was tender. 'You OK?'

'Mm-hm. You?'

'I'm very OK.'

He kissed her again, then rolled onto his back, leaving his arm around her, and she lay with her arm draped over his chest and her head on his shoulder, listening to the beat of his heart and the slow rhythm of his breathing.

I don't do love.

Maybe not, but he did mind-blowing, earth-shaking no-strings sex with bells on. Maybe she should have said heart stealing, too. Because that was what it was. She felt as if he'd reached inside her chest and cradled her heart in his hands, and nothing would ever feel the same again, and she wanted to cry...

He woke in the night to raging thirst and a dead arm.

She was fast asleep, her body lax, her breathing slow and regular. He eased his arm out from under her, tucking the pillow in its place, and went quietly out of the room, snagging his robe off the back of the door and wincing as the blood flowed through his arm again.

The dogs were silent, so he left them alone and went into the kitchen, downed a glass of water and then made a cup of tea and sat and drank it, his mind lost in thought.

Was she really OK? Would they be able to do this? He didn't know, and the very last thing he wanted to do was hurt her, hurt anyone, but she was young, only early thirties, and she had so much life to live, so much love to give.

It would be so easy to let himself love her, but she deserved a family, not a no-strings contract, and that was all he could offer her. All he *dared* to offer her. And it wasn't enough.

Idiot. You shouldn't have touched her.

He swore softly under his breath, and stared blankly out of the window. The sky was still dark, not even the slightest touch of pale along the horizon, but he was too wired to sleep. He scrolled through the photos he'd taken last night, Kerry dancing with James, a group one of the practice members, and then one of Ellie laughing at him that got him right in the solar plexus.

And then just because why not torture himself, he scrolled back through the photos, right back to ten years ago and his photos of Samuel.

There was one of him lying in Emma's arms, another in his own, one of his little finger in Samuel's tiny fist, another with Peter and Sally.

Four broken hearts, four lives plunged into grief and despair. A salutary reminder of why it could never happen again...

He switched off his phone, put it on charge and went quietly back into the bedroom. She was motionless, silent, and he let his robe drop to the floor and lay down, easing the duvet over himself.

'Are you OK?'

Her voice was soft, concerned, her hand finding his shoulder in the darkness, and he shifted to face her. 'I'm fine,' he lied. 'I was just thirsty.'

'You've been ages.'

'I made tea. We didn't drink the last one.'

'I know. I'm thirsty, too. What's the time?'

'Three twenty-eight the last time I looked. Want me to get you tea?'

'Tea would be lovely. Thank you.'

He made them both one, and took them back to the bedroom. She'd turned on the bedside light and she was in the bathroom, and she came out naked and beautiful and he wanted her all over again.

Yet again, the tea went ignored.

The dogs woke them at eight, and she ran up to her flat and showered and dressed while Hugo let the dogs out.

He was in the shower when she came down, so she made coffee and put some toast in, then sat on the sofa, Lola's head on her lap and Rufus curled up under her arm, wondering what would happen next.

He hadn't outlined the rules beyond the 'don't do long-term' etc., but was she expected to move in with him? Sleep in her own bed unless and until either of them wanted to be together? 'The Rules', as she was starting to think of them, needed a little clarification. And maybe some of her own.

He appeared a few moments later, while her list was still a work in progress.

'Well, you all look comfy,' he said, and perched on the arm of the sofa, the only place left for him. 'I can smell coffee.'

'You can. And toast. It's only just done. Come on, dogs, shift, it's time for breakfast.'

The dogs leapt off the sofa, and Hugo stood and pulled her up into his arms. His hug was brief, and then he let her go and led the way into the kitchen, the dogs trotting at his heels.

After breakfast they walked the dogs along the beach, and as they headed back she broke the comfortable silence.

'What are your plans for the rest of the day?' she asked him, because it was that or wait for him to tell her.

'I don't really have any. I mean, there's always admin to do.'

'Well, while you're doing that, you can do a bill for Lola's treatment,' she told him, and raised an eyebrow when he opened his mouth.

He ignored the gesture. 'Don't you think we're rather past that?'

'Or I can do it myself.'

'So what are your plans?'

'First I need to go over to my house to make sure it's ready for my first booking. They're coming this afternoon.'

'Can I come?'

'Sure. You can give me your first impression of it.'

They let the dogs in, rubbed them down with towels to get the sand off their feet, and then headed over to her house on foot.

'It looks really good,' he told her as they walked round, and she smiled in relief.

'I did my best. I just hope they don't trash it.'

'Who is it, do you know?'

'A couple with a baby, and their parents, his or hers, I don't know.'

He chuckled. 'They don't sound like they'll trash it.'

'No, they don't. It was a good idea of yours.'

So long as nothing happened between them to upset the status quo. Not that she was entirely sure yet quite what that was…

They went back to the practice, and while Hugo busied himself in the office, she went food shopping.

She had to drop a welcome pack in for her tenants, so she picked up those things and some stuff for the barbecue. His idea, and of course because it was a glorious early May day, everyone else had the same idea and the shelves were a bit depleted.

She threw a selection of things into the basket, then detoured up the last aisle and dropped a packet of condoms in on the rest. Just in case…

By the time she'd been to the house and got back it was getting hotter, and she carried the food upstairs and then hesitated. His fridge or hers? Or both?

They definitely needed to lay down more rules…

Hugo heard her come in, and followed her upstairs.

'What did you get?'

'All sorts of stuff. I just don't know where to put it,' she told him, turning to meet his eyes. 'Are we living together? Cooking together? Sleeping together? Or living independently and meeting up for sex when the mood takes us? Are we lovers? Friends with benefits? What the hell are we, Hugo?'

He blinked at that. 'Wow. Um—are you OK, Ellie? Because that sounds…'

'Confused? Uncertain? I mean, you have all these *rules*, but they're so vague—'

'OK, so we have sex on Sunday evening, Tuesday lunchtime, Wednesday morning—oh, and we might cram a quickie in between consults—'

'Don't be sarcastic.'

He scrubbed a hand through his hair and sighed. 'I'm not being sarcastic, Ellie, and frankly, I don't know the answers either.' His voice gentled. 'And I don't know what we call this. I hate friends with benefits, it's—it's not what it is. It feels—I don't know, more than that. And I certainly don't want to call all the shots, that's not what this is about. Maybe we just need to be honest with each other, like say, *I want to spend the night alone*, or *Let's eat in mine tonight*, or…' he shrugged '…*I want you now.*'

She stared at him, her eyes searching. 'Do you?'

He felt his body react instantly, and he couldn't stop the little huff of laughter. He closed his eyes briefly. 'Of course I do. I always have done. Right from day one. But only if you do.'

She was still staring at him, something primal stirring in her eyes. Her lips parted, then shut, pursing a little. He could almost hear her mind work.

'Um—maybe we should put the food away first?' she suggested after a sizzling pause, and he laughed and pulled her into his arms, folding her against his chest in a gentle hug.

'We probably should.'

Over the next few days, things sorted themselves out, because it turned out neither of them wanted to sleep alone, and it was easier with the dogs if they were in his flat rather than up the extra flight to hers.

And because they were there all the time, they cooked and ate in his kitchen, and hung out in his sitting room playing backgammon or watching TV or just talking about this and that.

Work was busier than usual, because people were going on holiday and so there were the usual panicked vaccinations that had been overlooked or forms to fill in for going abroad, and of course Kerry and James were on their honeymoon so they were a nurse down for that first week.

Then Kerry sent a group message, full of her honeymoon photos, both of them looking blissfully happy with life. And Ellie felt a pang of sadness that this wasn't ever going to be the case with her and Hugo.

Not in his rules. And yes, she understood where he was coming from, and in a way she was glad she knew where she stood with him, but underneath it all was an aching sadness that it couldn't be more, because she loved him.

She'd loved him since the day she'd met him, the day he saved Lola's life, and with every day she loved him more.

And he didn't do love.

So she kept smiling, got on with her work, and then on Thursday, just as she was about to take her lunch break, a client she'd seen before came in on the verge of tears. Ellie was in Reception at the time, and she ushered her into a consult room and closed the door.

'What's wrong?' she asked gently, because the dog looked absolutely fine, and her owner shook her head.

'My husband's—we've split up, and he doesn't want Bailey and I work full-time and I don't know where I'm going to live because I can't find a place I can afford where they allow dogs, and I can't leave him alone all day, and I can't work from home—'

'Do you want us to find a new home for him? Is that it?'

She nodded, fumbling in her pockets, and Ellie handed her a tissue. 'Thanks.'

She blew her nose and blinked away tears and met Ellie's eyes. 'It's just—he's such a lovely, gentle, kind dog, and I can't bear to think of him going to someone awful who doesn't understand dogs...'

'Let me talk to Hugo—in fact, hang on, if you can, and I'll see if he's free now?'

She went out the back into the corridor and heard his voice. He was in the office talking to Jean, and he looked up at her and broke off.

'Hi, what's up?'

'Client wants—no, she *needs* to rehome a dog. He's a Golden Retriever, three years old, absolutely lovely dog, they've split up and she can't find accommodation that'll allow her to keep him, she works full-time. I was thinking, Jenny?'

Jenny, who'd lost Nell in Ellie's first week, and was alone now.

'Who is he?'

'Mrs Williams' Bailey.'

'*Bailey?* I know Bailey, he'd be perfect for Jenny. Oh, she must be heartbroken. Is she still here with him?'

'Yes, she's in the consult room.'

'Jean, I'll be back. Ellie, let's go and talk to her.'

Bailey recognised him instantly and greeted him, tail wagging, smiling in the way that only a Golden Retriever could smile. He crouched down and gave him a fuss, then straightened up.

'I'm so sorry to hear about your circumstances, Mrs Williams. Are you OK to keep him a day or so while we make some enquiries? We have someone in mind, a lady who lost her dog recently who could be just right for him. She has grandchildren, and they visit her often and are used to dogs. They've had five over the years and she certainly knows what she's doing with them. I could call her? Would you mind?'

'Oh, could you? He loves children. I've got a baby nephew and he adores him, he's so gentle, and we thought…'

The tears started again, and it wasn't hard to work out why. A family dog, for a family that was never going to happen.

'I tell you what, why don't you stay here for a minute and let me go and make a call. OK?'

She nodded, and they left her there and went back to the office. Jean, reading his mind as ever, thrust a piece of paper at him.

'Jenny's number.'

'Thanks.' She picked up almost immediately, and after asking how she was, he said carefully, 'Look, I know it's still early days, but have you given any thought to getting another dog?'

'Oh, Hugo—I don't know. The house just feels so *wrong*

without a dog, but I can't cope with a puppy right now, and an older rescue dog might come with all sorts of issues.'

'How about a three-year-old Golden Retriever? Lovely boy, sweet, friendly, gentle dog, loves everybody, good with children, fit and healthy, and needs a new home through no fault of his own. Change of personal circumstances, but he's very much loved.'

'Oh, poor boy, he sounds… Oh, Hugo, I don't know. Is he with you?'

'He is at the moment.'

There was a long pause, then she said, 'Can I come now?'

'Sure. Come to the back door, you can meet him in the office.'

They sent Mrs Williams back to the waiting room and took Bailey through to the office, put Lola and Rufus in the kennels out of the way, and after a very few minutes Jenny arrived.

Hugo met her at the back door and ushered her in, and she took one look at Bailey and fell in love.

'Oh, the dear, dear boy…'

'Here, have a seat.' He turned a chair round and she sat on it and held out a hand, and the dog came over and licked it and sat beside her and leant against her leg, his head tilted up, staring at her as if she was his best friend.

'Oh, he's such a sweetheart… He reminds me of Rupert.'

'I'm sure he can be naughty.'

Jenny laughed and looked up at him, smiling the first real smile he'd seen on her in months. 'Hugo, all dogs can be naughty. It's part of their charm. Nell was still naughty. Oh, the poor, sweet boy. Can I ask why?'

'Divorce, and she works full-time.'

'Oh, no, that wouldn't work, Goldens need all the love all the time. Oh, Bailey. Are you a good boy? Are you?'

Bailey wagged his tail, tongue lolling, a silly smile on his face, and that was it. 'I'll take him.'

'Are you sure? You don't have to make a decision now. Do you want to think about it?'

She looked up and met his eyes. 'Hugo, I've thought about nothing else since Nell, and she would have loved him. I don't need to think any more. I want to take him home as soon as I can.'

'Let me fetch his owner. I'm sure she'd love to meet you.'

Half an hour later a tearful Mrs Williams said goodbye to Bailey and left him with his new owner. He whined for a moment, but a bit of a cuddle and a gravy bone treat brought him back to Jenny.

'She's left a bag of his toys and blankets in Reception, and also his bed, so you can take them home with you. I'll give you a hand out to the car.'

He saw her off, then went back inside and found Ellie up to her eyes with consults, and he took some of them off her.

Jo, their Thursday vet, was busy doing the first of two dentals, and Ellie was in dire need of a break. So was he, but hey, he was the boss.

'Are you sure you've got time? I thought you were busy with Jenny.'

'No, she's gone home with Bailey. Go and eat something, and after we've finished tonight we'll take the dogs for a walk by the river and go to the pub.'

It was a lovely walk, the dogs enjoying the change of scenery as much as she was, and she breathed in deeply and sighed.

'There's something so evocative about the smell of river mud at low tide,' she murmured, and Hugo chuckled.

'Only when it's in the river. When it's on the dogs it's less great.'

She laughed, picturing the two of them if they'd been off the lead. They couldn't be, of course, because of the ground-nesting wetland birds, but they were still having fun.

'So how did it go with Jenny?'

'Oh, she's in love. I think they'll be fine. She knows what she's doing.'

Ellie didn't reply. She was busy thinking about the comparison between them, Jenny in love with Bailey, who wouldn't have any rules or restrictions on the breadth and depth of her love for him, and her, falling deeper and deeper in love with an enigmatic loner with a broken heart and a rule book that lay between them like a minefield.

What on earth was she doing with him? Unlike Jenny with Bailey, she didn't have a clue. She just knew it was bound to end in tears...

CHAPTER NINE

Friday was as hectic as ever, and as soon as all her consults were done, she headed over to her house.

Her tenants had left this morning, and a new family were coming in tomorrow. She opened the front door with a feeling of trepidation, but the house was immaculate, and there was a note on the worktop thanking her for a lovely break and saying they'd like to book again later in the summer.

They'd be more than welcome. The bathroom and kitchen had both been cleaned, the beds stripped and the carpeted floors vacuumed, so there wasn't much for her to do. She put on the fresh bedding, ran a duster round the house, emptied the dishwasher and then headed back to Hugo.

She found him in his kitchen, busy stirring something on the hob, and she wrapped her arms round him and peered down into the pan. Chilli? 'That smells delicious.'

'Hopefully. So how was the house?'

'Brilliant. I couldn't believe it. They'd cleaned everything.'

'Wow. That's good. So when do your next tenants come?'

'Tomorrow afternoon, and they're here till Wednesday. I'll need to pop over first thing tomorrow with a welcome pack before we start. Then I've got another family from next Saturday for two weeks. Have the dogs been out?'

'Yes. Not far, but they've been out in the garden quite a bit today. They get on really well. Oh, and I heard from Jenny.

Bailey cried a bit in the night, but then he settled and she's really happy. She brought us some chocolates as a thank you.'

She rolled her eyes. 'More chocolates? We'll all be obese and diabetic.'

He threw her a wry grin. 'Don't worry about that, some days it's all that keeps us going. I have to say I'm glad Kerry's back on Monday, we've been picking up all sorts of things she usually does, so we might get time to eat actual food.'

It was a vain hope.

They were every bit as busy, and the week flew by. She went over late on Wednesday to get her house ready for the new people coming on Saturday, and then on Friday afternoon, as it was all winding down at the end of the day, Lucy walked in via the back door with her baby in her arms, and everyone who could downed tools and congregated in the office for a look at the new arrival.

Ellie was still busy while they were all cooing over baby Freya, but when she emerged after her last consult ended, she went in there for a peek.

'Oh, she's gorgeous,' she said softly, just as Hugo walked in, and Lucy laughed.

'She'd be more gorgeous if she slept through the night. Hey, Hugo, do me a favour and hold her while I nip to the loo?'

And without waiting for an answer, she dumped Freya into his arms.

For a fleeting second he looked paralysed, then Freya cried and instinct kicked in and he shifted her gently into a better position, smiling at her and murmuring reassuring nothings to soothe her, and Ellie stared at him, gazing down at Freya with such tenderness that she wanted to cry.

And then he looked up and met her eyes.

For a moment he froze, his face filled with longing, a deep yearning he'd never let her see before, and then his eyes went blank as the shutters came down. He turned away and walked out, still talking to Freya, but away from Ellie, away from the others.

Lucy appeared, and he handed Freya back instantly.

'Has she been OK?'

'Fine. Sorry, got to go. Congratulations, she's beautiful.'

He dropped a kiss on her cheek and walked away, heading for the door to his flat with Rufus at his heels, leaving Ellie standing there staring at the space where he'd been. She'd thought he was OK until he'd looked up, and then she'd seen the longing in his eyes—for Samuel, or for a child he'd never let himself have?

Oh, Hugo. Had that shown in her own eyes? The ache in her heart for him, and for a child of his that she'd never be able to hold?

Or the ache in his own heart, reflected back at him...

She needed to go to him.

He turned the latch on his door, went upstairs and locked the door to the back stairs, then walked into the sitting room and dropped onto the sofa.

He could still smell the baby—that evocative, unforgettable mixture of milk and nappy cream.

How? How can I remember that?

How could he forget?

He closed his eyes to shut out the images, but it didn't work. Of course it didn't work.

And nor did this thing he had going with Ellie. He'd been OK until she'd rocked up in his life and invaded the safe little cocoon he'd built around himself. He'd let her in because he couldn't help himself, but he couldn't do it any more, couldn't let her stay there, knocking down the protective walls around his heart brick by brick with every kiss, every touch, because he knew what would come next.

He'd seen the need in her eyes, the longing he could never dare to fulfil. It was a longing that was all too familiar to him, but Samuel was gone and he'd never get him back—

He heard her on the back stairs, the rattle of the door handle, the knock.

'Hugo? Hugo, let me in.'

Rufus ran to the door and scratched at it, whining, and he closed his eyes.

'Hugo, please, don't do this. We need to talk.'

She was right, they did.

And he knew exactly what he had to say...

Ellie rested her head against the door, her heart pounding, dread running through her veins.

Why wouldn't he talk to her? Why—

She heard the key turn, and the door opened.

Oh, Hugo...

He looked awful, jaw clenched, eyes blank and yet not. He turned away and she followed him into the sitting room. He walked straight past the sofa where they sat each night, over to the window, staring through it as if he was looking for something.

Words?

'Hugo, please talk to me.'

He turned, hands still rammed in his pockets, his back to the light, and she sat down on the arm of the sofa as if her strings were cut.

He was going to end it. She couldn't read the expression on his face but she didn't need to, she could see it in every defensive line of his body.

'We can't do this any more. You're getting in too deep, and I can't let you do that. I don't want it, and if you had any sense, nor would you. You deserve better. You deserve someone who can give you what you need, give you a family, a stable home life, the love you deserve, and that's never going to be me.'

No...

'Why don't you let me be the judge of what I need?'

'Because your judgement's clouded. Yes, the sex is great, but that's all it is, all it could ever be.'

'You're wrong, Hugo. I don't care about the sex, it's neither here nor there. It's way more than that—'

'Only for you. And I don't want it any more.' He closed his eyes and she saw him swallow. 'I can't love you, Ellie. And you need a man who will. A man who *can*.'

She stood up, legs shaking like jelly, and took a step towards him, but he held up his hand to ward her off.

'Don't—'

Don't what? Don't go and put your arms around him and tell him you love him? Don't tell him he's all you'll ever need, that you don't care about having a family, so long as you have him?

His face blurred, but for a few more seconds she stood her ground, and then she sucked in a breath and drew herself up. She wasn't going to grovel.

'Goodbye, Hugo,' she said softly.

And then she turned and walked out of his flat, her heart in shreds. Lola was torn between the two of them, and she called her, closing the door behind them and heading up the stairs on trembling legs.

Seven weeks. Seven weeks today since she'd hit the road and driven here, into his life. How was it only that?

She reached her flat and closed the door, somehow holding it together, her heart numb. She knew it wouldn't stay that way, but for now, she had to escape from here and get as far away from him as she could before the tears came.

She packed her things—not all of them, she didn't have enough bags or enough energy. Just the things she and Lola would need.

She carried it all downstairs, put it into her car, came back for Lola's bed, her food, her toys, and then put Lola in the car and drove away.

Hugo stood at the window and watched her go, his eyes dry, his heart thudding against his ribcage.

He'd done the right thing, for her, for him.

The only thing.

He just hadn't expected it to hurt quite so much.

His chest heaved and he fought down the sob, but it tore its way out of his chest anyway. He walked into his bedroom and lay on the bed, but it smelt of her, the lingering trace of her scent wrapping around him, engulfing him in pain.

Rufus whined and licked his face, and he realised tears were leaking out of the corners of his eyes and dribbling down onto the pillow. He let them fall. He owed her that, at least...

She didn't know where to go.

Her house? Too close, and anyway she had holidaymakers arriving tomorrow.

Oh, no. Welcome pack.

She pulled over into the forecourt of a mini-supermarket, left Lola in the car and grabbed a few things—milk, tea-bags, bread, butter, eggs, cheese, biscuits, jam—just some-thing to tide them over after a journey—and dropped them off at the house.

Seven weeks ago today, almost to the hour, she'd let Lola out into the garden and she'd been injured. Seven short weeks that had been the best and worst weeks of her life.

And now here she was again, back to square one, only now with an intact dog and a broken heart.

Where could she go?

Nowhere, at this time of night, but she couldn't stay here in Yoxburgh. Too close, too many memories of Hugo.

So she locked the house, left the key in the key safe she'd had installed and drove away.

Instinct and adrenaline got her down the A12 and round the M25, and then a near-miss as she went up the slip road and onto the M40 brought her to her senses. She drove to the motel she'd stayed at before, checked into a dog-friendly room and fed Lola, then lay on the bed, dry-eyed, cast adrift once more on the sea of life without a rudder or a compass to guide her, the future a yawning void...

Where could she go? What should she do?

Somehow she slept, Lola on the bed beside her, and when she woke it was just gone five. Too early for breakfast, not that she was hungry, but she fed Lola, picked up her bag, clipped her on her lead and left the room, dropping her key in the slot on her way out.

She drove on autopilot, and shortly after six she turned onto Jim's drive and cut the engine. The light was on in his kitchen. Of course it was, because her old boss and mentor had always been an early riser and the kettle would be on. His face appeared in the window, then the front door opened and he stood there, a familiar silhouette in a world that seemed suddenly alien.

She got out of the car and walked towards him, and he took one look at her and held out his arms. She fell into them, felt the warmth and strength of them close around her, holding her safe, and felt herself starting to fall apart.

'Oh, dear, dear girl. Come inside and have a cup of tea.'

'Lola,' she said, and he let the dog out of the car and brought her inside, ushering Ellie into the kitchen.

'This one looks as if she could do with a run in the garden, and you look as if you could do with a nice cup of tea,' he said, and while he opened the back door and took Lola outside, she sat down at his kitchen table where she'd sat so many times before, and finally, finally, the tears fell.

He didn't say a word when he came back in with Lola, just put a mug down on the table in front of her and handed her a wad of tissues.

'I'm sorry,' she managed, sniffing and scrubbing at her eyes, but he squeezed her hand briefly.

'No need to apologise. You're safe here, and you don't have to tell me anything.'

Just as well, because right then she was beyond making any sense. She cradled the mug, warming her ice-cold hands on it, but she didn't drink.

'I should have rung—'

'Nonsense. My door's always open to you, Ellie. You know that. I wish you'd come to me before.'

So did she, now, looking back, but then she'd never have met Hugo, never known just how beautiful love could be.

Or how painful.

The tears welled again, and she swiped at them, her hands shaking.

'When did you last eat anything?'

She stared blankly at him. 'Eat...? I—I don't remember, Jim. Maybe lunch yesterday? I'm not sure, maybe a chocolate? I had a biscuit in the motel last night, but—no, not really.'

She wasn't even making sense, but Jim just tutted softly and got up and put some bread in the toaster, took eggs out of a bowl and a pan from the rack and cracked the eggs into it, added milk, a knob of butter, a twist of salt and pepper, beat them together and set them on the hob while he buttered the toast.

Moments later he put their two plates down on the table and sat down.

'Come on, eat up,' he told her, pushing the plate of scrambled eggs towards her, and she suddenly realised how hungry she was.

She ate, and then when she'd finished every last morsel, Jim cleared the plates away, sat down again and met her eyes.

'Is this about Hugo?'

The kindness and sympathy in his eyes were too much for her, so she looked down at her hands, finding a crumb on the table and pushing it around with her fingertip until she couldn't see it any longer.

'I should have known better,' she said unevenly. 'God knows he warned me, Jim. He told me it wasn't going anywhere, and he gave me a whole list of rules, things he didn't do, like permanent or long-term or love, said he didn't make promises he couldn't keep—and I somehow managed to forget all about that and fall in love with him anyway—'

Jim's firm, kindly hand closed over hers and gave it a gentle squeeze.

'I'm so sorry. I thought you'd be all right with Hugo, I thought he'd take care of you.'

'Oh, he did. He was so kind, so decent, so—and he still is, Jim. That's the awful thing. It's not about us, it's about—'

She sucked in a shaky breath. 'He had a baby. Ten years ago, and he was born with a chromosomal disorder that was incompatible with life, and he died when he was eight weeks old. And it broke him, Jim. It broke him more than I'd realised. I suppose I thought at first I could stick to his stupid rules, but then I couldn't, I went and fell in love with him, and still I thought we'd be OK, and then… I'm—no, I *was* covering someone's maternity leave, and she brought her baby in, and she's about the same age as his baby was, I guess, and she gave her to him to hold, and the way he looked at her, the tenderness, the longing—I just wanted to cry for him, and then he saw my face, and…'

'And?'

'I went after him, asked him to talk to me, and he told me it was over, he didn't love me, he told me I needed to go and find a nice man and have babies with him, but I don't want to have babies with a nice man, I want to have babies with Hugo, and if I can't have babies, well, tough, but I want him, I love him, and he won't even give us a chance—'

The tears erupted again, and she felt Jim's hand on her shoulder giving it a gentle squeeze.

'Oh, dear, oh, dear. I'm so sorry, Ellie. Love can be a hard thing to bear at times.'

And then she felt a wave of guilt because Marion, his wife

of more than forty years, was in a care home and didn't know who he was any more.

She scrubbed away the tears and looked at him. 'How's Marion?'

'Oh, you know. Some days are better than others. But it is what it is, and we put one foot in front of the other and keep on going. That's what it's all about, isn't it?'

Was that what Hugo had been doing for the last ten years, putting one foot in front of the other? And then she'd come along and upset the fragile equilibrium of his life, and it had all come tumbling down on top of them.

'I'm so sorry. I shouldn't be here, you've got enough to deal with.'

He laid a hand on Lola's head, and Ellie realised she'd left her side and was leaning against his leg as if to comfort him. She looked around, puzzled, but there was no sign...

'Jim, where's Milo?' she asked softly, knowing the answer but not ready to believe it.

'He died—a month ago. His heart. I found him in the morning, curled up in his bed asleep. And the house doesn't feel the same without him or Marion.'

Like Jenny, when she'd lost her beloved Nell so soon after George. And now there was Bailey...

'Do you think you'll get another dog?'

He gave a soft, humourless little laugh. 'I'm not sure I've got the stamina for it, or the time. I spend most days with Marion—not that she realises, half the time. But I do, and I'm there because she's still my wife and I still love her.'

Of course he did—and she still loved Hugo. The difference was Hugo knew exactly who she was and he didn't want her there, didn't want her love...

'He may come round, you know.'

She could have laughed at that. 'Hugo? No. He's too—oh, gosh. Principled? Decent? He really seems to believe that being a mother is what I'm on the earth for, and it's not, or not the only thing. I'm thirty-two, Jim, and this is the first time I've ever met anyone I loved enough to even consider having a child with. And now it's not even for me, it's for Hugo.'

'Having another baby won't bring his dead baby back, Ellie. Was it planned, do you know?'

She shook her head. 'No. They were off and on, as he put it, and it was just a tragic accident. And it's broken him, Jim. He said he'll never have another child, and he'd be such a good father.'

'Maybe he doesn't want to be? Not everyone's cut out for it.'

'You've got four and I don't remember you complaining,' she reminded him, and he gave a rueful chuckle.

'No, and we've three grandchildren, now, and I wouldn't change it for the world, but if it hadn't happened for us, we would still have been happy together.'

'Maybe I should give you his number so you can tell him that.'

'It's not me that has to tell him that, Ellie. It's you. But not yet. Let the dust settle. Stay here, you and Lola, for as long as you need, and then when you're ready, go and talk to him.'

'He won't talk. He's got a stubborn streak a mile wide.'

'He's not alone in that. Don't give up on him yet, Ellie. Give him time. He'll be missing you, too.'

How could he miss her so much?

He hadn't slept all night—changing the sheets had got rid of her scent, but it didn't do anything for the memories of her lying there with him. So he'd got up and gone down to the office and changed the rota, emailed Jo and asked her to do Saturday morning, juggled things around later in the week so he or Jo were picking up the times Ellie would have been in surgery, then he took Rufus out for a run at stupid o'clock, ran for an hour and came back and showered, sent Jo a text to be sure she'd got his message, and then went downstairs to get on with the day.

Thank goodness it was only Saturday and he didn't have a full day of electives to fit in, but that didn't really help his mood. He was terse with everyone, and Kerry took him on one side after a short while and told him to get a grip or they'd all be leaving.

'It's not their fault you and Ellie have had a row—'

'We haven't had a row. She had to go away.'

'Had to? Is that why you're like a bear with a sore head? I wasn't born yesterday. You've obviously split up—'

'We weren't together—'

'Oh, come on, Hugo, tell it to the fairies! It's been blindingly obvious since the wedding. Everybody knows.'

'Nothing happened at the wedding.'

'Oh, don't give me that. The way you two were dancing? There was only one place you were going when you left— and don't bother to deny it. So why's she gone? What did you say to her?'

'It's none of your business, Kerry.'

'It's my business when you upset my nurses.'

He scraped a hand through his hair and gave a sharp sigh. 'I told her to go. She's left.'

'*Left?* You mean she's not coming back?'

'No. She's not coming back.'

Kerry stared at him for an age, then light dawned in her

eyes and her voice softened. 'Oh, Hugo… This is because of Lucy's baby, isn't it?'

He swallowed hard. 'Don't go there, Kerry, please.'

'Oh, Hugo…'

She hugged him hard, then told him to go. 'You don't need to be here. We can manage, Jo's in, she can do the consults. I'll shut up shop. Go and see Peter and Sally. Talk to them.'

'I can't just leave you all—'

'You can. Seriously, we can cope and you're no use to us anyway like this. Go.'

So he went, taking Rufus with him and leaving the practice in Kerry's very capable hands. Not that he had the slightest clue what to say to his godparents when he turned up on the doorstep at ten on a Saturday morning, but it turned out he didn't have to.

'Come in, Hugo,' Peter said, and he walked in and found Sally in the kitchen.

'Oh, you're here, darling. Sit down, coffee'll be ready in a minute. Would you like something to eat?'

'No, I'm—I'm fine.'

'Are you? Because you don't look it.' She pointed to a chair. 'Sit down, you're cluttering the place up. I'll make some toast.'

The light dawned. 'Kerry rang you, didn't she?'

'She might have done.'

'Interfering—'

'She's got your best interests at heart, Hugo,' Peter said quietly. 'We all have. And we're here if you need to talk.'

'I don't want to talk,' he said tightly. 'There's nothing to say. She's gone. End of.'

'Because of the baby?' Sally, this time, not knowing when to leave well alone. What was it with the women in his life?

'You, too? It's nothing to do with Lucy's baby—'

'I wasn't talking about Lucy's baby, Hugo,' she said softly. 'I was talking about Samuel.'

He felt himself flinch and looked away.

'So what happened with Ellie?'

She wasn't going to give up, but then nor was he.

She plonked a plate of hot buttered toast in the middle of the table, poured the coffee and sat down, waiting.

He picked up a slice of toast and bit into it, but he could hardly swallow past the tightness of his throat. He gave up and put it down again.

'Lucy came in with Freya, and I thought I ought to show my face, and she just handed her to me and went to the loo. And then Freya cried, and I—just knew what to do. It all came back, and the smell—it was so familiar, so—'

'So what happened then?'

'Ellie was looking at me, and her face—' He broke off and looked down, poking at the slice of toast for something to do, crumbling it into little bits between his fingers. 'She doesn't need me. She needs someone to give her children. She'd be a brilliant mother. She *needs* to be a mother.'

'And you need to be a father.'

'No. I've *been* a father. I *am* a father. Never again.'

'Why? Why, when you were so good with Samuel?'

'*Because* of him. I don't want—don't want to overlay my memories. I don't want to forget—'

His voice cracked, and he felt Sally's hand on his shoulder.

'You'll never forget him,' she said gently. 'He'll live in you for ever, Hugo. That's what happens, but it doesn't mean you can't try again—and even if you don't, even if you never have children, you'd have each other.'

She took Peter's hand and squeezed it, and he covered her hand with his.

'We were never blessed with children,' he said quietly, 'it just never happened for us, but there's no way we'd rather not have been together. We've had a wonderful life, we've been together for forty-five years, and we're still in love. And if we'd known at the start that one of us couldn't have a child, there's no way it would have made the slightest difference to how much we love each other and want to be together.'

'You weren't really childless, though, were you? You were lumbered with me—'

'We were never *lumbered* with you,' Sally said firmly. 'We were more than happy to have you, and you've brought so much richness into our lives, but even without you, we would still have felt the same. It isn't children that make a marriage, Hugo, it's love, first and foremost.'

'But—what if she really wanted a baby? What if she got pregnant? I can't—I'm not brave enough.'

'They said it was a one-off,' Peter reminded him.

'But it could be something else next time. I can't lose anyone else—'

'You've lost Ellie. Doesn't that matter?'

He sucked in a breath. 'Of course it matters! But a child—it would just open the wound…'

'Which will never heal unless you let it, Hugo,' Sally said softly, taking his hands in hers. 'You need to let yourself grieve.'

He snatched his hands back.

'Don't tell me about grief, Sally. I know enough about grief. I could write a book about it.'

'You've never grieved for Samuel. You just threw yourself back into work and carried on, business as usual—except it wasn't, was it? That's why you've worked so hard, spent all your time keeping busy, and you've never really let yourself love anyone since your parents died.'

'That's not true, I love you.'

'You already loved us, just as we loved you.'

They had. 'I was horrible to you.'

'You'd just lost your parents! That's huge. And we understood, of course we did, but you've never had a serious relationship, and ever since Samuel you've sabotaged anything that might lead to love. And now it's even worse, because you've found someone to love and you've sent her away. You're just hiding from your grief, Hugo, and you've been doing it ever since he died.'

Had he?

He pushed back his chair. 'I don't need to listen to this—'

'Maybe not, but maybe it's time to listen to your heart.'

CHAPTER TEN

HE DROVE AWAY, no fixed idea of where he was going, just anywhere away from the people who loved him and thought it was their business to sort him out.

If only it were that easy.

He couldn't go back to the practice while they were all there, so he drove down to the harbour, parked the car and took Rufus for a walk. Not that he needed one, not after their run that he'd thought was a good idea well before dawn. He had no idea what time he'd left or how long they'd run for, but he'd been back at five thirty and he'd felt wiped.

Still did, but he couldn't rest, couldn't settle to anything, so he walked, until Rufus finally sat down and refused to move. He sat beside him on the edge of the path, legs resting on the bank down to the river, the smell of the estuary reminding him of Ellie.

He'd walked here with her and Lola, the day Jenny had taken Bailey home because she missed Nell and she missed George.

He sighed, and laid a hand on Rufus.

'I miss her, Rufe,' he said softly. 'I had to let her go, but I miss her.' Just another ache, another loss to carry with him.

He blinked to clear his vision and got to his feet, picking up the exhausted Rufus and carrying him back to the car.

Listen to your heart.

That was what Sally had said to him, but he had no idea what it was trying to say. All he could hear was all the reasons why he'd done the right thing letting her go.

Had he?

Although actually he hadn't *let* her go, he'd sent her away. And he'd lied to her, but he'd do it again if she came back.

He'd have to, for her sake, because she wanted something he could never give her.

He drove away from the harbour on autopilot, turned off and found himself somewhere he hadn't been for ten years, his heart apparently leading him where he needed to go. He drove slowly into the almost empty car park and stopped the engine.

'Come on, Rufus, let's go for a little walk. It's not far.'

He clipped his lead on, and they left the car park and wandered along the pretty, tree-lined path. It led between gravestones, some ancient, others newer, and then it came to another area, set aside from the rest, with tiny headstones set among the bobbing heads of wildflowers coming into bloom.

His feet led him in the right direction, and he knelt down in front of the simple headstone and laid his hand gently on the grass.

Maybe it's time to listen to your heart.

He didn't have a choice. It was beating so hard it was deafening, but it brought him no answers.

Why?

But nothing answered his silent scream. Rufus leant against him, and he sat down cross-legged and pulled him onto his lap and held him against his flailing heart while he let the memories flood in.

Samuel, his poor body compromised, his brave little heart doing its best against impossible odds, but his eyes would look up as clear as day, follow you, watch you. He'd recognised people, would turn towards the voices of the people he knew, kick his legs in delight, and sometimes he'd reward them with a smile. He loved to be sung to, would listen intently to voices, react to their tone.

He remembered singing to him, an old-fashioned lullaby his mother had sung him as a child. He used to sing it to him every night, and Samuel had loved it. He'd sung it to him softly as he lay dying in his arms...

He hummed it now, rocking gently, his hand still lying on the grass, and as he sang his heart slowed and steadied. Yes, it still ached, and it always would, but coming here, singing that tender lullaby, had reminded him of the good things that he'd forgotten.

He stayed there an age, lost in his memories, until Rufus started to fidget. He had no idea how long he'd been there, but Rufus was telling him it was time to go, and he unfolded his legs and got stiffly to his knees, kissing his fingers and pressing them to the grass where his baby lay, surrounded by all the other little ones who'd gone too young.

'I'm sorry I've been such a rubbish father. I should have come before, but I'll come again soon, I promise. I love you.'

He slept that night, then spent the next day going through his photos, printing some out and framing them. He propped them on the bookcase in his study with the one of himself with his parents, and put one, his favourite, on his bedside table.

The memories still tore him apart, but in a good way, now, and he realised just how much of himself he'd shut away for the last ten years since Samuel died.

And on Monday morning, he apologised to all the staff.

'I've not been in a good place—that's nothing new, I've not been in a good place for a long time, but Saturday was—well, anyway, I'm sorry. Sorry I took it out on you when it was nothing to do with any of you, but it won't happen again.'

There were a few murmurs, and then one of the junior nurses said cautiously, 'Is Ellie coming back?'

He swallowed hard. 'I don't know. Probably not. But I'm going to start advertising in earnest for a new vet, and I'm going to try and get a locum in the meantime, and until then I guess we all need to work a bit harder, but I'll do my best to sort it.'

More murmuring, and then, realising he'd finished, they went back to their tasks.

'Well done.' Kerry patted his shoulder on the way past, and Jean met his eyes.

'Are you really all right?'

He smiled. 'As all right as I can be.'

'Peter rang. He said he could come and help out if we need him.'

Hugo swallowed hard. 'I think we'll be OK, Jean. I'll give him a call.'

He sent him a quick message, and then there in his messaging app was Ellie's photo. He was so tempted to message her, but he needed to get his head straight before he could do that.

She couldn't ignore it any longer.

She'd been with Jim for two weeks, and there'd been nothing from Hugo. Not that she'd expected to hear from him, but she'd hoped...

Would he talk to her now? Hear what she had to say? Because if these weeks away from him had proved one thing, it was that she couldn't live without him. And if that meant they never had a family, well, so be it. Lots of people were in that situation, some because it had never happened for them, others by choice.

And it could be their choice.

Jim was with Marion, so she wasn't able to talk to him, but she wrote him a note thanking him for all his kindness and understanding and promising to be in touch, and then she stripped her bed, packed up all their things and loaded them and Lola into the car.

Her tenants would have left this morning and she'd kept the next two weeks clear, so if all else failed she could live at her house while she worked out what to do with her life, but for now, at least, she wasn't giving up on Hugo.

He needed her every bit as much as she needed him, and she knew—she just *knew*—that he loved her. He'd lied to protect her, and for that she loved him even more, but she had to convince him that it wasn't necessary. She didn't need protecting, she needed him. Nothing else.

She was on the M25 when her phone tinged, but it was probably nothing, so she ignored it until she got to the South Mimms service area at the A1 junction. She found a space, dug her phone out of her bag and glanced at it.

Hugo?

She tapped to open it, her heart pounding.

Where are you?

She stared at it, the text blurring, her heart trying to escape from her chest. Why did he want to know?

She struggled to get her shaking fingers to work.

On M25. Why?

His reply was instant.

Need to talk to you.

To say what? She had no idea. She hesitated, then:

I'm on my way back.

Come on, Hugo...

Drive carefully. Call me when you get here.

She got Lola out of the car, her legs shaking, her whole body trembling, and led her to a patch of grass at the edge of the car park.

He wants to talk...

Her heart was pounding so hard she could hardly think, and she couldn't drive like this. She needed a drink and something to eat, so she put Lola back in the car, ran into the services, bought a bottle of water and a sandwich and ran back out. She shared the water with Lola, and sat in the car and took a bite of the sandwich and made herself swallow it, and the next one, and the next, until her heart had slowed a little.

Then she screwed the lid back on the water, put her seat belt on and headed back onto the M25.

Hugo sat on the sofa, staring at his phone.

She's coming back. Why?

Tenant change-over day, he realised. Of course.

His heart sank. For a moment there he'd thought…

No. He'd told her he didn't want her, didn't love her. Who in their right mind would want to talk to him again?

But maybe…

He went shopping. Just in case. He knew exactly what he was going to buy, and he had the recipe on his phone to remind him.

He found everything he needed, went home, did all the necessary prep and followed the recipe meticulously. And then, when it was done, he turned the heat off under the casserole dish, closed the kitchen door and went into the study, stood at the window and waited for her car to appear.

She turned into the practice, parked the car and sat there, her heart in her mouth.

Lola was standing up, tail thrashing, and she got out of the car and unclipped her harness. She shot out of the car, lead trailing, and ran straight up to Rufus, who was wagging furiously in delight.

And then she looked past them, and there was Hugo.

He looked drawn, thinner, his mouth unsmiling, and she walked towards him, her legs like jelly.

'You made good time,' he said.

It was the last thing she'd expected him to say, and her heart sank. Until she saw the muscle clenching in his jaw, and realised his heart was beating so hard she could see the pulse at his throat.

She walked up to him and then stopped, not knowing how to greet him or what to say. He saved her the trouble.

'Let's go up to my flat. I've cooked for us,' he said, and led the way.

She followed him, all her carefully rehearsed speeches forgotten. This was Hugo's gig, she'd let him do the talking.

For now.

He didn't know what to say, where to start. Except…

'I'm sorry.'

They were on the sofa in his sitting room, the room where two weeks ago he'd told her to leave. Told her he didn't love her. Told her to go and find a nice man and make babies with him.

Her eyes were fixed on his, searching.

'What for?'

'Lying to you. I said I didn't want you in my life any more, but it was a lie. I told myself I was trying to protect you, but I wasn't, I was trying to protect myself, and I wasn't ready to acknowledge the truth.'

'And now?'

'And now, I am. I've spent the last two weeks sorting my head out, dealing with a lot of stuff I should have dealt with years ago.' He took a breath. 'Losing Samuel was brutal. It broke my heart, and so I shut down and I didn't let myself feel any more. I didn't want to feel, didn't want to love. I just wanted to carry on being numb, because it was safe.

'What happened after the wedding really shouldn't have happened. I wasn't ready for what it made me feel, and I couldn't handle it. I hadn't dealt with Samuel's death—hell, I probably hadn't dealt with my parents' deaths, and I've never let myself love anyone. I've avoided it like the plague because I couldn't bear to expose myself to losing anyone else. And then you came along and blew all that out the water, and it scared the hell out of me.

'You'd broken through my defences, and you made me

want more in my life than I could bear, more than was safe. And so I lashed out, because I was afraid of unleashing all the feelings I'd denied for the last ten years.

'I didn't mean to love you, but I did, and I hadn't even realised. It hit me like a train, and I was scared. I was so scared. And I'm so sorry I hurt you.'

'So what now?' she asked, her face guarded, but she wasn't giving anything away and he had no idea where she was in her head. He could only hope.

'That's all down to you,' he said, and waited.

And then finally, she spoke.

'I thought I could cope with us being friends,' she said quietly, 'but I wanted more. I'd never found anyone I could trust with my heart, and then I met you, and you were so kind, so caring, so generous, and I thought I might be safe with you, that you wouldn't leave me like my father left my mother…' Her voice cracked and she swallowed, then went on, 'I thought you were different. And then you sent me away.'

His face creased with pain. 'Oh, Ellie… I only did it for you. I was too scared of the future, too scared we might lose a child, and I knew you wanted children. The way you looked at me when I was holding Freya—the longing. And I felt it, too, and I just couldn't deal with it.'

'So what's different now?' she asked, her heart pounding as she waited for his answer. She could see the sincerity in his eyes, but could she trust it?

'I am. I told Sally and Peter I was afraid of losing anyone else, and Sally pointed out I'd lost you anyway. And she was right. I had, and it left this yawning void…'

'So—what now, Hugo?'

'I want you back.'

'Really?' she asked, pushing him for the truth. 'For ever, or just for this week? Because right now you're sounding a lot like my father apparently did and I'm not sure I can dare to believe anything you tell me.'

His eyes prickled and he turned away. 'I guess I deserve that.'

'So why do you really need me back? Because you need a locum?'

He stared at her, shocked that she could even think that, but then what had he ever done that might make her think differently?

'Absolutely not. I have a locum. What I don't have is you, Ellie, and I love you, and I'm lost without you.'

His voice cracked, and she stared at him, searching his eyes, so readable now, if she only dared to trust what they were telling her.

'You really want me back?'

'Yes.'

'What, just to take up where we left off?'

'No—well, yes, but—no.'

'Hugo, you're not making any sense. Do you want me back, or do you not want me back?'

'Yes, I do want you back. Of course I want you back!'

'OK. And what about your rules?'

He looked puzzled. 'My rules?'

'"I don't do long term, I don't do—"'

He held up his hand. 'No rules—well, that's not quite true. There is one. We tell the truth. Always. And the truth is, I love you, and I want to be with you.'

Could it really be so easy?

No. It never was, and they'd only had nine weeks to get to this point, and they'd been apart for two of them.

'You honestly love me?'

'Yes, Ellie. I honestly love you. Honestly and truly and with all my heart, tattered though it is. And no, I'm not perfect, I know that, but I promise I'll do my best not to hurt you ever again.'

Her eyes were welling up, but she blinked hard and pulled herself together.

'And no rules? Because I don't want to get in any deeper and have you change your mind because you realise that actually you *don't* do long term after all.'

He smiled, a rueful flicker of his lips, a softening of his eyes. 'No rules. Only the truth.'

She swallowed, looked away, looked back at him.

'And this stuff you had to deal with…?'

His smile faded. 'Ah. When I went to see Peter and Sally, Sally pointed out I'd never let myself grieve for Samuel, never let myself move on. I'd cut myself off from any joy, any love—until I met you. And then I still wouldn't let it in. And then I lost you and everything seemed pointless— my work, my life—all of it. I went to Samuel's grave, and I talked to him, and then I came home and I cried. I'd never cried for him—'

'Oh, Hugo…'

She reached out to him, and then she was in his arms, and he was holding her close, his lips pressed against her cheek, and she tilted her head back and met his eyes. 'Are you OK now?' she asked, cradling his jaw in her hand, and he smiled.

It was a bit crooked, but it was there. 'I think so. It's still a work in progress, but I'm getting there.' He turned his head and kissed her hand, then stood up. 'I need to go and finish off in the kitchen.'

'Want any help?'

'No, you stay here and talk to the dogs. I won't be long.'

He warmed the food up, stirring it gently on the hob, blanched the green beans, drained the baby new potatoes and laid the table.

Nothing fancy, no candles, since it was four in the afternoon and candles might look a bit ridiculous. And he checked his back pocket, just in case.

Lord, he was nervous. What if—

'Are you sure I can't help?'

He turned and smiled, or tried to, but it was probably a pretty poor effort. 'No, you're fine, I'm done. Come and sit down.'

She sat, watching him curiously. 'Smells good,' she said, and he put the dishes down on the table and took the lid off the casserole dish.

She looked at it, then up at him, her heart starting to race.

'Is that...what I think it is?'

She saw his throat work as he swallowed. 'Yes, it is.'

He'd cooked her Marry Me Chicken?

She looked away, wondering if...then looked back up at him. Was she imagining it, or did he look nervous? She'd *never* seen Hugo look nervous. And now he was fumbling in his back pocket, pulling something out.

A—ring?

He knelt down beside her and met her eyes, and she bit her lips and tried not to cry.

'I love you, Eleanor Radcliffe,' he said, his voice low, soft and a little shaky. 'I know I'm a basket case, but I'm working on it, and I promise you that whatever happens, whatever goes wrong, whatever life throws at us, I will *always* love you. Will you marry me?'

'What about children?' she asked, not because she wanted them, but because she needed to hear his answer, whatever it was, before she gave him hers.

'What about them? If you want my children, then if it happens, I'm fine with it. More than fine. Yes, it might hurt, but it would also heal, and I'd love us to be a family. But there's no hurry, and I don't mind either way, so long as I've got you. But the thought of you with another man...' He hauled in a breath. 'I wouldn't try to stop you if it was what you wanted, but it would break my heart if I knew I'd driven you into someone else's arms.'

She cradled his cheek in her hand. 'I can't give you Samuel back, you do know that, don't you?' she said gently, unable even to imagine the depth of his pain, but he just smiled a sad little smile.

'Of course I do, and I wouldn't want that. He was incredibly special to me, but we always knew we would lose him. What I didn't know was how much it was possible to love someone so small, and how much it would hurt to lose them.'

'Oh, Hugo...'

'Don't be sad for me. I'm OK. And if you want to have a family, we can do that, but I don't want to put any pressure on you one way or the other. I just need to be with you. That's all I ask. Anything else would be a bonus.'

She leant in and kissed him, just a gentle touch, then sat back.

'I was coming back to tell you that I don't need to have a baby to make me happy. Yes, I'd always hoped that one day I'd meet a man, the sort of man who wouldn't leave me like my father left my mother, and that we'd get married and have a family, but nobody's ever made me feel even remotely like this before. I fell in love with you weeks ago, and then I found out you'd lost a baby, and my heart just broke for you.'

'Oh, Ellie…'

'I can't replace him for you, I know that, and I know you'll always feel a tinge of sadness around babies, but, children or no children, I want to be with you. I love you, Hugo. I know it's ridiculously quick, but I think I've loved you since you saved Lola's life and we sat and had that long talk and I realised what a truly decent and wonderful human being you are.'

He gave a choked laugh. 'Don't go too mad, I'm very far from perfect.'

She smiled at him, the love of her life. 'Aren't we all? I still love you. And yes, I'll marry you, of course I will. I'd be honoured.'

'I thought you'd never get round to saying that,' he said, and he started to laugh, then his eyes softened and he took her hand.

'I don't know if this will fit you. It—' He broke off and swallowed hard. 'It was my mother's engagement ring, and I know she'd be so happy for you to wear it. She would have loved you very much, and so would my father.'

'Even though I'm a vet?'

He smiled. 'Even though you're a vet.'

He slid the ring onto her finger, and it fitted as if it had been made for her. She looked down at it, a row of five simple but beautifully cut graduated diamonds, sparkling in the light. She touched it with shaking fingers, and bit her lip to try and stop the tears.

'It's beautiful,' she said. 'Thank you.'

He stood up and pulled her to her feet, and he wrapped her in his arms and held her as if he'd never let her go.

'Make love to me, Hugo,' she said, and the meaning wasn't lost on him.

'Nothing would make me happier.'

He put the lid back on the casserole dish with a smile. There'd be time to eat it later, but right now they had better things to do, and its job was done…

EPILOGUE

ANOTHER SCORCHING EARLY September day, just like it had been this time last year for their wedding day.

Hugo locked the gates and the front door, ran upstairs and showered, pulled on shorts and a T-shirt and went out into the garden.

A year ago, there'd been a marquee on the lawn for their wedding reception. They'd closed the practice at lunchtime on that Friday so all the staff could join them, and he and Ellie had had a quiet wedding with all the people that mattered to them.

Peter and Sally, of course, and Ellie's mother and her partner from Spain; Jim Harkness, all the practice staff, old friends—nobody had been left out. Ellie wore his mother's ring, he his father's dress watch, and in his breast pocket against his heart he had a picture of Samuel—they'd all been there in their thoughts and in their hearts.

And since then, there'd been a new arrival.

He could see them in the shade under the copper beech. Ellie had spread a rug on the grass, and they were all lying on it, Ellie on her side, head propped up on one hand, watching Lola and Rufus, who were, in turn, lying with their heads on their front paws and watching the newest member of the family.

She'd been born so fast he'd delivered her himself on the

bathroom floor, bright red and screaming with rage and utterly beautiful. It was a moment he'd been dreading, but it had been the best and most wonderful moment of his life.

The dogs lifted their heads and wagged their tails as he walked barefoot across the grass towards them, and he stopped and looked down at them all with a wry smile, his heart filled with love.

'You all look very relaxed,' he said, and knelt down beside Ellie and gave her a kiss. 'Everything OK?'

'Very OK, thank you. It's blissful.'

'How long's she been asleep?'

'I'm not sure. I fed her a little while ago but I'm sure she wouldn't say no to a cuddle.'

He smiled. 'I can't wake her, she needs her sleep and so do I. She was up most of the night.'

'Tell me about it.' She shuffled across and made room for him, and he lay down between them and drew her into his arms and kissed her.

'I love you, Mrs Alexander.'

'I love you, too. I'm glad it's the weekend, we've missed you.'

'I was never far away.' He kissed her again, his body stirring, but he ignored it. It wasn't the only thing stirring, and he snagged another kiss and propped himself up so he could look down at their baby. Charlotte, after his mother, but Lottie to them.

'Hello, my gorgeous girl,' he crooned softly, and she kicked her legs and smiled at him, just the way Samuel used to.

He swallowed the lump in his throat, scooped her up and cradled her in the crook of his arm. She was so precious, so easy to love, but it hadn't been easy. The first few weeks of the pregnancy he'd lived on a knife-edge, and only after the first scan had he dared to believe in her. And here she was, perfect in every way, three months old and the image of her mother, and he loved her more than he would ever have believed possible.

'Now, little Lottie, listen to your daddy,' he murmured, still smiling. 'You need to be a good girl tonight and sleep, because it's our wedding anniversary and we would like to celebrate it by sleeping all night…'

'*All* night?'

He dragged his eyes off the baby and looked at Ellie—his wife, his soulmate, his saviour. And he smiled.

'Well, maybe not *all* night…'

* * * * *

If you enjoyed this story, check out these other great reads from Caroline Anderson

Finding Their Forever Family
The Midwife's Miracle Twins
Healing Her Emergency Doc
Tempted by the Single Mum

All available now!

LAS VEGAS NIGHT WITH HER BEST FRIEND

TINA BECKETT

MILLS & BOON

To my family.

Thank you for being my rock!

PROLOGUE

EVA MILAGRE LOOKED at the first picture in the small stack and blinked. Tried to process what she was seeing. Her last name might mean *miracle* in Portuguese, but right now it didn't look like even a miracle could save her marriage.

"You investigated Brad?"

Her friend on the barstool next to her wrapped an arm around her shoulder. "I'm so sorry, Evie. After you told me his hours had been all wonky and that he'd been evasive about his last overnight trip, it sent up several red flags."

Her gaze didn't waver. The picture showed her husband hugging another woman. A raven-haired beauty that made Evie feel tired and rumpled in her scrubs with strands of hair escaping from her clip and falling wildly around her face. It could be something totally innocent. An embrace after closing a deal at his investment firm. But there was no way Darby would be showing her pictures of her husband hugging another woman if it wasn't something bad. Really bad.

Her thumb hesitated—Evie didn't want to see anything else. "And the rest of these?"

"They're worse. I hoped he'd prove me wrong. He didn't."

Her friend turned toward her, holding out her hand. "I didn't think you'd believe me without those. I know how much you love him."

The thing was, Evie was no longer sure that she did. The pictures just sealed the deal. She handed them back. "And his firm?"

Brad hadn't shown her the financial statements for his business this year, which she found odd as well. He'd always been so proud of what he'd accomplished, going out on his own almost three years ago. When she'd asked about them, he said he was late in filing them this year.

"He filed for bankruptcy a month ago and gave up the lease on his office space."

Bankruptcy? God. He'd been leaving home every single day at the same time, kissing her on the mouth and telling her he'd miss her before walking out the door of their home. She'd heard nothing about any kind of trouble. And she'd put a big chunk of her own money toward him opening that business and had trusted him to…

She'd trusted him. Too much. And it looked like she was going to pay the price for that. Swallowing hard, she bit back tears of anger and frustration. "Thank you. I just can't fathom how he would do something like this."

"I know. I can't believe it, either. We both went to college with the guy, and he was voted the most likely to succeed."

"It looks like he succeeded alright." Her laugh held more than a hint of desperation as her fingers tightened around the stack of photos. "Only not in the area I expected." All she could see in her mind's eye was the woman he was evidently having an affair with. Since they hadn't had sex in the last six months, the reason made far too much sense—he'd used the excuse of work overload and stress, and she hadn't challenged him on it. In fact, she'd been secretly relieved, since she could relate to both of those things. She'd been feeling stressed and tired herself recently, their talks of having a baby going up on a shelf until things settled down. Thank God they weren't still trying. What if she'd been pregnant?

"Do you want to stay with me for a few days?"

A sense of relief washed over her. At least she wouldn't have to face him. Tonight, anyway. "That would be wonderful." She held up her hand for another drink and after the bartender brought it over, she took a gulp of the spiked fruity drink. "I can't promise I'll be in any shape to drive after this." She put her glass back to her lips and drank again.

"Don't worry. I've got this."

"Thanks." She picked up her phone and pushed the button that would connect her with her soon-to-be ex. She wasn't surprised when it went straight to voice mail. She decided to just get it over with. "I won't be home tonight, but when I do come back to the apartment, I expect you to be packed up and gone."

The second she disconnected, her phone rang. It was Brad. She didn't answer. She was pretty sure he would figure out that the jig was up. But she hoped he did as she asked. Because tomorrow morning she was going to head to town, find a lawyer and file for divorce. It was something that probably would have happened, anyway, even without Darby's news. Neither one of them seemed happy with where they were anymore.

Her friend glanced at the phone she'd placed on the polished bar after silencing it. "Do you think he'll leave without a fight?"

Evie took another drink. "I don't know. I'm pretty sure he has someplace to go, unless she's married, too."

"She's not."

Another laugh came out. "You are nothing if not thorough, Darbs."

Her friend gave her a searching look. "I hope you know this is not how I wanted this to play out."

Now, that was the first thing her friend had said that she took issue with. "You and Max always had issues with Brad."

Ugh. Why had she even said Max's name in the same sentence as Brad's? She and Darby and Max had always been close friends. But something had changed between her and Max when she started dating Brad and they got married. He hadn't even come to her wedding, saying that he had a medical conference to go to. His absence had cut deep. And he'd made it pretty clear, even before the wedding, that he was no fan of her fiancé.

"We both cared enough about you to tell you there were some areas of concern."

Except Max really hadn't spelled out anything specific. He'd just seemed peeved whenever Brad was around. Soon, he'd practically dropped out of her life.

"And yet you never investigated him before now."

"I was a cop when you got married, remember? Running an illicit investigation is frowned on in those circles."

Why was Evie blaming her friend for something she'd

gotten herself into? "I'm sorry, Darbs. I had no right to say that."

Her friend's transition from being a police detective to a private investigator had been heartbreaking. A bullet to her leg would have left her friend chained to a desk, so she'd decided to resign and open up her own PI office, where literally chasing down suspects was no longer required. Instead, she chased them via a keyboard or, in Brad's case, through the lens of a camera.

"It's okay." Darby shifted in her seat, barely catching her cane before it fell from its perch. Her limp wasn't as noticeable as it had been years ago, but Evie knew it still hurt when she'd been on her feet too long. "I can investigate now, though. And so don't expect me not to run your next beau through the wringer."

"Next beau? Nope. I think it's one and done as far as that goes."

"Famous last words, Evie."

"Famous or not, they're true." And she meant it. She didn't see herself going down her current path with anyone else. How could she ever trust a man again? First Max backed out of her life, and now her husband. That didn't mean she'd be entering the nearest convent and taking a vow of chastity. It just meant she was no longer going to equate sleeping with someone with being in love with that someone. No matter whom it might be.

CHAPTER ONE

"DAMMIT." TODAY HADN'T started off well for Maximilian Hunt. He'd gotten numbers back on two of his patients and neither one of those reports had been good. He leaned back in his chair and pinched the bridge of his nose, trying to staunch the vague rumblings of a headache. He could appease the migraine gods by telling himself that neither of those patients were without options. Both had been newly diagnosed and were just starting treatment. But he always hoped for a misdiagnosis that went in the patient's favor, rather than the other way around.

He made a note to call both of them in for an appointment to discuss things. One of his least favorite tasks in his job.

A knock at the door made him push aside those thoughts. "Come in."

The door opened, and Evie peered past it. He could barely see her face.

He hadn't seen her in almost a month. And it's how he'd hoped to keep it. Ever since Darby had called him to tell him the news a year ago, that Evie's marriage was over and the reason for it, he'd had a hard time not chasing down Brad and letting him know how little he thought of him. The bastard had hurt someone he cared about very much.

But now, Evie was divorced, and she could move forward with her life. Darby had been on him to join them for dinner, like old times before Brad had come on the scene, but he wasn't sure he wanted to go back to those times or seeing Evie every week.

And he wasn't sure why.

Oh, hell, he knew. And that's precisely why he was so reluctant. Seeing her with another man had churned his gut in a way he hadn't expected. In a way he hadn't wanted to dissect. He still didn't.

His college friend opened the door a little farther and frowned from across the room. "Do you mind if I talk to you for a minute?"

"Not at all." He motioned to the two chairs that sat across from him. He did mind. Kind of. But there was no way he was going to say that. Especially not when she sauntered across the room, her hips encased in her snug skirt swaying ever so slightly with every step.

Dammit!

The word from a few moments earlier swept through his skull again, crashing into one side of his brain with enough force to make him wince.

He gritted his teeth and waited for her to take a seat. This was why he'd been happy to see a wedding band on her ring finger. He was attracted to her. Even when they'd been just friends. But he knew himself well enough to know that he was the last person that should be in a relationship with anyone. Work took up eighty-five to ninety percent of his brain cells, leaving precious little to invest in anything more than the friendship he, Evie and Darby had always had. Mainly because it had always been light and easy.

At least until one specific night had destroyed any semblance of light. Or easy. He and Evie had kissed under the glittering lights of the Las Vegas strip after the trio had gone to see a production of *Wicked*. Darby had caught a taxi and gone home, and left Max with Evie. She'd looked up at him, laughing at something stupid he'd said, and it just happened. That kiss. It had only lasted a second—a light playful peck that he hadn't expected to rock him to his core, but it had. And it was a mistake. Because just like the two main characters in the musical they'd just seen, their paths led them in opposite directions. He'd been married to his job. He still was. And Evie was married to… Well, he wasn't sure what she was married to now, but it wasn't Brad. Not anymore. And that made him feel…

Uneasy. Because that kiss had happened just before she started dating Brad. And he sure as hell didn't want things to go back to that time before her marriage. Because he might want to kiss her again. And he would end up hurting her. Just like her ex had. Well, not in the same way, since Max would never cheat, but he also wasn't good relationship material.

And Evie was not a one-night-stand kind of girl. She never had been, and he'd respected the hell out of that. But Max could never give anyone more than that. And he had no desire to change. Life was easier when it was just him.

When she made no move to say anything, he decided to push a little bit. "You wanted to talk about something?"

"More like ask something. I'm kind of desperate actually, but feel free to say no." Her mouth twisted in a way that might have made him smile under different circumstances.

"Desperate?"

"Yes. I've asked several other doctors, but they all turned me down."

For what? Did he even want to know? Especially since his head was imagining all kinds of scenarios. All of them revisiting that kiss from years ago.

"Turned you down for what?"

"The gala."

Hell. The annual hospital fundraising event? She'd always brought Brad in the past and he'd pointedly avoided crossing paths with the couple any more than necessary, other than the cursory greetings he gave most of his other acquaintances. And he'd made it a point never to go to those galas.

"Are you asking me to be your date?" The words slipped out before he'd had a chance to examine them for stupidity.

Her eyes widened as if horrified. "My...date?"

Okay, so that's obviously not what she meant. And he felt like a fool for even thinking along those lines. But did she have to look so stupefied?

Yes, she did. Because it helped him relax into his seat.

Before he could think of a funny rejoinder, not that there was anything humorous about the situation, she quickly added, "I—I wanted to ask for your help planning it."

Did that mean she already had a date? He pushed that question from his head. He was feeling more and more angry with the way this conversation was going.

"I thought there was a small committee that handled the gala every year."

"There was. But Dr. Parker, who normally headed it, moved to Texas to teach at a university there. And the rest of the committee stepped down, saying it was time to hand the reins over to someone else. I kind of fell into the role. And was assured that it was a piece of cake."

"How big of a piece?"

That made her smile. "Like maybe a whole sheet cake. And so far, no one wants anything to do with it. The venue has been the same for the past ten years, so that is already set up. And I'm hoping the same goes for the caterer and so forth."

He was evidently her last stop, since she'd been turned down by every other person she'd asked. So she actually was desperate, although it stung a bit that she acted like she had nowhere else to turn. But still, he wasn't sure he could stomach disappointing her. Especially after the year she'd had. She'd had to sell her apartment and split the proceeds with her ex despite the fact that she'd sunk a bunch of money into his investment firm. According to Darbs, anyway, who told him way more than he wanted to know. It made Max want to step in and fix everything, and he knew he couldn't. Not this time. But maybe this was one area where he could help.

"So what would you need from me?"

"Just to be a sounding board and maybe make some phone calls to past sponsors to see if they wanted to help with this year's gala. I know Darby doesn't work here, and she won't be involved, but maybe we can all meet for dinner—it'll kind of be like old times. I'm sure she won't mind if we talk shop for part of it."

Was she making sure he knew that they wouldn't be dining alone?

Darby had still been pestering him to join them, and he'd always managed to have something else to do. And he wasn't even sure why. Except that having Evie here in his office was messing with his equilibrium, the way it used to before she'd gotten married. It had to be some weird phenomenon like muscle memory that was coming back to haunt him.

But trying to explain that to her wouldn't be in anyone's best interest. Because she might think his interest in her was more than just friendship and it wasn't. He wouldn't let it be, because it could only end one way: with their friendship imploding in the worst possible way. Max was not interested in relationships. Never had been. But for now, all he could do was nod and repeat her words back.

"Just like old times."

"So you'll help me?"

"Yes. When is the gala again?"

She snorted. "That's right. You don't attend them."

"Nope. And don't expect that to change, just because I'm helping plan it."

Her head tilted. "Is that a challenge?"

"Just a statement of fact."

She gave a smile that had his libido sitting up and taking notice despite all of his inner speeches. "Well, we'll just see about that, shall we?"

What had she thought she was doing? Max had made it pretty clear that he'd been avoiding her for the last year—actually it had been longer than that—and she had to go and flirt with him?

It wasn't exactly flirting. It was the back-and-forth repartee they used to have before something had changed. When their friendship was light and easy, and so uncomplicated. Before her marriage.

She'd thought that had been the problem. He hadn't exactly liked Brad, and he'd made it pretty clear once they started dating. Had said that he didn't trust the guy. She'd laughed off his warnings at the time. But, looking back, it was easy to see who'd been the better judge of character.

But she wasn't about to admit that to him. Or to anyone, except for Darby, even though Max had to know by now what had broken up her marriage.

Maybe some part of her was still looking to get back to those earlier times, because they'd been happy. *She'd* been happy. Their little friendship trio. Her and Max and Darby. Her best friends in the world. In fact, at one time she thought that she and Max might even… But then he'd suddenly pulled away, and she'd been wounded deeply. Brad had come along soon after that with his smooth confidence and obvious interest. It had been a balm to her bruised ego. The rest was history. Only instead of bringing back Max, it had seemed to push him away even further. But then she'd gotten married and with the business of life had been able to push the friendship to a back burner. Until now. There'd been a reason that he was the last person she'd asked to help her with the gala, and she had fully expected him to refuse.

Only he hadn't.

She laid her head on her desk and groaned, letting the cool surface of the wood absorb some of the embarrassment over that coy smile she'd sent him as she'd stood to leave his office. She hadn't meant anything by it. But what if he thought she did? If she'd been hoping to mend fences with him, that was probably off the table now.

Her eyes tracked up to look at the clock on her wall. Time to get back to work. She had a busy day ahead of her. Especially now, since she'd just bitten off more cake than she could possibly chew. And there was a staff meeting at three with the hospital's new CEO about the gala. He wanted all department heads there. Evie wasn't a department head, but because she was now in charge of planning the event, he'd sent a memo specifically asking that she be there. So she would. Maybe the meeting would even land a few more volunteers to help with the planning.

Max's headache hadn't let up and he'd barely made it to the smaller of the two conference rooms before Arthur Robbins, the hospital's new CEO, got up to speak. He slid into his chair and caught sight of Evie sitting a short distance away. She hadn't noticed him yet, since she was talking to someone to her left, and it gave him a chance to properly study her. She was a little thinner than she'd been a year ago, probably due to the stress of the divorce. But it was good to see her smiling again. She hadn't seemed happy in…a while.

And how the hell did he know that? Because while he might not have been chummy with her over the last few years, he still found himself noticing things about her when he did see her. And the last year of her marriage with Brad had found her smiles few and far between. She'd become serious and focused on her work. Kind of like Max. Not that that was a bad thing. But Evie's personality used to be geared more toward being happy and lighthearted. She'd always had a witty rejoinder. But those had practically disappeared.

He'd glimpsed a bit of that lightheartedness just as she was getting ready to leave his office after asking him for help. She'd thrown him a look and a grin that had shifted something in his chest.

Dr. Robbins got up and received a smattering of applause as he took the podium. Max shifted his attention from Evie to the man. Robbins had once been a plastic surgeon and although he was in his mid-fifties, he could easily pass for early thirties. And with his easy smile and confident bearing, he was probably the perfect person to take on the role after Morgan Howard had retired last year.

"Thanks for coming. I've gotten to meet most of you in person over the last several weeks, but for those of you who don't know me, I'm Art Robbins, and I look forward to working alongside you to make this hospital reach its highest potential."

Something about the way he said that made Max shift

in his chair. Was he saying the hospital had lacked something under the last CEO? Morgan Howard had been much loved, his compassionate nature evident in almost everything he did.

Robbins went on to talk about the gala and how he'd looked at the figures the event had brought in over the last several years. "And there's no denying they're solid numbers, but I feel they could be even better with a little work. I'd like to thank Eva Milagre for heading up the committee. A committee that will make this the best event in this hospital's history."

The man had mangled the pronunciation of Evie's last name, making *Milagre* somehow rhyme with *pedigree*. And yet, when Max glanced her way, she hadn't moved in her chair.

"But we can only make it the best if we all plan our schedules so that as many of us are there as possible. After all, it's a party, and who doesn't like to attend a good party?"

Had Evie gone to the man and complained about him not attending the party in the past? Had that been what the smile in his office had been about? Whatever part of him that had been moved by it hardened to stone.

"And it *will* be a party, but I'd also like to think of this as a work event. Where we can go and mingle with prospective donors. Having faces to put with the names people see listed in the hospital's foyer is always a good thing. I really want to see those donations double or even triple this year. So I want each of you to pick up a flyer and a sign-up sheet that I have up here at the front. Please encourage your folks who aren't scheduled to work that night to attend if at all possible. Again, look at it as a work event, just like the meeting this morning."

Although the man smiled as he said the words, had Max sensed a vague threat hidden in there? When he glanced at Evie again, she was staring back at him, giving him a slight shrug. He had no idea what that meant. But he planned on finding out. Just as soon as this meeting was over.

Fifteen minutes later, it was, and he went up and got the flyer and sign-up sheet while the CEO was in conversation with someone else. He waited at the back of the room and watched Evie go up to the man and shake hands with him as if sealing a deal. He tensed further before ducking out of the room and waiting for her to appear. When she did, he struggled to keep his tone civil as he asked her to join him for coffee. She glanced at him, blinking as if surprised at the request, but nodded. Once they were in the cafeteria, seated with their cups, he studied her for a second before saying anything.

"Was Robbins's speech for my benefit?"

"Wh-what?"

"You know, talking about everyone needing to attend the gala. It's never been a requirement before and we both know it. Is that what you meant when you said 'we'll just see about that'?"

There was a long pause and then understanding dawned in her eyes. "No, of course not. My saying that was a joke. I had no idea Robbins was going to talk about any of that today. I'm as shocked as you are. And for your information, I don't agree with making it a required work event. It used to be looked at as part of the perks of being a staff member, that you could get dressed up in your finest clothes and have fun and eat a fantastic meal on the hospital's nickel. I think what he's done will kill the spirit of the event."

So she hadn't put him up to it. Now, Max felt like a jerk for even thinking it. He knew her better than that. At least he used to think he did. Was he just searching for reasons to be mad at her? If so, that wasn't fair to her.

"I'm sorry, Evie. I think I'm just looking for someone to blame and you happened to be a convenient target."

"It's okay."

He reached across and touched her hand, the warmth of her skin immediately waking up something inside of him. Pulling away, he smiled. "Thanks, Evie."

"Not a problem. And I hate to bring it up, but is there a good time when we can meet to talk about some of the specifics? I can ask Darby to come and we can make a night of it, if you want. But if staff is going to be, er, *encouraged* to attend, then our guest list just increased by about a hundred people from what we had last year. Robbins also wants me to try to increase our pool of sponsors by at least fifty. So that brings the guest list even higher."

"Maybe you should have told him you'd do that as soon as he learned how to pronounce your name."

She laughed. "I'm used to it."

Max lifted one eyebrow. "I remember being schooled on how to say it when we first met."

Her nose crinkled in a way he found adorable. "Because people who are my friends and family should be able to pronounce it."

Even after she'd gotten married, she'd kept her last name, just hyphenated it for documents. But at work, she'd always just been Dr. Milagre. He assumed if he and Evie had gotten married she would have done the same.

That pulled him up short. They weren't married and never would be, so it was a moot point. "Speaking of meeting to talk about logistics, most of my evenings are free." He didn't exactly have a big social calendar, and although he dated casually from time to time, there was no one in the picture at the moment. "And I'll see if I can come up with a list of people who might want to attend the gala as sponsors."

"That would be great, Max. I'll text Darbs and see what dates she has available." She stood. "I have an appointment in a few minutes, so I need to go, but I'll touch base later this afternoon on possible meeting times and places."

That was the third time she'd mentioned inviting Darby. Was that her way of saying that she was uncomfortable being alone with him? He was probably reading too much into something that he should be thankful for. Because she might not be worried about them being alone, he sure as hell was, and he wasn't sure why.

"Sounds good."

With that, she disposed of her trash and headed out of the cafeteria, leaving him at the table to mull over his options as far as avoiding going to the gala. From what Robbins had said, there were no options. And since he had patients of his own to see, he waited for the elevator Evie had gotten into to close its doors before he headed out there himself.

CHAPTER TWO

"HELLO, MRS. COLLINS. How are you today?"

"Okay, I guess." Even as Evie walked in the door, though, she could tell that one of her favorite patients was not okay. She was struggling. It was there in the increased rise and fall of her chest and in the breathlessness with which she'd said her words.

"Is your inhaler not working?" Margaret Collins had been Evie's patient for several years. She had controlled asthma, so it was odd to see her breathing so out of whack.

"It's been taking more puffs from it to get things back to where they should be."

Evie frowned. "Have you been sick recently?"

"No, which is why this is so weird. I feel fine otherwise."

"Why don't I give you a quick once-over first."

A list of possibilities scrambled through her head, each trying to make itself heard. Blood clot in the lungs, COVID and pneumonia were among the top choices.

She looked at the vitals her nurse had taken and then listened to the woman's chest sounds. Her left lung sounded clear, but when she listened to the right, she heard decreased breath sounds. And her pulse was hovering on the low end of the nineties. It didn't exactly knock any of her potential ailments off the pile, but it did shift them slightly. "Are you okay if I call for an X-ray?"

"Yes, whatever you need to do. I trust you."

She heard that a lot from patients, and she understood where they were coming from. But she also wanted them to trust their bodies. To know when they weren't working the way they should be.

Evie called down to Radiology to see if they had an opening and it turned out they did. Normally, she had to wait for a slot to become available. Since Margaret was her last patient before her lunch break, she opted to walk her down there and get her signed in. "Once they get the results they'll call and let me know, and then I'll get in touch with you, okay? I don't want to prescribe additional medications until we know what we're dealing with."

"I just want to be able to catch my breath."

"I want you to, too. We'll work on that."

"Sounds good."

Evie walked out of Radiology and headed for the cafeteria. She got her food and sat down, glad to be off her feet. She saw Arthur Robbins on the far side of the room and wished she had opted to go to one of the local coffee shops instead, but she was here now. And maybe he wouldn't even notice her. Right about then, his gaze swung toward her and he gave her a quick wave before rising and heading her way.

Oh, great. She wasn't really in the mood to hear about anything gala-related, but since she was in charge of it, she probably didn't have much of a choice. And it had been almost a week since the staff meeting, so he probably wanted an update. That was too bad because she'd called the venue where they used to hold the gala and while they said they could accommodate the projected hundred and fifty extra attendees, they couldn't add anyone else without them being over the fire marshal's limits. Which would mean they might have to find a new venue and, if so, they would lose their hefty deposit on this one. Maybe she could talk Dr. Robbins out of the new requirements and ask him to institute them next year instead. After all, then people would have more notice, since the gala was in two months. She was pretty sure trying to find a new place in that condensed period of time was going to be nothing short of a headache.

He stood over her table with a fixed smile on his face. "How's the planning coming?"

It was now or never. "I have some concerns that I'd like to talk to you about. Is there any chance of setting up a meeting?"

"My schedule is pretty tight right now. Can you give me a quick rundown?"

She did as best she could after being put on the spot.

"So what I hear you saying is that the current venue can handle our projections of a hundred and fifty extra guests."

"Yes, but—"

"We'll simply limit the number of tickets to that number and leave it at that."

"And if that leaves some of the prospective donors out in the cold?"

His smile widened, but the man didn't look pleased

at being pressed. "From where I'm standing, Nevada isn't looking too chilly these days. Besides, invitations to last year's donors have already gone out and we've asked them to RSVP by next week. That should give you a rough number and you can go from there."

Not *we*, but *she* could go from there. There was one more thing she needed to run by him. "Okay. Also, our previous CEO did the welcomes and so forth, so I wondered if you'd be carrying on with that tradition."

"I wouldn't miss it. I'm working on my speech even as we speak."

Actually, there was something chilly in Nevada. Their new leader. Whereas Morgan Howard had been warm and welcoming, Dr. Robbins seemed cool and aloof. And he wanted this year's fundraiser to double or triple in donations?

She forced a smile and thanked him. He then walked away to another table, that same smile firmly in place. Maybe she was misjudging the man, but something about him made her edgy. She couldn't read him like she could Howard. Somehow, unless he was a very good actor, she didn't think his persona was going to foster a lot of new interest in giving to the hospital. If anything, Evie was fairly certain that donations were going to be down unless the doctors themselves could make those connections. Maybe that's what Robbins was counting on and why he'd instituted the new attendance requirement.

Maybe that's also why no one else wanted to be on the committee. Had the man's reputation preceded him? Evie didn't usually listen to the hospital's gossip chain, but maybe in this instance she should have tried. Because if something didn't change, this gala could wind up being a colossal failure. And she could see that failure being dropped right in her lap. Not that she couldn't take a little criticism. But she loved this hospital and wanted it to get the funds it needed to grow and help more patients.

Her phone pinged, and when she glanced down, she saw it was the hospital's radiology department. Wow, that was fast. She'd just left Margaret down there less than fifteen minutes ago. She answered the phone and waited as the tech gave his findings.

The results made her close her eyes and let out a long shuddering breath. "Okay, thank you for letting me know. Is Mrs. Collins still there?"

"No, sorry. We sent her on her way. Did you want us to keep her?"

"No, it's fine. Thanks again." She disconnected and sat there, her lunch untouched as she tried to process the one possibility she hadn't put on her list.

Margaret Collins had a mass in the lower lobe of her left lung.

Max waited for Evie to arrive at his office, just like she had a week ago. But this time, she'd given him advance notice and said it wasn't about the gala. But her voice had been strained in a way that said she was worried about something. Something involving a patient.

Since Evie was a pulmonologist, her concern was probably related to a finding during a test. And that she suspected a tumor or she wouldn't be running to him with it.

He remembered when his mom had been diagnosed

with cancer. She'd come home and said she needed to talk to his dad alone. Because of the way she'd said it, he'd stood outside the door and listened, horrified at what he was hearing. Brain cancer? That couldn't be right. He'd burst into the room, a thousand questions in his mind and his eyes burning with tears.

His dad had sat motionless at the dining room table, and rather than being there as a support for his wife, he'd lifted a bottle of what Max later knew to be alcohol and drank deeply from it while his mom comforted them both. She had told them it would be alright, that the doctors had a plan and she'd be starting chemo in less than a month.

In the end, his mom hadn't had a month. Her tumor had hemorrhaged and she died on the operating table. And his dad hadn't stopped drinking. Not during her short illness and not afterward. He remembered checking the bedroom before going to school to make sure his dad was still breathing. Max, who was still grieving the loss of his mom, had been suddenly thrust into the role of caregiver, a job he neither wanted nor felt capable of. But it was either that, or end up an orphan. So he coaxed his dad to eat and put him to bed when he was too drunk to get there on his own.

And in that time, Max had decided that he was going to help people like his mom, because in doing so, maybe more people wouldn't wind up like his father, a shadow of the strong person he'd once been.

The knock at his door drove him from his thoughts. "Come in."

Evie entered and this time she didn't wait to be asked,

she just sat in one of the chairs. She had nothing in her hands, but that didn't surprise him, since all of the patients' records were now kept in an automated system. So there was no need to tote around physical X-rays or paper records. "I have a patient who I think has cancer."

"Give me her name."

He looked up the chart and went through the findings. "No MRI yet?"

"No, just the X-ray. I expected it to show pneumonia or something different, but not this."

"I get it. I take it she's gone home."

"Yes. And is waiting on my call."

"I'll need a biopsy to know for sure. But I want to do an MRI first to get a better look at whatever this is. Do you want me to make the call?" He wasn't sure why he asked that. It would be protocol for Evie to contact the patient and let her know that she needed to be seen by an oncologist. But he sensed something in her demeanor that said this was going to be a hard one. Besides, she had come directly to him rather than writing up an order that would land on the desk of one of his office staff, who would then call him to set up an appointment.

She paused for a minute as if thinking about it. "No, she's my patient. At least for now."

"She'll always be your patient, Evie. I'm only treating one part of her."

"So am I. But she's…a special one, even though none of my patients are supposed to be any more special than the others."

He was right. He'd always been good at reading Evie. Even during that quick kiss all those years ago, he'd sensed that she wanted something more from him. Something that he couldn't give her. Not just because he was afraid of ruining their friendship if something went bad. But because of his dad and how he'd become after his mom died. He'd become a shell of himself and had never recovered. Max had seen many partners lose loved ones. Every day a new one walked through the door of his office. But if Max didn't have a partner, he couldn't lose them. Couldn't grieve his way into a pit of despair.

He knew that kind of thinking was skewed, but he'd already lost two parents. And he'd lost his dad long before he'd died of cirrhosis last year, right before Evie and her husband split up. Max's soul felt as dry as the drought that was currently afflicting Las Vegas. It had been months since the last bit of rain had come their way and severe water restrictions were currently in force.

Evie was looking at him strangely, and he realized his thoughts had wandered for longer than he'd realized.

He stood up from his desk. "Do you have time for a walk out in the courtyard before your next patient?" He hadn't been much of a friend since her split from her husband, and if he wasn't careful, he was going to do exactly what he'd told himself he was trying *not* to do: lose her friendship.

"Thanks. I'd like that."

The relief in her voice said he'd done the right thing. "We can talk about the gala for a few minutes and kill two birds with one stone."

Except Max wasn't sure what the first bird was, except maybe the fact that he'd missed her. Had missed seeing her on a regular basis. Had missed laughing with her and going on their dinner dates and excursions with Darby. They still hadn't had that dinner she'd mentioned about planning the gala. Or had she decided she didn't need his help after all?

"Good. Because the venue the hospital usually uses can only accommodate a certain number of folks, and by requiring that staff go, Dr. Robbins is reducing the number of potential donors that can attend. It's one of the reasons that in the past, staff was invited but attendance wasn't required. I do get why they want department heads there, though."

He stood, waiting for her to do the same, his eyebrows going up. "Ah, so you think I've been remiss in my obligations by not going."

"Not remiss." She smiled. "Just antisocial."

That made him laugh. Because she knew him. In an even deeper way than Darby did. Darby had actually gone to medical school for a year or two before realizing the health-care field wasn't for her and had made the leap to the police, much to the dismay of her parents. She'd breezed through training. Had been the maid of honor at Evie and Brad's wedding, and then been wounded in the line of duty a year later, opting to resign when it became clear that her leg would never regain full function. But she seemed happy with what she was doing and claimed that there was nothing better than being your own boss.

Max was beginning to see the benefits of that after the doozy of a staff meeting they'd had. He'd even toyed with opening his own practice. But he loved hospital work. Loved working with other specialties—seeing the *life* that ran through this place. Oncology could be rewarding, but it was also draining and heartbreaking at times. The atmosphere at the hospital helped mitigate those aspects of his job.

Even the gala was probably not the onerous chore he'd made it out to be.

"So how do you plan to balance the staff-to-donor ratio?"

"I saw Robbins in the cafeteria and when I mentioned my concerns, he basically batted them back at me, saying he wasn't worried." One of her shoulders went up. "I'm hoping the sign-up sheet will give me a better idea of what we're dealing with. It's kind of short notice to say that everyone has to go. There are people who've already planned vacations and so forth. He did say that exceptions could be made for those folks who absolutely couldn't come."

"Hmm…maybe I should plan a vacation for that time."

"No way, chum. You know that you never take actual vacations."

It was true. Both Darby and Evie had gotten on him about that. He did take time off. But he almost always stayed home and didn't do anything special unless it was dinner with her and Darbs. Even when his dad died, he'd only taken off the day of his funeral. And he'd looked stiff and awkward whenever anyone approached him. But, Evie being Evie, she had said she got why he was that way. He'd told her the story about his dad's drinking and when it had started.

She also got why he abstained from alcohol and had always been her and Darby's designated driver. At least until he'd stopped coming to their dinners. Things had never been the same between the three of them since then. But now—with the gala—maybe he had a chance to rectify that. Unless—like the medications he prescribed—he decided that the risk outweighed the benefits. The jury was still out on that one.

They found themselves out in the large courtyard. The space was carved out of the middle of the medical center. It could only be accessed through the hospital. There was no lush greenery out here. Just interesting rock formations dotted with succulent plants and a central sculpture. But the place had a beauty of its own, just like the desert, as triangular sun sails and the tall walls of the hospital provided shade over a multitude of seating areas. And a flagstone path wound through the space, giving patients and staff alike a spot to contemplate their day. It was really lovely, and at night there were countless strings of fairy lights that gave it a beautiful, romantic appearance. Several staff members had even held their nuptials under those lights.

Max glanced around. "Too bad this space isn't being used for the gala. It would give visitors a chance to actually see the hospital and know where their dollars were going."

Evie cocked her head. "Actually, it probably would be big enough. It must be at least as big as the ballroom at the hotel. Tables could be set up throughout the space and a sound system could take care of making sure everyone could hear what was going on. But I don't know if it's possible to cancel the reservations at the hotel."

"If not this year, then maybe next year."

"Yes…"

She seemed to see the space with new eyes. And he loved watching her mind work. It was there in the way she perused her surroundings, in each twitch of those full pink lips. In the way her head tilted ever so slightly to the left.

He couldn't help but stare.

Since Max had never attended the event, he had no idea what the atmosphere was like, but surely the hospital could match or even surpass whatever was done off campus at these events. And with catering and being able to rent almost anything, right down to tablecloths and silverware, surely it was doable. Although no one could guarantee the weather would cooperate. But with rain looking like more and more of a luxury right now…

"I think it would be lovely. An intimate setting, rather than the formality of an elegantly appointed hotel. We could still erect a temporary dance floor from wood planking in the far left corner, where we have benches arranged in that large circle."

That area was often used as a venue for small lectures or for students and their families who were touring the hospital, hoping to be accepted into one of the local universities. They could visit and chat with other students, as well as staff who would talk about the hospital. So it was already set up as a gathering space, just not for the size or scale of a large event such as the gala.

She glanced at him with eyes that were bright and expectant. "Would you be more apt to come to the gala if it were held at the hospital?"

"Since it's now required, isn't that a moot point?"

"But what if it wasn't? What if this were any other year and held on the hospital grounds."

He thought for a minute. "Then, yes. Because I know that I could always go hide in my office if I got too bored."

"Exactly. I think more staff would want to come. Especially if they knew they could escape to either the staff lounge, the café, or any of the other waiting-room areas. They wouldn't be confined to a table or any one space. They could mingle and visit with each other the way they can't when they're at work. I think it would be a win-win. For everyone."

"You might be right." In fact, she probably was right. "The question is, will Robbins go for it?"

"Ugh. He's kind of a wild card. All I can do is come up with a plan and try to sell it to him. Do you think you could draw up a replica of what such an event might look like?"

She remembered that he liked to sketch? It shouldn't be surprising. During that awkward period after their kiss, he'd wanted to make up for his weird reaction, so he'd drawn a scene from *Wicked* from memory and had wrapped it and sent it to her house. She hadn't said much about it, but she had come up to him the day after she got it and had looked in his face, and simply said, "Thank you." But he could tell she was touched by the gesture. It helped them get past that terrible phase that could have turned terminal. He was grateful that it hadn't.

Was thankful he still had her friendship, even if he had been remiss in nurturing that over the last year and more. But like he'd thought earlier, maybe he could make up for that. At least a little. And as a friend, he could do this for her.

"Send me a list of what you want included in the drawing and I'll see what I can do. I can't promise it'll pass muster with Robbins, but maybe it'll give him a hint of what such an event could be like."

"Thanks, Max. I truly mean that."

He smiled. "I'm happy to do it."

"One more thing. If you have time in the next week or two, I'd like to call the hotel and see if they'll let us look at the venue. I was there last year, but don't remember exactly how things were laid out, since I wasn't involved in the planning. Maybe they'll even have pictures of what the room looks like set up. And I can walk out here in the courtyard and do a comparison, to see if we can fit buffet lines and the number of tables we'll need."

He glanced around before a thought came to him. "The courtyard opens to the atrium area of the hospital. Its size makes a big impression, with high ceilings, and it's not cluttered with a lot of furniture. We could spill over into it. Or maybe even set up the catering area in there. And I bet we could get some fans set up in strategic places to help keep things cool, although once the sun goes down that shouldn't be a problem."

"True." She smiled and gripped his hand, giving it a squeeze. "I'm liking this idea more and more. In fact, maybe we can even use it this year. We could have the formal part of the gala at the hotel and then have something set up in the courtyard, where people could come once that's over, if they want to see what the hospital is like. Something informal juxtaposed against the stiff formality of the event itself."

It was all he could do not to press the hand she'd squeezed against his pant leg to erase the feeling of her warm soft skin against his.

"I think Robbins would go for that. He has to have actually liked the hospital to have accepted the position as CEO of it. Surely he'd want to show it off?"

"I agree. And maybe that will make the idea of having the gala in house next year more appealing. That, along with the beautiful rendering you're going to draw."

One side of his mouth went up. "No pressure, though, right?"

"Oh, I'll press as hard as it takes to make you say yes."

And what if she'd pressed the night of that kiss all those years ago? What if she'd pulled him closer and deepened that kiss. Would he have taken her home? Carried her to bed and stayed there with her the entire night?

Not something he wanted to think about right now. Especially not with the way she was looking at him. As if he could do anything.

It's just a drawing, Max.

He needed to remember that, before he started ascribing personal motives to something that was anything but.

She pulled a pad out of her pocket and scribbled some notes on it. "Before I forget anything," she muttered.

Was she talking to him or to herself? A minute later she ripped the small sheet off and handed it to him. "It's just some of the things that I thought could be included in the drawing. If I think of anything else over the next few hours, I'll send you a text, okay?"

He perused the list. She wasn't kidding when she said she didn't want to forget anything. Ambiance, dance floor, seating that included tables and comfortable groupings of nice chairs, DJ station, food tables, bar, open doors to the atrium, additional strings of lights…

He sent her a grin. "I don't think we could fit anything else out here if we tried."

"You don't think it's over-the-top, do you?"

"I think this CEO is expecting exactly that. So, no." He glanced at the list again. "I'll start working on this tonight and hopefully have it to you within the next couple of days."

"That would be perfect. Thanks so much, Max."

"My pleasure." And it would be. He'd felt badly about what Brad had done to her, but hadn't known what to say or do to help her get over that. Instead, for the last year, he'd pretty much walked the other way whenever he caught sight of her. Not because of Brad, but because of himself. And he couldn't think of anything more selfish than that. Maybe he had a little more of his dad in him than he liked to think. The only thing he didn't do was drink.

Maybe it was time to make up for that lapse. And if a simple drawing would help, then he'd do ten of them.

"Oh, and about your patient with the mass, I'll let you know when we set up the appointment, if you're interested."

"Yes, thank you. I'd like to be there for the consult, if it works with my schedule. That is if you're okay with that."

"Yep. Not a problem at all."

"Great." She pocketed her notebook and glanced at her watch. "Speaking of patients, I'd better get back to it."

"Me, too. Talk soon."

They parted ways, and he realized he was looking forward to talking to her, even to collaborating with her on the gala. And he wasn't sure if that was a good thing or something that would come back to bite him. But he'd worry about that if and when it happened.

CHAPTER THREE

"Wow. You weren't kidding when you said you'd get me something in a few days."

He'd placed a large drawing of the courtyard against the wall and was now standing across from her, watching as she perused his work. Her office was slightly smaller than his, and although he had been in her space before, it was different this time somehow. And she wasn't sure how she felt about it. It reminded her so much of the time he'd gifted her that drawing from the play they'd seen, and even though this wasn't the same thing at all, it still brought back all of the emotions and feelings that receiving that gift had elicited. Especially since it had come after that disastrous kiss. And right before he seemed to go AWOL from their friendship.

And maybe it was because he'd been absent for so long that his very presence seemed to overwhelm the space...and her. Not so much with his size, but his sheer magnetism. It was there in his raw masculinity, the scent of his soap or shampoo or whatever he used, and, of course, those green, green eyes that made her want to get lost in them. She'd always felt that way about him no matter where they were. He'd always been a big part of their trio of friends. So his absence, especially over the last year, had been sorely felt. In fact, even when she'd been married to Brad, Max had been hit or miss as far as being there because she knew he hadn't liked her ex.

But at the time, his withdrawal had made processing that kiss a little easier. Made the realization that nothing would ever come of it a little more bearable, despite the tremendous hurt she'd felt. Because back then, she'd nurtured a tiny bit of hope that things might evolve from there. But he'd apologized and said he didn't want what had happened to affect their friendship. Except that it had. It was then that he'd started making excuses about why he couldn't go out with them. Not always, but enough that she deduced that it was because of her and what had happened. Darby had even asked about it, and although Evie was pretty sure she knew the reason for it, she didn't want to admit it. Didn't want her friend's sympathy over something that couldn't be changed.

She'd realized she had to make a life for herself. She couldn't go on mooning after a man who'd never had a steady girlfriend and had made it clear that he wasn't the marrying kind. Evie was. Brad had proved that. Or at least she'd thought he had, until Darby had presented her with those awful photos. The aftermath of her and Brad's breakup had been just as awful. He'd hounded her for two months, trying to get her to change her mind. And once he realized there was no going back, he'd turned nasty and had sued her for half of her earnings, forcing the sale of their apartment.

She'd lived in Darby's spare bedroom until the divorce was final. Three months in all. Only then did she feel like she could get her own place without worrying

Brad would somehow come after that, too. Only now did she feel like she was starting to recover from the trauma of that time.

With everything that had happened, she saw some wisdom in Max's aversion to relationships. And Evie could say she was now firmly on the side of Team Single. And she wasn't about to change that anytime soon.

She forced her mind back to the drawing when she realized she was staring sightlessly at it. Moving closer, she crouched on the floor across from it and took in what he'd done.

How had he gotten so much detail into it?

The courtyard space had been divided into four different zones. A section for hors d'oeuvres and drinks was right off the entrance to the foyer of the hospital. Rather than the buffet tables she'd envisioned in the atrium, he'd put romantic lighting on each table and drawn in wait-staff carrying trays of champagne and canapés.

Off to the left were the benches that were already in the space, but Max had put small side tables where people could talk and place the food and drinks they'd carried from zone one. It looked like he'd had potted plants brought in to give at least a small illusion of green space, and give people hope that there might be rain in the near future, even if none was forecast at the moment. A shortage of water was a very real concern in this part of Nevada. And there was no relief in sight. Just more sunshine and blistering summertime temperatures.

Fortunately, once the sun set, cooler temperatures moved in, which was one reason Sin City had such a booming nightlife. The gala setting looked like any one of those fancy resorts that were packed into the city. Only this had a vibe that was more intimate. A vibe that encouraged confessions…and maybe even huge donations. She glanced at Max for a moment before returning her attention to the canvas. The only colors on the otherwise black-and-white rendition were the faces of those populating the drawing. While featureless, those faces gave the appearance of life and warmth. And she loved it.

The third zone was the dance floor that they'd talked about. Twinkle lights hung overhead and lined the edges of the low wooden platform that appeared to be made out of hardwood flooring. On it, couples floated across the space in all of their finery.

"You're making me nervous." Max's low voice vibrated over her, causing her heart to skip a beat or two. "You're not saying anything."

"Because I'm blown away by it. All of it. This is beyond fantastic. If Dr. Robbins doesn't go for the idea, then I'll be shocked. Oh, and I like that you left the last zone as a strolling path."

There was one couple holding hands as they walked past the huge sculpture and rock formations that were in the area. It opened up a pit in her stomach that made it hard to breathe for a minute. Because she could imagine Max and herself in place of the pair in the picture. But it wasn't true and never would be. Because the fact of the matter was, she would stroll that path alone. Brad had betrayed her and Max hadn't wanted her.

The hurt from the past rose up all over again and threatened to swallow her.

But she wasn't really being fair to Max. He didn't want anyone—it wasn't a rejection of her in particular. And if she was smart, she would get rid of whatever vestiges of romantic notions she might harbor for the man before she lost him again. She'd been enjoying having him back in her life over this last week—she could see how it had been an impetus to start moving forward again after a year of feeling stagnant and unwanted.

And now she felt wanted again? Ugh! She hoped she wasn't pinning her self-worth on how Max acted or didn't act toward her. If she did that, she'd just end up pushing him away again. Besides, those feelings weren't real. They were from not having anyone in her life right now. Maybe she should think about dating again. After all, Brad had been gone for a year and even if he came groveling back, she didn't want him—would never be able to trust him after what he'd done.

"I thought after the meal at the other venue, people might want to move around a little bit to burn some of it off."

She forced a smile, glanced back at him and stood. "And holding hands as they do. That was a romantic touch."

He gave a half shrug, part of his smile fading. "Purely a selling feature. Just like the couples on the dance floor."

"Ah, I see. Because Max Hunt doesn't have a romantic bone in his body."

She wasn't sure why she said it, especially in tones that were a little more waspish than necessary as evidenced by the muscle that was now pulsing in his cheek. Probably feeling guilty over her thoughts from a minute ago, she sighed and added, "Sorry. That was un-called for."

"No, it's okay. I can wish romance on others, even if I don't want any for myself."

"You don't think you'll ever be involved with any-one?" And there she went again. She wasn't asking for herself—at least that's what she told herself. She just thought Max deserved the happiness that came with companionship. Despite the way that she and Brad had ended, she had been happy with him for most of their marriage—even if it was more a comfortable feeling of familiarity rather than a rush of chaotic emotions that she had trouble sorting out. At least with Brad she'd known what to expect. Well, except at the end.

He gave her a quick glance before looking away, but not before she caught something almost poignant in his expression. "I don't think so. My mom's death was hard on my dad. He became someone I no longer recognized and I'd really rather not go through something like that."

"Not every partner dies so young."

"No. But in my family's case that's how it happened. And the process leading from her cancer diagnosis to her passing is something I'd rather not put any kids I might have through."

Her head tilted. "And yet you became a cancer doctor."

He didn't answer for a second, but finally he nodded. "It was because of my mom. But that doesn't have any-thing to do with my not wanting a serious relationship. The fact of the matter is that I like my life the way it is now and I don't want to risk that over something that might not—that probably *won't*—last. After all, look at you and Brad."

"Wow, okay. I get it. It's none of my business."

He closed his eyes. "Sorry, Evie. I didn't mean it that way. I'm just trying to show that even when you think something is going to last forever, it doesn't always. I try to live my life honestly. And don't ever want anyone to get the wrong idea and be hurt because of something I've said…or done."

Was he warning her off? If so it wasn't necessary. She'd gotten his message a long time ago. "I get it. I'm really not interested in a relationship, either. Like you said, there's me and Brad."

He was silent for a moment, then she felt warm hands on her shoulders. He gave her a light squeeze before letting her go. "I'm sorry, Evie. That man deserved worse than what he got. And you deserved better."

He evidently knew her ex had tried to take her for everything she had. Probably from Darbs. Thankfully, once the divorce was final, he moved away with the woman he'd been seeing. She had no real idea where he was right now and had no interest in knowing.

She took out her phone and snapped a shot of the picture as a way of changing the subject. "I'll send this to Robbins. Can I keep the drawing in my office, in case he wants to see the original?"

"Of course. I thought maybe you'd want some tweaks."

"Are you kidding? This is a masterpiece. It's perfect the way it is. But don't be surprised if it goes up on the wall of the hospital somewhere, or if our new head guy ropes you into doing some other drawings."

"Nope. I only do them for a few special people."

And Evie was one of those people? All of her self-lectures from moments earlier flew out the window and in their place something warm and tingly stirred in the pit of her stomach. She had to bite her lip for a minute to stop the sensation from spreading. The last thing she wanted was for Max to realize how much those words meant to her. So she again changed the subject. "Any news on Margaret Collins?"

"The patient you referred to me?"

"Yes."

"I actually have an appointment scheduled with her for this afternoon. Do you still want to be there?"

She thought for a moment. It wasn't absolutely necessary that she attended. Margaret would be in good hands, since she trusted Max implicitly. But she would like to be. Would that seem odd to him that she would want to support her patient?

"I don't want it to seem weird or for you to feel like I don't trust your judgment."

"Why would it seem weird? Family members sit in all the time. As her pulmonary specialist, it makes sense that you would want to know what her treatment will be so that you can help carry it out."

When he said it like that, it didn't sound strange at all.

"Thanks, Max. I'll take you up on that then. What time is her appointment?"

"At three thirty. Are you free then?"

"I should be. My appointments tend to be in the morning. And I do a second set of rounds in the afternoon. So I'll just pop over to the appointment and then come back."

He nodded. "Speaking of popping over, I hadn't meant to stay as long as I did, so unless you have any other questions about the drawing, I'll head back over to my office."

"No questions, just a huge thank-you. I'll let you know what Robbins says."

"Great. I'll see you around three thirty, then."

Speaking of which, she needed to write that down before she forgot. Not that she was likely to. Her insides were already doing loops at the prospect of seeing him again so soon. Talk about a downpour in the midst of a drought. It had been a long time since she and Max had spoken so freely to one another, and she was going to turn her face up to the rain and enjoy it while she could. And ignore the fact that, like living in the desert, the rain wasn't likely to last.

As the day went on, Max became less and less sure about having Evie sit in on Mrs. Collins's appointment. There had been something unsettling about being closed in her office while she studied his drawing, especially since she'd asked him about whether or not he might consider being in a relationship.

Had she even realized that she'd used a fingertip to trace the couple he'd drawn who'd been walking together in the picture? He had shuddered, as if she'd been running her fingers along his skin rather than an inanimate object. He still hadn't gotten that image out of his head. When he'd kissed her in front of that theater, her palm had curled over the back of his neck. The warmth of her skin against his had served to jerk him back to awareness just as the mental image of them in bed had slid through his brain.

That same image had risen up as she'd touched that drawing, the intimacy of the act making him picture them together all over again. It made his nerves prickle to life, along with another part of him that needed to be kept on a short leash. Before something bad happened. Not that sex was bad. And with her it was guaranteed to be good. Very, very good. But it couldn't happen if he had any hope of salvaging their friendship—a friendship that was just now being brought back online.

Was the burst of lust something remembered from their past? There'd been that same shivery sensation that he'd thought he'd banished long ago. Or was this something entirely new? If so, he needed to put it in the past and leave it with his other baggage. Because if he couldn't...

Well, then there would be no more meetings in anyone's offices and no more collaborations on anything work-related or not. And the friendship that he'd hoped to salvage would be dead in the water. Again.

His phone pinged and his emotions went on high alert until he glanced at the reading and saw that it was Darby. He immediately relaxed and read the text. She'd actually written the word *squee* followed by an absurd number of exclamation marks. The message went on.

Evie texted me a copy of your drawing and I love it. She said she's headed to the CEO's office to show it to him.

He's going to go berserk. If he doesn't, then he doesn't deserve to run that hospital.

That made him smile. He couldn't picture Dr. Robbins going berserk about anything unless it was something related to dollar signs. He texted back.

Don't get your hopes up too high. He's not the most demonstrative man, from what I've seen of him.

Was he sad that Evie hadn't asked him to accompany her to the CEO's office? He'd be lying if he said no. But he'd also hinted to Evie that he had a busy afternoon ahead of him. Maybe she was afraid Robbins wouldn't like his plans, despite what she'd said. Except that Darby had also seemed to think his rendering was worth presenting to the man.

His phone pinged again.

Well, I think this will float his boat. Besides, he'd be crazy not to go for this. It'll give him a chance to show off his hospital to potential investors. I can't wait to hear what he thinks.

He smiled.

Thanks for the vote of confidence.

Once Darby signed off, he was left with a strange sensation. He had no idea what had caused it or why it was so unsettling, but it was. It could be that it was better for him not to be there. Because he didn't want to witness the sense of disappointment flit across Evie's face. He'd already lived through that once before and didn't want to go through it again. If only she knew that he'd saved her from a relationship failure that was as bad, if not worse, than what she'd gone through with Brad.

Oh, he wouldn't have cheated on her, except with his job. And he certainly wouldn't have gone after her money. But he knew himself well enough to know that he would be withholding some of himself. It was a defense mechanism that he'd brought into play while he was taking care of his dad. Oh, he'd taken care of his physical needs, but he'd felt powerless to help him with anything more than that. Because he'd expected to someday come home and find his dad dead, either by drinking himself to death or worse. Thankfully, it hadn't come down to that. He'd just damaged his liver beyond repair instead. That damage hadn't shown its face until Max was long grown up and out of the house.

The damage done to Max emotionally, back then, hadn't reared its head until later, either. Until he'd started thinking about Evie in ways that had nothing to do with friendship. It had paralyzed him and made him realize something inside of him was missing. Something that had to do with him trying to meet someone's needs in a way that went beyond the physical joining of two bodies. Because he knew that was all that he'd be able to give her. And she'd eventually come to hate him for it.

He shook his head and stood up to stretch his back. He needed to go do something besides just sit here and think about the past. Or about Evie. He glanced at his watch. It was lunchtime, so he might as well go out of the hospital. Maybe he could throw off some of his thoughts. Besides, he was pretty certain he would find out what Dr. Robbins thought of the ideas soon enough. And they weren't even his ideas. They were Evie's. All he'd done was put them to paper. So he'd go and eat and sit somewhere where his thoughts would not be consumed with hospital stuff.

So, he headed down the street, hopefully leaving the clutter in his head far behind.

Margaret Collins looked relieved, which struck Evie as odd. She would have expected her older patient to be defeated by a possible cancer diagnosis, but she didn't seem fazed. "Evie, dear, I'm so happy you were able to come."

She'd said it as if it was a birthday party or some happier occasion. An inkling of worry erupted in the back of her head. She'd never known her patient to think with less than a clear head, but this sounded... Well, it didn't seem like a normal reaction.

When she glanced at Max, she saw a troubled frown. Evidently she wasn't the only one to find Margaret's words odd.

"I thought Dr. Milagre should be here so that she'd know what treatment your tumor needs and would be able to know how to treat the breathing aspects."

"Of course. I never meant anything other than that. She's just always been so sweet to me, even before this, when I had COVID and no one knew if I'd live or die. But Dr. Milagre never seemed to have any doubts." She glanced at Evie. "You were always so encouraging and your sense of hope was contagious. It still is, which is why I'm glad you're here."

Evie's concerns eased. "Your willingness to follow a treatment plan and to never stop fighting played a major role in your recovery. I'm counting on that same determination to get you through this as well."

At seventy-two years of age, some might have not wanted to put the woman through cancer surgery or chemo, but other than her asthma, Margaret had always been remarkably healthy. At least from what her records said and what Evie herself had seen. She was an amazing woman, and she reminded Evie of her own grandmother, who'd come over from Brazil and had made a home in a new place with her family. She'd lived to the ripe old age of ninety-six. And if COVID hadn't come along, her grandma might still be alive. But instead, it had taken her life, even while sparing Margaret's. She sincerely hoped her patient had another decade or two to live.

"We're going to do an MRI today and get a better look at what we're dealing with. We'll inject a little dye into your system to see how much of the tumor is being fed by your blood vessels. Then we'll schedule a biopsy. Do you have family who can come and take you home from that, since you'll need anesthesia to do the procedure."

"My son can. He lives a few miles from my place. The only reason he's not here today is because I didn't tell him. Not yet, anyway. I wanted to have a better idea of what I'm facing before bringing anyone else in my family into it."

Max perched on a stool in front of her and looked

her in the eye. "You're going to want to call him for this one."

"You're that sure?"

"Sure enough. I really want someone here for you. There will be a lot of information thrown at you in a short amount of time. It would be good for someone else to be a second set of ears. No one remembers everything."

He was right. After Darby had shown her those pictures of Brad, her mind had been a mess and she'd barely remembered anything said afterward. It hadn't been a medical emergency, but she'd still been glad Darby had been there for her and had been her support system. She'd even come with Evie when it came time to tell her parents what was happening. Her dad had threatened to come for Brad, and at least give him a piece of his mind. She and Darby had talked him out of it, eventually convincing him that it wouldn't change anything and could only make things worse.

Brad hadn't been worth it. He still wasn't.

"I'll ask him as soon as you know for sure that it's cancer."

Max laid his hand on Margaret's. "We won't know that for sure without the biopsy."

"But you'll have a better idea of what it is with the test today, right?"

"We should have."

Margaret nodded and turned her hand over to squeeze his. "If the test seems to indicate it is, then I'll tell him."

"Good."

"Then let's get this show on the road then, shall we?

The sooner we know, the sooner we can get this thing out of my chest. Or at least I'll hope that we can."

Max turned to look at Evie. "How is the next hour looking for you?"

"I can't think of anywhere I'd rather be." She quickly added, in case Max got the wrong idea, "Than with you, Margaret."

The older woman swiped her fingers under one of her eyes before glaring at them both. "These damned allergies…"

Allergies or not, Evie was glad she could be here for Margaret, no matter what the results turned out to be.

She hadn't had time to even tell Max that Dr. Robbins had loved the sketch and had agreed, even on such short notice, that they should incorporate the ideas into this year's gala. They would still do the speeches and appeals at the hotel ballroom, but they would shorten that portion of it to an hour or two, enough to serve dinner and get through the fundraising portion. But then they would invite everyone over to the hospital to enjoy some desserts and drinks. Robbins had gone so far as to say they would hire a taxi service to drive those home who had imbibed more than they should have. And this way, staff members who were on duty would be able to pop into the courtyard for a few minutes and at least get a few refreshments.

So while Margaret was getting her MRI, she thanked Max again for the drawing. "He's giving us everything we wanted."

His eyebrows went up. "Maybe he's not as hard-nosed as he seemed. And since people can come and go as they please once they get to the hospital, there shouldn't be a problem with overcrowding."

"No. There shouldn't. They're going to rotate some board members and have them take people on tours of the hospital, so it won't be everyone out in the courtyard all at once."

His eyes focused on the images going across the screen as they were taken. He swore softly.

"What is it?"

"It's hypervascular," he said, pointing at the tumor. "And I'm pretty sure it's metastatic, probably from her breast, liver or somewhere else. An angiosarcoma."

"Oh, no." Her whispered words were part prayer. An angiosarcoma was a rare cancer and Max was right— lung involvement almost always originated from somewhere else. Which meant it might have also metastasized to the brain or other organs. "Will you still need a biopsy?"

"To be one-hundred-percent certain, yes. But if it's what I think it is, it'll be aggressive."

"I know." Evie's heart plummeted and all of a sudden fundraisers and whether or not they got to hold part of the gala on hospital grounds seemed so unimportant.

"I want to stay while you tell her."

He nodded. "I figured as much."

They helped Margaret down from the MRI table. She looked at their faces. "It's bad news, isn't it?"

"It's not the best."

"I see." She stood there for a minute before sitting gingerly down on the wheelchair they'd used to bring her into the room. "Are there treatments?"

"Yes. Chemotherapy and possibly some radiation. But we don't think the lung is the primary site. We think it came there from somewhere else."

She twisted her hands in her lap. "Oh, my. That is bad news, isn't it?"

"Like I said, I still want to do the biopsy. And it's time to bring your family members in on this and let them know what's going on. You mentioned your son lives nearby."

"He does. I have a daughter, too, but she lives in Maine at the moment. That's such a long way to travel…"

"Why don't you let her decide if that's too far or not."

They wheeled her to Max's office and Evie sat beside her and held her hand as Max continued to give her more information.

Margaret interrupted once to ask how soon he'd want her to have the biopsy.

"As soon as possible. We'll want to begin treatment right afterward. Will your son be able to stay with you?"

"He's married with three teenaged daughters. How can I ask him to do that?"

"I understand. But I have to be honest. You'll need support during treatment. I won't lie and say it'll be easy, because it won't."

She gave him a frank look. "Is it even worth it, in your opinion? If this were your mom, would you suggest she go through chemo?"

He paused for several long seconds and Evie's heart contracted. She knew the story of Max's mom and it was a heartbreaking one.

"My mom never got the chance to go through chemo.

Her cancer was found too late and she died before she could start treatment. But to answer your question, yes, I would want her to at least try one course to see if there was any improvement."

"I'm sorry about your mom. She must have been a special lady, because you're a good man."

Max smiled. "Well, some might argue with that assessment."

He glanced at Evie, his mouth twisting sideways. Did he think she was one of the people who might argue with that assessment? Not on her life. And she was going to make sure he knew it. Just as soon as his appointment with Margaret was over.

CHAPTER FOUR

"Do you think I don't think you're a good person?"

Max frowned. The question had come right on the heels of his patient leaving the room. "What? Where did this come from?"

"When Margaret said you were a good man, you looked right at me when you said there were people who might not agree with that assessment."

"I'm sure that was a coincidence." It hadn't been, though. He had looked at Evie, but he just hadn't realized she'd caught the movement. Until now.

"I'm pretty sure it wasn't." She took a step closer. "You are a good man. Why would you even think otherwise?"

"You're reading too much into all of this." His heart thumped hard a time or two before going back into a normal rhythm. She was standing just a foot away from him, her head tilted up to gaze at him, the brown of her eyes soft and knowing. As if she knew all of his secrets and was hell-bent on prying them from him one by one.

"Am I?" Her hand went up to touch his face. "Is this because of your mom? You were only a kid back then. You couldn't have stopped what happened to her."

"I know that." A coil of emotion unspooled from

somewhere inside of him. "There are days, though—days like today—when I wonder why I went into a specialty that is rife with so much heartbreak. Margaret is probably not going to survive this, you know."

"I know. But if it goes into remission she could have some good years ahead of her. Years when she'll be able to see her grandkids grow up and live her life to the fullest. That has to be worth something, despite the heartache."

Her fingers were still touching him, moving over his jawline in a way that made him shudder. And dammit, he needed this. Needed to feel something other than the desperation of all of the Margaret Collinses of the world, although she seemed remarkably at peace with whatever might happen.

"Evie…" He closed his eyes and balled his hands by his sides to keep from gripping her arms and pulling her closer. Much closer.

"It's okay, Max. You don't always have to be strong."

He felt arms go around him and her cheek pressed against his chest. She was hugging him. Hell, she was only trying to comfort him. So why did the urges going through his body right now have nothing to do with comfort? Or hugging?

But he did have to be strong. Because to be anything other than that would be dangerous. Not just for him, but for Evie, too.

He opened his eyes and looked down at where she was pressed against him. And God help him, his arms went around her and hugged her close, one hand sliding up into the silky strands of her hair and gripping it.

A tiny sound came from her throat, and at first he thought he was holding her too tight and was hurting her. But then he realized it wasn't about that. It was something else entirely.

His hands went to her shoulders and eased her away, and Max looked down into her face as he did. Her eyes, rimmed with impossibly dark lashes, were moist with emotion, and suddenly he knew there wasn't enough strength in the world to stop him from doing what he was about to do.

Except before he could even make a move to do exactly that, Evie went up on her tiptoes and pressed her lips to his in a kiss that was as soft as a butterfly's wings and as deadly as a cobra's strike. Because it ignited a maelstrom inside of him that took over all rational thought. And soon, the kiss was anything but soft. His hand went to the back of her head and held her as his mouth covered hers, his tongue sliding between her lips only to be welcomed home as she opened to allow him any and all access. And he accepted her invitation, his palms going to her back and sliding down until her hips were pressed firmly against his. And this time, the sound she made wasn't imagined. It was real, very real, and if this went much further she was going to be on his couch and rolled under his body until there was nothing separating them, and they could…

Hell, no. She didn't deserve this. Didn't deserve someone that would just take what she was offering and give nothing in return. Because even as his body clamored for it, his mind knew that was all that would be in it for him.

He pulled his mouth free. "Evie. Stop…please."

She tried to move closer again and this time he somehow summoned some superhuman strength and set her away from him. "We can't."

Evie stared at him for a second, the back of one of her hands pressed against her mouth. Then she straightened, her fingers going to her hair and dragging through the mussed locks.

"We can't what, exactly?"

He motioned to his couch, letting the bald implication speak for itself. He didn't want any warm fuzzies entering the conversation and muddying the waters. Hell! She'd tried to argue that he was a good man? Well, he was about to disabuse her of any such thoughts. Because what he'd been thinking had been the opposite of good or noble.

She frowned. "You think I was angling for you to sleep with me?"

"Weren't you? Because that was sure the direction my thoughts were headed. I'd be damned surprised if yours weren't there as well."

They stared at each other, both of them still breathing hard. Then she shrugged. "So what if they were? We're both adults. It's not like I'm asking you for a ring." Except there was a quick flash of pain in her eyes that cut him to the core.

God, he didn't want to hurt her. Had tried so hard over the years to keep from doing exactly what he was doing now. "Evie, I know you aren't. But I just can't give you what you deser—"

She took a step back. "Don't! I know all of the blah blah blahs you're about to recite. You're not the marrying kind. You don't do relationships. You don't want forevers. You'll remind me *again* of how Brad and I wound up. Well, let me let you in on a little secret, Max. I did learn something from my marriage, even if you think I didn't. I'm not after any of those things. Not forevers, not declarations of love, not emotional pleas for more than you can muster." She sucked down an audible breath. "So your overinflated opinion that anyone who sleeps with you must immediately fall head over heels in love with you is way off base. But just in case you're still worried, let me make it as clear as I can. You won't have to turn down a night of pleasure with me ever again. Because this truly was our last dance."

Is that was she thought? He gave a hard laugh. Because if he was worried about anyone immediately falling in love with someone, it was the other way around.

"Something funny?"

Only then did he realize how that had probably sounded to her. But there was no way he could explain that he wasn't laughing because of what she'd said. It was because the reality of those "blah blah blahs" she'd named was still true. Even after all these years.

Rather than respond, he just shook his head.

"Perfect. Well, I guess that about sums it up for both of us." She turned to go, and then said over her shoulder, "Please let me know when Margaret's biopsy is scheduled. I want to be here for it."

As much as he wanted this conversation to be over, he didn't want her to leave like this. "Evie—"

She stopped him with an uplifted hand. "Don't worry. This won't affect our professional relationship. Or our friendship. I know that was another one of your arguments the last time we kissed. But we got through that… kind of. So we can get through this, too."

"Wait."

She turned back and stared at him, eyebrows raised as she waited for him to say something else. But for once his brain was blank. Because what could he say? Everything that she'd just thrown at him was true.

He shook his head. "Nothing. Except, I'm sorry."

"Well, don't be. Because I'm not. See you around the hospital."

With that she was out the door, leaving him to wonder if she would ever speak to him again. Because despite what she'd said, he couldn't think of any way that this wouldn't affect their friendship. Not this time. Because this kiss wasn't the same as the last one. Not in any way, shape or form. It was way worse. Because it had meant something. If not to her, then to him.

Darby nudged her leg under the table. "What is wrong with you?"

"Nothing."

"No. Don't even try that stuff with me. It doesn't work. Since Max conveniently had surgery tonight— *again*—and said he couldn't make our dinner, I take it he's the reason for those slumped shoulders."

Yes, he was. But Evie honestly didn't know how to fix it at this point. When he'd laughed at her for saying that he expected her to fall in love with him if they slept together, a scorching pain had ripped through her. Because it might have been true. If they slept together she probably would fall for him. He'd helped her see what a huge mistake that would have been. But along with the pain, there'd been anger. Furious words had tumbled around her brain, and she'd had to grit her teeth before she lashed out and used them to cut him to the ground. Instead, she'd stormed out of his office like an indignant child.

But now that she'd had time to think, she realized she'd overreacted and hadn't given him a chance to say anything else. Because she'd been scared. Scared he would avoid her like he had the last time this had happened. And it looked like he was. Even Darby could see it for what it was.

She decided to come clean. "I kissed him and he seemed to kiss me back. Until he wasn't and started backpedaling so fast that things became a blur of anger and regret. I'm pretty sure that's why he's not here."

Darby's mouth fell open and her eyebrows shot up, reaching near her hairline. "You kissed *him*?"

"Well, I mean, I think he was about to kiss me, but then I just kind of…beat him to it." She tried to put her thoughts into words. "It just happened. I'm not even sure why or how."

"Wow. Did you guys talk about it?"

She shrugged. "I talked at it. And around it. And through it. And then I stormed out of his office."

"You didn't." Her eyes rounded. "I know it's not funny, but I'm picturing you slamming his door behind you. That is not like you. At all."

"I know." Her chin dropped into her hand and she

probably looked every bit as miserable as she felt. "But I don't know how to repair the damage."

"You go and talk to him again. And again. As many times as it takes for him to screw his head back on straight. I know the guy has a thing against commitment, but from what I'm hearing, you didn't ask for one."

"Correct. I don't want one. I don't know that I'll ever get married again after what happened with Brad. But he even threw that in my face."

"God. I can't blame you for storming out, then. Maybe we'll all just be groovy old singletons when we turn seventy."

Although Darby had nothing against marriage, she just hadn't met the right person yet. And after one failed engagement, it didn't seem like she was in a hurry to change her status on social media.

"Maybe. And you're right. I probably do need to go talk to him. The kiss was just impulsive. It meant nothing. I just need to get him to understand that."

"That's probably a good idea." Darby reached over and squeezed her hand. "Plus, it's hard to do the planning for the gala if you end up being the only one on the committee. And since part of the event will now be held at the hospital, there's a lot of last-minute things to organize, like caterers and DJs and linen services, right?"

"I know. I'll try to talk to him. And if that doesn't work, I'll have to find someone else who'll be willing to help out."

"He'll come around. He probably just feels awkward about everything right now. You could try to reschedule dinner, but until things are resolved between you two, it's probably just going to be lather, rinse, repeat, with him finding excuses not to come."

Although Darbs wasn't trying to make her feel guilty, she just felt more and more miserable as dinner went on and ended with her just picking at her food.

"You need to go home, Evie. Get some rest. Things will probably look better tomorrow."

Her friend was right. Even though Max was avoiding her at the moment, she couldn't really see him not following through with what he'd committed to do. He wasn't anticommitment in general, just when it came to relationships.

They paid their bill and then headed out the door. She turned when she heard her name murmured in a low, familiar tone. Shock made her stand completely still.

Max was standing there in black jeans and a turquoise polo shirt, looking completely at ease. And completely gorgeous.

Oh, Lord, what did he want?

She couldn't think of a single thing to say, just stood there looking at him like an idiot. It was Darby who broke the silence. "Sorry you missed dinner. I hope your emergency worked out okay."

One side of his mouth quirked. "The jury is still out on that. Sorry about tonight, though."

It was then that she realized he wasn't talking about his supposed surgery, but about what had happened between the two of them. She didn't think she could hash it out in public like this, though. It was one thing to tell Darby in confidence, but to then have things laid out like his surgical instruments?

Thankfully, Darby again saved the day as she leaned on her cane and said, "Well, I've got an early morning, and my leg is giving me fits tonight, so I'll say good night."

"See you later. I hope your leg feels better," Evie replied, giving her friend a hug.

Darby whispered, "Good luck" in her ear.

Ah, so it wasn't the leg giving her fits, she was just giving Evie a chance to talk to Max alone. He was here, so he must be ready to talk things through, right? Or maybe he was coming to say "sorry, but I can't help you with the gala after all."

Darby had caught a cab and was on her way home, leaving her and Max standing in front of the restaurant.

"Walk with me?"

"Okay."

They started down the street, heading toward the Vegas strip, where some of the most famous Las Vegas casinos were located. They strolled in silence for about five minutes before he spoke. "I don't like the way we left things the other day."

A sense of relief swept over her. "I don't, either. And I'm sorry for stomping off the way I did. I really do value our friendship and don't want to lose it over something stupid." She hesitated. "I feel like the last time this happened, you avoided me for a long time, and it hurt. And I missed you. Can we just forget that any of this happened?"

She'd spoken the truth. She had missed him. And it had hurt. Hopefully he would take those two things at face value and accept them for the apology that it was meant to be.

"I missed you, too. And I realized when I had to make up a story in order not to come tonight, then I was headed in the wrong direction. Again. I'm sorry, Evie."

"I'm sorry, too. So we're good?"

"We're good."

Her eyes closed and a feeling of gratitude washed over her. She wanted to hug him but was afraid it would ruin things if she did. So she simply smiled and thanked him.

"So do you want to give me a rundown about what still needs to be done for the gala?"

"I actually wasn't sure you were going to continue on the committee, but I'm glad you are." She pulled a list from inside of her purse and showed it to him. "Anything spark your interest?"

He pointed to an item on the list. "I actually know a guy who DJs for a living if that would help. Nothing off the wall and I think it would fit in with the atmosphere Dr. Robbins is going for."

"You mean cold and cranky?"

Max laughed. "I have to admit, that's a fair assessment. I bet his bedside manner was phenomenal."

"I bet. But at least he liked our idea. If it works out, he thinks we might be able to have it completely at the hospital next year. We can use the atrium for dinner and the presentations and then the courtyard for the after party."

"He actually called it an 'after party'?"

Her mouth twisted. "No. He called it a 'greet and mingle.' But, anyway, if you know a DJ, that would be great, if he's available for the time slot we need him for."

"Which is…?"

She thought for a second. "The actual gala starts at seven and Dr. Robbins wants it to go until around eight thirty. Then those who wanted to would all head over to the hospital. We're thinking that most will want to if we advertise that there will be dancing and a bar."

"So from eight forty-five until, say, eleven?"

"That sounds about right."

He made a note in his phone. "I'll call him in the morning and let you know for sure. Now, what else?"

They went through the rest of the items with Max selecting a few more things from the list. "Does that help?"

"Absolutely." She paused for a minute as something struck her. "Is Margaret's biopsy tomorrow? I was afraid that was the surgery you were talking about."

"No, I would have let you know if it was tonight. It's tomorrow at ten thirty. Her son will bring her in at six to do pre-op stuff. And then we'll go from there."

"Did her daughter fly in?"

"Yes, she did, actually. I was proud of Margaret for calling and asking her to."

"Her kids are great. I've met both of them over the years."

They stopped to wait for the light to change, signaling they could cross the street. "Having a great support group will help a lot. She's going to need it, if the biopsy tells me my suspicions are right."

"The hospital also has support groups for those with different types of cancers. I'll encourage her to try some of them out. I'm sure she will find one that she likes.

It'll help if there are some familiar faces in the infu-
sion room."

They crossed the street and found themselves in the
middle of a large throng of people waiting to get into one
of the shows. They moved to the outside of the cluster,
skirting it as best they could. Maybe they should have
gone a different way. But she actually loved the crowds
and the liveliness of Vegas. Just by walking its streets,
no one would ever guess that there was an unprecedented
water shortage going on right now. Except for the hotel
notices that had been posted saying that for those staying for extended periods, they would only change lin-
ens and towels once a week, things were pretty much
business as usual.

"I'm sure she will. And she has a great treatment team
behind her, too," Evie said. She meant it. Max and his
staff were good at their jobs and their reviews showed
it. Not that Evie herself put a lot of stock in those things.
After all, anyone could have an off day and either be
shorter than necessary with a patient, or too cautious
when it came to treatment.

"Well, thanks for that. But she has a good doctor in
you as well. If you hadn't found that mass on her lung,
who knows how long it would have been before it was
found. You may very well have saved her life."

"Well, mutual admiration society aside, let's keep on
trying to save her life."

"Not a question. We're all going to fight hard for her."
He glanced down the street and then back at her. "Do
you have room for some ice cream from Delacort? It's
just ahead."

She smiled. "Are you kidding. Delacort is my favorite spot. Their raspberry sorbet is to die for."

"I remember. I also remember the one time they ran out of it."

She laughed. "That wasn't one of my finer moments."

"You weren't rude. You just looked like you were going to burst into tears."

He remembered that? "Well then, let's hope they have some tonight, for both of our sakes."

He laughed and the sound sent a shiver over her. Maybe because she hadn't been sure she would ever hear it again. The urge to link her fingers through his made her curl her palm into itself until it was a fist. She wasn't going to risk doing anything that could be misconstrued. Especially not right after they'd kissed and made up.

Ha! No. Kissing could also be misconstrued. Even figurative kissing.

Instead, she took a deep breath of cool dry air and let herself enjoy simply being with him.

Delacort was a few stores ahead and although Vegas wasn't particularly renowned for its ice cream, it should be, she mused. Or at least this one store should be. It was churned fresh every day and if you happened to go in while they still had their machines going, the place was filled with wonderful scents of cream and sugar and the various flavorings.

The line wasn't too long and they were soon back on the street with their selections. Max's was in a little bowl, while her raspberry sorbet—which, thankfully, they had plenty of—was scooped into a chocolate-lined cone. The tip of the cone was also filled with chocolate and was so good when taking the very last bite of the confection.

"Yum." She took a small bite, and the fresh taste of fruit melted on her tongue, leaving it wanting more. "How's yours?" She glanced at him to see him smiling at her obvious enjoyment of her ice cream. "What? I don't get over this way very often. So it's a treat when I do."

"I know. And mine is as good as it always is."

"I can't believe you don't want it in a cone. But you never have, have you?"

"No. I never have. I like the ice cream all by itself."

Heading back the way they came, she happened to glance to the side and gasped before she could stop herself.

"What?"

"Oh, nothing. I just didn't realize that *Walter Grapevine* was showing here in Vegas."

"Walter who?" He looked so puzzled that she had to laugh.

"It's an off-Broadway musical I've been wanting to see. I was hoping it would come here."

"I've never heard of it."

She wasn't surprised. "It's a smaller production, but it's gotten rave reviews."

"I'll have to look it up."

The topic gravitated back toward the gala as they walked back toward the restaurant.

When they got there, he glanced at her. "Did you drive?"

"No. Darby and I both took a cab together—why?"

"I'll take you home."

"You don't have to. Really, Max, I'm out of your way."

He gave a light shrug. "Only by a few minutes. It's not a big deal."

The parking garage was just a block from the restaurant. Max paid the attendant and they waited as the car was brought up to them. "I'm sorry you ended up having to pay for parking when you didn't even get to eat."

"I had Delacort's finest. I can't complain."

She smiled. "Thanks again, Max. For being able to get past what happened."

"I could say the same for you."

The rest of the trip was made with the kind of small talk that Evie had missed. They talked about work and the gala, and just life. She gave him the address of the apartment she'd bought just after selling her and Brad's previous one. It was just a mile away from where she'd lived before and, despite the anger she'd felt at the time, she was thankfully free of memories that might have plagued her if Brad hadn't needed the funds from a quick sale. It had worked out for the best. And she was happy with the new place.

He pulled into one of the guest parking spots and turned to face her. "I'll let you know tomorrow about the DJ either before or after the biopsy."

"Sounds good. I have an appointment tomorrow after work to go look at the venue, just so I can see the space and find out when it'll be open to us to get the setup done. From what I can see we have a linen service, caterer, someone to set up the sound and a florist coming in. I'm pretty sure I understood that those companies were already contracted last year during the previous gala, but I want to make sure none of those changed. And since last year's coordinator moved to a new hospital, I'm not sure how much he can help us."

"Do you want me to come with you?"

"Do you have time?"

"I do. When does your shift end?"

She had to stop and think a minute. "Five o'clock or whenever I finish my rounds."

"How about if we meet in the lobby at five thirty? You can let me know if you get hung up."

"That works. You'll let me know, too, if it doesn't work?"

"I will."

With that, she said goodbye and stepped out of the car. He made no move to back out of the spot, so she started to walk toward the lobby of the apartment building, feeling his eyes on her with each step. He was just being polite, but it made her self-conscious, something it shouldn't have. Evidently, things hadn't gone completely back to the way they were before, but all she could do was give it time and hope that each day would bring a new sense of normalcy and friendship.

CHAPTER FIVE

SHE WAS UP THERE. Max could sense it. He didn't even need to look. He'd caught a hint of movement in the observation room around five minutes ago. She'd been held up with a patient right as the procedure was starting, but by the time he'd placed the camera for the video-assisted thoracoscopy he would use to perform the biopsy, he knew she'd made it.

He made the other two incisions he would use for his instruments and got back to work. They'd know pretty quickly what they were dealing with and if the mass was benign, he might even be able to get it out during this session. If it was malignant, they would need a PET scan to see where else it was and to help them figure out a treatment protocol.

Watching the screen to his right, he made his way to the tumor and used the grasping tool to hold a section of the lung while cutting off a small piece, then quickly moved in to cauterize the area. The danger with vascular tumors was they could hemorrhage, filling the surgical field with blood. Fortunately, it looked like he'd gotten all of the vessels. After pulling the sample free, he dropped it into the collection cup one of the nurses brought over.

"Can you get that over to the lab?" he asked, although he really didn't need to. She would know what to do.

"On my way."

Now, it was a waiting game to see if he closed her up or removed the tumor. This time he did glance up and saw he was right. Evie was up there. She nodded to him and he returned the gesture before turning back to his patient.

He had a piano concerto playing on the speakers, which was usually his music of choice during surgical procedures. It was soothing, with no distracting words to get tangled inside his head. Every surgeon had their own playlists, or none at all. He had one or two colleagues who wanted it completely quiet.

Ten minutes later, the nurse returned with a name. "Metastatic breast angiosarcoma."

Damn. There were times he just didn't want to be right. This was one of those times. He wasn't going to take the tumor out. And depending on the results of the PET scan...

Well, he would cross that bridge when he came to it. She would need to be in the hospital until the chest tube came out, probably a couple of days. And he would need to go out and talk with the family members who had come to the hospital. He knew her two adult children were here, but had no idea if Margaret had living siblings or not.

He glanced up at Evie and shook his head. Her eyes closed for a minute before she opened them and acknowledged his gesture. It was a damn shame that it couldn't have worked out in their favor. But you had to play the cards you were dealt. He'd learned that the hard way when his mom was taken from him. And then again when his dad drank himself into oblivion.

Both he and Evie were aware that with every patient who came across their paths, there was the possibility that a life would end and that there'd be nothing they could do to stop that death. And Max hated this part of the job. He hated even more that this patient was special to Evie, and that there was nothing he could do to change her odds of survival.

He checked to make sure there was no bleeding before he inserted the chest tube and withdrew the instruments he'd used to take the biopsy, then closed up two of the holes with a stitch or two and tightened the opening where the tubing was to keep it secure.

Then he made sure she woke up from the anesthesia without any problems before he started to head out the door. Margaret reached up with a shaky hand and squeezed his, making him swallow hard. He squeezed back. "I'll come check on you once they get you in your room, okay?"

She nodded, but didn't say anything. Not that he expected her to. He wouldn't tell her the results of the biopsy until she was truly awake and could understand what was going on around her.

Evie met him at the door. "You were right, weren't you?"

"Yes, but it doesn't make it any easier."

She leaned her shoulder against his for a second. "You're doing what you were trained to do, Max. You're not responsible for whether or not it's a good outcome."

Evie's voice was low and soothing, and he realized she was trying to comfort him. Shades of what his mom had done with his dad filtered through and he stood up straighter. "You don't need to tell me what I already know."

As soon as he said the words, he clenched his teeth. "Ah, God, I'm sorry, Evie. It just bites that things like this happen to people who don't deserve them."

"I know. And you don't have to apologize. I was trying to talk to myself as much as I was you. I wished for so much better for Margaret."

"We might not be able to take away the diagnosis, but we can do our damnedest to make sure her treatment gives her the best quality of life possible. I've never believed in extending life just to extend it, though, if those months are going to be lived in misery. I wouldn't want it for myself and I don't want it for my patients."

"I'm in complete agreement, Max."

"Do you want to come with me while I talk to the family?"

"Yes. Her kids will recognize me, and I went to Thanksgiving dinner at their house after Brad and I… Well, my parents were in Brazil visiting extended family at the time, and I didn't want to be alone so I accepted their invitation."

And Max had been too busy trying to avoid her—to avoid the complicated feelings that came along with her divorce—to recognize that she might have been lonely during those first holidays without her ex. She'd been staying with Darby, so he'd just assumed… He sighed.

"I haven't been a very good friend, Evie. I don't know why you put up with me."

Her head jerked to look at him. "I didn't say that to make you feel bad. It was more to let you know that I have a history with this family."

"I know. And somehow, that makes it worse. I'll try to do better."

She smiled. "You are. Just don't disappear from mine and Darby's lives again, okay?"

"I won't." It was a promise he hoped to hell he'd be able to keep. Especially as he'd made an impulsive purchase yesterday evening. He wasn't sure what he'd been thinking, or if she'd even go with him. He could always offer the other ticket to Darby and let them go together. But he truly wanted to make it up to Evie and he couldn't think of a better way to do that than to offer her something she loved. And while Darby had liked *Wicked*, she'd confessed that musicals really weren't her thing.

They got to the waiting area and presented a united front when talking to Margaret's family, telling them what they knew so far—that this tumor was aggressive and they needed to find out where else it might be hiding before coming up with a treatment plan.

When her son asked if this was terminal, Max nodded. "I'm afraid so, but I can't give you any more information until we've done some other testing."

As soon as those words were out in the open, brother and sister embraced, with Margaret's daughter breaking into tears. Evie went over and hugged each of them, then promised they would do all they could to keep Margaret comfortable.

After they left the room. Max stood in the hallway for a minute, his own eyes burning before he said, "I do have some more patients to see and I want to check on Margaret. What time is our tour of the venue?"

"At six, so we can meet in the parking lot at five thirty, like we planned. I can drive, or we can catch a taxi, whichever you prefer."

"You drive?" He gave a half snort. "The last time I was in a car with you, you nearly killed us both."

Her eyes widened. "Because some jerk came through a red light and nearly T-boned us. It was my quick thinking that saved you from being squashed like a bug."

"A bug, eh? Quite the opinion you have of me, Dr. Milagre."

"Just stating the facts."

It should seem strange that they could joke after that meeting with Margaret's family, but sometimes inviting some lighter moments in was the only thing that kept him going in the midst of difficult diagnoses. And he was thankful Evie had played along rather than chase the sadness that was Margaret Collins's case.

"Wow." It was the only thing Evie could think of to say as she stood in the cavernous room that would house the initial part of the gala. "It's hard to comprehend how big this room is when it's full of tables and chairs and decorations."

"It is pretty big." Max stood there, his hands shoved in his pockets, and glanced around. "I can see why they chose this place."

"Yeah, me, too."

Right now, the room was devoid of anything except for scaffolding, which was set up in the middle of the room. Some workmen were hanging what looked to be paper lanterns from the ceiling.

With walls that were off white with just a hint of green, the space was bright and airy, a large chandelier giving it an opulence that the hospital's courtyard couldn't match. But maybe it didn't have to. The two places had a completely different feel, but the hospital space would perhaps come across as somewhere that everyone could let their hair down and shrug off the cares of the day. Heaven knew that's what Evie used it for on an almost daily basis. In fact, as her divorce was dragging out, she'd spent many hours out there on one of the secluded benches, needing time to find herself again.

But getting away from the hospital grounds was proving to be nice, too. Margaret Collins's diagnosis had been heartbreaking, something that would haunt her for a while if the PET scans came back with the cancer in multiple places. At least here she could think about something else for a little while.

Really? Then why was it still running through her mind? She did her best to shake it off.

"I think I remember the buffet tables over on the right by the door. Probably because that allowed things to be refilled without staff having to drag food and drink carts through the seating areas."

"That makes sense," he said.

Movement out of the corner of her eye caught her attention. One of the workmen was straining to reach a lantern that was hanging askew, and was leaning way past the railing on the metal scaffolding. She shuddered. That was definitely not a job for the faint of heart. Evie was not a fan of superhigh places. Darbs had talked her into going on one of those drop towers and had said it wasn't as high as it looked from the ground. But it was. It was every bit as high. Once she'd gotten to the top, she'd been pretty sure she wasn't going to survive the plunge to the ground. She expected her heart to give out halfway down. It hadn't given out. But she had given Darby a piece of her mind. One look at her face must have told her something, because her friend had stopped laughing and hugged her instead. "I'm sorry, Evie," she'd said. "I didn't think you would be that scared."

But she had been. Almost as scared as she'd been when Darby had shown her those pictures of Brad and she'd realized that her life was about to radically change. The last year had been harder than she ever could have imagined, and while the betrayal had eroded her confidence in her ability to judge character, it had also caused her to grow stronger and more independent. And it looked like she and Max were on their way to mending their friendship. A silver lining, for sure. Only time would tell if it would last.

One of the hotel's staff came into the room and headed their way. "Do you have any questions? Or any special requests?"

Evie shook her head. "I can't think of anything at the moment." She glanced at Max, who shook his head.

"Well, if you do, please feel free to get in touch with me." The woman handed her a card.

"I will, thank you."

She left and Evie sighed. "Can you think of anything else we need to see?"

"Not off the top of my head, but then again, I haven't been to one of these events."

She grinned up at him. "Well, that's all about to change."

"I guess so." There was a pause and then he added, "Speaking of events, would you be interested in—"

Just then, she heard a shout from above her and glanced up just in time to see the scaffolding tilting to the side. The man who'd been leaning quickly moved back to the middle, but it did nothing to right the structure. Instead, like something out of a movie, it continued to tilt farther and farther, gaining speed as the legs on that side collapsed inward. Two of the men were clinging to the side boards, but one of them slid down the side and hit the ground with a loud thunk and lay there unmoving. Max hurried over to him, and as the same employee who'd talked to them a few minutes ago appeared in the doorway, Evie yelled, "Call 911!"

A cell phone appeared in the person's hand and she assumed she was calling for help.

Max was near the collapsed side of the structure, taking vitals, but when Evie glanced at the scaffolding, she realized if it fell farther, or boards started to rain down, they were going to land right on Max and the victim. And if those men holding on for their lives couldn't maintain their grip, they were going to have two more injuries, or worse.

"Hold on!" she yelled up to them. "Help is on the way."

At least she hoped it was. She made her way to Max.

"We need to move him. That thing could collapse completely and come down on both of you."

"His leg's broken at the very least, and I'm thinking he has head trauma. One of his pupils is blown."

She knew the dangers of moving someone with unknown injuries, but if the scaffolding continued to fail…

The sound of something mechanical caught her attention and she saw a small skid loader being driven into the room. The driver moved the vehicle to the collapsed side of the scaffolding and raised the mechanism so that it bolstered the structure. Smart. Maybe that would help hold it in place until help could arrive.

As if summoned out of thin air, two firefighters appeared in the doorway and immediately entered the room and assessed the situation. One of them nodded at the forklift operator. "Thanks."

Max continued to monitor the downed man as they waited for the EMTs to arrive.

The other firefighter moved to the far side of the scaffolding and called up, "Are you injured?"

Both of the men stated that they were okay.

"Is it safe to try to climb down?" one asked. "We don't want it to completely collapse."

"If you feel you can. If not, we have some harnesses being unloaded even as we speak."

One of the men swung his legs over the side and picked his way down diagonally. The second soon followed his lead, taking the very same path.

Evie held her breath as they continued down, but they both seemed sure about the placement of their hands and feet. When the first one got to the firefighter who'd spoken to them, he allowed himself to be helped onto the ground, where he sat down in a rush. The second firefighter had him put his head between his knees. Evie hurried over to them.

"How is he?" she asked the firefighter.

"Honestly? He's extremely lucky."

Squatting next to him, she took his pulse as the other man was helped off the structure.

Then the place was suddenly teeming with police and EMTs, who rushed in with their bags and each went to a different victim. But the men who climbed down were found to be in perfect condition, except for having the living daylights scared out of them. And this was nothing like the drop tower, because while Evie had been scared out of her mind, the rational side of her knew that she was in no real danger. These men, however? They'd known very well that they could die at any given moment. It gave her a hard dose of reality. In all her years of practicing medicine, that whole scenario of "is there a doctor in the house?" had never happened to her. Until now.

She asked one of the emergency services guys, "Which hospital are you taking them to?"

"Vegas Memorial."

Their hospital. "That's great. We're both doctors there."

"I thought I recognized you, although we normally deal more with the ER crew. Looks like it was lucky you were here when it happened."

She glanced at where Max had handed off his patient to another paramedic. She was glad she didn't have to do what these guys did on a regular basis. She was sure if she'd had to climb that scaffolding, she would have. But she was so, so thankful that it hadn't come to that.

She nodded at the forklift driver, who looked like he couldn't have been older than nineteen or twenty. "We were lucky that hotel staff member thought quickly and brought in the skid loader. He may have saved those two men from having the whole structure collapse."

"Agreed."

The EMT guy went over to speak to the man who was leaning against the wall, looking a little pale himself. He shook his hand and patted him on the back. It made Evie smile. She was glad he'd received a little recognition for his act. She doubted he would forget this moment. At least not for a very long time.

She knew she wouldn't, either.

She went back to stand by Max, and nudged him with her shoulder. "You okay?"

"Yes. I'm happy as hell we didn't have to make the decision to move him." The EMTs had stabilized the man's neck and slid a backboard under him.

"They're taking him to our hospital, so we should be able to check in and see how he's doing."

Max's phone pinged and he got it out to look at it. A second later, his lips twisted. "It's Margaret Collins. She's asking to go home."

Her heart cramped. She understood where the woman was coming from. If Evie thought she was going to die, she wouldn't want to be in a hospital, either. She'd want to go home to her own bed. "She can't. Not yet."

"No. That chest tube has to stay in for the next day or so. I need to go."

"I'll come with you. I think we've done everything we can here." Besides, she wanted to ask him what he'd been about to say to her before the scaffolding collapsed. Something about an event she might be interested in?

A police officer came over and asked if he could take a statement from one of them. She guessed she'd have to ask him later. Looking at Max, she said, "You go on. I'll stay here and talk to him."

"You sure?"

"Yes. Tell Margaret that I'll be there to see her in a little while."

"Will do. See you back at the hospital."

As she watched Max's strong back retreat through a doorway, she closed her eyes for a second. That had been so scary. And the thought of that heavy support structure collapsing on top of Max and the victim had rippled through her head and filled her with fear.

It would have been the same if had been Darby.

No, it wouldn't. She loved her friends dearly and would never choose one's life over the other's. But the thought of Max being severely injured or dying hit a visceral spot inside of her.

One that she knew existed, but that she tried to keep buried and out of sight. It was the same one that had held a tiny hope when he'd kissed her all those years ago only to have it snuffed out in an instant.

The police officer asked her a question and she shook off her thoughts and tried to concentrate on what he was saying, thankful for the distraction.

But what was going to happen when the distractions were all gone and she had time to think?

She didn't know. But she'd better figure it out before that happened, or she was going to get herself into a situation she didn't want to be in. And she had no doubt that Max wouldn't want her to be there, either. Because it would mean that she cared about him a little too much and in the wrong way, and that would not be good. For either of them.

CHAPTER SIX

EVIE ARRIVED JUST as he was getting ready to leave Margaret's room. He had talked her into staying until the drain tube came out, but just barely. She was in pain, which was understandable given the procedure she'd had. But it was also her breathing. She feared she was having an asthma attack and the nurse had refused to give her an inhaler without Max's permission. The nurse had evidently called when he'd been in the throes of helping their scaffolding victim, and he'd missed it. He couldn't imagine how scary it must have been to have had her meds withheld. But it wasn't the nurse's fault, either—she'd been following what the chart had said, and Max had wanted either he or Evie to check on her if her breathing problems got worse. And neither of them had been there.

But once he'd gotten to the hospital and had okayed a breathing treatment, Margaret felt a little better. But it was as if she knew her days were numbered and didn't want to spend the remainder of them in the hospital, despite the fact that both of her children were there with her.

He sat with her and shared that he wanted to get a PET scan and that would give them some more information.

It was a tricky balance of not giving the family false hope, but also not bringing down doom and gloom before they knew what they were facing. He might "think" he knew, but until he had the evidence to prove it, he tried to always err on the side of hope. At least whenever it was possible.

He paused just outside the doorway to share with Evie what had been said. When he finished, she nodded. "I would have done the same. I'll go in and visit with her and if she asks I'll reaffirm what you just said."

"Thanks. I'm going to see if our scaffolding guy has arrived yet. Do you want to be updated?"

She glanced at him as if in surprise. "Of course."

"Alright. I'll give you a call once I hear something."

"Sounds good. Thanks." She stopped him before he could leave with a hand on his arm. "Wait. What were you going to say to me at the hotel? Something about some event?"

Damn. In the chaos, he'd totally forgotten about the two tickets he'd bought for the musical. And the doubts he'd had about them going together had seemed to grow the more time that passed. "It was nothing."

"No, seriously. I want to know."

He shifted from one foot to the other. "I actually have two tickets to the musical you wanted to go to. And was wondering—as an olive branch for some of my less intelligent moments over the last couple of years—if you might like to go to it."

Her eyes widened. "Are you serious? You really want to go?"

"Why wouldn't I?" Actually he could think of a hundred reasons why it might not be such a good idea. But now that the words had been tossed into the universe, there was no way he could retract them.

"I wasn't sure if satire was your thing."

"If you decide to go with me, I guess we'll find out."

She laughed. "Well, in that case, I absolutely want to go. When is it?"

That was something he hadn't even given thought to. What if she had to work that night? He found himself hoping they could somehow make it work. "Next Tuesday night at eight."

"Really? That's perfect because I get off at five that night. It'll give me time to go home and change."

Her eyes were sparkling and he was suddenly glad he'd asked her. It made her happy to go, and that made him happy. And he wasn't sure why, other than what he'd said, which had been the truth. He did see it as a way of making up for being an absentee friend. He just hoped it didn't backfire on him. "Well, then that works out for both of us. Talk to you in a little while."

With that, he left the room and headed down to the emergency room, glancing at the courtyard as he crossed the atrium on the ground floor. The sun was out in full force and the sidewalk outside looked dry and parched, a sign that there still hadn't been a drop of rain in almost two months. It was good that what Evie liked to call the "after party" of the gala wouldn't begin at the hospital until after the sun had gone down and things had cooled off.

There would be no mist machines set up or temporary fountains or anything that involved water, since there was no end in sight to the restrictions that had been set in place. Nothing but a good long rain would remedy any of that. Even an ice sculpture, although not forbidden, would probably be frowned on by some of their bene-factors. Evie hadn't wanted anything that could be seen as wasting that precious resource.

When he glanced at the large television as he passed by, there was a report talking about the rain levels being much lower than normal, even for Nevada. They were hovering near the lowest recorded rainfall in the history of the state. The people in Las Vegas who'd opted to try to maintain lawns had found that even the smallest patches had turned brown. Some had decided to rip them up and turn to xeriscape landscaping instead, which had always been popular in desert climates. The hospital had been one of those places that had recently changed landscaping companies to focus on water conservation.

He sighed and kept moving. He'd been born and raised in Las Vegas and had never thought of moving, but some-times the reality of living here could be frustrating with the constant traffic and how busy the strip could be, but it was also full of life and laughter, and people who ex-ited the shows and casinos smiling. Those chapels of love were also a big draw for the area, probably pro-ducing some of the shortest-lived marriages in the his-tory of the US, but even those were fun and light. His parents had been married in one of those chapels, but theirs was one that had endured, at least until his mom's death had cut it short.

And why was he thinking of any of that? Their mar-riage wasn't one of the happy-ever-after stories from the pages of a storybook. And yet, they had been happy. At least until his mom's diagnosis.

Thankfully, the emergency room was bustling with activity and pulled him from his thoughts. He went over to the nurse's desk. "Any idea where the man injured in a scaffolding accident is?"

The nurse glanced at a computer screen. "He's actually in room one. Dr. Wilson is with him."

"Thanks." That was a good call. Todd Wilson was the head of neurology and a great doctor.

He headed over to the room and gave a quick knock before entering. Todd was leaning over the patient, whose eyes were actually open. The neurologist glanced his way. "Ah, Max. I hear you played hero today."

"No, Evie Milagre and I just happened to be in the right place at the right time."

He smiled. "That's not how I hear it. Grady here was just telling me that the rest of that scaffolding could have come down at any time."

Max moved closer. How had the patient even known that? He'd been unconscious at the time. He looked down at the man. "Glad to see you're awake. How are you feeling?"

"I have a massive headache." Grady's voice was rough-edged, probably from pain.

"I'm not surprised. That was quite some fall." Max glanced at his colleague with an unspoken question in his eyes.

"He's pretty lucky. He's got a big knot on the back of his head, and we're going to send him for a CT scan to make sure I'm not missing anything, but I think he's going to be okay."

"Thanks to you, Doc." Grady forced a smile. "Where's your lady friend? I'd like to thank her as well."

Oh, hell. Thank heavens Evie wasn't here to hear that. "She's actually a doctor here at the hospital as well."

"Oh, I thought you were at the hotel looking to see if it would work for your wedding reception. Sorry."

Todd's eyes twinkled. "Wedding reception, eh? Is there something I should know about?"

The neurologist no doubt knew exactly why he and Evie had been at the hotel. "You know my philosophy on marriage."

"Actually, I don't. Care to enlighten us?" He winked at the patient, who smiled.

"Not really. Suffice it to say I won't be visiting any of the area's wedding chapels anytime in the foreseeable future."

Just at that moment, Evie poked her head in the door. Great. This was all he needed. To have this little joke expanded on and dissected.

"I thought I'd come and check on him myself," Evie said. She came into the room. "I'm glad to see you're awake."

He nodded. "I'm glad to wake up and find I'm not sitting on a cloud playing a harp."

He was right. That scaffolding was heavy. If one of the pipes had broken free and landed on him, things might have turned out very differently. But it looked like this was one story that might have a happy ending. He was sure Todd saw his share of tragic outcomes himself, given the line of work he was in.

Evie came closer. "I'm glad you're not, either."

"So you're a doctor, too?"

"Yep. Evie Milagre, nice to meet you. I was there at the hotel as well. Dr. Hunt and I were looking at the venue for the hospital's gala."

Although it was normal to use titles in front of patients, it always seemed weird when Evie referred to him as anything other than Max. Or Maximilian, if she was feeling playful.

The man nodded before wincing. "I thought you were there for a different reason, but Dr. Hunt set us straight pretty quickly."

Her head tilted sideways, and Todd said, "He thought you and Dr. Hunt were getting hitched. Max jumped right on that and assured us that wasn't the case, nor would it ever be the case."

A strange look went through her eyes before she masked it with a smile. He frowned. It had to be a figment of his imagination. After all, she'd married Brad, and other than that kiss in front of the venue where *Wicked* had been playing, there'd never been any indication that she had any interest in him as anything other than a friend.

Except, then there'd been that second kiss, too. That one had thrown him for an even bigger loop. Because he'd been about to let things go a whole lot further than they had. And Evie certainly hadn't seemed opposed to that happening, either. At least not from the way she kissed him. There'd been a slow thoroughness to the way her mouth had molded itself to his. To the way her fingers had tightened their grip on him—as if she never wanted to let him go. It had set him on fire and made it almost impossible to pull away. But he'd had to. For both of their sakes. Because what he'd wanted out of that encounter had been purely physical. And Evie? He had a feeling she wanted more. More than he could give.

Her smile held steady. "Dr. Hunt and I have been friends for a very long time. But we wouldn't last two seconds as a couple." She gave a quick laugh.

What was that supposed to mean, that they wouldn't last for two seconds?

"That's right. Evie is far too picky and controlling for me."

After a second of no response, she finally made a face at him. "And you are far too overbearing and ridiculous for me."

"Oh, really?"

Evie thought he was overbearing? That was kind of a punch to the gut. But was it any worse than him calling her picky and controlling?

No. So maybe she felt like it was just as mean-spirited. But he'd been joking, choosing words that didn't describe her at all. Because the ones that he would have chosen in real life were the ones that made her hard to resist. Even for an old friend.

But he did want to explain that he didn't see her as either of those things, he'd just been trying to be funny in a not-so-funny situation.

He moved closer to her, so that he could shake Grady's

hand. "It's good to see you awake and in good spirits. Let's not have any more scaffolding accidents."

"Yeah, I think I'm going to keep both feet on the ground for the next couple of weeks."

"Good plan. Take care."

Grady nodded. "You, too, Doc. And thanks again."

"You're very welcome."

He went outside to wait for Evie, although he wasn't sure that was the best idea. Maybe he should just leave well enough alone. But he never wanted to hurt someone even unintentionally. And that look she'd given him…

A minute later, she came sailing through the door, throwing a comment behind her as it closed. Her eyes widened when she saw him there.

"Is something wrong? Margaret?"

There was something wrong, but this time it wasn't with Margaret.

"No, I just wanted to make sure you knew I was joking in there, earlier."

"Joking? About which part? About us never being a couple?" She crinkled her nose as if to show him that she was not serious.

"No, about you being picky and controlling. I don't think you're either of those things. It was meant to be funny, but as soon as the words left my lips, I realized they could be construed as something that I really think. I don't."

She nodded, eyebrows going up. "I assume you want me to say that I don't think you're overbearing or ridiculous?"

"It would be nice."

And just like that, their relationship had shifted back over to the fun friendship they'd always had. Except for the last couple of years, when things had gotten so weird. He was suddenly glad he'd gotten those tickets and that he'd asked her to go with him.

"Sorry, Charley. No can do."

He laughed. "Why did I know you were going to say that?"

"Because, like I said to Grady, we've known each other a very long time. And I need to prep you for that musical we're going to see."

"Yes, you do." He paused. "I'm glad you can go."

This time there was no mirth in her smile, but there was a sincerity that came through in her eyes. She touched his arm. "So am I, Max. So am I."

He glanced at his watch, almost sorry that he was due to see a patient in a half hour. "Sorry to seem overbearing and ridiculous, but I need to go."

"Sorry to seem picky and controlling, but so do I. See you around, Max."

With that, she walked away, and damn if it wasn't hard to look away from the curve of her butt as she retreated. But he forced his eyes up and turned, then strode down the corridor at a pace he hoped would leave the mental image of his hands sliding over that shapely derrière behind.

She and Max had a dinner meeting scheduled with Arthur Robbins in a half hour to discuss where they were with the plans for the gala, which was coming up in just over a month. It was hard to believe that much time had passed since they'd agreed to work on it together. She had to admit, it had brought them closer and had seemed to iron out the creases of neglect that had plagued their friendship over the last couple of years. Three weeks ago, she'd never have imagined they'd be going to the theater together.

She'd even purchased two new dresses. A blue cocktail dress for the theater and a long black sequined affair for the gala that was off the shoulder, but had a detachable chiffon mini train in back that just scraped the floor. She would definitely be removing that for the courtyard portion of the gala, so that it didn't get snagged on the concrete walkway. It had been years since she'd bought anything for the galas. She normally just recycled some of her old formals for the events. But she found she just wanted something new this time. And she wasn't sure why.

She was nervous about the meeting. Maybe because the other two times she'd gone to see Dr. Robbins, he'd always seemed underwhelmed by the hard work they'd done on the gala, even when she'd gone to him with Max's sketch. Oh, he'd said he liked it and wanted it to happen, but there'd been no warmth in his voice to back up his words. Was he really that cold?

She also found his choice of restaurants a bit odd. A pancake house. For dinner. Somehow, she couldn't see the formal CEO eating a stack of strawberry pancakes, so this should be interesting. She and Max were going to meet outside the hospital and walk the two blocks to the restaurant. As soon as she got outside the building, though, she started having second thoughts. It was blistering hot, and most of that heat seemed to be emanating from the blacktop. She was pretty sure her rubber-soled shoes were in danger of melting into the pavement.

She glanced around hoping to see Max so they could be on their way, when a car pulled up next to her. When the window rolled down, she realized it was the man in question. "Care for some air-conditioning?"

She closed her eyes in bliss as a hint of cool air drifted toward her from the open window. "Oh, God, yes, yes, yes!"

As soon as she opened the door and stepped into the chilly space, she realized her words could have come across as orgasmic. She let out a laugh. It wouldn't be too far off the mark.

"What?" he asked.

She cast about for an explanation for her ridiculous laugh and came up with a quick response. "I was mentally moaning that it was too hot to walk, and here you came with your already cooled car. It was as if you could read my mind." Actually, she was pretty glad he couldn't because she would be mortified. Just like she was about choosing the word *moaning*. What if those were both Freudian slips? Then she'd just have to make sure there were no more of those.

"I went out to the courtyard to kind of refresh my memory about the layout before the meeting and thought the same thing. That this heat is unbearable. It's why I don't jog during the day."

That's right. The man ran marathons. He'd dragged her to one of them years ago and she thought she was going to die. She'd been short of breath and had sweat buckets, even in the cool of the evening. "It's why I don't jog at any time. Day or night."

"You haven't given running a chance."

"Yeah? Well, it didn't give me much of a chance when I tried it that one time."

His mouth twisted, as if he was amused, then he pulled away from the curb. "I should have insisted we train together, then you would have been fine."

Train together? She was pretty sure that wouldn't have gone any better. Because she would have just stared at his legs and physique, and probably ended up tripping over something and winding up on the ground in an ungraceful heap of sweatiness, which Max would never be able to unsee.

"I'm pretty sure I'm not cut out to run, training or not."

Maybe it was like Max, who'd once told her he wasn't cut out to be married. It was after he'd kissed her after the showing of *Wicked*. And it could have been construed from his reaction that she'd been looking for a proposal. She definitely had not. But she certainly hadn't expected him to overreact to the point that he made it seem that being with her in that way was the most hideous thing he could imagine. She'd been glad when he'd stayed away from her for a while. But then she'd missed him. And ended up regretting what had happened as much, or almost as much, as he'd seemed to.

But at least there was none of that today. In fact, over the last month they'd seemed to have drifted back into their old pattern of friendship. Margaret had gone home and at their appointment a few days ago, she'd seemed to be feeling better. She even acted like she was looking forward to starting treatments next week.

The PET scan had not revealed any lesions in her brain or liver, but had found one in her right breast and a mass in her lung. Chemo, while it wouldn't be curative, could help extend her life while maintaining the quality of it, hopefully for a few more years, depending on how the tumors reacted. But the hope was that they'd shrink enough that they could both be removed through surgery. The chance of recurrence was high, since the cells had already traveled once and were likely to again, but maybe they could keep that from happening for a long while.

He glanced her way. "Well, I certainly wouldn't recommend starting in the middle of the summer."

"Starting what?" Surely, he hadn't read her mind about Margaret.

"Running."

Oh! She'd forgotten that's what they'd been talking about. "I wouldn't recommend my starting it any time of the year. I'll stick to hiking. But you're right. Nothing seems very appealing when it's this hot. I wasn't looking forward to walking to the restaurant."

"Me, either. Speaking of which, we're here." He turned into the lot and they got out of the car and walked into the entrance of the restaurant.

"I wonder if he's here yet."

At that moment, Dr. Robbins came around the corner from the dining area. "I wasn't sure you saw me in there, so thought I'd come over and show you where our table was."

There were only three of them, but the CEO had evidently chosen a large corner booth at the very back of the restaurant. The table could have held double their number, but maybe it was just so they could have some privacy.

They sat down. Evie ended up sandwiched between Max and Dr. Robbins, which was kind of awkward. But at least the CEO was sitting on the other side of where the table formed an *L* so they weren't side by side. The former plastic surgeon intimidated her, for some reason. Then again, she'd heard rumblings from others that she wasn't alone in that feeling.

Just in case, she'd brought her spiral-bound notebook with all of the vendors' names and numbers and had hunted down pictures from last year's gala, since the decor was being done by the same company, who said they would make it almost identical to the previous gala. She figured it was better to play it safe, since having part of it at the hospital was already changing things up quite a bit.

He motioned for a member of the waitstaff. "I've already ordered."

Evie glanced down at her watch as surreptitiously as possible. They were still fifteen minutes early. How long ago had the man arrived? A tickle of dislike made the back of her throat itch. She cleared her throat to banish the sensation, trying to tell herself he wasn't trying to make them feel small and unimportant. But, trying or not, he was. And she didn't like it.

He waited until they'd ordered their meals before saying anything else. "Thanks for coming. I just wanted to see where we were and ask if there's anything you need me to do before the event. I collected the sign-up sheets and see a lot of our folks are planning on being at least here for the hospital portion of the gala."

Evie had wondered where those sheets had gone. One minute they'd been up, and yet when she went to gather them this morning, she'd found they were already gone. So he had her at a disadvantage, since she hadn't actually seen them yet. "I'm glad of that. Max and I went to see the venue last week and it looks like it'll be plenty big to handle the guest list. If I could look at those sign-up sheets, I would appreciate it, just so that I can get the final numbers to the caterer." The sheets had a place to check whether or not the staff members would attend both events—the hotel venue and the hospital—or just one, or neither. She was surprised Robbins wouldn't have realized that she would need them.

"Of course." He pulled out his briefcase and handed her a sheaf of papers. "If I could get those back afterward, I would appreciate it."

That made her frown even as she promised that she would return them. What did he actually need them for? Was he going to keep track of attendance or something? If so, that rankled and the tickle grew stronger. Really, it was none of her business how he ran the hospital. But if he was going to treat the staff like preschoolers that would not go over well with the nurses' union or any other job representatives.

Their drinks came out and so did Dr. Robbins's meal. "Sorry, I have another meeting in an hour, do you mind if I start?"

When she hesitated, Max's leg pressed against hers,

reminding her that she was the head of the committee. "Of course not, go ahead."

As he ate, she and Max shared what they'd gotten done from their prospective lists. And she was proud of both of them. They'd worked hard and had completed everything that could be done at this time. All that was really left to do was to finalize the numbers with the caterers and get a copy of Dr. Robbins's speech for the sound people in case he needed a teleprompter. But when she asked, he set down his fork and fixed her with a look. "I actually try not to give those out in advance, or at least not until the legal department takes a look at it. Just in case something gets leaked that shouldn't be."

Although he wasn't accusing her directly, it still bothered her that he would say something like that. They'd each done their jobs well and had given him reports without anyone fearing that something untoward would be done with those reports. But again, maybe something had happened in the past that made him leery of trusting anyone. But he would eventually have to trust his staff, or else he was going to find working at Vegas Memorial very uncomfortable.

"Will we be able to get a copy at all? The reason I'm asking is that we can have a teleprompter set up if you would like one."

Their last CEO had treated the staff more like family, and most of those people were still here. If the atmosphere changed too drastically, she could picture a mass exodus, making the hospital a shell of what it had been under Morgan Howard's term. She wondered if Morgan was keeping up with the goings-on at the hospital or if he was just content to go about his retirement with nary a thought about any potential problems crossing his mind. She kind of hoped it was the latter. She didn't think he'd like the direction things were now taking. In fact, she didn't, either. But she wasn't the one in charge.

Dr. Robbins finished his bite and then leveled another look at her. "No teleprompter needed. Do you need a copy other than for that?"

Max again pressed his knee to hers as if sensing her blood pressure was shooting through the roof. And it was. But he wasn't the only one who could keep a level head. She could be as civil as the next person.

"No. No need."

When he set down his napkin, she wondered if he had heard the undertones of her response without her being aware they were even there. But if so, he didn't mention it. "Well, I'm off to my next meeting. Thanks for all your work on the gala. The hospital thanks you and will pick up the tab for your meals."

Oh, you mean the meals in the place that you chose for this meeting?

But, of course, she didn't say that, just smiled and thanked him back, as did Max, who seemed a lot more sincere than her words had been.

Then he was gone, leaving his empty plate and a bad taste in Evie's mouth.

"What a dick." Her half-muttered words made Max laugh.

"Tell me what you really think."

She rolled her eyes at him. "I think Darby has the right

idea about being her own boss. That's looking pretty attractive right now."

Their food came out and was placed in front of them, while the waitress whisked away Robbins's empty plates.

She glanced at Max. "Any thoughts?"

"None that I'd better voice aloud."

She relaxed, scooting away from him a bit so he had more room to eat, since the CEO was gone. His eyebrows went up, but he didn't say anything.

She thought he'd be glad to have a little more elbow room, so why did he look just the tiniest bit perturbed? But she wasn't going to ask. She was glad Darby wasn't here. That woman was an expert at cataloguing facial expressions and would have been sure to let her know what they meant.

She rolled her eyes even at the thought of having that conversation. But for all of Darby's quirks, they got along great—she was fun and loved to go out for a night on the town. Whereas Evie liked staying at home and relaxing, for the most part. But they balanced each other out and they were all for compromising.

It was one of the problems she and Brad had had, because he wasn't happy spending a lot of time just chilling with a glass of chardonnay and whatever show she happened to be binge-watching. And he didn't like compromising, so Evie had often forced herself to go out for a night on the town or to a casino with him, even when she was tired and grumpy after a long day at work. Instead of each giving and taking, she often found herself on the giving side, growing more and more resentful each time she gave in.

Maybe she'd contributed to him looking elsewhere, but if he'd been that unhappy with their relationship, he should have come to her and talked to her about it. But he hadn't. Instead he'd put in longer and longer hours "at the office." One she'd come to discover he no longer had. And those long hours? Well, they hadn't really been about his job at all.

She shook off the thoughts. "So do you think we'll even get a copy of that speech?"

"I'm actually wondering if he's even written it yet. There's just something about the way he avoided the subject that struck me as more than being worried about leaks or the legal department."

"Well, that's just great. But why? This is his chance to show what a good leader he is and that he can be trusted with their donations. You'd think he'd be anxious to prepare for that. Instead he acts like he's more worried about how we're going to make *him* look."

Max shrugged. "We did our part. And since he couldn't think of anything to criticize or recommend, I'm going to assume he's happy with how things are set up. Now, it's up to him to be a voice the hospital can be proud of."

He'd said it well. And frankly, Evie *was* worried about what he was going to say. The reason past donors had given so freely was due to the warm and caring manner in which Howard conducted himself. If Dr. Robbins hoped to compete with that, he was going to need to step up his game and adopt some of that warmth. He might be an excellent administrator, but the jury was still out on whether or not he would be a good boss. She was surprised the hospital board hadn't pinned him down about what he was going to say. Or maybe he'd given them a copy and she and Max were the only ones he didn't trust with it.

Whatever it was, she could only hope things would go smoothly with the gala. All of it.

She pushed away her plate. "Well, I think that does it for me. Can you think of anything else that needs to be done?"

"Nope. Are you headed home or back to the hospital?"

"Home. I got off work a few minutes early to go to the meeting."

"Great. Do you have time to make a quick pit stop on the way back to the hospital, since your car is still there?"

"Sure? I'm assuming it's not a bathroom break since there's one here in the restaurant."

"Nope, not the bathroom. I'll tell you about it on the way."

CHAPTER SEVEN

MAX WANTED HER opinion on the playlist the DJ had sent him. But rather than just show her the list, he wanted to take her to hear some selections from it so she could get the flavor of the music. The songs would be piped throughout the courtyard, but the booth would be set up behind the temporary dance floor, so that people would feel free to dance or to sit around and watch as others danced the night away.

In the fifteen minutes that it took to get to his friend's little out-of-the-way studio, she didn't say much. Until they arrived and the sign out front proclaimed that this was where DJ Electric Nights was located.

"Oh! I've heard of him. *He's* the friend you were talking about? Why didn't you say so at the meeting?"

"Dr. Robbins isn't the only one who doesn't tell everything he knows. Besides, the guy is from New Jersey, so I doubt he even knows who Dale Night is, or would recognize his stage name."

"His name is Dale? I didn't know that. He always seems so mysterious with that mellow voice and those playlists he comes up with on his show. I can't believe you got him on such short notice."

DJ Electric Nights also had his own radio show, which

made him one of the most sought-after DJs in Vegas. The right side of Max's mouth quirked up. "Fortunately, he had his vacation scheduled for that week, so he's just pushing it back one day for us."

"Oh, I feel bad that he's going to miss vacation time."

"Believe me, I'll owe him. Probably my football season tickets. He hasn't decided yet."

That made her laugh. "That hits you where it hurts."

"But it'll be worth it, won't it? Dale's worth it."

"Of that, I have no doubt." She leaned over and gave him a hug. "Thank you, Max. This means a lot to me. And to the hospital."

She pulled away just before his arms came up to go around her. An instinctive move, but one that he probably shouldn't act on. It was bad enough that he'd wanted to at all. And yet he did. Seeing the happiness on her face when she heard who his DJ friend was made things warm up inside of him.

"You're welcome. Shall we?" He motioned toward the studio.

"Oh, absolutely. Just kick me if I start salivating."

That made his jaw tense. He knew that Dale had this effect on a lot of the women who crossed his path, but somehow the thought of Evie being one of those women made him uneasy and he wasn't sure why. Maybe because she said she'd sworn off marriage and Dale was newly divorced, like she was.

That didn't mean anything. Lots of people got divorced. They didn't marry the next person that crossed their paths, though. Not that either of them were. Dale was also of the no-more-marriage camp. So even if Evie were taken with him, it wasn't likely to be reciprocated. At least he hoped not. Again, why it would even matter was beyond him.

Wasn't that the way he'd been about Brad? Except that Dale was a good guy, and Max had never had a good feeling about Evie's ex. Something that had turned out to be true.

And if she really did like Dale?

Then it was none of his business.

They got out of the car, and headed toward the door. Before they could get there, it flew open and a man bearing a slight resemblance to Jason Momoa stepped out. He wasn't as broad as Momoa, but his stage presence was every bit as striking as that of the actor. And Dale knew it and used that to good effect.

"Max! So good to see you." The man peered past his friend. "But who is this? Don't tell me you have a *girl-friend*?" His friend's eyes were trained on Evie with an interest that made Max tense further. He knew that look. It was on the tip of his tongue to lie and say that yes, he and Evie were involved. But then, he'd have a lot of explaining to do afterward. And that was one conversation he could do without.

"No. No girlfriend. But she is a friend. A *good* one." He tried to inject a subtle note of warning in there, but Dale had never been good at subtle. It was one of the things people found so endearing about him. "Dale Night, meet Eva Milagre."

Dale gave her a slow smile. "Oh, *miracle*. Very nice name. I think I'll call you my miracle girl."

Evie laughed, and it set Max's teeth on edge.

His friend went on. "You came at just the right time. I need *you*, Eva, to listen to a song from the playlist and tell me if I should include it. Or lose it."

"Oh, but I'm sure I don't know anything about playlists or how they're chosen."

"That makes you the perfect person to give me an opinion. I'll show you the ones I already have on the list. The one I'm on the fence about is very different as far as genre goes, but I think the message is perfect for the night." He pointed both of his thumbs at himself. "And *this* Night."

Evie actually giggled again, the sound light and magical. What wasn't magical was Dale calling her his miracle girl. He'd become somewhat of a serial dater since his divorce, but there wasn't much of a chance of him dating Evie. At least, Max hoped not. As far as he knew, she hadn't gone out with anyone since her divorce.

And if she chose Dale to be the first? Hell, what did he do if that happened?

Nothing. You sit back and let it happen.

Like he'd done with Brad?

Every time he'd seen Evie and her ex together, it had made a screw tighten in his gut. The sensation had grown so unbearable that he'd eventually stopped accepting invitations to things where he knew the pair would be. Which meant that his and Evie's friendship had suffered. And in the end, she'd been hurt terribly by someone who was supposed to love her.

That same screw was beginning to turn inside of him. Why now? Just when they were starting to get back on track.

All he knew what that bringing her here might have been a huge miscalculation on his part. He'd hoped she'd be impressed, but this went way beyond that. But he couldn't very well rip her away and say they were leaving. Because she and Dale would both want an explanation for why he was acting that way, and he had none. Not even for himself, since he had no idea where this feeling was coming from. Or what it even was.

They went into the studio and neon lights surrounded them. They were one of DJ Electric Nights's gimmicks. He took a neon light to each gig he had, and whichever one he chose, it was the theme for the music of the evening. Whether it was Lovers in Peril or Love Overcomes or Lovers Inc. Every show he did had a calling card that was a play on words, just like the playlist he selected.

He pointed to one of the lights on the far wall and Max's fingers clenched at the words on it. It said Friends to Lovers with an artistic heart added after the words. Yeah, that was not going to be the theme of the gala, if Max could help it. But Dale was doing him a favor. And if he suddenly overruled the man on his lighting choice, he was going to ask why, and that wasn't something Max was going to admit to under threat of death. Although it was better than Strangers in the Night, right? Maybe, but not by much.

Max had fantasized once or twice about what it might be like to make love to Evie—okay, make that fifty or sixty times—but he wasn't willing to risk what they had on something that couldn't be permanent. It would be the same thing if he was fixated on Darby and acted on that fixation. Things between them would change. They would have to.

And if Dale and Evie spent the night together?

Not something he wanted to think about right now. Or pretty much ever. The last thing he wanted was for her to be hurt again.

Was that all it was?

He chanced a glance at her. She was gazing at his friend expectantly. *Ah, hell.* Why had he even mentioned having a friend who was a DJ?

"Isn't anyone wondering why I might have chosen that as the theme?"

"Theme?" Evie blinked as if coming back to awareness.

Dale laughed. "Okay, well, I'll tell you even if you aren't wondering. This is a fundraiser, right? Where you're hoping that people will be coaxed into donating for the good of the cause. *Right?*"

The emphasis on that last word told Max that his friend was waiting for a response.

He forced himself to answer. "Yes. That's the hope."

"Well, then all of those who aren't already involved with the hospital financially are friends who are basically coming to play dress-up and eat some great food. But the hope is that they'll go from being *friends* to being *lovers*. Let's call it a subliminal message."

Evie laughed. "Aren't those illegal?"

"All music at its heart, Miracle Girl, carries subliminal messages. Even orchestral music with no lyrics. Even the scores to movies. They're all meant to elicit an emotional response—in other words, they hope to move a listener to react in a certain way."

"True," she admitted.

"And *we* hope that listeners at this gala react by opening their pocketbooks and donate to something that gives back to the community in ways that go far beyond its exceptional health care."

Despite his uneasiness, that explanation made sense in a way that Max couldn't argue with. It had gone from a knee-jerk response about Max thinking about how it would be if he and Evie spent the night together, to seeing how carefully his friend had crafted a message for the event. He didn't realize how much work Dale put into these gigs.

As long as he didn't let his job venture into more personal territory.

As if waiting for something more, he turned to Max. "What do you think? Do you think it'll work?"

"I think it will. And we honestly need any help we can get this year."

Evie came over to stand beside him. "That we do."

They glanced at each other, and at her nod, Max saw that she'd had the same thought he had. That the new CEO was going to make it tough to get new sponsors. It actually made him relax a little bit. Maybe all of her attention hadn't been on Dale after all.

And if Dale could inject the warmth that Dr. Robbins lacked, maybe it wasn't going to be as much of a disaster as he'd feared.

"Well…" Dale spread his arms wide. "I'll give you any help I can muster. Now, let's look at the playlist and then I'll tell you about the outlier that's begging me to include it."

He put the list on the table and Max saw that it was a good mix of pop, rock and some lighter ballad-type songs. Most all of them dealt with love of some type. But then a lot of songs had love at the heart of their message. There were a couple of things that Max didn't recognize and Dale played those for them. One was a tearjerker ballad of regret and Max nodded, trying to see the choice through the eyes of the DJ. "The regret of not giving?"

"You got me, man. That's definitely the message for anyone who's hesitating."

Max put a hand on the man's shoulder, relaxing even more. "I've got to hand it to you. There's a reason you're the best in Vegas."

The man's head went back as if shocked by the words. "Just Vegas?"

That made Max laugh. "A little humility might do you some good."

"How about you, Miracle Girl, do you think I'm lacking in that department?"

Max noticed she hadn't said very much, but had instead listened to Dale give his spiel. That Miracle Girl thing bothered him, though. And he wasn't sure why.

"Do you want my honest opinion?"

"I do."

Max would have expected Dale to look a little less confident, but if anything, he had a half-expectant smile on his face. One that he kind of wished he could wipe off. All he could hope for was that Evie was going to knock him down a peg or two.

"I think you're kind of a genius."

Max could feel his eyebrows crunch together, even while the DJ's arms spread wide again.

Far from knocking him down to size, she'd just added to the man's overinflated ego.

"And there it is. Humility, huh?" Dale said. "She can see where I'm going, even if you, my friend, can't. But you will. When you see those dollars pouring in."

What if she really did start dating the man? How would he feel then?

He groaned internally. He felt just like he had when she'd started dating Brad. All he could hope was that it didn't happen. And so he wanted her to be alone? No. But he also knew that Dale wasn't going to give her what she needed. Especially not after what Brad did to her.

"Well, I hope you're right about those dollars." He glanced at Evie. "Are you about ready?"

He hadn't meant to add that last part, it had somehow just slipped out. But now, Evie and Dale were both looking at him like he had two heads. Maybe he did. And one of them was taking exception to what was happening in this room.

He finally put a name to the feeling that was jabbing him in the gut. Jealousy.

Oh, hell to the no.

That's not what it was. It couldn't be, because that would mean…

It would mean nothing. And it would *change* nothing. Max didn't want a relationship. Not even with Evie. No… *especially* not with Evie. He wanted their friendship to go on exactly like it had over the last few weeks and in the years before her marriage. It had been fun and easy, at least for the most part. He was just being protective of her, that was all.

By admiring her body when she moved, or hoping she'd throw a little extra attention his way?

Like she was at Dale?

No. He wasn't hoping for that. Because—again—he didn't want a relationship.

"I still haven't played the outlier," Dale said.

Right now, the only outlier Max saw was himself. And he really didn't want to be played. Not by Dale. And not by Evie.

"What is it?" Evie asked.

He handed her a piece of paper. "You two read it. And tell me if the lyrics fit the situation or not. Then I'll explain my dilemma."

Max started reading and every muscle in stomach that wasn't already knotted went tight. The song talked about being let down so many times before. About being tired of getting hurt. About being tired of searching for answers.

The words could have been lifted straight out of his childhood. About his mom's death and his dad's descent into alcoholism. And his own pain and the hopeless anger he'd felt. And at the heart of it, the inability to change any of what had happened.

And then the chorus kicked in about someone special walking into the singer's life and how it had made a change for the good and how the person had transformed his life. It ended with saying she was his best friend.

He swallowed hard, and the jealousy he'd been feeling

toward Dale seemed to fade away. Because right now, he had bigger concerns. Namely, not seeing himself and Evie in those lyrics. They were just words written by some writer and sung by a random artist. He couldn't even put a tune to the words as he didn't know if he'd ever heard the song before.

Evie glanced up. "Wow. I know this song. And it *has* to be included."

"Ah…okay, Miracle Girl. Tell me why."

"I just think a lot of people will be able to relate to the message. I mean how many of us have been let down by people we care about? I know I have."

He swallowed. She had been. And not just by Brad. Max had let her down as well.

Her soft voice went on. "But then along comes someone who makes us believe that not everyone is like that." She shrugged. "Can't it be said of corporations as well? That we've all been let down by a business or other entity. But then along comes one that goes above and beyond and makes us believe that there's goodness in the world after all. That not every person and business is out for themselves."

Max nodded. He could see her point, and it sounded exactly like what Dale had talked about. How he wanted to make people believe that they were doing the right thing by giving to the hospital. And they would be. They could help more folks who, for some reason or other, couldn't afford medical care.

Dale smiled, a very broad smile that said Evie had given him exactly what he'd wanted to hear. "And that is why I wanted your opinion and exactly what my dilemma is. You say you know this song. What genre is it?"

Evie didn't hesitate. "Country and western."

"Yes! So will it sound off for it to be mixed in with all the others?"

She seemed to think for a minute. "I think the singer is well enough known that a lot of people will recognize it. I'm sure the song has been played at countless weddings at these little chapels around here. It's not an outlier."

Dale steepled his fingers and regarded her, and then he went over to his computer and tapped some keys, before stepping away. The sound of a printer starting up made Max turn to look at a long shelf where several machines were set up. A piece of paper came spitting out of one of those machines, then a second sheet, then a third. Dale went over and collected the pages.

"One for my friend Max. One for me. And one for my Miracle Girl, who gets me."

Evie smiled. "Glad I could help."

Yeah, Max was glad she'd been able to help, too, but if he heard the term Miracle Girl one more time he was going to tell the DJ exactly what he thought of him.

No, he wouldn't. Because for one, he liked Dale. The man had a good heart. Plus, if he said anything, Evie would want to know what was going on with him. And he did agree with them both about including the song. At least the business side of him did. The personal side of him said it was a very tricky business, which could get him into a lot of trouble. Because he knew himself well enough to know he was going to go home and play that song. And then it was going to wander around in his head until after this damn gala. And then, all he could hope was that he never heard it again.

But until then, he was stuck with it. And he had a feeling even if he objected to the tune being on the list, it was going to do no good. It was two against one, which made Max almost want to laugh. Because he didn't have to wonder long to realize that he really was the outlier in this mix. And he didn't like the way that made him feel. At all.

Max stopped in front of her apartment building and turned to smile at her. It was weird, because technically, the curving of his lips could be considered a smile, but it looked more like a pained grimace. In fact, he'd been strangely silent ever since they left his friend's house and she wasn't sure why.

She'd been wildly happy about what the DJ hoped to accomplish by letting his playlist get his message out. And she was pretty sure that every DJ gave an intro here and there to a specific song, or talked about the occasion, whether it was a wedding or birthday party or whatever. He would try to hammer home his message. And from everything she had witnessed, he was going to be successful at it. Who could resist that low sexy voice?

Her lips twisted. Actually, it looked like she could. He'd gotten her alone, while Max was looking at some equipment behind his desk, and asked her to go out with him. She'd had to tell him no, as gently as she could, and she wasn't sure why. Darby had been after her to get back into the dating scene, and Evie had been trying her best to start thinking in that direction. But when it actually came down to acting on her words, she'd chickened out.

DJ Electric Nights would have been the perfect person, because she had no doubt that he was a casual dater who went out with a lot of different women, sleeping with some of them and not sleeping with others. But there was no doubt that when a woman was out with him, he would make them feel like the most special girl in the world.

And God, she needed to feel that way. But she was scared to. And despite her words to Max a couple of weeks ago about not wanting to be in a relationship, the thought of going out with someone who would simply move on to the next person after their time together was done didn't sit as well with her as she'd hoped it would.

In fact, it didn't sit well at all. Maybe because that's exactly what Brad had done. Moved on to the next person. And she was pretty sure nothing was going to change her mind, which was why she should thank her lucky stars that the kiss she'd initiated with Max had been summarily rejected. What if it hadn't been? What if they'd slept together and he'd simply gone on, as if it had meant nothing to him?

She would be devastated.

Which is why she was not going to bed with him.

No, but she would be going to a musical with him in a few short days. What had made him get those tickets? Did he feel sorry for her?

She blinked back to awareness, realizing they were still sitting in front of her place and she'd made no move to get out. Did he think she was expecting a kiss?

Oh, God. She snapped open the mechanism that would allow her to get out of the car and practically fell to the ground in her haste to escape.

"Are you okay?"

"Of course. You?" She couldn't help throwing the question back at him, because he'd seemed to find too much pleasure in watching her try to roll gracefully from the passenger seat. She'd stuck the landing at least.

He turned to look at her. "Can I say something?"

"Sure." Although she wasn't sure she wanted to know what it was that he wanted her to do.

"Be careful around Dale. He dates a lot of women."

She blinked, trying to digest his words before the meaning hit her. "You don't think I can figure that out? I've seen articles about him. I know he's been divorced and that he dates a lot. But I'm not sure what business it is of yours."

"So you're going."

"What?" She stared at him. "What are you talking about?"

"I know he asked you out. When he mentioned the vinyl he had under his desk, I was pretty sure that was just a ruse."

She crossed her arms over her chest and bent down to peer inside the car, wanting to see his expression. "You're right. He did. What of it?"

"I just don't want to see you hurt." His low, gritty voice diffused some of the anger she felt over him acting like he could tell her what she should or shouldn't do.

"I'm not some fragile mouse who can't stick up for herself, Max. And for your information, I'm not going. I knew who he was the minute I met him. But that doesn't mean that I didn't enjoy him flirting with me."

"Flirting? Really?" The faux shock in his voice made a trickle of amusement go through her. "Flirting with Miracle Girl?"

She laughed, suddenly not offended anymore. Max wasn't just being nosey and giving her unwanted advice. He was concerned, and she appreciated that concern, even if it wasn't necessary. "I thought that was rather clever, didn't you?"

When Max didn't say anything, she climbed back into the car so she could face him on his level. "He didn't mean anything by it, Max. It's all part of his persona. I'm sure every person who steps into his studio is presented with the same one-dimensional caricature of his stage name."

"But you bought it. Told him you thought he was a genius."

"I wasn't lying about that. I do think he's a genius, when it comes to what he does—how meticulous he is about preparing for each job. But that doesn't mean I want to go out with him. Yes, it would be fun and exciting, but it could only be taken at face value. I think Dale has problems separating his stage presence from who he is outside of his job. And that's okay. It makes him happy. But when and if I ever decide to date again, I don't want it to be an act. Even though I'm not interested in marriage at this point in my life, I still want things to feel real and important to whoever I'm out with. I don't like games. I never have. So it's a lot, and not even I am sure of what I hope to get out of dating someone. After Brad it's…well, everything is jumbled in my head."

He linked his pinkie with hers for a second and squeezed before letting go. "You don't owe me any explanations. And I'm sorry for intruding. I just…" He shrugged, his voice dropping off in a way that touched her.

"It's okay. I know I don't owe you an explanation. I just didn't want you to think I'd been taken in by anything Dale said or did. Because I wasn't." She reached across and touched his face. "But thank you for being the good friend that you are. It means the world to me that you care enough to not want to see me hurt."

She wasn't prepared for the rough stubble that met her fingertips. It was earthy and real and made her shiver. Made her want to know what it would feel like in the morning after a long night of…

She pulled away, suddenly feeling shaky and uncertain. What had that been? That sudden awareness of him as a man, and not simply as a friend. She'd felt it before, but this was… She was not going to analyze it. She was just going to get out of the car and walk up to her apartment. While she still could. "Well, anyway, thank you."

She started to leave only to have him grab her hand and stop her, his eyes holding hers for a long minute before letting her go. "You're welcome, Evie. Have a good night."

"Y-you, too." With that, she got out and closed the door. With one more look through the window, she gave him a little wave and then walked away as fast as her shaky legs could carry her.

* * *

"That was so good, Max. Thank you for getting the tickets."

"You're welcome. It was fun."

They'd decided to go to Delacort's after the musical, and strolling down the street was reminiscent of the last time they'd gotten ice cream from the place. Only this time, both of them were dressed up. And when he'd seen Evie come to the door in that teal dress, his mouth had gone dry.

Dressing for the theater in Las Vegas meant just about anything went. Ranging from jeans to formal-wear, people basically wore whatever they felt like. And her dress...

The dress was cut so that her shoulders were bare, and it clung to her curves in a way that turned heads—he found that he'd had trouble looking at where he was going. And yet, Evie seemed relaxed and happy and to-tally unaware of all of that. Maybe because of the show. The musical satire had been both witty and subtle, and the actors had truly been good at what they did.

Max had expected things between them to be a lot more stilted than they'd ended up being. When she'd touched him in the car a few days ago, he hadn't wanted her to get out. He'd wanted to pull her close and hold her in his arms in a way that had nothing to do with friend-ship. And hell, he'd listened to that song that Dale had chosen for the gala and then had to play it again before turning it off with an irritated sigh.

"It's a shame that Darby isn't a big fan of live enter-tainment. I think she would have liked this."

Probably, he thought, but right now, Max was glad to have Evie to himself. Seeing her at Dale's had been a wake-up call. Someday she might find that special someone and they would lose their connection again. To hope that it might not happen was not only improbable, but also downright selfish. It would be the same if Darby started dating someone seriously. Most of her time and energy would go to whomever she was in love with. It was the way of the world. Except no matter how many times he told himself that was the case, he knew deep down it wasn't. It had been different when Evie had gotten together with Brad. She hadn't been the one to leave the friendship. Max had. Maybe if he hadn't, he could have spotted the danger signs before it was too late.

And that wasn't quite true, either. It was more than that. But he couldn't quite decide how it was.

He was not in love with Evie. He could not let himself be in love with Evie. To go down that path would just bring so much heartache on both of them. He knew he had a problem with being intimately involved with anyone, but that trait had been seared into his conscience many years ago. He didn't know how to change, nor did he want to. He'd given his all to his dad. Had tried to protect him and be the emotional support he needed after his mom had died. And it hadn't worked. No matter how much he tried, it just hadn't been enough. Max had just ended up burned out and used up emotionally.

Evie's bare shoulder bumped his arm and he swallowed, realizing his ice cream was melting in his cup.

"What are you thinking about?" she asked.

He cast around for an answer, then said, "I wonder if

Walter Grapevine was ever happy." Okay, it was stupid, but at least sticking to the topic of the musical was safe.

"I don't know. I think he just got so used to wallowing in the bad that he never opened himself up to opportunities that could have changed his life. Like when he had the chance to leave his job and go away with Tammy. He didn't. He chose to stay where he was."

This topic was safer? The musical hadn't had a happy ending, even though it couldn't be considered a tragedy, either. At least not from his perspective.

"Is that what you would have done? Give something up for love?"

"I think I tried to. With Brad. But I've learned there are no guarantees in life."

She took the last bite of her raspberry sorbet and dropped her napkin in a nearby trash receptacle. He did the same with his unfinished dessert.

"I've learned that, too."

She glanced at him. "Your mom."

"And my dad. He was completely lost without her."

"I remember you telling me that." She reached for his hand. "I think your dad was kind of a Walter Grapevine figure. He chose to stay in his unhappiness, never looking for anything beyond that."

"I know. But he was so sure there *was* nothing beyond that."

"Like I said, there are no guarantees in life. But it was his choice not to try, wasn't it?" They got to the parking garage and Evie let go of his hand. He immediately missed the connection. As they waited for the valet to bring Max's car, the topic changed yet again, and for that, he was grateful. Because Evie was right. His dad had made his choice and there'd been nothing anyone could do about it.

But hearing her say what he'd known in his heart to be true was somehow freeing. It took the burden off a kid who'd tried so hard to change things, but who couldn't. A ball of emotion rose up, threatening to overwhelm him. He glanced at Evie, and it was as if he was seeing her for the first time.

And yet, he wasn't. These temporary bursts of feeling for her had erupted from time to time over the course of their friendship. Usually when she'd had some sort of insight or tried to make him see hope in situations that seemed bereft of it. In a few days' time it would run its course. It always did. He just had to wait it out.

And if he couldn't? If he did something stupid and ruined everything? Then he was in for the biggest pity party in the history of man.

She might be Dale's Miracle Girl, but Max had to remember she wasn't his. Because there'd never been a big enough miracle to save him from what his past had made of him: a man who, like Walter Grapevine—like his dad—was too afraid of pain and loss to let himself take a chance on love and everything it meant.

CHAPTER EIGHT

Evie touched a finger to the picture Max had drawn for her years ago. It was in the entryway of her apartment, exactly where it had been when she'd been married to Brad. Her ex had never asked about it, maybe assuming she'd bought it at some out-of-the-way market. And he'd never seemed bothered by her friendship with Max, although Max had made it fairly clear that he and Brad would never be friends. And he'd pretty much stayed out of the picture during her marriage.

It was funny how Max had much the same reaction to his friend Dale's interest in her that he'd had when she'd been in the initial phases of her relationship with Brad.

Was that a coincidence or something more?

The musical had been so, so wonderful and sitting there next to Max had been…heady. It was the only word she could find to describe it. And it was totally different than when their little trio had gone and watched *Wicked*. Maybe because so much had happened since then. Evie had learned to treasure their friendship again. Was learning to be grateful for this new season in her life in a way that she hadn't been since her divorce from Brad.

She didn't want to be Walter Grapevine. She wanted to live. To enjoy life and friendship and lo— She stopped herself before she could go any further and ruin how lovely last night had been. Max hadn't kissed her when they stood there on the sidewalk in front of her apartment. But he had hugged her and thanked her for a wonderful evening. It had taken her a long time to get to sleep, despite the late hour, and she was still on kind of a high this morning.

She glanced at her watch. Ugh, she needed to get busy or she'd be late for work. After taking one last look at the picture, she headed to the bathroom to get ready.

When she arrived at the hospital, she was shocked to see workers out in the courtyard. She hadn't scheduled anything to be done until two weeks out from the gala, and they were still four weeks out at the point. Maybe Dr. Robbins had requested some repairs or something.

She met Max in the atrium to find he, too, was looking out at the courtyard space, hands shoved into his pockets. "What's going on?" she asked.

"I have no idea. I thought maybe you knew."

"No clue." She blew a breath out. "I think maybe it's time I went to see our new CEO and see if he's behind this."

He glanced at her face. "Are you sure you want to do that?"

"You bet I am. It's one thing to refuse to let us have a copy of his speech. It's another thing to start interfering with our plans without even notifying us. I have workers scheduled to come in two weeks. I have no idea if these are the same ones, or if Robbins has gone out and gotten his own."

"I'll go with you."

"No, I can handle this on my own. Besides, if he fires me, he'll still need you to carry out his plans."

"No way," he said. "If he fires you, I'm gone, too."

That stopped her in her tracks, and she stared at him for a few seconds. "Don't do that, Max. People like Margaret Collins need you."

"They need you, too. If you haven't noticed, you're the first person she calls because you're the one she trusts the most. And I wouldn't have that any other way."

"I promise to *try* not to get myself fired. Does that help?"

"Yes. Let me know how it goes, okay?"

She bumped his shoulder, like she'd done last night. "I will." Looking up into his face, she stopped for a minute. The sun came through the window and cast a light on him that made him glow. He was gorgeous. Why had she never noticed that before? Well, she had, lots of times, but more in the sense of how one friend knew another one was good-looking. But this was a take-your-breath-away kind of response that only came with attraction. Maybe it was because of last night's outing. He'd looked incredible in his suit.

So what? She'd always been attracted to Max. Otherwise, those two kisses—one years ago, and one more recently—never would have happened. But she'd never let herself actually think about what they meant. Until last night and this morning. There'd been an intimacy between them during their trip to the musical that had stopped her cold, even without a single kiss.

Could she really afford to dwell on that, though? It had already gotten her hurt. Twice. That picture in her foyer, as much as she loved it, only served as a reminder of one of those hurts. And yet, she could never bring herself to part with it. He'd made it. For her. And she loved it.

Just like she lov—

No! Do not even think it!

That half-formed thought from this morning threatened to break through yet again. And this time, there was no doubt about what it meant. She needed to get away from here.

"Okay—well, I'm off. I'll let you know how it goes."

He repeated her shoulder-bump move from a moment earlier and it sent another shiver of awareness through her.

"Good luck," he murmured.

"Thanks. I'm going to need it." In more ways than one.

Forcing her thoughts to something else, she went to Robbins's office and checked in with his assistant. Yes, he was in. And no, she wasn't sure if he was busy or not. But she would check.

Evie dropped into one of the chairs in his waiting room and wondered if he was even going to see her or not. If not, then what did she do from here? Just sit around and wonder if her workers were going to have anything to do when they arrived in two weeks?

Hell, she had no idea. But one thing she did know— she was not going to head up any more committees that Robbins had anything to do with. That included next year's gala. As much fun as she'd had with Max planning this one, she didn't think she was ready to sit in front of the CEO and watch him smugly inform her that she wasn't getting a copy of his speech. She hoped the board saw through the man before he did something that would hurt the hospital. He was either really, really smart, and would surprise the heck out of her, or he was a clueless narcissist who only wanted his own way in everything no matter what it did to anyone else.

Robbins came out of his office, and she stood to go shake his hand.

"What can I do for you, Evie?" Was it her imagination or was there a slight edge of irritation to his voice?

"There are some workers out in the courtyard, and I'm not really sure what they're doing. I don't have the preparations for the gala scheduled until two weeks from now. Does this have something to do with that work?"

"Ah, I see. No, this isn't for the gala. Not specifically, anyway. I just thought that maybe there needed to be another sculpture out there to go with the first one. It'll make more of a statement that way, don't you think?"

Except she'd only taken one sculpture into account when it came to the walkways. And if, as he'd said, it was going to be a statement piece, then it might change her plans for out there. "Is it going to be a big? Because that might mean we won't be able to fit as many people out there."

"Hmm, you yourself talked about having people in other areas of the hospital, did you not? So not everyone will be out there at one time."

That was technically true. But when she'd said that she hadn't meant that they could cram the courtyard with a bunch of new stuff, either. But to stand here and argue with him would accomplish nothing. And since he hadn't offered to show her a picture of the new addition, she was stuck. "Okay. I'll wait and see what goes in and then reconfigure the walkways to accommodate it."

"Good. That will work just fine then. Is there anything else?" He brushed his hands together as if he was already done with this conversation.

"I think that does it. Thank you."

With that, she turned to walk away, her jaw set into stiff angry lines to avoid telling the man exactly what he could do with his new sculpture. And God help him if the man erected a statue to himself. She might take a sledgehammer to the thing herself. Of course, she wouldn't, but it didn't hurt to at least pretend that she could.

Blowing out a breath, she suddenly felt a lot lighter. People weren't stupid. She had to believe the board of directors weren't blind, either. And since it wasn't just her who felt this way, others would catch on as well. Max felt the same way as she did.

She wasn't alone. And that was all that mattered. She had a feeling that things would work themselves out. One way or another.

The breathing treatment had an immediate effect on the young athlete, as the ragged coughing stopped, and she was finally able to take deeper breaths. The fourteen-year-old track star had wound up in the emergency room complaining of coughing and shortness of breath during training. There was no history of asthma, but Evie had seen this before.

"Did that help?"

"Yes. I feel so much better. I'm not sure what happened." The girl took another deep breath and let it out with a sigh.

"Have you had this happen before?" She glanced at the girl's mom, who was seated beside her daughter.

"Sometimes at the end of a run, I feel extra tired. But today, I couldn't even finish the race."

Evie held up the spirometer for Delilah to try again now that she'd had a treatment. The girl took it and blew hard. Looking at the result, Evie smiled. "Much, much better than when you came to the hospital."

"So why is this happening?"

She took the instrument and put it on a tray to be sanitized, then came back and sat on a stool in front of the girl. "I think you're experiencing something called exercise-induced bronchoconstriction. It causes the airways to constrict, making it hard to breathe. It's similar to asthma. We actually see it in a lot of asthma patients."

Her mom spoke up. "Does this mean that Delilah has asthma?"

"It's kind of something in between. They used to call it cold-induced asthma, but obviously, we're in the middle of summer here in Nevada and it's not cold. But the thought now is that dry air is the real culprit, and since cold air holds less moisture…" She let her voice trail off before restarting. "We're in the middle of a drought, and although we live in a desert climate where it's almost always dry, there's even less moisture in the air right now. It dries the lining of the lungs and causes them to spasm when she's breathing hard."

"But why does it happen to me and not everyone?"

"We don't really know why it affects some people more than others."

"Does the mean I have to give up track?" Delilah's tone was one of devastation. "I love it so much."

"No, you absolutely don't have to. We're going to start you on an inhaler that you'll use before you start running. It'll help keep the airways open. A longer warm-up period before you start your practice may also help. If those two things don't do the trick, we have some other options we can try." She patted the girl on the shoulder. "The fact that you responded so quickly to the albuterol is a good sign."

Delilah broke into tears and hugged her mom before returning her attention to Evie. "I was so afraid you were going to tell me to quit running."

Evie smiled. "I'm not a runner, so I can't quite relate to the lure of it, but I know someone who is. And he would be pretty devastated if he had to stop, too. I know you guys are a dedicated crew. So keep on running. And I'll keep on doing my best to keep those airways open. Deal?"

"It's a deal."

She gave the girl's mom her card. "I'd like you to call and schedule an appointment so we can follow up on how things are going. Until then, I'll give you a prescription for the inhaler. If there are any questions, give me a call. My cell-phone number is on there."

"She has another meet the day after tomorrow, is it okay for her to go?"

"I'm going to say yes, but do the inhaler before you

start and if you start feeling short of breath at all, stop. We may have to tweak things a bit, but I'm very hopeful."

The mom looked at the card. "Are you sure you don't mind if we call?"

"I'm sure." She didn't give her actual card out to all her patients, but this one was special, and she could tell that running was Delilah's passion. She'd told her the truth—she was going to do everything in her power to help keep that dream alive.

"Any other questions?"

Mom and daughter looked at each other. Then Delilah's mom said, "I don't think so. You'll give us a prescription for the inhaler?"

Evie nodded. "I will. Your breathing seems to be back to normal and the test we just did shows a vast improvement to how you were when you arrived at Vegas Memorial, so I think you're good to go. I'll get your discharge papers and prescription ready, and the nurse will be in to give you everything. And call and let me know how the track meet goes."

"We will."

Delilah jumped off the table, came over and hugged Evie tightly. She hugged the girl back, feeling a kindred spirit. Evie had had people in her corner helping her achieve her dream of becoming a doctor, and she'd vowed to do everything in her power to help other people fulfill their dreams.

She smiled down at the girl. "Take care and I look forward to hearing from you."

After Evie left the room and gave instructions to the front-desk attendant about the girl being discharged, and handed them a prescription, she headed to the elevator. It opened and she was surprised to see Max standing there. "Well, hi there. Fancy seeing you in a place like this." She was in a good mood that no one was going to ruin. Seeing Max just made that mood even better. "Not as fancy as Tuesday night. But then again, neither are you."

He grinned. "I'm crushed."

"Do you have a patient in the ER?"

"No. I was looking for you, actually."

Her heart sailed in her chest. "You were?"

It had been two days since she'd last seen him and the new sculpture in the courtyard had been installed yesterday. She wasn't quite sure what it was. It was oval-shaped and almost looked like some kind of tall obelisk. It stood side by side with the sculpture that was already out there, but the two pieces had nothing in common. But she'd taken measurements so that she could somehow maneuver the pathway between the two structures. It would be a tight squeeze, but there was nothing she could do about it at the moment, since it was obviously there to stay.

"Do you have any more patients?" Max asked.

"No, the one I just saw was actually my last for the day." He was acting a little odd. "Did you want to talk to me about something?"

"Yes, and it could affect the gala."

Her mood suddenly plummeted. "Oh, God, what now? Is there a third sculpture going out in the courtyard?"

"No, but… Can we go somewhere outside of the hospital? I don't know if what I have to say is common knowledge yet."

Okay, those words were as obscure as the new sculpture. "We can. But I'm actually starving, so can we go someplace we can eat? I skipped lunch today."

It had been a crazy day with three emergency cases sprinkled in among her normally scheduled appointments. It had put her behind, so she'd worked right through her lunch break.

"Yep, how about that little Italian place we used to all go to?"

That "little Italian place" was actually a hole in the wall that the three of them ended up falling in love with. It held a lot of great memories of friendship and laughter. And, of course, since Max didn't drink, they had a built-in designated driver, which they always teased him about. But they both respected his reasons for abstaining and were careful not to overimbibe and bring back bad memories for him.

"I love that place. I actually haven't eaten there in ages. And right now, anything's better than the place we went to with Robbins."

"I don't think you're going have to worry about that anymore."

Her head cocked. "I don't understand. Did that restaurant get shut down?"

"Even better. I'll explain over dinner."

As soon as they got settled in the restaurant and she had a glass of wine in front of her, she prodded him. "So what's all this cloak-and-dagger stuff?"

"Cloak-and-dagger pretty much describes it."

She blinked. "Are you being serious right now? Did Darbs investigate someone other than my ex?"

"Huh?"

"Never mind. Tell me what it is."

Max settled back in his seat. "It seems all of us department heads were brought in for a meeting this afternoon with the board of directors and told that Dr. Robbins is no longer with the hospital, effective immediately. They don't want to make a public announcement at this point until they figure out how to proceed."

She stared at him, looking for any sign of humor in his face. Because if he was kidding right now, he was going to be in big trouble. "Tell me you're serious."

"I am. They looked for you when they called us in, since you're in charge of the gala, but you were with your ER case and so they asked me to notify you."

She took a sip of her wine, trying to wrap her head around the fact that the man she'd tangled with about the new structure going up was no longer there. "How did this even happen?"

"His personal assistant went to the board with some concerns she had."

"And they fired the man based on that? And what about the gala? Will it be canceled?"

"No. It's going on as planned, including all of your ideas for using the courtyard for a type of after-party."

"Did Robbins even notify them of our plans?"

"He did, but he didn't tell them about a lot of other things, like his going to a couple of our donors and asking for a personal loan."

Shock held her speechless for a second. "What?"

"They evidently did a background check before hiring him, but missed the fact that the man has a gambling problem and there were some hefty private debts that don't show up on any credit reports. We weren't the only ones who noticed that he was behaving kind of oddly. Some sketchy characters came to his office not long ago when he wasn't there and freaked out Amanda, his personal assistant. That's when she started looking at what he did a little closer. The meeting he was in a hurry to get to when we were with him at the restaurant? Well, it ended up being with a loan shark who was calling in an overdue note, hence the phone call to the donors."

"God. I can't even believe this is happening. Who's going to be the keynote speaker at the gala?"

He leaned even closer, forearms braced on the table. "You're not going to believe this."

This time she laughed. "I pretty much don't believe anything you just told me."

He leaned back, putting his hand on his heart. "It's all true, I swear it. Anyway, the new speaker is going to be Morgan Howard. They're trying to coax him to come back at least until they can vet some other candidates. And do a more thorough job of it this time."

"I love Morgan. I don't begrudge him his retirement, but it'll be hard to fill his shoes. I just think they tried to rush things and didn't dig deep enough into Robbins's finances. I bet they don't make that mistake again."

"Let's hope not."

Their food came. She'd ordered the eggplant parmigiana and Max had chosen the rigatoni. She couldn't help but smile. "Some things never change."

"What do you mean?"

"Isn't the rigatoni what you always got?"

"It is. And you liked the eggplant." He took a bite of his food. "And this is just the same as it always was. I'm glad the owners have always kept things simple, even though they're a lot more popular than they were seven or eight years ago, when we started coming."

"Me, too. And Darbs always liked the Caesar salad."

"With anchovies, of course."

She laughed, feeling inexplicably happy all of a sudden. "Those tiny fish always looked so sad lying on top of a bed of lettuce. I'll have to tell Darby the news. She's had to listen to me moan and grumble about gala stuff for the last few weeks."

She cut into her food and took a bite, as a thought hit her. Once she'd swallowed, she had to ask. "What are they going to do about that ugly thing in the courtyard that Robbins had commissioned?"

"The board didn't say, but I can't imagine them keeping it."

She blew out a breath. "This day has suddenly become perfect. I didn't have to kill a young girl's dreams and now the CEO from hell just got booted out of the hospital."

"Back it up a step. You didn't have to kill a young girl's dreams? Care to elaborate?"

"Just a patient I had today." She rubbed the back of her neck. "Some stories really do end well. And, as doctors, we need those, you know."

"Yes, we do. And then there was the man who fell from the scaffold. His story ended well, too, don't forget."

She sighed. "Yes, and in light of what could have happened, I'm grateful. It could have been so much worse. You could have ended up on the bottom of a pile of heavy metal along with our patient. And those other two men could have—"

"But none of that happened. It was a good day."

"Yes, it was." She thought for a second. "And so was today. First with the news from the board. And then eating at this restaurant again. It brings back so many good memories, doesn't it?"

"Yes, it does. Very good memories." His eyes locked with hers for a minute.

She couldn't stop herself from reaching over and catching his hand and giving it a soft squeeze. "Thanks for being there for me during the gala planning. And for the musical. You don't know how much either of those meant to me. It was like light at the end of what's been a long dark tunnel."

"I know I haven't been there for you during that, and I'm sorry. I know I went MIA during that whole thing with Brad. I kept feeling like I needed to somehow fix things, and yet, I knew I couldn't. And so I stayed away and let Darbs do the heavy lifting."

"I have no doubt if I'd have called, you'd have come."

He hesitated for a minute as if examining some deep part of his psyche. "Yes. If you'd have called, I would have come."

She let go of his hand and took the last sip of her wine. And that was enough sad talk for the night. "Hey, why don't you come over for some coffee. We can watch a movie or something. It's too early to go to sleep, but I don't really want to go out and do anything, either."

Again, he hesitated, and for a minute she thought he might refuse, saying he had something else he had to do. But then he smiled. "Sure, coffee and a movie sound good. And I'm not really in the mood to try to go out, either. How about if I run you back to the hospital and we can pick up your car."

"That sounds perfect." And just in case he was looking for an out, she added, "Don't feel obligated to come, though, if you'd rather just go home and decompress from the day."

The waitress came and handed them their bill. "Just pay at the front desk as you go out."

They waited for her to leave, and then Max said, "I do want to come. Sitting with someone who understands what a 'day in the life' is like is probably just what I need. I'm actually looking forward to the gala now."

"Even though it probably won't be a requirement for staff anymore now that Robbins is gone?"

He nodded. "In retrospect, I knew I should be attending it, but after so many years of sitting it out, it just became a habit. Kind of like Walter Grapevine. Maybe the nudge was a good thing."

"I think Robbins's method was more of a shove."

"Shove or nudge, I'm still going to go. Especially after seeing how much work goes into it."

She smiled. "And since DJ Electric Nights is our disc jockey for the evening?"

"It'll be good to see him do his thing. Just don't let him get too chummy."

"Define chummy." Before he could say anything, she laughed. "I'm kidding. You got your point across last time we talked about him. He's nice, though. I can see why women fall for his charm."

"But not you."

"Not me. Not after what happened with Brad."

"Good call." They paid their bill and headed out to the lot to get Max's car.

Once inside, it only took a couple of minutes until they were at the hospital and he was parked beside her car. "I'll lead the way."

"Sounds good."

With that, she got out of his car and jumped inside hers, then started it and backed it out of the spot. And then she turned it and headed toward home.

CHAPTER NINE

EVIE'S APARTMENT WASN'T far from the old one. Maybe just a block away. She'd said that moving her things from the old place had been a lot easier than she'd thought, since she'd left all the furniture behind for Brad to take with him. All she'd had to do was pack her clothing and her most precious possessions, and she was out of there.

He pulled into a guest spot and turned off the car, then joined her on the sidewalk. "I've only seen your place from the outside. It's nice, though. And I'm sure starting fresh was the better option than staying where you were."

"It was really the only option, since Brad had been out of work for a while and needed the other place to be sold. But it worked out for the best. This apartment doesn't have any memories attached to it other than the ones I put in it. And I tend to be pretty careful about which ones I let in."

He could understand that. When his dad had died, his childhood home had automatically become his. It was paid off, and so he could have moved into it and saved himself some money, but the thought of doing so just made him queasy, so he'd sold the place. He'd donated the money to a well-known cancer-research place in honor of his mom.

Her apartment complex was a tall structure that curved partway around a pool, so that all of the units had at least one window that overlooked it, a great selling feature. They took the elevator up to the third floor.

"Very nice."

"It is nice. But it feels odd to have a big body of water sitting in the middle of the lot when the drought has caused so many changes in our personal usage. I mean, car washes are only allowed on a weekly basis and they've had to cut back on the amount of water per wash."

"Looks like they've saved water in other ways. Didn't there used to be lawn here?"

"There was. And they took it out. But I kind of like it. It's a nod to the reality of where we live, although it would probably be hard if the city were devoid of green spaces."

They stepped into her apartment, which was blissfully cool after the heat that had enveloped them outside. The marble floors probably felt wonderful on her bare feet when she padded around in the mornings.

And just like that, the image of Evie in a silky robe that was loosely belted around her waist came to mind, her nipples standing out in sharp relief against the thin fabric.

Hell, coming here had probably been a huge miscalculation on his part. Because he'd envisioned this as each of them watching a movie enveloped in their own little bubble of space. But when he glanced through the door into her living room, he saw that she had one couch and a chair—which he was certainly going to use. She didn't need to be sharing anything besides room space with her.

Just then, something hanging above the glass table in the foyer caught his eye. He stared at it for a second, realizing what it was. It was the picture he'd drawn her from *Wicked*. She'd taken the canvas and had it framed in black wood that looked ragged and bubbled along the edges, as if it had been in a fire. It was the perfect contrast for the pristine white of the canvas and the black inked images that seemed to jump off the page. He'd almost forgotten what it looked like after all these years.

"Wow. You kept it."

She glanced at where he was looking and gave a half shrug. "I really like it. And the fact that you drew it makes it that much more special."

"And the frame?"

"My dad actually made it, using a flamethrower to blacken the surface and make it look older."

"It makes the black of Elphaba's robe stand out. I never would have thought to do that."

She smiled, touching the frame with light fingertips. "My dad can't draw, but he does have a great eye for putting the right frame with the right print. He did all of the frames in the apartment for me."

As he glanced back into the living room, he saw several other pictures each with a different type of framing material. Most were informal, made out of wood that was either painted or stained. As far as he could see, this was the only one made with a charred appearance. "I'll have to remember that. Does he do them for friends?"

"For you, I'm sure he would."

She tossed her keys in a wooden bowl on the hall table and motioned for him to come into the living room. He took one last look at the picture and followed her.

He wasn't sure how he felt about his work being given such a prominent place in her home. It created a warmth in his chest that could transform into a more dangerous heat given a little encouragement. Encouragement he didn't intend to give it.

So he turned his attention to the living room. Just like he'd seen from where he'd been standing, she only had a few pieces of furniture, including a TV stand with some drawers and another wooden bowl that held a couple of remote controls. She took one of them and turned on a ceiling fan that was suspended from a vaulted ceiling. He was glad because he was still a little warm—both from picturing her in a thin robe and from seeing how much care she'd taken in displaying his artwork.

She motioned him to the sofa, and so he gingerly sat on the long piece of furniture, hoping that she was going to sit in the chair adjacent to it. "Do you want some coffee or tea?"

"Coffee if you have it."

Maybe the coffee would help center him and keep him from falling asleep on her couch, something he did at home quite regularly. He'd kick his shoes off, stretch out on his long leather sofa and sleep an hour or two. But that was not something he was going to do here.

"I do. Black, right?"

"Yes, thanks." He tried to remember how she liked her coffee but came up blank.

When she came out with a tray that held a thick mug

and a more dainty cup with the string from a tea bag dangling over the rim, he knew why. She liked tea rather than coffee. With her Brazilian heritage, he just assumed that coffee was a cultural norm. And yet, she had it in her house. For company?

"You don't drink coffee?"

She bit the corner of her lip. "Not a lot, but buying it is still a habit. Plus when I have company I serve it."

The way she said it was still a habit to buy it made him pause before he realized Brad had probably preferred coffee. Which explained why she always had it in the house.

He wished he could go back and change what had happened to her, but he couldn't any more than he could change what had happened to his mom. Or to his dad. Sometimes, it just had to be accepted that bad things happened and that there was no rhyme or reason for them. There wasn't necessarily a grand scheme that demanded they happen.

He tried to think of something to say about coffee or tea, but came up blank, so instead he asked, "Do you use your pool a lot?"

"Almost never. When I'm home, I'm normally in for the night, and to change into a suit and go down there just seems like work. But most complexes have pools as part of the amenities, so I just go out on the balcony and sit and enjoy looking at it."

"May I?"

"Of course. There's a ceiling fan out there, too, and it's nice and private."

She followed him out to the balcony and unlocked

the sliding glass door. Outside, she had a few potted plants, including rather healthy-looking tomato and pepper plants. There were small red tomatoes on the one bush, but nothing on the other. "Does your pepper not produce?"

"Oh, it does. They just never last because I eat them almost as soon as they're big enough."

There was a double glider swing on the side of the balcony and they settled on it together, thighs lightly touching. Maybe coming out here hadn't been such a good idea after all. He'd been worried about being too close in the living room. This was ten times more intimate. He set his mug on the table beside him and looked through the glass barricade that was the only thing standing between them and falling over the side of the building.

It was warm and dry, and there was no sign of grit on the tiled flooring from the dust storms that periodically rolled through the area, obstructing visibility and creating a mess. Part of the "blessing" of living in the desert.

"It's nice. My house doesn't have one of these. I'd probably be out here every evening." With the fan above them twirling and sending air over his skin, he stretched his legs out and glanced out over the empty pool area.

As if sensing his unspoken question, she said, "The pool normally gets busy after dinner, when the kids are out of school. An hour or so from now. It can get pretty loud."

"I can imagine."

"Are you okay if I go put some shorts on? It tends to be pretty warm out here."

"We can go back in, if you want."

She shook her head. "I like it out here. I just need something a little cooler. I'll be back in a minute."

As soon as she went in, he got up and looked over the balcony at the hardscape below. The sun glinted off the pool with enough force to make him squint. And yet he loved the desert, even during times like then when the heat became unbearable. Because once the sun went down, it almost always cooled down enough to open the windows and let some fresh air in.

Other than the *Walter Grapevine* production, he couldn't remember the last time he and Evie had gotten together and done something that didn't involve work or, more recently, the gala. Or that hadn't included Darby. To be here with her alone was…nice. It had a comfortable feeling, like wearing a favorite pair of jeans. Which made sense, since Evie was one of his favorite people.

She came back out a minute or two later and he turned from his spot to look at her. She had on black Lycra shorts that hugged her frame and made every curve of her hips and backside stand out. And she was wearing a white racerback tank top that showed off thin pink straps that were probably to her bra. The sight made him swallow.

A pink bra? The urge to trace his finger down the path of that strap on her back came with a strength that surprised him. When she leaned over the glass railing, making even more of that tanned skin visible, it became even harder to resist. Because he could just follow the path down, continuing its trajectory even past its boundaries, going over the small of her back until he reached the curve of her buttocks.

He swallowed and when her head suddenly turned and caught him staring, she blinked. "What?"

Hell, what could he say?

"I thought you weren't a runner?"

"Why do you say that?" She glanced down. "Ah, the outfit. Is there some kind of special runner's law that says no one else can wear spandex?"

"No. And it looks good on you."

Why he'd said that last bit was anyone's guess.

"Thanks. I'm normally out here alone. But once I get home from work, I'm ready for the clothes to come off."

"I guess you are." The image of that bathrobe came back to his mind and he wondered if she would lean over the railing just as easily when she was wearing just that. Wondered what it might be like to come up behind her and slide the hem of that robe up the backs of her thighs and…

She turned around and grinned. "That didn't come out quite right."

In a voice that sounded strangled, he said, "I was pretty sure you didn't mean you come out here and dance in the nude."

"You know, when it's dark and the lights are completely off, it probably wouldn't matter if I did. No one could see." Her throaty chuckle did nothing to erase the image of her doing just that.

"Evie…" Did she even know what she was saying? How every picture she painted was being burned into his brain?

"What?" Her eyes widened as her gaze took a quick trip down his body, where he was pretty sure every one of his thoughts was there on full display. "Oh! I didn't realize that you... That what I..."

She bit her lip, then propped her hip on the glass barrier as she stared at him. "Would it really be that awful, Max?" Her words were so soft he'd barely heard them. But she'd said them all the same.

He could pretty much guarantee that whatever might happen between them wouldn't be awful at all. At least not on his end. But was it the smart thing to do?

Hell, did it really matter? She'd made choices she probably regretted and so had he. That didn't mean that this would necessarily be one of those choices, right? They'd kissed and their friendship hadn't gone up in flames.

But he knew something else that might go up in flames. Him. The moment that he touched her.

He should stop with those thoughts. Right now. But the note of uncertainty that he'd heard in her voice as she'd whispered those words had cut him to the core. So, reaching out, his hand encircled her wrist and tugged her closer. "No. It wouldn't be awful. And the way you're making me feel right now says it would be the opposite."

She took another step closer, until their bodies were touching. "Would it?"

Doing what he'd wanted to do just moments earlier, his free hand went to her shoulder and followed the hellish path of that bra strap until it disappeared under her stretchy shirt. He came back up and dipped his hand under the strap, loving the feel of the elastic across his skin as his thumb brushed against her soft skin. The sensation sent prickles across every nerve ending he possessed.

"Hell… I want to go back inside."

He could only hope she could guess why that was and that she was in full agreement with it.

"So do I. But I don't want to watch a movie. Not anymore."

"I was hoping you were going to say that."

With his fingers still around her wrist, he towed her behind him as he reentered the apartment and closed the glass door behind them. Then he turned her to face him. "Are you sure you're okay with this?"

"Yes. More than okay."

As if to emphasize that point, she stood up on tiptoe and kissed him, her lips soft and pliable against his. It only took a second for him to wrap an arm around her waist and fasten her to his body. Then his hand pushed deep into her hair and he kissed her in earnest, his tongue sliding along the seam of her lips until she opened to him. If she thought what she'd seen on the balcony had been obvious, then feeling the effect she had on him must be all the more apparent as he pushed his hips against her belly, loving the pressure along his length.

Except he wanted more than this. So much more. And this time he wasn't going to pull away with some glib speech about saving their friendship. Because if it could survive two kisses, surely it could survive sex. And it would be very good sex. It was in the way she whimpered against his mouth. In the way her mouth closed around his tongue and drove him wild with need.

He needed to find a horizontal surface. And soon. Or this was going to be over before it had even begun.

After pulling away long enough to mutter the word

bed, he moved back in without waiting for a reply, his hand leaving her hair and traveling down the front of her body until he reached her left breast. It was perfection in his palm as he squeezed, finding her nipple in a millisecond.

"Bed." This time it was her voice repeating his earlier thought.

Oh, yeah, he'd wanted to find a bed. He'd almost forgotten. Scooping her up in his arms, he let her direct him to the first open door down a short hallway. Not bothering to shut it behind him, he entered the room and found the bed in the middle of the room. Instead of tossing her onto it and following her down, he turned his back to the mattress and lowered himself onto it. Lying back on the mattress, he took her with him. She quickly scrambled so that she was on top of him, the breast that he'd cupped now pressed tightly against his chest.

It was heaven on earth having her like this. Something he'd never in his wildest dreams ever pictured happening. But it was real. Evie was here with him, kissing him like there was no tomorrow. And maybe there wasn't. But right now he didn't care.

He cupped her bottom, pulling her tight against him and wishing she'd already shucked her clothing. But because she hadn't, he found the waistband of her shorts and pushed his hands beneath it and encountered smooth rounded flesh that sent his body into a frenzy of want and need.

"Evie." He pushed the clothing over her hips, and as if sensing what he was trying to do, she stood up and stripped them off her body, kicking free of them. His mouth watered. But when her hands went to the hem of her shirt, he sat up and stopped her. "Let me."

Pulling her onto his lap so that she straddled his thighs, he gently slid her shirt up her flat belly and over her breasts. When she held her arms high over her head so he could get it off her, he paused for a minute after he'd discarded the garment, one palm sliding up her arm and trapping her wrists in place so he could enjoy the decadent sight of her lacy bra against her skin, her breasts pushing tightly against it as if wanting to be free.

Soon. Very soon. But not before he did this. Letting go of her wrists, he eased her forward until his mouth was against her breast. With it still encased in fabric, he found her nipple and used his teeth to grip it, wetting the lace and scrubbing his tongue across the sensitive part of her.

Evie moaned and pressed closer before she reached down and freed her breast from the cup and drew him back to it.

The sensation was incredible as he pulled hard against the nipple, her hands cupping his head and holding him in place. He finally couldn't take it anymore, so he undid her bra and tossed it across the room. Then he lay back as she remained where she was, her thighs on either side of his.

All that stood between them were his jeans and briefs. But first... He bucked up under her enough to slide his hand into his back pocket, then withdrew his wallet. He hoped to hell he had something in there. It had been a while.

Flipping it open, he found not one, but two condoms.

Plans for how to use that second one were already form-
ing inside of his head, but he put them aside for now,
along with the second condom, barely able to reach her
nightstand with his fingertips. The he used his teeth to
rip open the packet he still held in his hand.

Before he could try to maneuver himself to where
he could reach, she took the condom from his hand and
went up on her knees. Setting it beside his hip, she made
short work of undoing his button and fly and freeing
him, her hand warm against his oversensitive skin. Her
eyes came up and met his with a secretive smile as she
pumped up and down with the perfect amount of pressure.

It was too much.

"God, Evie. Stop for a minute."

She did, halting her movements and reaching for the
condom. She slowly unrolled it down his length while he
muttered under his breath and tried to hang on to what
little control he had left.

Her fingers drew circles across his abs, making his
nerve endings crazy with the mixture of pleasure and
ticklishness. He was so attuned to that that he completely
missed her hips moving over him until she pressed down
hard, taking him deep within her with a single movement. He swore out loud, gritting his teeth at the intense
rush of pleasure that swept over him.

His fingers gripped her hips in an effort to slow down
the wave that was starting to grow and gain strength.
But she was relentless, as if needing something only he
could give her.

The feeling was mutual. Because what he needed, only she could give.

And there was still that second condom…

Giving himself permission to just go with what was happening, he slid his fingers in between their bodies and found moist curls and that tiny sensitive nub that lay at the very heart of her.

She moaned as he stroked her with both his fingers and his body, using them both to bring her as much pleasure as she was bringing him.

"Max. Yes." Her movements quickened, taking him deeper with each strong pump of her hips. And the wave, which was traveling toward shore, grew to monstrous proportions, and he knew it would soon overtake him.

Just as it hit, she cried out, her hands gripping his shoulders and wildly driving herself onto him. Her body spasmed, once, twice, and then it contracted rhythmically around his flesh, finally forcing him over the edge. He saw white for several long seconds before he became aware of anything other than their frenzied movements and the ragged sound of their breathing.

She slowed the friction just before it became too much, her gripping hands easing their hold and smoothing over his chest.

That had been… More, much more than anything he'd experienced before.

When she finally came to a stop and sat atop him, her eyes landed on him as if seeing him for the first time. And it did something to him. Touched a part of him he wasn't sure he wanted exposed, so he put a hand in the middle of her back and eased her down until she was lying against him. But at least she could no longer see his eyes. Because what he'd seen in hers threatened to rock his world and topple everything he believed to be true.

But those thoughts could wait until tomorrow. When he would be seeing the world with more rational eyes. Until then, he could just lie here and enjoy the slight aftershocks that were still coursing through his body and making him jerk against her a few more times.

He was spent. Didn't want to move. Didn't want to think.

But he didn't really have to, did he? Not yet. He could just relax, revel in the release his body had just had and enjoy the feel of her body against his. Although the fact that he still had clothes on was starting to rob him of some of the joy of lying here with her. He could fix that later, too. But right now…

She wasn't moving and it took him a few minutes to realize she was breathing in deep steady movements that made him smile. She was asleep.

And part of him was glad. Glad she hadn't tried to rationalize what had happened or try to talk through things. He didn't want any of that. He just wanted to be here with her.

If she'd been anyone else, he probably would have already been up and out of here. Or at least up and in the shower. He rarely took the time to wallow in the afterglow of sex. But this time was different, and it stole the part of him that sought to escape.

He didn't want to escape, because this was Evie and she was his…

Max didn't finish that thought because the word *friend* didn't seem to fit in this context.

Don't try. Just lie here and be with her.

So until she woke up, or morning arrived, whichever came first, he was going to do just that. Enjoy being with her.

CHAPTER TEN

THE SOUND OF something buzzing somewhere near his head woke him up. At first, he brushed his hand across his head as if chasing away a pesky insect. Then his eyes opened, and he wasn't sure where he was. Someone's leg was draped over his.

Evie. The events of the previous night rolled over him like a freight train.

They'd had sex.

He swallowed, all of the implications that he'd swatted away yesterday came rushing back. And this time he couldn't just ignore them.

He'd told himself that sex wouldn't affect their friendship, but now that it was staring at him in the cold light of day...

What was he going to do? He'd broken all of the promises he'd made to himself. Not about sex, because that had never been off the table. But his rule was that he not be with someone that he was emotionally involved with.

Had he really broken that rule, though?

Hell yes. Because he was emotionally involved with Evie, he'd just refused to acknowledge it. So again, how was he going to fix this?

The buzzing started again and this time he realized

it wasn't an insect. It was his phone. What time was it, anyway?

He reached for the item on the nightstand and felt the second condom, instead. It, too, filled him with foreboding. He'd had every intention of using it last night. Except he'd fallen asleep. Strike two for his promises.

Grabbing the phone, he sat up to answer it, and felt something on his shoulder. Lips. Very warm lips that trailed up his neck and sent a shudder through him. His eyes lighted on the condom again, and this time it didn't look quite so evil. Quite so nefarious.

He pressed answer on his phone in case it was something urgent and muttered, "'lo?"

"Max, is that you?"

He was awake in a flash when he recognized the voice of his personal assistant. "It is. What's going on?"

Evie stopped kissing him and came around the side to look at him. He held up a finger to signal he would be just a minute. And then what? Was he going to actually move on to round two with her?

The question swirled in his head as Sheila's voice came back to him. "Max, I have some news. Margaret Collins was scheduled for her first treatment today."

That's right. She was. He glanced at his watch. It was only eight in the morning. He wasn't due at the hospital for another hour. "She is, but that's later this afternoon, isn't it?"

"It *was*…"

Those two words came down like a hammer, shattering whatever had happened last night.

"What happened?"

"We're not sure. But her son went to wake her up this morning and found her unresponsive. She died in her sleep."

She died in her sleep.

The guilt that he'd not felt last night came pouring over him in a flood that wouldn't be stopped. His eyes burned and his throat went bone-dry. While he'd been rolling around in this bed with Evie, Margaret Collins had been taking her last breath. A sense of déjà vu went over him that wouldn't stop. She hadn't even made it to her first treatment.

Shades of his mom. Shades of people leaving those they loved. Loved ones being left behind to somehow carry on.

It's not the same thing.

He knew that, but it still didn't stop his heart from trying to jackhammer its way out of his chest.

"Thanks for calling." It was all he could manage to get out before he hit the end button.

He was somehow able to get his feet under him and lever his way out of bed as a fog of regret settled over him, every bit as dark and heavy as the dust storms that ravaged this part of Nevada.

Then Evie was in front of him, wrapped in the bed-sheet. "Max, what happened?"

"Margaret…died last night." He took her by the shoulders, even as he wanted to jerk away from her, the urge to escape beating through his skull. "I'm so sorry, Evie."

Her eyes closed and two tears escaped. "Did she suffer?"

"I don't think so. She passed in her sleep."

Brown eyes stared at him and a hurt almost as deep as when he'd learned his mom had died held him in a paralyzing grip.

He couldn't do this. Couldn't bear to see the devastation in her eyes over what had happened.

Margaret had been Evie's patient for years and so he understood those emotions. But what about the other ones? Like the fact that Margaret Collins had never gotten the chance to prepare? Had never been able to say goodbye to her family?

What if it had been him? Or Evie?

He didn't know. And things right now were so jumbled he couldn't make sense of anything. All he knew was that he couldn't stay here and think about any of that. It was why he'd been so adamant about not getting close to anyone.

And now, he'd gone and done the very thing he knew he shouldn't have. Gotten close in a way that had nothing to do with what they'd done last night.

He let go of her and closed his eyes, hoping he could do what he needed to do. "Evie, I'm sorry. Really, really sorry about Margaret. But I just can't be here right now."

Grabbing his clothes from the floor and pulling them on with a frenzy that came out of nowhere, he tried to put his thoughts on hold. Only they wouldn't go away, and kept swirling inside of him.

"Max, stop a minute."

"I need to get to the office."

"No, you don't." She moved in front of him and threaded her fingers through his. "Please. Talk to me."

"Not now. Maybe later. I just need time to process this."

"Process what? Margaret's passing? Maybe it's better that it happened this way. There was no pain. No suffering."

Maybe not for Margaret. But for her family?

"Not just her passing. I just need time to think. About everything."

"Okay. I get that."

But she didn't. He could tell.

"Call me if you need anything, okay?"

Her hand fell back to her side. "I will." She paused for a second. "Does some of what you need to think about revolve around what happened last night?"

"We can talk about it later."

"So it does."

He swallowed. He didn't want to hurt her, but wasn't that inevitable at this point? The thought of being involved with someone caused a queasiness to churn inside of him that no amount of talking would abolish. It was a knee-jerk reaction that made no sense, and yet, try as he might, he'd never been able to rid himself of it. He was like Walter Grapevine, forever stuck on a dead-end path, but not able—no...not *willing*—to change.

He moved forward and took her hand. "Evie, last night was a mistake."

"A mistake. Why?"

"I can't explain it. But I don't have what it takes to truly give myself over to someone else. Maybe it's from my childhood. Maybe it's engraved into my DNA. I don't know. But I only know I'm not what you need."

She jerked her hand free, her eyebrows going up. "I think *I* should be the one to decide that. But since every single time we start to move toward something deeper, you stop and call it a mistake... Well, this time, I'll believe you. So let's just say it's over and move on."

Hearing her cast the very words he'd been thinking into the universe was a shock. And for a second, he wondered if he'd done the right thing. But right or not, it was too late now.

As if emphasizing her point, she went over to the table, snatched up the condom and walked back over to him. She put it in his hand and curled his fingers around it. "Take it. You'll need it for the next woman you decide to have sex with. Only let me give you a piece of advice. Don't tell her it was a mistake."

Before he could say anything else, she walked past him to the bathroom and went inside, softly closing the door behind her.

He should be glad. Evie had let him off easy. But something about the way she'd said that he'd need that condom for the next woman sent a knife deep into his chest. Is that what she thought he did?

Don't you? Didn't you just think about how you don't have sex with women you care about?

He stared at the object in his hand, horrified at the truth that was staring him right in the face. And then he went over and dropped it into the garbage can by the bed. He finished dressing and left Evie's apartment, getting into his car and driving with no destination in mind. The only thing he wanted to do was escape. Escape the news of Margaret's death. Escape the fact that what had happened with Evie was done for good. And that there was no going back.

* * *

"In short, it was a mistake. According to Max."

She'd met Darby at her office shortly after he'd left her apartment. She couldn't believe how easy it had seemed for him to throw words at her that hurt her to the core.

"Maybe give him some time. I always felt like there was something he wanted to tell you, but just never could."

"I think he pretty much said everything he wanted to say. And when I told him it was over and we should move on, he didn't say a word."

"Do you love him, Evie?"

Those words shocked her into silence for several minutes. Then, in complete misery, she nodded. "I do. I think I have for a very long time. I was just too afraid to admit it to myself." She let out a hard laugh. "And it looks like I was right in being afraid. Thank God, I didn't say it this morning or last night. Because I'm pretty sure he would have thrown it back in my face."

"You don't know that."

"I do. You didn't see the look he gave me when I asked him to stop and talk to me. He acted like I was made of poison."

"I'm so sorry, Evie. Do you want me to talk to him?"

The thought of that filled her with horror. "No. Please don't say anything to him. I don't even want him to know that you know."

"There's no way he won't. He knows how close we are."

She thought for a minute. "You're right. Because here I am less than two hours after he left my apartment. And

I don't really need advice. I just needed to tell someone. Losing Margaret and Max in one day…"

Darby put her cane against her desk and caught her up in a tight hug. "I'm sorry, honey. So, so sorry. I thought… Well, never mind what I thought, because that doesn't matter. And I know you don't want advice, so all I'm going to say is that you need to give yourselves space and time to heal. Maybe you'll both either realize that what happened isn't the end of the world. Or you'll realize it is and that you can't live without each other."

"I don't see that second option ever happening, but I do think you're right about the first one. And since Margaret was the only patient we had in common right now, there shouldn't be a lot of reasons to see each other."

"What about the gala?"

"That planning is all done. No need for any more meetings, and as for the event itself, there should be enough people there that we can avoid crossing paths during it." She shrugged. "I've never thought about leaving Nevada, but maybe I need to go visit some of my relatives in Brazil for a couple of weeks. I have a lot of vacation time saved up. I can be back in time to make sure all of the gala stuff is ready to go."

"I think that's a good idea. I'll miss you. And please don't leave Nevada. Not permanently. Not without giving yourself a lot of time to think and grieve. And this is worth grieving over, Evie. You love him. Let yourself cry and scream and shake your fist at the sky. But don't make a permanent decision while you're feeling like this."

"I won't. I have a few patients I need to wrap up over

the next week and then I'll spend a week or two in Brazil. Once the gala is over, I think I'll be able to screw my head back on straight and figure out my next step."

She wanted to make sure that Delilah, especially, was doing okay before she left. She had a track meet today, so Evie would call this afternoon and find out how it went. And then she had another two patients who were in the middle of adjusting meds and she wanted to see those through as well. And then she'd be free to go to Brazil and try to clear her mind of anything that had to do with Max or what had happened between them. And he was right. This could never happen again, because it would destroy her. So even if she had to walk away from him, from his friendship, she was going to do what she needed to keep from being hurt by him ever again.

Max twirled a pencil between his fingers, then tossed it to the top of the desk and groaned out loud. He'd gone to Margaret's memorial service two days ago and had seen Evie from afar. He'd toyed with going over to her afterward to see how she was doing, but she must have slipped out as soon as it ended. When he looked for her, there was no sign of her.

He hadn't seen her in the hospital, either, but that wasn't all that unusual. Unless their paths happened to cross because one of their patients needed services that the other specialized in, they pretty much kept to their own departments. But he hadn't even caught sight of her since the service. And he couldn't stop thinking about her. About how they'd left things.

No. Not *they*. Him. Max was the one who'd had the

meltdown and had said a lot of things he didn't mean. A lot of things he regretted. And a week after Margaret's death he could see that he'd mentally blamed Evie for getting through to his heart, when all along it had been Max who'd opened the door and let her in.

Blaming her was probably just an excuse to run for the door. What he really hadn't been able to face wasn't Margaret's death—it was what had happened in Evie's bedroom.

But why had he made it into such a tragedy? Why had he felt like the world was ending, when it really was still spinning on its axis just like it always had?

Everything inside of him went silent for several seconds. All thought ceased. His muscles froze, breathing stopped, then it all started back up again when the truth he'd been avoiding exploded onto the scene, scorching everything he thought he knew.

He loved her.

And that was why he'd been so horrified. And so adamant that it had meant nothing, and tried to convince not just himself, but her.

All because of the baggage he carried from his mom and his dad. And it wasn't even their fault. It was his for taking on their problems and acting like they were going to be repeated in his life. They weren't. Max hadn't gone out and drunk himself into a stupor when Evie had let him walk out of her life. Evie wasn't the one who'd died, it was one of their patients. And while that fact made him sad and he had grieved the things that she would never get to do, he was going to be able to move past it and keep on living.

What he wasn't sure of was whether he was going to be able to move past Evie. And he suddenly knew he didn't want to. He wanted to hold her in his arms and say he was sorry for every stupid thing he'd ever said to her. Sleeping with her hadn't been a mistake. It had been the smartest thing he'd ever done. Because it had made him stop and take a good look at what was staring him in the face. What had been staring him in the face since before she'd met Brad. That he loved her. It was why Brad and Dale's interest in her had bothered him so much. Why he hadn't been able to stand the sight of her with another man.

So what was he going to do? He was going to find her and do what he'd just thought about. He was going to take her in his arms and tell her how much he loved her. And beg for her forgiveness for wasting so many years of their lives.

He took a deep breath and picked up the pencil, then tossed it in the air and caught it by its point. But he couldn't do any of that sitting here at his desk. He wasn't sure she could forgive him, or if she even should, but what he was sure of was that he needed to try. Right now. After telling his assistant where she could find him, he headed down the elevator to her department and went to the desk. "Is Dr. Milagre here?"

"No. She actually left for vacation this morning."

A cold wind washed over him. Was that a euphemism for leaving? For good?

"Do you know when she'll be back?"

The woman glanced at a calendar in front of her. "She

said if things went well she'd be back…let's see. Yes, here it is. A week before the gala. July twenty-fifth."

If things went well. And if they didn't? "Okay, thanks."

He left and did the only thing he could think of. He called Darby.

"Nao sei."

God, how many times was Evie going to have to explain to her well-meaning relatives that she didn't know if she was ever going to get married again. Or if she was going to have children before she was forty years old.

She thought coming here had been a good idea, but a week in, it looked like it might have been the worst idea of her life. She missed her job, missed her apartment, but most of all she missed Max. Despite what they'd said to each other, she regretted leaving without getting some kind of closure, even if it meant the end of their friendship. She regretted not having her say and not telling him the truth once she'd realized it: that she loved him. Confessing it didn't demand that he feel the same way, it was simply telling him the truth. How much worse could it be than leaving things the way they had?

Her aunt was saying something and she'd missed it.

"Como?"

"I asked if you'd mind riding with me to the airport to meet a friend. I hate driving in that traffic alone."

"Why don't you take the bus?" The bus that went from São Paulo to the international airport was a lot easier than driving. And it only took about forty minutes.

"It's a special friend, and I want him to be comfortable."

Evie's eyebrows shot up. "Aunt Maria, do you have a *namorado*?" Her aunt had never been married and she was pushing seventy.

"Of course not, *moça*. Grab your purse, we need to go."

Okay, so it had gone from asking Evie if she wanted to go to assuming that she would. But what else did she have to do? She still had two more days before her own flight for the States, and the way she felt right now, it could not arrive fast enough. "Okay, I'll be right back."

Then they were in the car and driving through the snarls of rush-hour traffic, but her aunt, to her credit, was very good at weaving in and out of traffic at just the right moment to keep inching forward. If you made eye contact with the next driver, it was an unspoken rule that they had to let you in. And Aunt Maria was a force of nature when it came to getting people to look at her.

Once they were at the airport, Maria checked the flights while Evie moped in silence. "I found it, let's go."

Her aunt pulled her behind her until they were at the arrivals area. Evie hoped whoever it was got here quickly. All she wanted to do was get back to the house so she could start packing for her return flight. Darby had kept her apprised of how the gala preparations were going—since she and Max were still on speaking terms. The workmen had almost completed the courtyard and the obelisk structure had been carted away to parts unknown.

"There. He is here."

She glanced up, only half interested in whoever it was.

She'd been gone from Brazil for so many years that it was doubtful that she even knew the person. "Where?"

"Just look. You will see him."

Oh, brother. She looked at the throng of people, not seeing a single familiar face. Then her attention snagged on something. An easy move of masculine hips that looked familiar. She frowned and looked closer at the people coming toward them. Then she blinked, every emotion in her suddenly rushing up and getting stuck in her throat.

It couldn't be.

She lost sight of him for a second, then as she frantically swept her gaze across the group, he reappeared behind someone. Oh, God, it was.

Max!

She jerked around to look at her aunt, who only nodded. "Yes, *querida*, it is him."

"But how?"

"Your friend Darby called your mother, who called us and told us he was flying into Brazil. It is why I insisted you come."

Was he here for a conference and her mom had somehow found out? The shot of happiness she'd felt vanished. What if he wasn't here for *her* at all?

Then their eyes met and he stopped, right in the middle of the moving line of people, forcing the crowd to part and go around him like water flowing around a rock.

Then he was moving again, his lanky frame eating up the distance before she had a chance to catch her breath.

Then she was in his arms and he held her so tightly that she really *couldn't* breathe.

Was this happening? Maybe this was all some dream or wishful thinking. Maybe her longing was so strong that she'd summoned a hallucination. And yet, his arms felt real. And he was murmuring something in her ear over and over.

It was her name.

And for some reason it broke her, and she started sobbing, clinging to him like he was the only thing that could save her world. And maybe he wasn't, but he was the closest thing she was going to find.

He pulled back, looking into her face. A thumb came up and captured a drop of moisture. "Happy tears or sad?"

She sucked down a shuddering breath. "That depends on why you're here."

"I'm here for you."

Her eyes closed and she pulled his face down to her, pressing her cheek against his. "Happy. They're happy tears. I love you, Max."

He kissed her, the softest touch, almost making her cry again. She thought she knew what it meant, but she wanted to hear the words. Needed to hear them. He looked at her and nodded. "I love you, too. I was just too afraid to admit it. Or to believe I deserved it. And so I ran. And worse, I called something beautiful a mistake, hoping it would make you pull away. And it did. But it was the stupidest thing I've ever said and it wasn't true. It wasn't a mistake. You'll always be my best friend, Evie. But I'd like the chance for it to be more than that."

"Yes."

He laughed, pulling back and putting an arm around her waist. "Yes, what?"

"Yes to whatever you suggest, as long as it includes having you in my life."

"That's a nonnegotiable." He glanced to the side and saw an older lady who looked far too pleased to not be a part of how he'd gotten to Brazil. "Is this your aunt?"

"Oh, yes." She turned red. "I'm sorry. Aunt Maria, this is Max, my..."

"Teu namorado. Ja sei." The woman stepped forward and kissed him on either cheek. *"Bem vindo ao Brasil."*

Max's head tilted, and Evie laughed. "I'll explain what she said later. But right now, all I want to do is this." She went up on tiptoe and kissed him again. "I just want to hold your hand all the way to my aunt's house. And then I still want to be holding it in two days, as we head home."

"Home," he said. "I like the sound of that." With that, he gripped her hand and followed her aunt to the airport's exit, where they stepped out into brilliant sunshine and the promise of a thousand more days just like this one.

Just then her phone pinged, and she glanced at the readout. "Oh, my God," she whispered.

"What is it?" Max sounded worried.

"It's Darby. She said it's raining in Las Vegas and more is predicted over the next couple of days. The drought is over."

"It certainly is." Only Max wasn't looking at her phone. He was looking at her. And in his expression was more love than she ever dreamed possible.

She squeezed his hand in silent agreement. The drought was over. And she thanked God for the rain.

EPILOGUE

Two years later

MAX CAUGHT SIGHT of Evie coming toward him across the courtyard. It was their second gala as husband and wife and he would never get tired of the sight of her in an evening gown. Even eight months pregnant, she was the most beautiful woman in the room. And she was all his.

At thirty-eight, she was considered a high-risk pregnancy and Max had to fight the urge to coddle her and make her slow down. But Evie swore she would not do anything that would put their baby at risk. Her mom and dad and whole extended family were ecstatic with the fact that their family was about to grow. And Max had been welcomed in as if he'd always belonged, and he loved it. Loved them all. He was even trying to learn Portuguese, although Evie always translated for him.

He tucked her arm through his and dropped a kiss on her head. "Have I told you I loved you lately?"

"Hmm." She hummed the sound in that low throaty way of hers that drove him crazy. "Only about forty times."

"Then I'm behind schedule." He nodded toward the left. "Come dance with me."

"Now? I'm not sure I'll make the best partner." She cupped her belly.

He tipped up her chin and looked into her eyes. "You make the best partner all the time. Please. For me."

"Okay." They walked over to the area where the dance floor had been set up. The same dance floor that had been used for the last two years, since the hospital portion of the gala had been everyone's favorite part. And Evie was still head of that committee. Morgan Howard's successor had finally been chosen and it was actually his son, who was also a doctor. And Morgan Howard the second was every bit as compassionate and savvy as his father was. Everyone loved him.

DJ Electric Nights saw them coming and winked at him. "All set?"

"Yes, we're all set."

Evie looked up at him in question and the music started softly, then slowly got louder. She bit her lip. "Max, you know this song always makes me cry."

"That's why I wanted him to play it." He took her in his arms and slowly moved in time with the music, the country singer's voice coming through with a sure sincerity that said he knew what he was singing about.

Evie laid her head against his chest and closed her eyes as they swayed together. No one else in the world mattered, except the woman in his arms. The first verse moved into the chorus and then flowed to the second stanza. Through each word and phrase, Max took them in and made them into a vow he would never go back on. She was the best thing that had ever happened to him.

The chorus came for the last time and the singer

seemed to hang on to those final words for a long time. Long enough for Max to sing them softly in her ear. "You're my best friend…my best friend."

* * * * *

*If you enjoyed this story,
check out these other great reads from
Tina Beckett*

Reunion with the ER Doctor
ER Doc's Miracle Triplets
Tempting the Off-Limits Nurse
A Daddy for the Midwife's Twins?

All available now!

MILLS & BOON®

Coming next month

HEALING THE BABY SURGEON'S HEART
Tessa Scott

'Well, let me at least walk you back.'

'I'm fine, really.'

'Well, if you get bored and want someone to talk to over the next few weeks, I'm here every Tuesday evening with my fellow louts.'

'I'll keep that in mind,' Claire said, truly appreciative of his offer.

Kiernan's lips curved into a slight grin. 'Oh—and one more thing. If you decide to hit up the usual tourist spots, you might want to spray down the Blarney Stone with a strong antiseptic before kissing it. Just saying.'

Claire chuckled quietly. 'That's good advice.'

Kiernan smiled and nodded. 'Well, you take care.'

'You, too.' Claire said as she walked past him.

Once outside, she took a deep breath and allowed the cool night air to seep into her lungs. For a split second, she questioned her decision to close the door on any further interaction with Kiernan. But she had no choice. She had come to Ireland to make a difficult decision that could potentially alter the course of her life from hereon in. The last thing she needed was to tempt another complication that would only create more heartache. She had had enough of that for a lifetime already.

Continue reading

HEALING THE BABY SURGEON'S HEART
Tessa Scott

Available next month
millsandboon.co.uk

COMING SOON!

We really hope you enjoyed reading this book.
If you're looking for more romance
be sure to head to the shops when
new books are available on

Thursday 16th January

To see which titles are coming soon, please visit
millsandboon.co.uk/nextmonth

MILLS & BOON

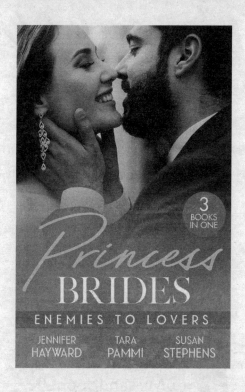

LET'S TALK

Romance

For exclusive extracts, competitions and special offers, find us online:

f MillsandBoon

X @MillsandBoon

⊙ @MillsandBoonUK

♪ @MillsandBoonUK

Get in touch on 01413 063 232

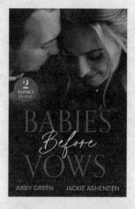
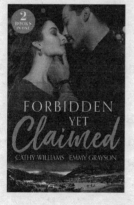

afterglow BOOKS

Afterglow Books is a trend-led, trope-filled list of books with diverse, authentic and relatable characters, a wide array of voices and representations, plus real world trials and tribulations. Featuring all the tropes you could possibly want (think small-town settings, fake relationships, grumpy vs sunshine, enemies to lovers) and all with a generous dose of spice in every story.

♪ @millsandboonuk
⃝ @millsandboonuk
afterglowbooks.co.uk

#AfterglowBooks

For all the latest book news, exclusive content and giveaways scan the QR code below to sign up to the Afterglow newsletter:

SCAN ME

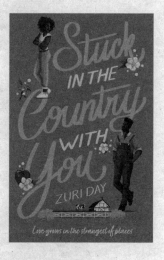

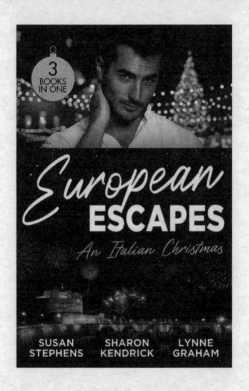